Her Will

Her will drives her far and beyond...
Ego exposes her to the inevitable truth...
She just wants to be set free

Floranova B. Msc.

HERWILL
A fiction book / published by The Flame Remains

PUBLISHING HISTORY
First edition © 2010
Second edition © 2014

ISBN-10: 0615453155
ISBN-13: 978-0615453156
Library of Congress Control Number: 2011930380
Facebook.com/HerWillToBeORnotToBe

A WORD FROM THE AUTHOR

Her Will novel is based on my own life experiences, Hermetic truths, the seven Hermetic Principles as well as Holistic and Metaphysical Sciences; the prefix '*meta*' from Greek origin means 'beyond' thus Meta-physics is a science that studies not only what the physical eye can see (the tangible) but also the unknown (the intangible) which theories comprise physics and beyond.

The seven Hermetic Principles are:

Principle of Mentalism (Not to be confused with mentalist)

Principle of Correspondence (As above so below…)

Principle of Vibration

Principle of Polarity (Negative and Positive are 'poles' not Energy. Energy is neutral.)

Principle of Rhythm

Principle of Cause and Effect (generally referred to as Karma)

Principle of Generation/Gender (Creation of everything that exists with its Masculine, Feminine and beyond)

Hermetic axiom:

"One may change his mental vibrations by an effort of Will in the direction of deliberately fixing the Attention upon a more desirable state. Will directs the Attention and Attention changes the Vibration. Cultivate the Art of Attention by means of the Will and you have solved the secret of the Mastery of Moods and Mental States. To change your mood or mental state; change your vibration." —Hermetic Philosophy; the Kybalion

Hence I titled my novel "Her Will" wherein I employ fiction to illustrate how the principles and mechanics of the Universe consistently affect all aspects of life whether an individual is aware or not; as no soul is free from being part of this world and it is a tale of inescapable truths but not necessarily facts being the difference that truth has no beginning and no end whereas a fact ought to happen to become true.

The candle flame meditation is a simple exercise to discipline focus through the third eye; however in due course and after practicing long enough, anyone is able to enter a meditative state without the aid of the flame.

According to studies and proven by American psychiatrist William Glasser, one learns only 10% of what one reads; therefore you might want to read *Her Will* more than once for regardless of the characters and the storyline, each and every chapter holds valuable information which might not be assimilated at first sight.

There are unfamiliar theories exposed especially in chapter 8, 9 and close to the end of the tale which are only like dialing buttons calling your own heart to speak, as every word enclosed in this book has been carefully selected in aim to guide you into a path of self discovery; so after reading the story, one day, you will find yourself listening to a silent wave whispering from your heart and following it. Do not allow the buttons pushed to stop you from meeting the character named Valentin. Ego resists and at times impedes discovering the greatness hidden in the deepest areas of one's soul. Every being possesses their own truth; thus fear not the truths you will uncover because unless you trust them; they won't have an effect on you at all.

The Science of Metaphysics encourages the use of proper vocabulary, especially in writing, with the intention for those words to manifest with a successful effect just as the story will illustrate further ahead; so I do not practice phonetic dialog in my writings. I made the conscious decision to expose my prose genuinely and in an unaltered form avoiding the services of editors on purpose to maintain the gist of the story authentic and pristine. And even though I employ narrative dynamics to keep the sequence of the tale consistent; this novel is intended to reflect a rhythmic Metaphysical glint vibrating throughout the leafing of the book and not intended to represent the literature field; for I am a Metaphysicist above being a professional writer and I dedicate to the study and research of Scientific and Spiritual fusion not necessarily the study of literature. Therefore, the same as in life, which is filled with correctable mistakes, there might be a few academic grammatical errors along the written lines that will become part of my tale's charm and won't change the essence of the story in any way.

I trust that the blend of words with my prose will flow from page to page inviting the reader to absorb and embark on *Her Will* journey enjoying the tale from the beginning to the end.

Floranova B. Msc.

"When the philosopher points to the stars, the fool's eyes are fixed on the finger."

DEDICATION

To my loving husband
To mama
and
To the residents in my heart that encouraged me to write.

PROLOGUE

&3

$\mathcal{L}$ove, peace, and harmony were in the air as Avon was meditating that morning; except it wasn't going to be an ordinary day because her father had passed away and she didn't even know it.

She sat in the dark with her eyes closed bonding to the surface by inhaling deeply, exhaling gradually and sensing truth from each of her heartbeats. Stillness and silence combined filled the space as she connected to her soul and experienced an instant of bliss. In the midst of the darkness; her smile reflected delight like she had just joined infinity.

Suddenly, the sound of a spark broke the silence as she opened her eyes to light a candle placed on a table facing her. The tiny flame illuminated the entire room in which she spent hours breathing, reading, researching, thinking, writing, and learning about the aspects of being, existence, and life-force. As a humanitarian, Avon dedicated her research to create goodwill projects and assist the community where she lived.

She observed the small candle flame growing firmer and larger appreciating the fact that not long before the space was as dark as matter in the sky at night beyond the stars and she absorbed the flame flickering glow brightening the room powerfully. She sat still gazing at the flame until her eyelids naturally closed and a bright reflection of the flame remained floating in her mind's eye and just as she was beginning to focus on the flame remains in quest for her intent to develop a project; a knock at the door interrupted her.

She asked who it was keeping her eyes closed. "I do not mean to disturb you my dear," the doctor replied behind the walls. She opened her eyes calmly and as soon as she got the door; he cleared his throat and said, "Your niece Mae left a message. Your father passed away."

Not having much of an option, Avon received the news with grace. She stared down aimlessly for a moment. Then she raised her eyes looking at him and with an untraceable but refined accent in a soft tone she said, "I am deeply grateful for your assistance in this matter—"

"It is my pleasure. Let me know if you need me for the trip arrangements my dear." He said interrupting a bit tense, for being the emissary of such a message didn't seem to suit him well.

She smiled saying, "I might in fact need help. I have not been in Bangkok since mama passed away and considering the situation I foresee a confrontation with my siblings approaching my way." Hesitant she asked, "I guess I could not elude being present at father's will distribution, could I?" In response, he looked into her eyes concurring with her guess by shaking his head and he walked away. Avon closed the door behind him and turned around gazing at the candle flame from the distance while sensing Arolf whose presence had been motionless all along. She sighed deeply and quietly said, "Father is gone."

☙☙

Two weeks later…

It was an afternoon full of activity at the Plaza Athenee Bangkok hotel where Avon and her siblings had been summoned to attend the reading of their father's will. In the middle of summer it was hot, humid and smoggy while the gorgeous blue skies were in disguise behind the pollution in the active and heavily populated area. The thickness of the air provoked one to nearly stop breathing generating a distinctive scent uniquely perceived in Bangkok, Thailand; locally referred to as "The City of Angels."

In the hotel, a few levels up, were the attorney assigned to execute the will and his assistant sitting by the elevator in the hall. They waited for Avon to escort her to the meeting suite like they did with her brothers Chet, Kyet, Nikom, and her sister Kalaya who weren't patient enough to collect the fortune their father had left. The four siblings waited in the suite which was informally arranged with a desk for the attorney, relaxing armchairs for the family members, as well as refreshments and butlers at their service. While enjoying the appetizers and drinks; they protested because their estranged sister Avon was coming from abroad to be present for the distribution of the funds. The attorney and his assistant perceived, from where they were out by the hall, an argumentative family encounter on the verge of happening before the session started at all and they just looked at each other.

Everyone in the suite was getting more impatient by the minute and after exhausting every unpleasant word they could think of complaining because Avon was coming to claim part of a fortune that belonged to them, Kalaya came out to the hall beckoning the attorney and they spoke inaudibly in a corner. Then Kalaya went back to the suite and persuaded her brother Nikom to entrust her with his share of the inheritance. Kalaya sat next to the forty-eight-

"When the philosopher points to the stars, the fool's eyes are fixed on the finger."

year-old man and rearranging his hair with her hand she enticed, "Nikom why don't you trust me? My brother, your money will be safe with me sweetheart." At the same time sitting opposite from them Chet interrupted arguing that *he* should be the one entrusted with everyone's share of the fortune because he was their older brother.

Chet tried to win them over saying in a devious tone, "I told you, I can multiply everyone's share of the fortune in no time through my friend's investments." After filling his mouth with caviar on a cracker, Chet licked the tips of his right hand fingers holding a mother-of-pearl caviar serving knife in his left hand and when the others ignored him and his mouth was still half-full; he pointed the knife at them and he menaced, "As your older brother I could just take every cent from you anyway!" Kalaya and Nikom just glanced at him with a mocking grin. Then Chet chuckled realizing the fragility of the threatening weapon he held in his fist.

In the interim out in the hall, the assistant asked the attorney what Kalaya had said and he replied, "Well, she offered me a percentage of her inheritance in exchange of my collaboration to distribute the funds in her favor." Smiling, the assistant asked what he responded to such an irresistible offer and he replied, "I told her that I was quite tempted yet not interested in the nature of her bribe." Then the assistant asked if Kalaya was the oldest of the siblings, "Yes, followed by the oldest male Chet, their brother Kyet is next; then follows Nikom and the youngest is the one that we wait for," he replied.

Sometimes people keep financial secrets, but not Nikom. Everyone knew that any amount of money vanished when passing through his hands and even he disagreed with Kalaya and Chet's dishonest propositions.

Meanwhile, Kyet stood by the window sipping a drink observing and listening; but not paying much attention for he was thinking *I want my money at once! I don't even want to split the fortune with them, much less give them my share.* Anxiously, Kyet walked out complaining, "This is taking too long!" While walking from the suite to where the attorney and his assistant sat by the elevator in the hall; he carried on saying, "We should begin without delaying any longer and Avon should be—" But whatever it was that he was going to say got interrupted, because right at that moment a bell rang, the elevator door opened and Avon stepped out. Arolf was with her. Kyet's expression of disappointment when realizing that Avon had just arrived didn't surprise the attorney who stood up and introduced himself to her as Leopold.

Avon, a middle-aged brunette whose big black eyes expressed astuteness, determination and experience through the glasses resting on the bridge of her nose was wearing jeans and a plain top. Her five-foot-seven-inch height often intimidated others and she wore no jewels, save for a tiny sapphire pierced earring in her left ear. A few hidden grays, thanks to her exposure to life, highlighted her shiny long locks. However when she finally arrived; she expressed no regret for making everyone wait. Avon's full lips stretched smiling while glancing at the blonde attorney-assistant's blue eyes whose hair was as bright as the sunshine. Then enhancing her smile; she looked up at Leopold's emerald eyes whose hair, beard and mustache were whiter than gray and she shook his hand responding to his greeting with her mysterious accent, "It is a pleasure Leopold."

Kyet rushed to the suite and announced to the others that Avon had just arrived expressing unkindly. While Leopold and his assistant escorted Avon there was complete silence. When they entered, Avon sat away from everyone at the left corner and aside from papers rustling between Leopold's hands and water chime pouring into glasses by the butlers, everyone waited motionless

"When the philosopher points to the stars, the fool's eyes are fixed on the finger."

and unvoiced. Until suddenly, Kalaya stood up addressing Avon and expressing aggressively she said, "What are you doing here? You have no dignity! You came back just for father's will distribution!" Followed by Chet, Kyet and Nikom's protests; Kalaya seemed as if she was restraining herself from physically attacking Avon and she sat back in her place. They were speaking all at once and it was hard to tell who was saying what. In any event, they reminded Avon that she had left their family and their country behind. They complained because she wasn't at their father's funeral. They seemed to see eye-to-eye in dividing Avon from themselves.

They all agreed when Nikom accused, "Avon you thief! You returned to steal a fortune that belongs to us!"

Meanwhile, Chet said in anger, "Bear in mind that you've never been a member of our family. You don't deserve a cent Avon!" Clearly, they were sending Avon back to wherever she had come from. They were justifiably claiming their birth right and their argument escalated gradually to the point where Leopold had to interfere to prevent their voices from getting any louder.

During their dispute Avon remained calm. The only thing she heard while they were blaring and voluble was her heartbeat and the support of Arolf's presence. Avon understood that her attendance was of the essence and she didn't say a word. She wasn't the least surprised by their attitude as she clearly remembered visiting from abroad when their mother was still alive and thanks to her siblings' rivalry those visits were miserable each and every time.

Leopold tried to get everyone's attention and everyone quiet down but Kyet who had much more to say. Kyet spoke demanding to annul Avon's name from the will and to assign him as the official treasurer. Apparently he spoke on behalf of the other three saying, "We've agreed to exclude *this* estranged sister from the inheritance our father had taken a lifetime of effort and hard work to accrue for his children. I volunteer to manage our father's fortune henceforth." He also said that as far as they were concerned, Avon didn't deserve to have anything from their father's hard labor. In addition he mentioned Avon's absence during their father's illness and he reminded her that she wasn't at their dad's deathbed.

Then the others joined reminding Avon, as if she had forgotten, that she had left their family when she was a teenager and Chet said in anger, "Visiting occasionally doesn't give you the right to claim any money from our father's riches." Mostly they were repeating what they'd just said, like by going over the same Leopold would change his mind, as if it was up to him to decide how to distribute the funds. Or perhaps they thought that by saying their words over and over, the actual document would rewrite itself then and there.

At any rate, their frustration was blocking their attention and they weren't aware of their own words. Then Kyet carried on and on. He seemed oblivious to the fact that he was insisting to reopen a closed subject in vain. So, Leopold claimed voice giving Kyet no option but to stop and Leopold said with composure, "With all due respect Kyet, despite the differences among you as siblings it is nobody's place to amend the will, much less my place; for an attorney is entrusted precisely to ensure that each word in the document remains unchanged."

Leopold was finding the situation challenging, because everyone was expressing their own reasons to be divided. To some extent, he had to figure out a way to manage the circumstances allowing him to execute his duty in truth and integrity. Virtues he found hard to identify among the family members sitting before him. They weren't reciprocating respect, as Leopold couldn't perceive truth or integrity from them. Everyone was acting as if they'd never seen each other before and they were looking after their individual interests, not accepting limits for the distribution of

"When the philosopher points to the stars, the fool's eyes are fixed on the finger."

the funds. Leopold took a moment to reflect thinking of something to break the energy of envy and greed quickly without adding any more tension to the emotions that were already in turmoil. By then, he knew that explanations wouldn't accomplish much; especially when everyone was lacking consideration and talking over one another; for he couldn't begin to address the contents of the will unless everyone was at least quiet and possibly calm.

Overall it was a sad situation, because if they only waited to learn about the good-willed intentions behind the words in the document; they could have realized and clearly understood that the contents of the will were a gift to them, not a right to be claimed or an obligation to be given. Perhaps then, they could have appreciated their new financial status without arguing and instead, seizing the opportunity by enjoying each other in the occasion. Still there was very little Leopold could say apart from performing his duty. He felt sad witnessing such ill-will knowing that the document was definite and simple for him to execute in an expedite process. Because basically the only requirement from the family members was to extend their hand and receive money and if they extended the other hand; they would receive more money yet. However, their individual emotions were mismanaged. Nobody seemed to understand and it was like their hearts were into acquiring the most money, not being grateful for whatever the amount was. Their individual ambitions combined seemed greedier every minute that passed during the time they had been in that meeting suite.

Avon's siblings' appearances were smart, as though they had gone shopping for the occasion and began spending money not yet in their possession. They were already planning to spend each others' money without even considering details for a moment. The idea of receiving money, with no effort on their part, seemed to blind them; like once the word *money* crossed their minds they had lost their sight. No one was interested to learn the ethics, values, integrity and the degree of responsibility tagged along with the acquisition of an amount of money that, they could have dreamed about spending; however, they might have never dreamed on managing such an amount of money through a lifetime. Not one of them bothered to find out where the money came from. No one cared that they have never heard of the attorney before. They weren't even curious about who Leopold was. Provided that their father left them money; they assumed that as long as the attorney represented their dad, they should claim their given right to collect without questioning the funds source. For them it didn't matter if the money originated from corruption, dishonesty or fraud. None of them could hide their apparent materialistic appetite. In any case, Leopold took a moment to figure out a way to break the greedy energy increasingly flowing in the meeting suite while they were there.

The ambiance was tense. Energy of wrath, greed and ill-will was replacing the oxygen in the room bit by bit. After reflecting for a moment, Leopold discreetly requested from one of the butlers to light some candles he noticed adorning the end tables, a tactic Leopold had learned to crystallize energy. Everyone was so focused on snatching as much money as they could from one another; the candle lighting was ignored.

When the butler lit one candle, an instant stagnation of air was sensed. As the butler lit a second candle, the air in the entire room changed to the opposite course. Then, as soon as the butler lit a third candle, neutralized energy filled the ambiance at once.

When Leopold cleared his throat to begin; the energy in the room had entirely crystallized, not decreasing nor increasing for the surroundings were yet tense, but it allowed him to get everyone's attention and at that point, he didn't even bother reading the will.

"When the philosopher points to the stars, the fool's eyes are fixed on the finger."

Leopold just commenced saying in concise detail, "Your father's will grants an equal amount of money to each of you which I present in individual envelopes enclosing five certified checks in the amount of one million dollars each." In addition, Leopold showed them a sealed package containing pertinent information explaining, "In order to have access to the contents of this package, one of you ought to exchange it for the one million dollar certified check."

Just then, Chet, Kyet, Nikom and Kalaya, didn't hesitate to claim their certified checks; as none of them would renounce to one million dollars for a package. Avon was silent and distractively thinking. The next thing she knew, her siblings were about to assign the package by unanimous decision to her. At the same time, they also noticed that there would be an unclaimed certified check for one million dollars from the package exchange and, except for pensive Avon; everyone was asking what would happen with the one million dollars left.

Leopold then clarified, "If you are interested in the contents of the package collectively; the certified check is not required in exchange for the package. If all of you decide to share the contents of the package openly, each of you will get a check for one million dollars evenly." Leopold paused for a moment allowing them to assimilate and he added, "However, if you do not unite and reach an undivided agreement to share the contents of the package openly; the one million dollars check from the package exchange will be divided among the four siblings who express no interest in the package granting an extra quarter of the million dollars to each and leaving the package to one sibling without sharing the contents with the rest nor the one million dollars certified check."

Just then, assuming with certainty that their father didn't mean to leave any money to Avon; Chet, Kyet, Nikom, and Kalaya showed no interest in the contents of the package and they claimed as much money as they could ensuring that Avon didn't get a single penny.

Avon remained silent, save for a couple of nods in agreement with whatever her siblings decided. She perceived that despite of the distribution of the funds; their father's intention was for his children to make a unanimous decision and since everyone appointed the package to her; she concurred to unite with them. Although she was assigned the package by her siblings' undivided decision influenced by their sense of avarice; Avon was influenced by their father's intention for his children to agree collectively and unify. Clearly, Avon wasn't focused on the one million dollars check, as she could have shared the contents of the package with them and everyone could have kept their money share. But the event was taking a direction that she was not willing to entertain and she was ready to let it be. Leopold voided the check that was made out to Avon in front of everyone and while he was writing the extra checks, dividing Avon's share of the fortune among them, they were mocking her reiterating that even *she* realized not deserving any money for not debating her rights.

Her sister Kalaya uttered, "You belong in a mental health hospital Avon. While you're here, we should submit you for treatment at once. My sister, you're crazy. I feel sorry for you sweetheart."

Avon was seated, serene and calm. She was waiting patiently and looking down; but when Kalaya brought up sisterhood she reacted. Raising her eyes slowly, Avon looked into Kalaya's and said firmly, "Are you referring to me as '*sister*' Kalaya? I am no one's sister." She paused glancing around at everyone in the room and changing pitch to a low tone she added, "You and I are 'One.'"

"I told you! She's insane!" Kalaya exclaimed. Avon just smiled sensing the support of Arolf's presence.

"When the philosopher points to the stars, the fool's eyes are fixed on the finger."

No one cared about Avon's witty remark and ignoring her; they became involved in signing papers. When it was Avon's turn, Leopold placed the package in a briefcase, handed it to her and advised her to open it in private. Avon absorbed the instructions and as soon as she signed; she left the meeting suite with Arolf.

Given that Avon had traveled from abroad for the distribution of the funds; she was by the hotel lobby waiting for the valet to bring a car she had rented and thinking *this might be the last time I am stepping on the soil where I was born*. All of a sudden, she noticed her nephew, Chet's son, standing outside by the hotel entrance door talking on a mobile phone. She had also noticed two suspicious men roaming around the hall during the meeting and at that point, the two men were at the entrance of the hotel wandering again. She was aware of the corruption, danger, hijacks, kidnaps and risks she took when traveling around the world and Bangkok wasn't going to be the exception. So, Avon was prepared for the worst but hoping for the best while there. Then when the valet brought the car to her; she rushed because after witnessing her siblings' greediness she tried to protect the package. As if Kalaya was ready to put her in a mental institution, it was natural for Avon to suspect that they might want to take the package from her as well. So, she quickly opened the car trunk. She switched the package inside the briefcase for another one that she managed to find among the things she was carrying in her suitcase. She hid the original package in a jacket liner. She put the jacket on. She tossed the briefcase holding the swapped package on the car backseat and she drove off.

The steamy evening was slowly dissolving the scorching beams from the sunset reflecting everywhere and as Avon looked through the rear-view mirror; she spotted a car following her. Soon after, she spied a helicopter above monitoring her course. She became alert but she didn't panic. Clearly, she didn't want the followers to find out her destination. So she drove through the main streets and, thinking that she might lose the car behind her; she even drove around in circles but she ended up in a secluded area. She got to a point where she had to stop. The car following her stopped short. Two individuals disguised behind ski masks got off. Avon noticed one of them talking on a mobile phone and she wondered if he was Chet's son. The other guy took out a long blade knife that looked like the *Rambo* one and approaching Avon told her to get out of her car.

"Arolf, at times you are just a presence, aren't you?" Avon said wondering while opening the car door.

"Always, not just at times; we got into this mess, we will get out of it no doubt" was Arolf's response.

As Avon was getting out of the car, the individual pointed the knife close to her face. He demanded the briefcase from her or else she was to go with them. Not resisting him nor giving-in right away either; she was saying, "I will give you what you are looking for, as soon as I feel safe—"

Unexpectedly, the helicopter came down startling everyone. The two suspicious men she'd seen roaming around the hall during the session and at the entrance of the hotel, jumped off the chopper rushing toward her. Avon noticed that at that point; they were armed and wearing bullet-proof jackets. They grabbed her and loaded her into the copter which flew up in the air without delay. They took Avon away with the original package but at least Arolf was with her.

The car was left available to the aggressors who didn't bother taking it. They just grabbed the briefcase from the backseat leaving at once and under the impression that the original package was inside.

Just like Avon suspected, one of the aggressors was her brother's son and he brought the briefcase to his father at the meeting

"*When the philosopher points to the stars, the fool's eyes are fixed on the finger.*"

suite in the hotel where Avon's siblings were still having appetizers, drinks and celebrating. The attorney and the assistant were already gone. Chet checked the briefcase and it was unlocked. He took out the package and handed it to Kalaya. The package looked like one of those bubble padded mailers and when Kalaya opened it, she revealed the content: a book. Kalaya tore off the bubble padded wrapper looking for more and there was nothing else inside. The only thing in the package was a book. None of them paid attention to the title of the book and they failed to notice what it was about. They just passed the book among themselves from hand to hand leafing through the pages quickly in search of something valuable hidden inside. After that, they didn't seem disappointed for not finding anything valuable in between the pages of the book. Blinded by greed, they were satisfied for having claimed as much money as they were able to obtain and they continued celebrating putting the book out-of-the-way.

Kalaya's daughter, Avon's niece Mae, assisted organizing the meeting for the distribution of the will and even though she didn't attend the session, Mae had made the hotel suite reservation. So the following day, after the will distribution had taken place, a hotel representatives phoned Mae conveying that there were some personal effects left behind in the hotel suite the prior evening. When Mae arrived at the hotel reception desk to pick up the personal effects, she was told to wait. They said that the manager wanted to talk to her in person. After Mae waited for a few minutes; the reservations manager duly appeared holding a book between his hands.

The manager greeted Mae apologizing for the condition of the book and explained that the book was found inside a garbage can by the overnight cleaning crew and he also said, "Haven't been for the printed dedication inside the book, I wouldn't have requested for you to come and recover it Ms. Mae" and "Does this book belong to you?" he asked. Mae replied with a hesitant smile. The manager handed the book to her opened on a specific page and expressing respect because the book was dedicated to her. She received the book reading: *From heart to heart to my siblings and to my beloved niece Mae.*

Mae leafed through the book looking for hand-written words or notes, but the book was new. Apart from the cover that was exposed to some garbage, the book was unread. Then, Mae recognized the *nom de plume* realizing that the author of the book was her aunt Avon. At that moment, nothing was making sense to Mae and expressing her gratitude to the manager; she left the hotel and took the book with her.

Well aware of the rejection her mama Kalaya felt toward her aunty Avon, Mae decided to conceal from everyone that the book was in her possession. Not only because a voice inside told her that she would discover more by reading the book, than by listening to the stories her mama would tell to justify the reason why the book was left behind and inside a garbage can; but also, Mae had overheard Kalaya talking on the phone saying that she wouldn't pay a single penny for ransom; because at that point, everyone was aware that Avon had been kidnapped.

A true revelation unfolded before Mae's eyes when reading the book page by page. She discovered the source of the unique connection between her aunt Avon and her. She learned the circumstances involved when Avon left Bangkok for the first time and she understood why her beloved aunt remained afar. She also found out that Avon had bounced from continent to continent, country to country and yet, she came back. Then, she was able to appreciate the situation finding herself enraptured in an awe-inspiring revelation that Avon's siblings didn't care to learn about or to understand.

"When the philosopher points to the stars, the fool's eyes are fixed on the finger."

The title of the book read:

My Childhood Dreams

The book contained Avon's most treasured memoirs and despite of the challenges that she'd encountered when growing up and through life's path; in her writings Avon highlighted the experiences that taught her the most extracting the lessons from her most cherished reminiscences in life. She revealed her journey from phase to phase beginning from her childhood and reaching the end at a defined period of her past aiming to disclose her essence mainly to those who ignored the intention from her heart. The story unraveled from one phase to another unfolding gradually but concise and she revealed some of the sources of her learning keeping others for herself.

As an adult, Avon had the opportunity to listen to people disclosing in confidence their adversities as they grew up, so when she realized the adversities she had confronted in life herself, her so-called adversities didn't seem as surprising anymore; because after contemplating about it, she didn't consider her journey as an exception but the norm and as far as she was concerned, she could have been born anywhere in the world and it just happened to be that she was an average girl birthed in "The City of Angels," Bangkok.

1

꧁꧂

*A*von's learning journey commenced with one of the first vivid memories stored in her heart when she was in Bangkok as a little girl and she didn't have dolls of her own to play with. Nevertheless, she never felt like she missed the joy of playing with dolls, because she played with her next door girlfriend's Barbies she often recalled. Besides, since she would've played with any doll with the same enthusiasm, enjoyment and care, as an innocent girl; she couldn't tell the difference between owning a doll and borrowing her friend's.

When Avon was about five-years-old, the little one wasn't allowed to play with the only doll she supposedly ever owned; and clearly, it wasn't a Barbie doll. The baby-doll was selected by Avon and bought by her mama, of course; but her mama persuaded her to keep the doll clean and being a child Avon agreed to keep the doll in the original box where the doll remained untouched. Hence, Avon's treasured memories of looking at her only doll from the distance through the cellophane cover of the original box and placed in a high up shelf by the hall, sufficed for her to appreciate the fact that she had a doll of her own one day. And at that age, pleasing her mama was more than a pleasure to her.

"When the philosopher points to the stars, the fool's eyes are fixed on the finger."

When Avon was about seven-years-old, she had pretty much grown out of playing with dolls and one day, Kalaya's one-year-old daughter wanted to play with Avon's only doll. Avon's mama was just observing when Avon's sister Kalaya said, "Avon, I know it's your only doll but you don't even play with it, give it to Mae. Thus far, she's your only niece, sweetie."

"Is Mae allowed to play with it?" Avon asked looking at her mama who was silent.

"Yes, silly! What else is a little girl supposed to do with a doll, look at it?" Kalaya replied while taking the doll's box down the shelf and handed it to Avon to give it to Mae.

Then holding the box between her little hands; Avon looked at the doll inside thinking *why shouldn't I give the doll to Mae? Mae plays with me. Mae moves by herself. Mae is a real doll not like this one or the Barbies, dolls are lifeless. Mae is not only my only niece, she is my only doll* and Avon happily agreed to give the doll to Mae.

Avon took the doll out of the box for the first time and gave it to her little niece who sat on the floor. But what impressed Avon the most was that when receiving the doll, Mae kept her eyes fixed on hers smiling as though she knew what was going on in Avon's heart. The doll must have been half Mae's size back then and dragging the doll through the floor, Mae crawled toward Avon giving her the sweetest kiss and the biggest hug she had ever received before. Therefore, Avon experienced more pleasure by giving the doll to her niece, knowing that at least she would be allowed to play with it, than keeping the doll for herself—looking at it from the distance through the cellophane cover of the original box placed in a high up shelf.

And so, the doll episode exposed Avon to the joy of giving without regret for the very first time in her short experience in life. The emotion she felt by giving the doll to Mae was such a profound bliss; Avon stored the memory in her heart developing into an affectionate relationship as years passed by between her and her nice.

On the other hand, being the happiest little girl when giving her only doll away, in her childish mind, Avon reflected on the pleasure her next door girlfriend must have felt every time she lent one of the Barbie dolls to her. However all in all, Avon wondered trying to understand, how come her next door girlfriend didn't allow her to play with any of the dolls in her Barbie's collection at times. So as a child, Avon often pondered if perhaps the pleasure of *lending* a doll might have not been the same pleasure of *giving* one.

When Avon was a little girl, rather than playing with dolls like other young girls did, she had unlike interests and ideas in her mind. She had sort of been exposed to worldly experiences. She had a slight sense of what a plane was and what traveling from one country to another meant. Not that she had traveled herself; but her mama spoke often and highly about family friends who were coming and going in planes and they told stories about what other countries were like. So, Avon had dreams from an early age and at that point; she had already allied with her one and only friend: Arolf.

Avon and Arolf bonded instantly and they became best friends. She confided in Arolf like kids do sharing fantasies, dreams and imagining different exciting things. And although so young, Avon perceived that Arolf was rejected by many, in particular by her family because while she was supposed to follow tradition and the culture's beliefs, Arolf encouraged Avon to pursue her desires and dreams opposite to what the little one was expected to feel. Naturally, Avon couldn't help being enthused about the ideas Arolf inspired her with, as usually, Arolf was in agreement with her.

Avon shared with Arolf genuinely elaborating about the dreams she wished to attain as she grew up. She dreamed of speaking

"When the philosopher points to the stars, the fool's eyes are fixed on the finger."

different languages and traveling the world. She dreamed of taking planes from continent to continent and country to country. She dreamed of the countries she wanted to live at and the countries she would visit. What's more, secretly, Avon confided her ultimate dream to Arolf pointing out with her little right index finger on an old dusty Earth globe the specific country where she really wanted to live at one day and Arolf response was inspiring the child twice as much. Avon's certainty to attain her childish dreams was almost arrogant. Yet, being just a kid it was clear that her assurance was based more in self-confidence than in arrogance. When Avon imagined herself traveling all over the world, at times, she acted as if she was already gone to Paris, London, Tokyo, New York and all the exciting cities she could discover on the old dusty Earth globe. Avon communicated with Arolf articulating the way only children can express within their own soundness genuine sense.

However as rejected as Arolf seemed to be by Avon's family, so were the little one's imagination, desires and dreams; as she learned the hard way one day when she shared her aspiration of speaking different languages and traveling the world with them. Because ever since, Avon was called crazy and except for her dad, each family member teased her in different ways. Avon noticed that no one paid attention to the true intention from her heart and she used to think *since my dad named me; he probably would understand*. But her dad was seldom around.

As Avon grew older, she realized that her desire to leave and explore the world had increased, and so did her connection with Arolf because by then, they had improved their communication to an extent. Avon had learned from books she read that if she only listened to her heart, her aspirations and dreams would take her far. So, she was determined to go after her dreams with or without her family's advice. She was rather young when she began being curious about what she felt deep inside, and often, she would ask questions to Arolf trying to identify the voice from her heart; but from time to time, the little one didn't know when to stop.

"Arolf, how do I listen to my heart to be able to follow it?" she would ask ready to take notes; because by writing Arolf's words, Avon validated the oomph she felt inside.

Then Arolf would explain, "Avon, one day you will learn by your own that you were able to listen to your heart all along." Since Avon appeared a bit puzzled and not quite satisfied, Arolf would go further, "Avon, when the time to make decisions come, you will sense your heart's voice and you will know where to go."

Inquisitively, Avon would ask, "How?"

Then Arolf would patiently illustrate, "Well, there is no particular order when allowing the heart to guide, Avon." Describing that sometimes she would follow her heart first and listen to it later, and other times she would listen to her heart first and follow it later.

"How?" she would ask again.

So, Arolf would explain, "Trust is hope, Avon, hope is trust!"

"How do I trust? How do I hope?" she would question still.

And as Arolf had explained many times, Arolf would repeat, "Trust the voice within as your heart's voice Avon. Sense it, feel it and trust it. Then, you will sense *hope*."

Something was for sure; Avon usually gave up the inquiring before Arolf gave up the expounding. Then, Avon would carry on dreaming not really understanding what Arolf meant and putting her notes away until she felt inquisitive again. Although the only thing the twelve-year-old girl could sense from her heart when trying to listen was the determination and desire to leave her family, country and everything she was familiar with; not allowing her to

"When the philosopher points to the stars, the fool's eyes are fixed on the finger."

fully identify the voice from her heart as her intentions vibrating silently in her mind.

Avon's family didn't seem to have financial means for her to be dreaming of such things. Her family was rather struggling and pretending to keep their social status higher than the middle class. Her Thai mama was married to an English man and she did as much as she could to prove that they were better off than most pretending to have what they couldn't afford.

Unaware of the facts and unable to identify her emotions; Avon was full of hope. She had self confidence and she didn't stop dreaming. She trusted that one day she would speak several languages and travel all over the world. The only thing Avon knew was that something would happen and things would change. She sensed emotions that she couldn't explain ignited by a passionate burning flame in her heart that no one would validate, along with an oomph driving desire reassuring her that her dreams would become true someday.

Not having idea of how her childish dreams would be attained, she had heard of the country known to everyone as America and *there* was where she really wanted to go. Due to the disdain she experienced by sharing her dreams with her family in the past; she dreamed quietly then not sharing with them what she really wanted deep inside. Clearly at that point, Avon felt disgraced around her family most of the time; especially when they ridiculed her in front of relatives and friends.

Years passed by. Avon reached adolescence and her determination to leave only increased more and more. At that point, she was able to realize that the way she was being brought up was making her feel out of place among her own culture, tradition, family and friends. She was being taught to desire nothing while her desire to attain her dreams was stronger than ever. She was supposed to learn to eat her own misery and to swallow other people's bitterness while her heart erupted with cheerfulness and sweetness. Then, she began to think *when I finally leave, I would probably return to visit but I won't live here ever again*. Her parents' conduct and the way they were leading their own children to get ahead made Avon feel even more out of place. Their parents would inculcate principles and values to them, but no one was led to practice what they learned. She sensed pressure from her parents leading them into a path that didn't appear to be in accordance with the principles she felt deep in her heart and being Avon the youngest of five; she had to learn most of everything by example. So, many times she rather followed examples from strangers by instinct, for her intuitive conscious didn't allow her to follow the guidance she got from her family.

During Avon's late teenage years, her brother Chet brought a friend named Lek to have dinner with the family one evening. Lek said that he had left Bangkok many years earlier and that he lived in Canada at the time. He also said that he would return to Canada after a few days because he was in Bangkok visiting family and friends; but from the moment Lek met Avon; he was infatuated with her. However, Avon wasn't attracted to Lek and she didn't reciprocate his intentions toward her. Lek was from Thailand and just like her mama; Avon was attracted to foreigners instead. Besides, she didn't like Lek's gluey mustache covering his missing teeth. Also, he had greasy looking hair and what's more, the man must have been at least fifteen years older than her.

Avon was young and thus far, she had only had one boyfriend named Clive who was originally from England. She liked Clive but not long before Lek's visit, Clive had gone back to England without signs of ever returning again. Avon became attracted to Clive because of her friend Jaidee's fiancé, who was a handsome

"When the philosopher points to the stars, the fool's eyes are fixed on the finger."

executive French man working in a project in Bangkok named Xavier. After dating Jaidee for some time, Xavier proposed marriage to her and when Xavier finished the assignment; he took Jaidee away to live in France with him just like in a fairytale. Avon had always admired Jaidee because she spoke fluent English and when she wedded Xavier, Avon was excited for her friend because Xavier spoke fluent English as well. Then Avon thought *if I meet someone like Xavier, he would take me away the same and when joining my ideal prince charming, we will be as happy as Jaidee and Xavier are.* Not long after Jaidee and Xavier went to France, Avon met the English boy, Clive, and she was attracted to him thanks to his physical resemblance to Xavier. Little did Avon know, because Clive wasn't Xavier nor she was Jaidee and when the time for Clive to go back to England came; he didn't ask for Avon to come along, let alone propose marriage to her, bringing Avon to be exposed to her first romantic heartbreak.

After experiencing such an intense heartbreak, Avon was even more determined to leave her family, country and everything she was familiar with and she only wished for an opportunity to come her way to be able to go away. Back then, Avon was completely unaware of the fact that every wish she had would manifest and by not being specific when wishing; her wishes manifested adrift, just like she wished, and sadly, her wishes not always manifested in her favor.

Not long had passed after Avon's devastating heartbreaking experience when one evening her mother approached her asking, "Avon do you still have those crazy ideas of traveling around the world?" Avon looked at her mama in wonder as her mama added, "If you still do, we will make your crazy dreams come true." As Avon expression went from surprised to happy, and then, extremely excited. She listened to her mama say, "Your father closed a business deal and we'll send you to America in a student exchange."

Avon was naïve and she didn't question her mother about the type of school or what kind of studies she was supposed to attend. Not only because she wasn't allowed questioning her parents; but she was excited. So expressing appreciation and happiness, her full lips smiled stretching from extreme to extreme and without hesitation she confirmed with thrill, "But of course I do mama!" Full of enthusiasm Avon went on jumping and exclaiming, "A trip!" "I will travel!" "Is this really happening to me, mama?!" "I will travel, mama!" She accepted her mama's generous offer without ado.

Although at the time, Avon didn't realize that she didn't apply for such a student exchange in any way. She was so excited about her dream of traveling becoming true; she just follow her heart without even knowing it and graceful Avon only knew that she was the happiest girl in the world for she was going abroad.

"When the philosopher points to the stars, the fool's eyes are fixed on the finger."

2

⚜

From Bangkok to America

On a matter of weeks, Avon's parents had processed her passport and they got her a ticket to fly out of Bangkok. However Avon had no idea where she was going and she didn't pay attention to details. For instance, she didn't notice if the ticket had a return portion; to which country she was going to fly, or in which city she would be studying. America! She was going to America being the only thing that matter to her. After briefly showing the passport to Avon; her mother said that the documents needed to be safe and she trusted her mother to keep the passport and the ticket until the day she flew away. Avon was so excited gathering and packing two suitcases with her most valued effects; she just kept wondering if she would ever return once she'd left.

When Avon was younger her mama had given a pair of tiny sapphire pierced earrings to her and she wore them all the time. As Avon was in the excitement of packing; her mama approached with a book for Avon to take on the trip and asked, "Avon, would you leave the sapphire earrings to me as a souvenir or are you taking them with you?"

"When the philosopher points to the stars, the fool's eyes are fixed on the finger."

Then Avon replied teasing, "Oh Mama, how could I leave these earrings to you if I had never taken them off since the day you gave them to me?" Next, softly and tenderly Avon described, "These tiny earrings are ideal to keep as a souvenir mama because no one could take away the bond between you and my flesh." At the same time, Avon had reached her right ear. She had taken off one of the earrings and she had put the tiny earring in her mama's left ear. Then she whispered, "Now, we are connected forever, mama. We share the earrings no matter where I go." Avon had kept the other tiny earring in her left ear, and just then, both of them touched their left ears and as mother and daughter they confirmed saying together, "We are connected!" Praising how thankful they were that earrings came in pairs so they could share wearing one earring each.

The anticipation of the trip meant everything to Avon and rightfully so; as in many ways she was a fortunate girl by having an opportunity not many did, or so she was told. Avon had heard of people who had lived a lifetime and they were still wondering if they would get to travel a short distance, to the next region, or to neighboring towns. And there she was, at her young age, ready to leave one continent and about to explore another one.

Avon's traveling day arrived and as she walked through the gate at the airport to present her passport with a visa stamped on it; at the last minute when there was no time to hesitate; just then was when Avon first noticed that the visa stamped on her passport was certainly taking her to America, but the visa was Canadian not a visa to the U.S.A.

Avon felt her legs shaking and her wits gradually dismaying standing like a lifeless cold tree while countless thoughts were wildly flashing through her uncontaminated mind. That was the very first time that Avon ever recognized the voice from her heart.

Because then, then was the time to make a decision and either find out exactly where she was going or seize the chance ahead of her. If she refused to get on the plane questioning her parents to satisfy her curiosity of the unknown, most likely she might have never seen herself in that side of the airport gate again; except when dreaming to reach as far as she was at that moment. Clearly, it was up to her to decide and accept the once in a lifetime opportunity facing her. Instantly, Avon sensed like a *wave* from her heart clearly saying *Cross the gate! Follow me to the plane! Fly away, Avon! Let's fly away!*

So, off she went waving and cheering goodbye to everyone; Avon decided by her own to explore the unknown and she truly followed her heart's voice.

Although from the moment Avon saw the Canadian visa on her passport; she suspected that the student exchange had something to do with the man named Lek. The man that she wasn't attracted to and she didn't have romantic interests for. By knowing her family's conduct, Avon thought *Lek could have arranged with my parents to send me to him.* Leading her to also suspect that Lek was behind the business deal her mother said that her father had closed. Then, Avon began having valid concerns, as she figured that Lek could have expectations at her arrival. Next, she thought *it could be just a coincidence.* But deep in her heart she sensed it. Her intuition was telling her that the student exchange had something to do with the man named Lek. So, she thought *if that is the case, I could learn to be attracted to him and things would be just fine.*

As Avon boarded the plane, she looked at the ticket and when she realized that she was going to Montreal; she forgot about every concern because going to an American city meant everything to her. Avon thought *even if it is not the U.S., stepping on American soil is worth anything and everything,* or so was her mind-set back then.

"When the philosopher points to the stars, the fool's eyes are fixed on the finger."

Enthused knowing that her destination was one of the greatest cities in the world; she went with the flow embracing what was to come.

Eventually, she realized how ignorant she was as she knew nothing about the meaning of *worth anything* or *worth everything* back then. Not until months later after encountering an extensive world out there; because when thinking about her dream of stepping on American soil being worth anything or everything she did not consider the fact that, without exception, actions were followed by consequences. She had no notion that every cause had an effect. Especially when pursuing childhood dreams by her own in a foreign soil; as if it wasn't difficult enough pursuing dreams in the soil where she had been born. Unawares, Avon was full of hope when she first thought that something out in the world was worth anything and everything for deep in her heart anything or everything didn't entail her body, her truth, her soberness, her integrity, and certain things that she was firmly not willing to negotiate; not even in exchange for her most precious dream of stepping on American soil or any other soil on the entire Earth.

While flying out of Bangkok, after looking at her documents, Avon noticed that she was holding a thirty day return ticket. So she was confused, for she felt that such a short period of time for a student exchange wasn't giving her dreams much of chance to be attained. And she thought *a month might not be long enough to learn much of anything. I wish I had a student exchange for life.*

When Avon arrived and entered Canada, she spoke some English and not French. She was briefly questioned by Customs and Immigrations and she was allowed into the country right away. Then the fact that the Immigration Inspector stamped her passport granting her a stay as a tourist and not as a student; confirmed that she was holding a visitor's visa and not a student visa. After that, it was clear to her that her trip had nothing to do with a student exchange. Avon followed the crowd at the airport and just like she suspected, Lek was waiting for her at the baggage claim. The man greeted her as though she had been the one who had agreed with him to come and visit. Yet, she remained calm and she didn't panic or expressed any emotion of concern. Regardless of what seemed to be the beginning of an endless nightmare; it was just the beginning of childhood dreams becoming true to her.

Lek took Avon to a friend's house where she was supposed to be welcomed or so he said. Naturally, she didn't know anyone and everyone was from Bangkok. There wasn't a single Canadian person in the social gathering. Avon was exhausted after flying for so many hours and she couldn't even refresh before attending a welcoming party; except it really didn't matter, for everyone was drunk and whatever they were celebrating had nothing to do with her arrival at all.

When Lek and Avon first arrived at that house, a lady who could hardly keep her eyes open, holding a beer in one hand and a cigarette in the other, greeted them at the door. The lady cheerfully invited Avon into a room where she put her suitcases down and when they came back into the living area to join the party, Lek was already gone. It turned out that Lek had brought her to his friend's house because he had suspicious businesses going on and he didn't have an established home. Therefore after Avon's arrival, he rented an apartment for her to stay and the man decided to move-in along.

Avon didn't quite understand what she had gotten herself into. Lek had the habit of going out not telling her when he would be back. From time to time, she went days without having a decent meal; but as weeks passed by; she figured out ways to endure and she survived. When Lek was around, she made sure to get some tea, cookies, dry packed drinks and instant noodle soups. Because except for an electric kettle to boil water in, the small apartment

"When the philosopher points to the stars, the fool's eyes are fixed on the finger."

didn't have a proper kitchen for her to cook or even a fridge. It was more like a room than an apartment it seemed. Although when Lek came by, they went out to eat at the corner restaurant once a day dividing one menu special between the two of them.

Revealing gently, Avon was suppressed under physical, mental and emotional abuse by Lek and even his friends. They used to tell her that no other man in the entire world would notice her and that she should be grateful that Lek did. They disrespected each other using insulting names among themselves and her as well. Avon's sensation of feeling her wits gradually dismaying like a lifeless cold tree intensified as weeks went by sensing her self-esteem progressively retreating into hidden areas that she ignored possessing deep inside. Lek was generally intoxicated exposing her to risky situations; especially when he took her to visit his friends. Time after time, they dared Avon to drink or to practice certain habits which she refused to engage. In exchange, she conformed to become Lek's punching bag so to speak, because she was embarrassing him, he used to say. Those experiences taught Avon more than she had bargained for. However, she didn't complain nor had anyone to blame; for she was where she wanted to be. Besides, she sensed that there was a light at the end of the tunnel and she began learning to trust the voice within as her heart's voice like Arolf had advised her in the past.

In the midst of her torment, Avon felt a sense of hope, the hope Arolf spoke of; and trying to understand the gravity of the situation she thought *the circumstances do not own me. I am in the moment and I am capable to decide either to leave or to stay.* Leading her to understand that it didn't matter how low her self-esteem was; for there was another sensation within her, an oomph driving her forward with certainty and not doubt. Lek and his friends could diminish her self-esteem all they wanted; nevertheless no one, including Lek, was competent to take away the source of her dreams, her drive, a faculty that she was inescapably bonded with, but she hadn't quite identified within—*Her Will.*

Even though, identifying some of the circumstances didn't allow her to act upon the situation automatically. Later in life, Avon discovered that she had to go through a process assimilating and then, appropriating her thoughts and ideas before being able to practice them. Back then, she was far from understanding her insight and she earnestly felt in her heart that she had to go through much more to attain her aspirations and dreams because she didn't even finish school in Thailand not giving her foundation to protest, as if she did, her options were limited for she could have been sent back to Bangkok as a result of her complaints.

A few months went by and the period that Avon was granted to stay in Canada came to an end. Her return ticket had already expired and she didn't know what the future held for her. Regardless, she truly hoped to come out of the situation without having to return to the place everyone around, except her, called home. Miraculously, Lek had made arrangements to change her immigration status by sponsoring her as an employee which she discovered a couple of years later when she learned to speak fluent French. In the dark, not knowing much of anything; she was accepted as sort of an *immigrant in probation* by the inspector who questioned her at the Canadian Immigration. The translator was Lek's comrade who was the incarnation of an angel, or so it seemed to her. By Lek's good deed, Avon obtained a legal work permit to remain in Canada giving her the chance to become an official Canadian resident, if she complied with the rules and regulations of the Canadian Immigrations Department. Then, she was forced to remain in the situation thinking *once I become an official resident*

"When the philosopher points to the stars, the fool's eyes are fixed on the finger."

I could detach from Lek, and then, I will carry on by myself pursuing my aspirations and dreams.

The conditions to become a Canadian permanent resident were to demonstrate her ability to communicate in English and French; she had to work legally and reside in a permanent address. And so, she thought *I should tolerate the situation a bit longer, and then, I will attain my dream of learning different languages. If I only find a job where I am not required to speak, I could work during the day, and after that, I could attend the school provided for free to immigrants in the evenings learning both languages at the same time.* Not giving up, full of enthusiasm and hope; she decided to stop resisting Lek's demands which she had to endure every time he came by and she took a chance intending to alter measures.

During those past months she had not contacted her family, except for a short phone call that she was allowed to make to her mama the day she arrived in Montreal. And so far, she wasn't ready to call her mama; not only because she felt embarrassed to expose her situation, but also, she couldn't figure out how to convey to her mama that she had been staying with Lek; as at that point, Avon still didn't know how the arrangement was made between Lek and her parents fabricating the story of the student exchange.

So one day, she thought of someone who would understand her, accept her and give her the best guidance and support without judging her. Avon had heard of some people having a friend who they could call at any time of the day; call through an operator collect or call direct and as best friends, they were always there for them, thus she was thinking of her best friend. However she struggled, because she seemed to have lost contact with Arolf. Avon felt like when she needed the most support, Arolf was unavailable and unreachable to her and it took a long, long while for Avon to establish communication with Arolf again; but once she did, Arolf was present in Montreal with her.

To avoid confrontations with Lek, Avon made sure to be with Arolf by herself and when they finally joined again, in safe privacy, Avon shared with Arolf her new idea to approach Lek saying, "I will propose to Lek to turn our association into a romantic relationship. I am not attracted to him but I sense that his intention is for me to like him."

Arolf explained to her common sense, "It seems as though Lek's frustration is provoked from not being able to attract you naturally, and as a result, he is aggressive with you Avon. Lek cannot force you to like him or force you to do anything against your instinctive will." Avon perceived Arolf's words with an open heart, and as usual, she took notes when Arolf explained, "Avon, where there are no wounds there is no healing. Without wounds and without healing, there are no scars in the soul. To expand to a maximum potential in life, scars in the soul are anticipated because experience and wisdom are merely the result of such."

Avon listened to Arolf absorbing as much. However, Arolf sort of knew that Avon had only absorbed that no one could force her to do anything against her instinctive will. Arolf advised her to find the positive aspects in Lek accepting the circumstances as they were. But, from the time when Avon arrived in Montreal, she and Lek hadn't confronted each other about their alliance and while for Arolf was simple to understand Lek's resentment toward Avon, causing her to feel trapped and as a result Avon resisted the sensation of feeling trapped by refusing Lek even more; being in the situation, Avon was unable to understand her feelings. Besides considering Avon's upbringing regarding emotional denial, she was convinced that by changing her attitude toward Lek, he would stop abusing her physically and mistreating her altogether. What's more, at that point, thanks to Lek's intimate demands Avon had already experienced her first orgasm without an option to reverse the facts

"When the philosopher points to the stars, the fool's eyes are fixed on the finger."

and she thought that she would be better off focusing on the light at the end of the tunnel; even if it meant passing through the tunnel submissively and in a numb state of mind.

Arolf suggested to Avon not to be intimate with anyone else, specifically expressing, "Avon, you should not focus on being faithful to Lek. You should focus on being faithful to yourself." Avon continued taking notes perceiving Arolf's words, "Your actions should originate from integrity and confidence within. You should respect your conscious above all by maintaining liberation of guilt, do not be faithful to please anyone else, do it for yourself." Arolf tried to enlighten her regarding what intimacy should represent for a couple as well, but Avon didn't understand what those issues meant back then. Still, Avon sensed hope again and she felt that eventually everything would make sense if she only kept the notes she'd taken and read them now and then. After that, Arolf didn't have much more to express; for Avon would have to expand in mind and soul learning by her own experiences in life. The time Avon and Arolf spent together came to an end and assuring her that everything happens for a reason; everyone has a purpose to be where they are; and clarifying that the emotions making her feel sad at times were only a sign of hope when approaching situations confidently, Arolf left.

Afterward, Avon was looking out the apartment's window and she distinguished Lek by the sidewalk approaching the building. She wave smiling and glad to see him thinking that she would be able to share her new approach with him.

As soon as Lek opened the apartment door Avon greeted him excitedly. In response, Lek abruptly smacked her in the face so hard, she landed on the floor. He said annoyed, "I don't know what makes you happy all of a sudden. Your laughter is ugly and you look awful when you smile." As she wept still laying on the floor, he kicked her adding, "From now on, you better don't smile at all. I forbid you to smile, much less laugh." Then, mocking her smile and laughter, Lek walked back toward the door. He locked Avon inside with the bolt key from outside as she was before, leaving Avon for a couple of days without being able to open the door to go out once more.

She cried and cried feeling sorry for herself and not having a TV or anything else to pass time; she read the only reading book she had which was titled: *The Greatest Salesman in theWorld*. Avon had read the book so many times it was falling apart and she almost had the entire book memorized. She got the book from the passenger sitting next to her in the plane when she arrived in Montreal. She accepted it enthused ignoring that each thought and word in the book would keep her company during countless hours while she waited for Lek to return every time he locked her indoors.

Some time had passed and it didn't take long for Avon to realize that nothing had changed between Lek and her; except for her understanding and acceptance of the consequences of her actions. Because after she finally had conveyed her approach to Lek, he continued being as bitter and resentful as he ever was. Avon's change of attitude didn't appear to have affected him in any way. Simply what Avon did, made no difference to Lek. Exposing Avon to observe that there wasn't much Lek could do to change her or for her to change Lek, other than accepting expansion at their individual own pace. Avon hardly spoke to anyone back then and she had time to think. When experiencing the incapacity to change another person, she realized that her thoughts could influence the manifestation of certain things happening around her. But she didn't understand why she couldn't influence Lek to change. Little did she know back then, because she had no capacity to change her own self; let alone someone else. She didn't know then what she later acknowledged, for as a human being she was

"*When the philosopher points to the stars, the fool's eyes are fixed on the finger.*"

only capable to expand in life, not to change humanly. Yet, it was a bit too early in life for her to fully understand her ideas; since practically the only thing in her favor was her determination to practice everything she had learned from Arolf and the book that she had read so many times. Therefore, her limited knowledge combined with the mind programming method illustrated in the book provided her with the enlightenment she required at the time to create a foundation during that specific stage in life. The girl had such lack of guidance when growing up; she could have lost herself engaging into addictions of alcoholism, drugs, prostitution, antidepressants, or whatever pills were provided to people afflicted by emotional and physical abuse. But instead, Avon's integrity and the oomph driving her within prevailed over the temptations she was exposed during a long term. Although eventually she clearly understood that addictions do not develop and destroy a soul due to contamination of intoxicating substances; but addictions develop due to contamination and manipulation of thoughts being what one thinks that destroys.

So, back then Avon ignored what she later discovered; as Lek had sponsored her to have a legal working permit with the intention to send her to work. After she worked legally long enough, Lek would manage to claim unemployment on her behalf. Then, he was planning to give her a job as a server paying her cash and collecting social benefits at the same time. Lek's affairs were dishonest. However at the time, even if it wasn't obvious to Avon, things were sort of working in her favor because being sober and Lek's woman was her protection; as she could have just become another dancer at the strip-club where Lek held his affairs. On the other hand being in the situation, Avon could only perceive that Lek wasn't supporting her to fulfill the requisites to become a legal resident, much less a Citizen one day.

In any event, Lek allowed Avon to spend some time with a lady allied to one of his friends in order to help her to find a legal job and in the process she opened up to Avon, Yada was her name. Yada was a couple of years older than Avon and she had tried to get away a few times; but for some reason the man allied to her always managed to find her bringing her back to the same situation. Yada was usually under the influence of intoxicating substances and one day riding in a bus Avon who just happened to be there heard every complain Yada had to express, "Most people in this vicious circle are in limbo. I know what it feels to have an excuse for every failure not being able to progress in life. There's always a problem."

During those days, when Avon was around Lek and his friends, she heard the word *problem* in every other sentence and since Yada opened up, Avon felt comfortable to ask, "Are you saying that they use the word *problem* as an excuse, Yada?"

"Yes, it's an excuse to avoid responsibilities and rules. They create their own problems focusing on getting away with something all the time, instead of facing solutions and take the responsibility of making decisions. The worst part is the guilt afterward." Yada referred about the men allied to them.

"Feeling temporary satisfaction, eh?" Avon added.

"Maybe" Yada wondered, admitting, "Temporary satisfaction alright; but after I feel like my conscious rebounds exposing me to the inevitable truth no matter what; because I'm in the same situation as they are."

"Probably they use intoxicating substances to forget the guilt for what they had gotten away with." Avon thought out loud.

And Yada didn't have a doubt confirming, "Yes, but I can only speak for myself."

Then Avon thought *seems like they try to fool the law and end up drowning into addictions depending on external sources to superficially*

"When the philosopher points to the stars, the fool's eyes are fixed on the finger."

be seeking liberation of guilt. They don't seem to get away with much, as depending on intoxicating substances is not liberation after all. No wonder she calls it a vicious circle. Only that time, Avon didn't think out loud out of respect for Yada because like she said, she was in the same situation as their men were.

At that point, Avon only had a slight idea of what was going on and she began to notice that for the most part Lek's contacts were immigrants and regardless of the years they had been living in Canada, they didn't speak English or French fairly. They didn't contribute as part of the society and they kept further away from becoming citizens. Avon speculated that even if they held residence permits, most of them still lived illegally in the country due to fear of learning the languages or perhaps for not to report their income tax. Lek and his friends didn't seem the kind who cared if society supported them through the social aid they claimed. It wasn't until then that Avon began to understand what being illegal in a country meant. She realized that illegality wasn't only about not having a visa; or a social insurance number; or resident documents; or a citizen passport. What for most people at her age was considered common knowledge, she was just learning. She figured out by herself that breaking any of society's laws and rules was illegal despite where she was. Not until being in a foreign country, she grasped the concept of a civilized society and she became aware of the fact that once she was somewhere, whether visiting or residing, she was automatically responsible to follow laws and rules; for illegality wasn't applied only to immigrants. Then she remembered situations when she was back in Bangkok living with her parents and she realized that many people naturally born in a country and in a civilized society, not necessarily in Canada, led an illegal lifestyle.

Learning from Lek and his friends, Avon recognized that making illegal decisions was up to her, but she didn't have to pursue her family's prototype. She felt that she could find the chance to become a good member of society anywhere in the world with the option to expand to the fullest of her potential or not. Back then, she could hardly wait to practice what she was learning in her mind because she was involved in a situation allowing her to think, however she was unable to practice her insight. She perceived the system from a different view as well, because she realized that even if the people around her earned cash wages while also claiming social aid and unemployment benefits; the funds they generated and supposedly saved by evading taxes wasn't allocated wisely. She didn't understand if they were smarter, making more money than others, how come cash wasn't abundant when passing through their hands. In essence ignoring the facts, Avon sort of figured out that since Lek and his friends didn't have aspiration to prosper in life, Lek assumed that just because she was also born in the same country that they were, she should follow the same path.

By exchanging a few words with Yada, Avon learned that the word *problem* was used as an excuse by some for not to move forward in life. And as a result, she intentionally expunged and removed the word *problem* from her mental vocabulary; hence if she didn't think it, she wouldn't speak the word either. While the people in Lek's circle seemed afraid to encounter bliss naturally; Avon didn't accept the idea of carrying a problem around as if she was holding a book under her arm. She considered that problems didn't have much use while unresolved and having the time to think, she established that she would find ways to resolve conflicts as they came to her without dwelling on them. She used the time to reflect. She created ideas by writing reminders for her not to forget and to be able to put into practice someday.

In due course, writing and reading loads of books became one of Avon's habits; however it was then when she wrote her first

"When the philosopher points to the stars, the fool's eyes are fixed on the finger."

words of reflection from her heart sensing a mild *wave* going into her mind like tossing thoughts to the air, ignoring that later in life those reflections would become priceless to her and to others when she shared.

Tossing a reflection to the air...

"A problem is nothing but the root of a solution. Otherwise mathematicians wouldn't make the slightest effort to discover blooming results in the midst of an infinite numerical art."

3

With Yada's assistance, Avon was able to find a legal job where she wasn't required to speak at all. She began working at an exclusive ladies fashion factory in the quality control department performing the task of general labor. Her function was to focus on performing her best to meet expectations. The designs they created were fashionable, limited, selective, and strictly, few mistakes were allowed. She had to deliver a hundred percent without doubting the importance of her post and just like she had planned; she worked during the day and with Yada's back up, Avon registered at school to learn English and French alternating classes in the evenings.

As time went by, Avon tried to ignore the incidents with Lek while she also tried to focus on her personal objectives. She met people from different countries at school and at work. Many people from Asia worked in the same place as well; however, Avon captured the attention of the designer and the pattern maker which created the sophisticated garments in the factory and she began to socialize. The designer was an average brunette Quebecoise young lady, married to an average Vietnamese man; and the pattern maker

"When the philosopher points to the stars, the fool's eyes are fixed on the finger."

was an average blonde French young lady, married to an average French man.

In one occasion, the designer and her husband invited Avon to spend the weekend at their lake house. Lek wasn't invited, because Avon had told both of her friends that he wasn't kind to her. Pointless for Avon to mention, as her friends and peers at work had already noticed many times Avon's black and blue eyes covered with excessive makeup. So to avoid conflicts with Lek, she declined the invite hoping to be able to come along some other time. Also, Avon was embarrassed to accept the invitation because she had never been on a weekend getaway. In general, the situation was a new aspect of Western living for her to adapt. As due to past experiences, she wasn't used to hearing the truth and even though her friend's invitation sounded like a story someone would fabricate to impress others, Avon trusted that the couple had a house by the lake which they only used during the summer weekends and remained vacant the rest of the year. As a matter of fact, when Avon first interacted with people out of Lek's circle in Montreal, she thought that being an honest worker, sober, truthful, kind, considerate, and a healthy-minded person was part of the Canadian culture. In essence, she felt sorry to decline the invite because the winter season approached leaving little opportunity for her to experience the getaway summer weekends her friends spoke about so much.

In addition to the emotional mix that Avon was experiencing, from the day that she arrived in Montreal, she felt an emotion she couldn't identify. At any rate, not that she could identify emotions easily but the feeling was torturing her. She felt sad. She sensed some emptiness deep inside bringing tears to her eyes and she couldn't explain why. Sometimes when she felt the emotion; she felt relief thinking of the future and that she was fulfilling her dreams; but she couldn't explain why sadness was eating her up inside. So an uneventful afternoon she was with a classmate doing homework and she mentioned about the emotion she felt. Avon explained describing the feeling more in detail allowing herself to search deep inside and she discovered that every time she felt that way was when she remembered her family and the past, realizing that her memories were what made her feel so sad. Then, her classmate recognized the emotion at once and told her that feeling sad was natural because she was just homesick. Avon had never heard of that term before, but at the time it gave her some peace of mind to learn that there was a word to refer to the emotion she felt. Although, she was unaware that such identified emotion would remain within her for as long as her mama lived.

Meanwhile, it didn't take long for Lek to realize that Avon was actually moving forward and he was obsessed to obstruct her development in the Canadian culture and society. Despite of the oomph Avon projected indicating her potential to discover many more cultures and societies in the world, it seemed as though Lek wouldn't let her be, unless she proved her ability to conquer her own culture first. So an ordinary evening, on an effort to stop Avon from taking language classes, Lek decided to lock her out of the apartment without keys. He could no longer lock her inside like he used to because Avon had to have her own bolt key to go to work, but despite the many times she begged him not to; he pushed her through the door locking her out of the apartment and leaving her outside for the rest of the night. It was cold and a snow storm was coming, she was just getting familiar to the winter in Montreal and naturally, adapting to the first winter was shocking and difficult for her as she had to manage with the clothing and the footwear provided by the ladies allied to Lek's friends. Yet, not being used to freezing conditions or having proper clothing to welcome the

"When the philosopher points to the stars, the fool's eyes are fixed on the finger."

winter season, Avon found herself out in the slightly heated corridor where she spent the night shivering. Similar incidents happened over and over, until there was a time when Lek went too far. It was late in the evening and few people were out and about. After having the meal of the day, Lek and Avon were walking on the sidewalk in direction to their place, and suddenly, Lek pushed Avon over a big pile of snow followed by gradually discharging urine all over her.

The following day at work during lunch break, Avon shared with the designer and the pattern maker the unpleasant incident that had taken place. Timidly embarrassed and totally mortified Avon requested their advice. Her friends' response was most obvious for they thought that Avon would never ask. And so, they assisted her to understand that she was no longer in Bangkok and that in Quebec women had civil rights. They also explained that couples seldom got married in Quebec; therefore, women weren't supposed to be submissive to men. They said as well that she was legally protected and that she was allowed to claim her rights at anytime. They explained that, even if Lek assisted her with the paperwork to change her immigration status, she wasn't required to stay with him in order to remain in the country. They gave her details about the Canadian-Quebecois law clarifying that Lek didn't have any rights over her. Both of her friends said that they would declare and testify if necessary about the mistreatment she had been exposed to during the time they have known her.

On that particular occasion, Avon felt for the first time in her entire short life's journey, a sense of alleviation; bringing her to almost feel complete peace of mind. As if it had not been for the challenges that she was about to confront, being around those ladies, she would have sensed complete peace in her heart. Her appreciation brought to light her best friend's presence as she recalled a time when Arolf conveyed to her *"The same as you found people to follow their examples Avon, you will find strangers who will be kind to you;"* and she expressed her gratitude to both of her friends who sort of reflected Arolf in flesh as tears rolled down her face.

Avon felt fortunate having encountered such humanitarian people at her workplace; because while more often than not, she had been exposed to cruelty for no reason; those two young ladies, although strangers, for no reason were amazingly kind to her. She accepted her friends' good advice sensing the true intention from their hearts, and just then, ignoring what her rights were or what rights meant; Avon wondered what made people react the way they did; good or bad, kind or unkind. And back then, she already knew that everything happened for a reason which wouldn't always reveal at once. So, she wasn't going to be waiting to find out why such things were happening to her. All she understood was that she had to act quickly, making a decision of either staying where she was, or moving forward by acting upon her friends' advice.

Looking back, Avon remembered those moments as slightly funny; because the way she communicated with her friends was a bit humorous. During that phase, Avon used to look up every other word in the dictionary to express and when speaking French, she must have sounded like *Tarzan* would in a way which was a tad amusing for her when she revisited her memory lane.

Mostly, Avon cherished the memories of the many people she found in her path who were kind and gave her hope to look forward and not back. Although she was willing to help herself; she often wondered if her friends ever realized how much they impacted her to learn and to carry on in life.

Soon after, Avon recognized that it was up to Lek and his friends to figure out their own reasons to be in Montreal. As for her, she took what she could gather from the factory work earnings and she decided to move on. She found an apartment a bit bigger

"When the philosopher points to the stars, the fool's eyes are fixed on the finger."

than the room that Lek had rented for them; except that she would be able to cook because her apartment had a small kitchenette.

Surprisingly, moving out of Lek's room wasn't difficult at all, as Lek wasn't around that much. However, facing responsibilities was a new challenge for her to confront; because the few things she had been responsible for to that point, she had been handling out of common sense. So when facing the commitment to rent her own place, she struggled; not because she didn't have the money but because she didn't know how to allocate it. The only thing Avon sort of gathered at the time was paying the rent on the due date; because she remembered when her parents used to send one of her older siblings with a false excuse for not paying the overdue rent every time the landlord came to collect it, and as a result, her family was evicted a couple of times from their home. It was unclear to her how come they frequently lacked of utilities and certain things while there were other expenses set as higher priorities than the family's basic needs. So, being such the notion of responsibility she had; she shifted the example and followed it in reverse. Avon figured out by herself that she couldn't live without a roof over her head and she inverted dishonesty into a lesson of integrity learning from corrupted financial examples which back then, was the only financial guidance she possessed. Therefore, the first thing she learned as a responsible member of society was to pay rent on the due date and ignoring the connection between willpower and ego, Avon was embarrassed and too proud to ask the designer and the pattern maker about how to run her finances thinking *everyone should know these matters at my age.*

The courage sheltering Avon during the following phase could only be attributed to her instinctive confidence by not defying her inner-self. For No one could really prepare to the degree of danger she exposed herself without foreseeing the consequences of her actions. She left Lek without looking back not thinking ahead. By leaving him, she risked being harassed, stalked and she even jeopardized being part of a passionate crime; all consequences which simply didn't cross her mind. She had provoked a man of the irrational kind and although it was evident that Lek had pushed her away, most likely she caught him by complete surprise because Lek never expected Avon to leave him and, from then on, a new facet began.

During many weeks, Avon had been evading Lek from his startling appearances at the bus stop line; or next to the employees' door at her workplace; and she had managed to conceal from him where she lived. On the other hand, Lek had to figure out where she was, so he calculated that if he only followed her unnoticed, rather than stalking her in the streets, he would discover where she had moved at and he did. After Lek followed Avon unseen and found out where she lived; he made a corny but apparently efficient plan, just like he has seen on TV. Then, one evening, he sneaked inside the building where Avon rented her apartment and he waited quietly for her to arrive. Once she entered the building, he figured out in which floor and door she went in and he was ready to attack.

After a long working day, Avon was preparing dinner and suddenly, a knock at the door. For the first and last time ever, she opened without looking through the peephole.

It was Lek. He forced himself in. He pushed the door against Avon, and as usual, she landed on the floor. The kitchenette was a couple of feet from the entrance to the right. While she was picking herself up from the floor, Lek jumped to the countertop and grabbed a butcher's knife. He said nastily, "If you don't return to me, I come prepared to kill you, and after, I'll kill myself." Avon had just connected the telephone landline not long before and when she reached the phone, he pulled her by the hair dragging her

"When the philosopher points to the stars, the fool's eyes are fixed on the finger."

toward him on the floor. He grabbed her from behind pointing the knife to her face and neck, "I'LL KILL YOU!" he yelled.

She had managed to get the phone and she was holding it between her hands; but not afraid of his alleged intention; she struggled to look at him in the eyes and, penetrating his most profound senses possessing a force above all, she told him straight forward, "If you have the courage to kill me Lek, do it quickly. Except you better kill me as in dead; for if you do not and you just injure me, you ought to face the consequences." She paused briefly, and added, "Once I am dead, if you would like to kill yourself, go ahead." After that, she didn't resist him. She relaxed her entire body and she released her wits to death. Because she would rather die than to go back to be Lek's punching bag, much less his public urine aim. With a calm and serene tone she said several times, "Go ahead" "Go ahead" "Go ahead."

She clearly conveyed to him that she rather died than to be forced to do something that she wasn't willing to do by instinct. Then, he realized that she didn't even try to stop him by calling the police. It was obvious that she was serious and not playing games like he was. Without fearing him or trying to calm him down, she had faced him and confronted him directly.

She was determined not to allow him to manipulate her as she had sensed his false intentions. Besides, her thoughts traveled faster than light thinking *no killer will undertake a victim to commit a premeditated crime as Lek claims without at least bringing their own weapon.* Avon quickly realized that if she didn't have the butcher's knife handy, Lek wouldn't have had the courage of threatening to kill her with his bare hands. Simply Avon didn't seem to fear much including death itself. Then again, she frightened Lek by the audacious young woman he had found. Certainly, she wasn't the fragile girl who he had suppressed during months under his control.

It was clear that his abusing behavior toward her had bounced back at him making her not weaker as he intended, but stronger instead.

Lek didn't know how to react to Avon's words, and suddenly, the police arrived in response to a call that the next door neighbor had placed due to disturbance of the peace. After that, Avon's words *"Go ahead"* resounded like an echo in Lek's mind for as long as he lived. By the police taking Lek to jail, basically took care of Lek once and for all because Avon didn't hesitate to place a restraining order preventing him to come nowhere near her ever again.

At last, Avon was free of obstacles to pursue her dreams or so she thought; because later in life, she realized that when confronting freedom, there might be a sense of imprecision.

Tossing a reflection to the air…

"One's detachment of all material things would bring a sense of freedom while no one can detach from being submissive to life-force."

It didn't take long for Avon to discover that as irrational as Lek was, so was his kind; especially those closest to her. Her family, her so-called bloodline, her parents and her own siblings; those were the worst kind. For when Avon left Lek, all the challenges to attain her precious childhood dreams really began.

Of course Avon didn't disregard the fact that she had been birthed among the same kind. However, it didn't mean that she belong to them, as she didn't know it back then, but she was on

"When the philosopher points to the stars, the fool's eyes are fixed on the finger."

her way to discover her true and only source. Mostly, Avon needed awareness for not to fall into the trap and the same frame of mind that her family members were, because naturally, she had already identified some differences between the kind she sensed within and her bloodline; as she couldn't tolerate the corruption, dishonesty, hypocrisy, irresponsibility, pretence, and unconsciousness from her own family making her feel completely out of place when she was around them. Nevertheless, as much as she tried to focus on pursuing her dreams, she struggled, because the same willpower led her to decide to prove herself to her family; she got caught into the trap of pretension which her family exercised on regular basis manipulating and controlling one another without accomplishing anything in life. And even if Avon understood deep in her heart that following the same route would lead her to limbo like many others were, due to lack of awareness, she wasn't exempt from falling right into the trap by her own self; for at that point, there were no excuses or anyone else to blame. Lek was no longer an obstacle and Avon possessed freewill to decide how to pursue her own path.

Of course eventually Avon was able to understand that, except for a rainbow of skin tone colors and gender issues; in the world there seemed to be only one kind of people, the humankind. Later in life, she was exposed to different cultures understanding that people like her family were all around despite of their cultural origin.

At any rate back then, as she detached completely from Lek, she focused on learning languages and the meaning of words bringing her to an instinctive fascination in perception because as a foreigner, she found herself perceiving things others didn't have to think twice about when speaking on a regular basis in their mother tongue. While learning foreign languages, Avon noticed that many words were similar in phonetics or spelling between English and

French, but the words didn't mean the same nor could be employed in the same sense. And she wasn't thinking of homonyms or homographs within one language. She was thinking of the contrast between words in two different languages. Hence, she realized that possessing the ability to communicate in foreign languages wasn't just a matter of translating and there was much more involved when learning a foreign language in effort to convey a message properly amid the society that spoke it. Once again, what might have been general knowledge for others, she was just learning by herself and she became fascinated with the process. Also, since she couldn't yet understand every word when people spoke to her, she began expanding her perception. She sensed with passion the intention applied behind vocal words captivating her attention by observing people's reaction and their approach to different situations when they spoke. When exploring her perception, she observed that some people were kind, others were unkind; respectful or disrespectful; cheerful or depressed; energetic or lazy; martyrs or sympathetic; distinguishing the envious from the resentful. And once again, she wondered what made people react the way they did. Turning into an extensive lesson preparing her for what was yet to come, because her attention was captured externally and Avon had no idea that there would be much more for her to discover in her very own inner world.

As time went by, in the midst of her homesickness and her satisfaction for overcoming obstacles in a foreign country, culture, and environment by learning different languages; Avon was eager to share her accomplishments with someone. So one day she thought *mama will be pleased to learn about my accomplishments and I should call her.*

In a way by calling her mama, Avon was in search for support but didn't know it; and although her mama was familiar with the

"When the philosopher points to the stars, the fool's eyes are fixed on the finger."

situation her daughter had been facing during the prior months, the lady was displeased when she learned that Avon had refused Lek and had decided to move on; when Avon said excited, "I have a working permit, I found a legal job in a factory and I am attaining my dreams mama!" The lady reacted upset.

"You are a shame to our family Avon, you're place is next to Lek," was her mama's response. The lady disapproved of Avon's decisions and her reaction to Avon's great news was ordering her to go back to Lek. Avon absorbed her mama's remarks. Then, the lady began manipulating her and said, "These worries and concerns about you being alone in the other side of the world will provoke my heart attack."

Avon continued absorbing her mama's rejection; however she was thinking *mama talks about a heart attack as her possession and like it is waiting to happen, I wonder if the homesick attacks belong to me.*

The lady also disapproved Avon's effort to work legally and the type of job she was performing. She tried to discourage her saying, "You'll soon fail. Most likely you'll get fired from that job. You'll end up in the streets without means to survive child." Clearly, the lady insinuated Avon's inability to be independent and to support herself. She implied that Avon was incapable, irresponsible and unskilled to earn money honestly. The lady was inducing Avon to go back to a situation which she knew was common for women to tolerate, whereas Avon had already been enlightened, leaving both, mother and daughter with a valid point; yet, unable to understand one another even though they were speaking the same language. The lady couldn't comprehend what her daughter was unsuccessfully trying to convey when saying that she had surmounted a miserable situation.

Especially the part where Avon explained, "I am learning other languages as I always dreamed mama." For Avon's mama those matters weren't vital. She seemed to project different interest toward her daughter. She was deviating Avon by insisting that her place was next to Lek, or else, she was to return to Bangkok. Avon sensed the same pressure she felt when she was younger and her parents misguided her and her siblings making Avon feel from such requests as though her mother was asking her to trade her soul for money; and on top of it, Avon wouldn't even get to enjoy it. The lady spoke as if Avon had been in total agreement to ally with Lek; she even told Avon that Lek was the only man for her. Avon respected her mama and didn't contradict her nor mentioned about Lek's expectations and intimate demands when she arrived in Montreal; much less bringing up the topic of the alleged student exchange.

At the beginning of the phone conversation Avon hesitated, as she almost agreed with her mama to return to Bangkok if it would please her; however Avon was not willing to please her mama by going back to Lek. When listening to her mama's voice, Avon vulnerably thought *mama is just looking after me*. Besides, going back to Bangkok would have taken care of the homesick attacks once and for all. But when Avon perceived each word like she had been learning in foreign languages; she was able to sense through the conversation that different intentions disguised behind her mama's voice. Her mama wasn't looking after her like Avon first innocently thought. Avon also noticed that apart from the homesick attacks distance had benefits. So taking advantage of the distance she spoke frankly and said, "Mama, I called to convey that we are only a phone call away; however I am not asking permission from anyone to approve my decisions. I am afar and responsible for my own actions now. In fact, I am the best capable person to take care of myself." Not letting the phone call to last much longer after articulating the point made, Avon reminded her mama of their earring connection.

"When the philosopher points to the stars, the fool's eyes are fixed on the finger."

Her mama confirmed that she hadn't taken the earring off since Avon had left allowing loving words between mother and daughter to be the end of the call.

Time went by and despite of Avon's success when overcoming the obstacles that she had confronted so far; the homesickness attacks gradually intensified. She experienced sleepless nights and extreme sadness most of the time; to the degree that she wasn't embarrassed to express her feelings anymore. So one day, she shared the homesick sensation with her good friends at work during lunch break and after learning how sad Avon was, the pattern maker and her husband invited her to their home for dinner on the weekend and to stay overnight.

Avon accepted the invite and when she entered their apartment she felt cozy and welcomed. She was amazed with their home and although their furniture seemed well preserved, Avon thought that it looked a bit old not knowing the worth of Western antique furniture at all.

Dinner was the most delicious French cuisine Avon had ever savored in her short experience in life and she felt like a special guest, because they allowed her to sleep in the guestroom. Avon rested like she had never slept before. She sensed peace and respect because back in Bangkok she never had her own room and even though at the time she already had her own apartment, she felt something different being in a room by her own but in a peaceful atmosphere which she didn't know how to identify—a home.

The next morning, they also had French cooking for breakfast and they spent the rest of the day practicing French. When it was time for Avon to leave, the pattern maker said, "Avon when you're ready, we'll drive you home."

To avoid abusing her friend's kindness, Avon tried to decline the offer saying in her broken French that she would be fine taking the metro home but they insisted. And then, Avon noticed that the pattern maker and her husband had a gift for her right by the door. The couple thoughtfully gifted a TV to her, so that she could distract herself from the homesick sensation keeping her awake at night. Avon didn't know how to respond. Although a plain *thanks* would have been well deserved she was wordless. Even if she had the words in her mind, she didn't seem to succeed when trying to link her thoughts with her tongue and she was unable to express in any language at all. Regardless, the couple was satisfied absorbing the most profound expression of silent gratitude all over Avon's face which they have never sensed before.

Tossing a reflection to the air…

"Receiving is just like giving, as long as a gift is exchanged with grace from a heartfelt loving intent."

"When the philosopher points to the stars, the fool's eyes are fixed on the finger."

4

⸱⸱⸱

The TV brought Avon comfort and when she was distracted, her homesick symptoms lessened a bit; however, when she was sleeping, she began having nightmares about her sister Kalaya trying to do something terrible to her. Avon always woke up in the middle of the dream and she wasn't able to see the end. She felt anguished by depression roaming around luring to invade her and ignoring what was happening to her, she became confused because at the same time, she also felt the oomph within not letting her to give-in. Desperate, she went through her notes and she found Arolf's words, *"The emotions making you feel sad at times are a sign of hope when approaching situations confidently."* Then, life-force defeated the depression torment and Avon perceived Arolf's presence instead. The next thing Avon knew, she was immersed learning about her essence and she was able to sense her childhood dreams once more. Avon was assimilating a unique inspiration from Arolf taking notes and writing each and every word. She still didn't know how her dreams would be attained, but Arolf reminded her to listen to her heart and follow it. At that point, Avon ignored what later she discovered because that time,

"When the philosopher points to the stars, the fool's eyes are fixed on the finger."

Arolf had emerged with no intention to fade away from Avon's wits ever again.

As time went by, Avon noticed that being with Arolf was like gliding in the clouds with the moon beams and the stars. They soared together so high, Avon didn't remember any of the past. The longer Arolf remained, the more Avon's sadness diminished and she was learning from Arolf to appreciate former times instead of feeling sad when remembering. Through their heart-to-heart Avon understood that remembering the spoiled memories from her experiences would not allow her to expand through life. And even though she couldn't change what went before; she could create new good experiences each present moment to have pleasant memories to remember in the future.

Avon was focused on creating joyful memories feeling glad for being where she was, and gradually, she was detaching from the homesick attacks. She gained strength around Arolf and she learned to appreciate the path looking back and not lamenting. Arolf encouraged her with simple words and Avon would take notes, "Avon, if you had not experienced the past, you would have never gotten where you are and you will never experience a future; past, present and future are purely correspondence: as above, so below and vice versa."

Not until then, Avon recognized emotions that unlike her people at her age learned as general knowledge from elder generations at a rather early age. She was able to understand the value of the experiences she had confronted thus far and she figured out that for her to assimilate the actual value of an experience; she had to extract the lesson from it. Because usually when she was remembering the past she felt self-pity most of the time. Interestingly enough, Avon was used to revisit her memory lane focusing on sad situations and adding a dose of melancholic drops which nourished the melodramatic memories that caused her the most pain. Opposite than the norm, she didn't think about the lessons she could learn from her memories at all. While remembering challenging experiences should've taught her a lesson and remembering unchallenging experiences should've caused her to be happy. When remembering, Avon was sad about the past unable to distinguish the bright memories from the shady ones and by concentrating in the dimness, her memories surfaced through the emotion she learned to call homesickness.

One thing in Avon's favor was that she didn't blame life or others for the consequences of her actions and decisions. She didn't complain for the challenges she had confronted and Arolf reminded her about the dreams that she had when she was a child cheering her to look ahead by pursuing her already defined dreams and to create new goals by following the voice from her heart. She learned through Arolf that, a bright present would become a bright past, resulting as the foundation of a bright future. So being with Arolf, Avon began learning to find peace and harmony when remembering the past. In fact, she was thinking of the past instead of remembering and not feeling self-pity anymore. Avon was extracting lessons from her past allowing her immersion into bliss, and unaware, she was falling in the realm of Love bit by bit.

In the interim Avon had obtained her Permanent Resident Permit presenting her with revelations and options that she had not yet considered. Once becoming a Canadian Resident; she learned that from the moment when she applied to change her immigration status, she wasn't allowed to travel out of the country until she was officially admitted into Canada. Therefore she wondered *have I returned to Bangkok when mama gave me an ultimatum; I could have lost the chance of becoming a legal resident and to ever return to Canada again.* Bringing Avon to realize that she had been fundamentally

"*When the philosopher points to the stars, the fool's eyes are fixed on the finger.*"

confined by the Canadian Immigration Department from the moment that her status was pending, and not that she minded, but she didn't even know it. She only learned those details after her status was established as a legal resident and the Immigration Officials informed her that she had permission to travel out of the country. So it was then when she decided to learn as much as she could about her legal status preventing to find more surprises along the way. She asked information about the rules, laws, and regulations to avoid future mistakes. She found out how long she could stay out of the country without breaking the law if she ever traveled abroad. She learned what she was liable for. She had to fully understand what her new status meant to her and to others. For instance, she learned the consequences of getting married to a citizen from another country, a Canadian citizen, or someone who was in the country illegally. She was beginning to understand that her new permanent resident status wasn't like when living in Bangkok as a native. She had to learn what being an immigrant was all about which made her realize that she had detached from her origin; for she had lost her roots and she had to start all over.

As a result, Avon realized that living in a society based on laws, regulations and rules, didn't allow much freedom to any; let alone to an immigrant with a status under process without background and a thick accent hoping to become a citizen one day. She also realized that apart from society's laws, regulations and rules, she was responsible for her own decisions and whatever became of her. Because from then on, no Immigration Officer would be evaluating her aptitude; or how well she was doing in general; unless she decided to become a Canadian Citizen at some point which would take her a few years to qualify for.

Therefore, she understood that the pending future was in her hands and she had to decide what she wanted to become; for the only evaluations she was to encounter afterward were temptations from society like anyone else and it was her responsibility to conduct herself with integrity and truth in all aspects of life. With her limited knowledge of the languages, Avon learned as much as she was able to understand about being a legal resident and what she was entitled and not entitled to do in a foreign land. She wasn't planning on going anywhere; so she had the Permanent Resident part covered. Then embarrassed of her accent, she made an effort to ask questions finding out about objectives that she could accomplish in order to advance within society as a reliable Canadian resident. Among the things she found out, she discovered that she was not only eligible to transfer her school equivalences from Bangkok but also to attend College. However, she still needed to learn much more of the languages to engage formal education; and so, she commenced to put more emphasis on the language that she thought would make the process simpler for her to achieve a new goal.

Eventually, Avon learned enough French to communicate fluently such as speaking, reading, and understanding others to the extent that she didn't need the dictionary when conversing anymore. But French writing was challenging for her. On the other hand, English seemed to flow out of her mind right through her mouth and when writing, she felt more comfortable in the English language realm as well. So just then, it was her option to either leave the language studies at a mediocre point, or to continue learning like a thirsty sponge. After learning the Modern Basic Latin Alphabet, understanding the languages phonetically became simple for her, and in due course, she accomplished to learn English and French simultaneously. Plus as an additional benefit, she even had a couple of classmates teaching her Spanish. At the same time, she excelled at work, getting a promotion as a supervisor in the

"When the philosopher points to the stars, the fool's eyes are fixed on the finger."

quality control department and a raise in wages allowing her to work closer to her friends, the designer and the pattern maker. Meanwhile, she focused on learning English writing and she spoke French everywhere she went to practice both.

Her writing practice was nothing like a prepared writer would write though, not even close; as when Avon practiced English writing was to work on the basics combining the letters of the alphabet. Because while her ears agreed with the sounds and, phonetics had not been that much of a challenge, the script and grammar were quite unfamiliar to her. In essence, she had to memorize how to form each word and also learn by heart the conjugation of each verb; since verb conjugation in foreign languages could be torturous for some. And so, she practice writing like a five-year-old with great ambition to be able to take notes from professors aiming to pass the evaluations which would allow her to attend College in Montreal at some point.

Over the years, Avon recognized that she accepted a great opportunity, because although she wasn't fluent in both languages, the Canadian Immigration Officials granted her the chance to develop to the fullest of her potential if she was willing to; whereas she could have perfectly opted to refuse the opportunity due to fear of discovering precisely how far her potential could reach. She also realized that not being able to communicate properly; her aspirations might have seemed beyond her reach. However she had nothing to lose by aiming for the stars, even if she ended up hitting a bird; because if she aimed for the bird, she might have ended up hitting a boulder. Besides she had heard some said that the sky was the limit; yet, when being with Arolf, Avon's mind traveled far and beyond the skies bringing her to realize that when learning and expanding in life there was no limit unless *she* established it.

She had certainly memorized the book she had read over and over again and instinctively, she was practicing everything she learned. Even though she didn't fully understand what she eventually acknowledged, because she didn't actually experience much until she had practiced what she learned, otherwise she wouldn't acquire wisdom in life at all. That far, while enjoying Arolf's presence and connecting with her instincts, Avon had managed to get used to be without her family and she was detaching from the homesickness slowly but surely. Until one day, her mother took care of reminding her by calling and writing dramatic letters to her. Just as if misery was seeking for company. Because every time Avon got news from her mama, she called Bangkok trying to solve every issue and conflict her mother exposed to her in the letters and phone calls. Avon allowed her mother to transmit an intense sense of pressure and responsibility to her making her feel as though without her financial help the entire family in Bangkok would starve to death.

Looking back, Avon wondered if perhaps the attachment to her mother and family was more important than all her goals, her precious dreams and her own objectives; as she couldn't resist feeling responsible for her family's misery. Avon didn't seem to know better when she trusted that it was beyond her family members' reach to find honest jobs to support themselves financially and to live according to their means. Each family member justified their constant financial demands with emotional guilt trips and the repetitive excuse of being in a country under development while Avon was in an already developed country. Their excuses led Avon to call her mama ending up falling into the emotional drama; for every time Avon called, she was presuming to remedy their situation by helping everyone to be.

Eventually, Avon did admit in her heart that the only reason why she got involved in the drama was to feel self-important due

"When the philosopher points to the stars, the fool's eyes are fixed on the finger."

to ego, since she wasn't exempt from contamination of thoughts entrapment. So as a result of all the telephone conversations, Avon only spent extra money in long distance calls, ignoring that all the words were going with the wind without specific meaning at all. Basically, Avon ceased being responsible for her own thoughts, going entirely against the values she had learned in the book that she read so many times and she was convinced that each of her family members required money from her in order to prosper in life.

Her mother claimed many times that for Avon's father to find an income source, they required money from Avon. Obviously, Avon didn't understand that *she* was the money source covering certain expenses her family incurred. She failed to pay attention to what her mother was actually telling her. Avon didn't stop for a moment to think that, she didn't need any money to find an honest job in a foreign country. And so, why would her family members need money to find jobs in their own environment. Avon didn't seem to understand either that, being able to support herself didn't mean that she could support the entire family without their individual help. Every family member must have seen Avon as a money symbol, not considering that if only one person in the entire family worked, wasn't going to be enough to support them all. In essence, every conversation with her family was related to money and she sent as much money as she could. And despite her mother's protests, Avon always managed to end every call with loving words between them reminding her of their connection through the sapphire earring.

Thereafter, Avon took the responsibility of enabling her mama's cash demands and she had to learn by her own experience to deal with the effect of that cause; for no one forced Avon to manipulate her own thoughts deciding to feel self-important; as she made the decision alone. Her compassionate intention could have been justifiable; however, as she continued learning some and experiencing more, one day she realized that there was a difference between giving and helping. Because helping with high expectations to receive acknowledgment in exchange had nothing to do with giving from the heart without regret assuring that what she gave wouldn't incur recognition in exchange.

As a result, during a good period of time, Avon deprived herself of everything in order to be able to send every extra dollar to her family and at the same time, the sense of great responsibility was slowly beginning to consume her inside. The pressure she allowed herself to experience caused her the homesick sensation again intensifying gradually and it was torturous at times. Arolf could hardly endure sensing Avon hurting so bad; still Avon's frame of mind couldn't process that it wasn't only homesickness what she was experiencing, since she was also allowing herself to absorb the manipulative thoughts her mother and siblings persuaded her to trust. Avon was in denial thus didn't accept that the way she felt was her own doing and she had to go through it alone; or so it seemed in the surface of it all, because although she was unkind to Arolf; her loyal friend lingered around waiting for her to understand. Avon took Arolf for granted back then, and yet, Arolf remained; because Arolf had nothing to lose by waiting patiently for her; as Avon would encounter a point in life where she would understand that Arolf meant much more to Avon than she pretended to admit to herself.

The fact that Avon managed not to get involved in drugs, alcoholism, or any other physical vices, didn't exempt her from manipulation and contamination of thoughts, and consequently, there was a period of time which emphasized her analytical state of mind and she began to distant from her inner senses. Perhaps

"When the philosopher points to the stars, the fool's eyes are fixed on the finger."

being analytical might not have been as far from being sensitive; but when she analyzed without perceiving she became quite a stubborn individual in certain ways. And as much as Arolf tried to bring Avon back to her inner senses and perception again, Avon seemed to be distancing further and further from her own self.

Tossing a reflection to the air...

"It is not the same to isolate to be within, than to isolate from within for not to be."

Meanwhile, Avon was focused on working, studying English, practicing French and fulfilling her responsibilities and she paid very little attention to her personal appearance. She didn't spend extra money to be able to send it to her mama and she hadn't bothered to buy clothes or fashionable garments to wear. She dressed basically just to cover herself and the clothes she wore were already quite outworn.

In one occasion, the designer and her husband invited Avon to spend the weekend at a condominium they rented in a private development.

Avon gladly accepted the invitation thinking *it will be just like when I spent the weekend with the pattern maker and her husband.*

In any event, the experience could have been similar; yet, they were different people as Avon realized the moment she entered their home. Clearly, her friends' individual taste for interior decoration was for the most part opposite. Avon had never been in the position to distinguish décor styles between Traditional French Country and Contemporary before. So inescapably the interior decoration of the designer's apartment impressed her from tip to toe.

When the designer and her husband walked Avon through the condo and she noticed the matching appliances in the kitchen, the color combination throughout the walls, including laundry room and bathrooms; she was speechless. Nothing in the entire place had much to do with her modest and tasteless way. Those were unnecessary details that she had never considered in the past. While having a roof over her head meant a great accomplishment to her, interior decoration might have seemed superfluous. In essence, the experience seemed like a new world to her because the couple was fashionable, stylish and sophisticated.

The designer's husband worked managing the fabric cutting department in the factory and many times if it weren't for the matching attires the couple wore; the designer's Vietnamese husband would have been mistaken for any other Asian worker among all. Avon saw them every day as a couple at work, but they hardly spoke to each other. However their nest, their home, where all those designing ideas were born, was everything and much more than what the twosome projected when doing their jobs. There was no clutter in the whole apartment, nowhere. It didn't matter where Avon went. The place was dustless, impeccable and well organized. So much so, that the table was set ready to serve dinner when they arrived from work that evening. They had offered a ride to Avon in their car at the end of the working day and when they entered into the apartment, Avon was embarrassed as usual and she didn't know whether to sit or to stand. Her friend had always been kind, but that evening, the designer was as affectionless as she had shown to be at work. There was no particular attention given to the guest; so Avon felt as if she wasn't important enough

"When the philosopher points to the stars, the fool's eyes are fixed on the finger."

for the designer to show some special notice to her. On the other
hand, the designer's husband was polite, but he didn't say much at
all making Avon doubt to receive something like the TV the pattern
maker and her husband had gifted to her, not implying that she was
expecting something from them, but the designer's husband was as
dry as only a brick could be.

Dinner was Vietnamese and the most delicious homemade
Vietnamese cuisine Avon had savored, or so it seemed. Regardless
of their similar Asian cultures, Avon was surprised by the designer's
husband, because he stayed in the kitchen with his wife the entire
time. Or perhaps it was the other way around, as *he* was the one
who cooked, served, cleaned up the table, and took care of placing
the dishes in the dishwasher after dinner.

Their interaction during the meal was about the different
food names and the proper way to combine the sauces enhancing
the flavor of each skillfully prepared dish, which seemed to Avon,
a real feast. Even though so geographically close; they engaged in a
conversation comparing the differences between the two cuisines,
Thai and Vietnamese. Avon explained that she was familiar with
most of the etiquette but that she had never had the opportunity
to actually practice it; then the couple shared with her that the
designer had to learn his cooking habits as her husband had to learn
hers and that they continued learning from each other as life went
on.

Out of respect, Avon had fun practicing how to use the
chopsticks the Vietnamese way and the couple's combination was
entirely a new experience for her to observe, because after being
with them for awhile, Avon understood that the couple was naturally
indifferent, cold and affectionless. Their individual personalities
had nothing to do with her presence. They acted naturally as they
were individually and as a pair. They didn't adapt to who they were

with pretending to be who others would accept. So, Avon became comfortable not feeling the need of special notice anymore for not having to respond to extra attention granted her liberation after all. She enjoyed the couple's simplicity of expression, and yet, sophistication when it came to cooking, design and decoration.

The next day, breakfast was French Canadian. Although somehow, someone managed to set up the table and prepared everything as if they did it in their sleep, or so was the impression Avon got.

Most likely the unfamiliarity woke her up earlier than the norm and as she entered the kitchen, following the coffee smell, she wondered if they had prepared everything and then, they had gone back to bed. Turning out humorous for the designer and her husband, because the coffee maker was automatic and the couple worked in such a team mode; together, they managed to do things as a routine taking them no time to set up the table for meals. The twosome had left the whole thing ready for the next day the previous evening; just like they did every night before going to bed and it was quite an experience for Avon to learn how the auto-coffee-maker magically turn-on every morning by itself.

The three of them spent the rest of the morning together doing different things and in the afternoon, the designer approached Avon asking her to come to the guestroom where she was staying. While walking to the room Avon mortified herself trying to guess what she could have possibly done wrong. When they entered the guestroom; the designer pointed out the sofa for Avon to sit and frostily said, "Get comfortable." As Avon sat absolutely embarrassed, the designer stood next to the sofa and looking at Avon with her cold penetrating dark eyes; she disclosed her intentions saying, "I don't want to offend you Avon, but I'd like to show you something." Then while Avon remained seated the designer walked to the closet

"When the philosopher points to the stars, the fool's eyes are fixed on the finger."

and she pulled out two big black garbage bags from inside. The bags were not empty though, the bags were full packed tight. The designer brought the bags next to the sofa—where Avon sat timidly in wonder—and said unemotionally, "Go through the contents of these bags. You may take home anything you like." She paused rearranging the bags next to Avon and she added with an indifferent tone, "I'll give away what you won't take to the same charity that I always do, and in fact, I almost did. But I thought you might like to check them out first." In addition, each hanger inside the closet hung a little surprise especially for Avon. Then, the designer said with an uncaring tone, "I don't care if you don't take anything from the bags; but I would be pleased if you accept the garments inside the closet; because you were my inspiration for those designs and I created them with my own hands." The designer left the room for Avon to spend some time at her leisure with the full packed tight black garbage bags which had a big tag on them marked: *GOODWILL*.

Of course, the contents of the garbage bags were fashionable garments that Avon's designer friend didn't wear anymore. To Avon, every piece looked newer than she had ever touched before and the outfits in the closet amazed her even more. Most of the clothes were about Avon's size and there were so many pieces, she really needed the rest of the afternoon to try them on. After awhile the designer's husband wondered if something was wrong with Avon, for she wasn't coming out of the guestroom. Then, the designer explained to him that Avon barely had a new garment of her own before. Because when they had asked her during lunch breaks at work, Avon had shared with the designer and the pattern maker that she always wore the clothes her sister passed on to her, being those over used garments her entire wardrobe which she modestly still wore. So, considering that Avon must have been overwhelmed trying-on new and moderately used clothes; the designer conveyed to her husband that Avon just needed to be left alone.

The couple prepared dinner giving Avon the time and space she needed. When Avon finally came out of the guestroom; she was wearing a dress that she found in one of the bags appropriate for the evening. Not one word was mentioned regarding her appearance; except for a glimpse and a frigid gesture from the designer nodding once expressing approval for Avon's selection. Avon spent most of the following day folding and sorting out clothes, as she modestly accepted each and every garment including the ones in the bags.

In the evening, the affectionless cold penetrating dark eyes designer and her dry as a brick husband, drove Avon back home, all the way in silence, no one said a word.

There were moments in life that Avon felt that she had not bargained for. However, there were other moments that she didn't even know that were available for bargaining at all, being those the memories she treasured the most and gave her strength to carry on.

Tossing a reflection to the air...

"Fashion isn't much for display but to wear as a second nature gratifying the inspiring passion behind its creation."

After finishing the required equivalences of the studies Avon had completed in Bangkok; she successfully passed the evaluations for the credits required to pursue her education. Therefore, the

"When the philosopher points to the stars, the fool's eyes are fixed on the finger."

time for her to register in College arrived and she enrolled in the
Tourism and Travel Masters Degree Program in English and not in
the Fashion and Design Program in French as everyone expected.
Avon suspected that her decision would disappoint her friends.
However, when she received the results of her vocational and
aptitude assessments, it was clear to her that she should pursue
the Tourism and Travel Degree recommended by the College
counselors, and so, she did.

Therefore, in the middle of working, language studies and
fulfilling her responsibilities, there were other decisions Avon had
to make. Since she wasn't going to be able to work in the factory
full time and attend full time College, she organized a schedule
with the assistance of the designer and the pattern maker. Then
she was given the opportunity to continue working at the factory
on weekends which was a chance the boss didn't offer to every
employee. After that, she had to find an evening job, because she
was to attend College from early morning to mid-afternoon the
first semester and during the summer breaks, she could work in
the factory adjusting her schedule to keep both jobs.

So according to Avon, she had little to no option being an
immigrant without much of a background and a thick accent looking
for work and without complicating matters, she accepted an offer from
a friend of a friend as a cleaner in an Office Maintenance Company.
Also by the College counselor's advice, she was able to get a grant
from the government to pay part of her tuition, just like most of the
students did, year after year. She needed an extra job to cover her
financial responsibilities as well as to pay the tuition that the grant
didn't subsidize and cleaning offices was one of the highest paying rates
she was able to obtain in her permanent resident, but immigrant class.

The College program was to last several years, if the students
decided to graduate, that was. Because as student, Avon had the

option to change her mind after attending the program for some time making her eligible to transfer the credits already obtained to a different métier. However, those years attending College and working two jobs went like water between Avon's hands for the next thing she realized; she was graduating from College and she had finished the program as she first committed. She didn't change her mind like many students did accruing credits for every métier offered year after year who didn't graduate at the end of the day and even had a moniker; those were the *professional students*, or so they called themselves.

Many years later, uncommonly looking à la mode, Avon reflected on the tremendous input the designer and the pattern maker had in her personality development. Considering that she never had a role model, she felt like the designer's role had been the one of the character sketcher who outlined and illustrated what character meant to her, just like a design is made. On the other hand, she felt that the pattern maker's role had been the one linking the sketch and the design to form illustrating individuality to her, just like a pattern is made. Then, Avon assumed the role of the maker sewing each stitch of the pieces at her leisure adopting her own personality in life.

Avon realized that when a design came to the pattern maker and then the pattern was sent to the textile cutters, the fabric arrived to the hands of the maker in larger pieces than what the actual size entailed allowing the maker to fit the garment as many times as required until the creation was completed to the ideal form.

So, she thought *from the moment these two ladies appeared on my path as role models, I felt like a fabric where life lines were delicately*

"When the philosopher points to the stars, the fool's eyes are fixed on the finger."

marked. Then, it was Avon's option to sew the pieces together and finish the design by adjusting each and every seam of her learning lesson with integrity and respect toward herself to be able to fit in life.

Regardless of the fabric color, origin, or texture used for the design created; Avon took the process as an illustration, appreciating that her personality was the result of the influence the designer and the pattern maker had on her during her very own alteration from being a girl and becoming a woman.

Therefore, as far as Avon was concerned those two ladies needed not to be called by any other name, as their profession labels seemed to suit perfectly to each of them.

Tossing a reflection to the air...

"Life's path is created by each individual; adjusting mistakes each step of the way until reaching an ideal fit."

5

⚘

$\mathcal{D}$uring the last year in college when Avon had to practice in the tourism field; she worked as an intern in a prestigious worldwide Corporation providing travel amenities to elite clientele; so, following her graduation, the Corporation made her an offer that she couldn't reject. They just offered her an entry level position; however, the proposal meant quite an offer to her. Therefore she resigned from her humble jobs embarking into a new endeavor and pursuing a career in the corporate world.

Prior to actually start working at her new job though; she had to attend training for several months and she wondered about the degree that she had just finished in College, as it didn't appear to have prepared her to begin delivering and performing. She felt as if she didn't learn much from her studies for everything she was learning at work was totally new to her. Clearly, her confusion at the time was eventually clarified resulting as a great opportunity; as not everyone got to be trained and well recruited right out of College while being paid, she was told. As a result, she managed to get caught up in the instant gratification or microwave generation sort of mode; because there was a phase when Avon wasn't patient

"When the philosopher points to the stars, the fool's eyes are fixed on the finger."

enough to experience one thing at the time. She almost forgot about following rules. She wanted to move up as if she could get away without paying society's dues and for a while, she struggled with the concept of starting at the bottom. But as she learned some and experienced more, she understood that paying social dues was a duty she couldn't escape, unless she failed her own integrity which would affect her in all aspects of life.

So, by the time Avon began chasing a career, she had already adopted an undetectable speech accent. Meaning, her origin was unrevealed reflecting an air of mysterious sophistication when she expressed and allowing her to interact professionally as an educated English speaking person, rather than a formal communicator. Naturally, Avon articulated certain words diverse than the norm captivating people's attention and making interaction gracious when she spoke, and at the time, she ignored what she discovered later; as her speech accent skill was an asset to the Corporation in the area of marketing strategies and sales.

Also, since Avon's father was from England, her eyes and skin tone reflected her mother's Thai lineage while her British bloodline accentuated her natural beauty and her unusual female height. Therefore, everyone would wonder where Avon was from encouraging diversity which was one of the values that the Corporation recognized and ingrained to the employees by motivating them to practice those values daily. Although, Avon did learn about being a Good Samaritan, success, loyalty, good citizenship among other values as well. So, she was being educated in many areas besides the computer programs, systems, and internal company functionality along with professional vocabulary; and having memorized the words she knew from the dictionary, she had sort of an advantage by not expressing through slang or popular idioms, because overall, she knew the definition of the words she spoke.

During Avon's University years and some years that followed, while Arolf observed her from a close distance, Avon expanded within and throughout many areas in life as well as learning different ideas, theories, and concepts adapting to society and her circle of friends. In the course of those years, Avon had attained to obtain her Canadian Citizenship and respective Canadian passport. She had been present when the designer and the pattern maker moved from rentals and purchased their own houses. In the summers, Avon had experienced the weekend getaways at the cottage that the designer and her husband had by the lake discovering that in fact, they used it only during the summer season and it wasn't a made-up story trying to impress. Avon had also reacquainted with her friend Jaidee who was still in France, married to Xavier and having children.

Furthermore, Avon had traveled a few times abroad to visit her family in Bangkok returning discouraged from the encounters with her siblings who projected envy, jealousy and demanded money from her; because the fact that Avon appeared to be in a better financial position than they were seemed totally unfair and they thought that it was Avon's obligation to provide for them. And yet, no amount of money was enough to satisfy their needs. Every time Avon went to Bangkok; she returned dejected as well as pressured by her mother who manipulated her with constant predictions of soon dying from a heart attack.

In addition, Avon had been married for some years, and at that point, she was trying to get divorced from the individual who she didn't care about anymore because the marriage didn't even last long. She never spoke of what occurred between the two of them. She didn't disclose what took place to any of her family members

"When the philosopher points to the stars, the fool's eyes are fixed on the finger."

or mutual friends. Avon's discretion and prudency didn't allow her to reveal a personal matter which only the individual that she had married was to relate to others. In any event, only the two of them knew what came to pass, but whatever it was that exploded right in front of Avon's sad countenance one day, turned her into a bitter, resentful and skeptical being. Naturally, she had to make another decision in life projecting disappointment to herself, her family and her circle of friends.

Avon's resentment intensified when thinking that, if the individual she married would have been honest not only with her but with others, perhaps she wouldn't have felt like the cover of a rusty pan on a stove burner simmering putrefied contents. So despite of the house, furnishings and things obtained jointly through that marriage, which were supposed to be important and valuable to her, Avon accepted a new job offer from the Corporation and she transferred. Totally disenchanted due to his dishonesty; she left behind her well selected home and her most appreciated friends who wouldn't understand her motives unless Avon unveiled his covert.

Therefore by not providing detailed explanations to her friends about divorcing the individual; her *role model* friends were led to believe–not by Avon, but by what seemed to be–that Avon was a cruel person following a career opportunity while the individual married to her was unable to transfer. Evidently, the idea of making everyone think that Avon was cruel suited *him* better than disclosing the truth behind her actions because he wouldn't disclose the secret himself.

As a result, regardless of everything Avon had shared with her *role model* friends, they lacked objectivity when the time to make a serious decision came for her. Because at the end of the day, the designer and the pattern maker didn't trust Avon's decision nor respected her discretion, being judging accusations the last Avon ever heard from her *role model* and well selected friends.

The job transfer opportunity came to Avon like the first rain of the season when the grass would be thirsty, crisp and waiting to sprout; simply sent from above she thought. For after a few years of working in the same division and having been promoted, Avon was satisfied with the course her career was taking. However, during the horrific situation she was experiencing by prudently trying to convince the individual she had married to cede and to divorce her once and for all; then was when the Corporation offered her a position in another division. Avon accepted the transfer without hesitation mostly because of her devastation causing a turmoil of emotions revolving through her entire being like a cyclone but gradually destroying her within when wondering how in the world she had managed to be such a fool ending up married to a person who wasn't much different than Lek, or different from what she had ran away from Bangkok to begin with.

When accepting the transfer to another division the last thought that crossed Avon's mind was the dreams of traveling from country to country she used to share with Arolf when she was only a child; because there was a catch for the new position. Avon had to move to another country. And to be able to relocate; the Corporation sponsored her as a permanent resident given that the division where she accepted the position was located in the State of Florida U.S.

After finding the suitable opportunity to blame Avon justifying himself; the individual married to her finally accepted to divorce her under the condition that she would leave everything to him; which she did without looking back ever again.

"When the philosopher points to the stars, the fool's eyes are fixed on the finger."

Tossing a reflection to the air…

"In the end, issues derived from a bad cause tend to reveal a good effect."

From Canada to The United States

The Corporation allowed standard time-off for employees to relocate and since Avon didn't have much to take to Florida with her; she used the time-off to go to England intending to breathe different air.

In the midst of her disillusion, a vague idea of her first boyfriend Clive gave her some comfort thinking that he might have been the man for her. Avon managed to contact Clive and he invited her to spend some time with him and his family in London. When she arrived at Gatwick airport, Clive greeted her excited holding a bouquet of gorgeous red roses between his hands. They intended to spend a great week together and they did.

On the other hand, planning to impress them during her visit, Avon arranged in detail to host Clive, his parents and his granny for the afternoon High Tea at the hotel where she was staying. Naturally, Avon was getting familiar with luxury travel because by offering the services on a daily basis to her elite clients, it was only likely for her to also practice opulence.

So, when the afternoon outing for the High Tea arrived, Clive conveyed to Avon that his granny would rather stay home and Avon decided to intercede trying to convince his granny to come along and she said, "Granny, it would pleased me greatly if you join us."

"No. Thank you," replied the granny firmly.

"Ooh granny, I have planned the afternoon High Tea for the family and you certainly wouldn't want to miss visiting such a prestigious place, would you granny?" Avon added.

"No. Thank you," repeated his granny firmly.

Yet, Avon insisted, "This is the last opportunity we have, because I am leaving in two days and we might never see each other again. Come with us granny."

The granny looked at Avon intensely in the eyes and she articulated calmly, "Avon, I have lived a lifetime without knowing you and without you planning my family outings." The granny paused grasping some air and added, "I will perfectly live the rest of life left in me without seeing you again. Don't take me wrong, you seem like a lovely young lady Avon. However going out for *High Tea* at *The Ritz* won't make much of a difference at my ninety-eight-years of age. Let it be Avon, I'll enjoy the afternoon tea by myself."

While Clive and his parents reprimanded the granny for her candidness, Avon sat in silence but in wonder. She didn't fully understand what she eventually acknowledged, because that specific trip to London was meant for the granny to transmit a truth to her. The granny's words were recorded in Avon's mind resulting in a lesson she actually assimilated, appropriated and ended up practicing herself. Through the course of life, the granny's words resounded more and more like a wise melody enchanting Avon's ears of understanding.

Clive was a musician and he played in the nightclubs. He told Avon that he didn't want to interfere in the projection of a bright future ahead of her career. At that point, Avon had adopted and developed a fashionable dressing style. Clearly, after working in the factory, fashion had become a second nature to her. Clive also mentioned that he couldn't adjust to living abroad and start all over as a musician in the U.S. Avon's looks rather intimidated him as well

"When the philosopher points to the stars, the fool's eyes are fixed on the finger."

as the air of professionalism in which she carried herself reflecting in many ways; especially when she verbally expressed. Clive wasn't planning to leave England and considering that Avon had just accepted the transfer to Florida; turned out to be a bit too late for him to propose for her to come and live with him in The U.K. Avon quickly realized that Clive had no intention to expand in any other area apart from his music. She sensed the passion he reflected when he played. He seemed happy and her intention wasn't to thwart his purpose. They felt relieved when seeing each other again as they didn't have to go through life wondering what could've been if they didn't give each other another chance. Yet, there wasn't a chance to be given and they both knew it their hearts. Back then, Avon wasn't paying attention; therefore she didn't realize what passion was all about, let alone purpose in life.

Tossing a reflection to the air...

"Passion isn't finding purpose for other's in one's path; let it be on purpose and passion will be found."

When Avon arrived in Florida, Arolf had simply followed her. Yet, Avon felt bitter and betrayed; because except for a great job opportunity, she had two suitcases and nothing else. She didn't even have a kettle to boil water in and she became indifferent to change. Evidently, that wasn't the first time that she had to start all over again and henceforth, change began to develop into a routine for her.

She leased a furnished condo by the ocean with one of the best views she could find; it wasn't the most expensive but expensive enough for her to feel comfortable and fine. She also leased a black BMW convertible and clearly, after a promotion and another salary increase, Avon was still sending money to her family; but not with the same sense of responsibility as she had done it in the past. From the time when she began working with the Corporation, she decided not to deprive herself anymore and she always sent money; however after her last visit to Bangkok, she felt disgraced because her father was in jail and she was becoming aware that no one in her family was even trying to help themselves. In addition, the impact of her divorce caused her a sensation of failure intensifying the resentment she sensed when remembering her past. Avon felt totally rejected because her mother didn't approve, recognize, or validate anything she did. Especially the last decision she made becoming a divorced woman. According to her mother, Avon had to have a pretentious explanation and justification for every action appearing what she wasn't. The lady didn't feel like facing her daughter's decisions making Avon feel that if she didn't report to her mama and obey her advice, she wasn't a good daughter.

Little did Avon know; because later in life she understood as clear as the sunshine that labels didn't turn people into good or bad. She didn't know at the time that despite of the labels of daughter or sister attached to her, what turned her into being good or bad was her conduct and actions reflecting from her heart. She couldn't be a good person and reflect to be a bad daughter; or be a bad person and reflect to be a good daughter. Eventually, Avon had to recognize and learn to identify her essence by making firm decisions when selecting either to be or not to be without labeling herself, who she truly was deep in her heart.

"When the philosopher points to the stars, the fool's eyes are fixed on the finger."

So, having just arrived in Florida, in an unfamiliar area and being alone, Avon had some time to think again. As a result, she realized that her mama didn't cross a fine line when it came to approve her decisions, much less her accomplishments. Her mama wouldn't cross the line in order to control and manipulate Avon to keep sending money her way. Therefore, certain emotions Avon had never sensed began awakening within her. Full of resentment, Avon decided to stop accommodating her mama's demands. Every time her mama asked for money she confronted her. Before sending any funds to her mama; she called her siblings corroborating what their mama was telling her about them. Because at that point, Avon couldn't help to absorb the ill-will her mama was creating among them; bringing Avon to suspect that her mama was telling her siblings pessimistic things about her as well, or else, during Avon's visits her siblings wouldn't have been as antagonistic as they were. In essence, Avon was unable to trust her mama. Turning into a difficult phase for Avon to experience, as her emotions were mixed; feeling at times as if her only drive to live was to please her mama and other times she felt so distant from her mama, Avon couldn't cope with the fact that the lady had actually birthed her and unaware, she began to withdraw and gradually detached from her family.

Right after her trip to England, Avon was possessed by being single. She didn't think about never getting married again; actually, she didn't even consider it. So, she dedicated herself to her career completely and not having any friends in a new area, country and State suited her perfectly allowing her to spend most of the time working. She brought projects home to occupy the weekends intending to get distracted from the homesick attacks and thinking *I'll be better off immersing into my career* which seemed to be her objective at the time. She still had not gotten around creating new objectives in life. Besides graduating from College, she didn't set any other goals and seemed as if from the time when she decided to enable her mama's demands, her personal interests were put aside and by not dedicating any time to herself; she kept in the dark about what her passion was. Observing her from a close distance, Arolf sensed that most likely Avon would take their connection for granted for a good while.

On the other hand, her new job kept her occupied traveling all over the country. Soon after Avon arrived in Florida, she was traveling to Atlanta, Boston, Chicago, Dallas, Detroit, New York, Orlando, Philadelphia, San Francisco, Las Vegas, and most of the metropolitan cities in the U.S. And although most of the time she was working, she did manage to meet a young lady named Angelina who worked in the same division as she did. Angelina and Avon bonded instantly when they met for the first time. They never made promises to keep in touch ignoring how much their friendship would mean to each other as years passed by. They went out for cocktails at times, they enjoyed a good conversation, and afterward, they both continue on their respective paths.

However the approval Avon yearned from her mama; she received from Angelina. Avon never thought of a stranger understanding her dreams in such a way, recognizing and approving her undertakings; as Angelina was much younger than her. But back then, it was Angelina who gave Avon the encouragement to persevere and to pursue her dreams going after the stars if she willed. Avon stored Angelina's words in her heart when saying "*Avon I admire you. I am impressed with your determination. Not any teenage girl would leave their country, family, friends, and everything they are familiar with, enduring the experiences you have been through, only to pursue childhood dreams.*" Of course at the time, Avon didn't understand a word Angelina said, but by storing the words in her heart after

"When the philosopher points to the stars, the fool's eyes are fixed on the finger."

years passed by, she was able to assimilate and appreciate Angelina's acceptance one day.

Angelina's big blue ocean eyes adorned with her perfect sparkling pearl teeth when she smiled and her radiant golden hair, inspired Avon to call her *sunshine*. Still back then, in spite of Angelina's acceptance and consent; Avon's need of approval was still empty deep inside. She didn't even know what she was longing for and unconsciously, she wanted her mama's approval or nothing else, while Arolf simply observed.

During that phase, Avon got in touch with Arolf at her convenience and just like when she was in Montreal with Lek; she felt as if Arolf wasn't available when she needed the most support. Avon seldom came to her senses and when she gave attention to Arolf, energy wouldn't flow. Over time, Avon realized that she had much more to experience before understanding that, even though Arolf was more humble than proud to be present; it was Avon's freewill to decide and select to be or not to be and openly admit to herself who she really was inside. For Arolf wasn't going to force Avon to expand into the Love realm like stretching a rubber band. Avon had to learn to expand from within and at her own pace which required the abundant patience that only Arolf's everlasting Love possessed reflecting to Avon in moments of despair. However back then, Avon wasn't paying attention distancing more and more from her own self.

Roughly one year after Avon relocated in Florida, she applied for another transfer within the Corporation at a different division located in the State of Arizona. The new position entailed international travel covering regions in Europe, South America and Asia. Avon was one of the most qualified candidates for the job thus she was hired with another salary increase right on the spot; being Angelina who encouraged her to move on and motivated her to apply for the post. So, off she went leaving her dear *sunshine* friend. Avon transferred to Arizona afresh and they kept in touch via occasional phone calls and e-mails. Meanwhile, after being confined by immigrations because she couldn't leave the country for a full year, Avon had obtained her Green Card making her a Permanent Resident in the U.S. and eligible to travel abroad in her new job with the option to become a Citizen one day. Avon was totally distracted developing and sprouting in many ways, mostly superficially though. She spoke to others of attaining her childhood dreams, but due to her bitterness, distrust, and resentment; she didn't connect her accomplishments to her childhood dreams herself.

Avon's unique taste in clothes was distracting her to focus even more. After she adopted a fashionable, sophisticated and elegant dressing style, her physical appearance turned into her highest priority. There was a time when she was attracted to suede and most of her shoes had a trace of suede feature on them. Also her garments had to have some sort of suede finish as a detail. She dressed according to the city where she lived but conserving a fashionable style everywhere she went and when living in Scottsdale, her wardrobe accentuated color tones of desert and Earth. Despite of her particular interest in fashion, she didn't enjoy shopping in person at the stores; so, she shopped through exclusive catalogues and the internet ordering her accessories, garments, and shoes from the comfort of her home and everything was delivered directly to her door and during that time; she didn't even try the clothes on; she would order carefully combining her complete attires blindly relying on the size and since she traveled internationally most of the time; she had two suitcases for cold and warm climates organized. Then, when she received the deliveries from the orders she placed; she unpacked directly from the boxes into the suitcase.

"When the philosopher points to the stars, the fool's eyes are fixed on the finger."

Her job in Arizona was related to negotiate rates with the vendors that provided fine accommodations, air and ground transportation to the Corporation's elite clientele. Therefore, Avon wasn't only traveling, but she was also staying in the most exclusive castles, palaces and mansions that had been converted into the finest hotels and resorts around the world. Naturally, she became familiar with flying business and first class everywhere she went, and at times, she was greeted by a stretch limo or a sedan. She was traveling the world just as she dreamed when she was a child and absolutely not backpacking throughout; for she was traveling in comfort, opulence and style. So actually, she was better off getting used to living well; because had she continued depriving herself of everything; living a simple lifestyle and sending every additional dollar she had to her mama; she wouldn't have been able to absorb all the luxury providing her with the aptitude needed to perform her job up to the clients' expectations, standards and demands which were essentially, *la crème de la crème.*

In the midst of her distraction, besides traveling the world, Avon met a special young man named Frank at work. They not only became close but also romantically involved. They used to meet at her convenience at one of the finest resorts in the area and they enjoyed a romantic weekend getaway now and then, keeping the relationship casual, because her highest priority back then was the impeccable performance of her job. She didn't mixed business with pleasure which might have been one of the key factors in her successful individual career experience, as her professional responsibilities were totally divorced from her personal affairs. She handled accounts and negotiated contracts involving extraordinary amounts of money. She was entrusted with affluent clientele's confidential information and details. Nevertheless she performed her job with integrity and honesty, being loyal to the Corporation.

All qualities her *sunshine* friend Angelina also admired about her. At times, Avon witnessed associates who authorized certain personal expenses on their corporate charge cards. However, when she went on personal trips with Frank; she paid her expenses out of her own personal account. Avon had the ability to perform under the parameter of her function and she was aware that she hadn't been hired to be a spy; so, if she was able to learn what others were trying to get away with, it wasn't her place to disclose it; as following guidelines allowed her to understand that anyone could have noticed the mistakes or dishonest actions from any of the employees, just as easy as she did. Besides, the Corporation had a specific division dedicated to monitor every transaction made by the staff. So if the workers were dishonest, they could've perfectly been discovered through the most sophisticated equipment without needing her assistance. Hence, while some of her peers allowed others' actions to interfere with their job performance, and as a result, they misused their paid time spying, gossiping and telling; Avon preserved her integrity. She understood that she hadn't been appointed to watch others; but the only responsibility she had regarding integrity was to watch her own self.

Tossing a reflection to the air…

"Ethical action is most important when no one is watching at all; for the mind's eye does not sleep and inevitable brings up guilt when one performs an unethical act despite of what others might think."

"When the philosopher points to the stars, the fool's eyes are fixed on the finger."

6

⁂

$\mathcal{A}$von found herself pointing out touristic destinations as she reported to her superiors in meetings regarding her travels all over the world on a rather dustless and stylish Earth globe. Turning into an unobserved fast phase of intense inner-growth for her, because once again during that time, the last thing on her mind was being a child eagerly pointing out on the old dusty Earth globe all the exciting places she wanted to explore as she grew old. Avon was disconnected from the intensity of her senses because just like she had aimed for as a little girl; her aspirations, desires and dreams were manifesting as she wished and she had forgotten. Yet, there she was superficially living to the fullest and apparently enjoying every minute of it.

Avon's career seemed to be at its peak, while her personal romantic desires were inconclusive. She still hadn't focused on creating new goals nor did she try to identify what she wanted in life like she used to when she was a child. Seemed as though once she began working in the Corporation, she had blocked being creative. Not that she was able to stop creating; for eventually she discovered the beauty of it all, as her mind never stopped

"When the philosopher points to the stars, the fool's eyes are fixed on the finger."

and continually thought whether she was focused on creating constructive objectives or not. Therefore, while living the moment and the now, Avon didn't notice, but she was basically momentarily living and during the following phase, most of her thoughts were unenthusiastic which manifested right under her nose. Years later she reflected on that period of time, wondering if perhaps she was thinking pessimistically for not being connected to her senses, because back then, seemed as if she was allowing her thoughts to spread wild all over her mind. When she could've been focusing on affirmative thoughts and even considering a companion to truly share intimacy with; she opted to remain single which might have been best so as to assimilate what was coming her way.

And so, it didn't take long for Avon's intimate young friend, Frank, to propose marriage to her and instead of refusing the proposal for she was determined to be single; she led Frank on and persuaded him to move-in with her without commitment. Frank was a handsome young man, well educated and spiritual. The only thing that might have been wrong with him was being eight years or so, younger than her. Other than the vague detail, his gorgeous blue eyes and bronzed complexion captivated Avon's attention immersing in a different dimension when they were together. Yet, both of them had career responsibilities and they couldn't be together at all times. So, the time away from each other, also turned out to be a disadvantage for Frank; because when they were away from each other, working, Avon misused energy thinking of ideas and creating the most terrible scenarios in her imagination. She couldn't possibly be jealous, because there was no one else; however, for Avon *that fact* wasn't an obstacle; since she employed time, energy and effort to create another woman in her mind's eye. Avon actually created and pictured a younger woman in her wits, who *could* also work in the division where Frank did. Perhaps,

Avon was focusing with similar intensity than when she was a child. At any rate, her mind was possessed with thoughts of Frank being romantically involved with her just for his advantage because she was older than him; causing Avon to fear with certainty the moment when Frank would cheat and leave her for a younger woman. A woman Avon created in her mind, intensifying the bitterness, resentment and suspiciousness throughout her entire being. All emotions she had been restraining since her divorce silently within, because by ignoring her feelings, her inner-deception led her to unawareness going through life with no specific flow and affecting her tremendously. Avon wasn't allowing her heart to open up and let it be. She still had to deal with the homesick attacks, as those emotions weren't going anywhere without warning. On top, getting involved with a new partner didn't seem to be a wise idea either and Avon knew it deep inside. But she was in denial and out of her frustration she employed in a wasteful manner the gift of creation reflecting the lifestyle she had adopted so far.

Over time, Avon recognized that back then, her mind was reacting to the unfilled extravagant thoughts she was experiencing during each and every luxurious trip connecting to her emotions and projecting in pretense, due to the bitterness, resentment, and mistrust she held silently in the deepest areas of her heart. However at the time, she was practically blind and she didn't understand the adage "It takes two to Tango;" for Avon blamed the unfortunate young man, Frank, for her pain and suffering which she had unconsciously selected to experience all by herself. But she wasn't in the frame of mind to admit such things back then. Being in denial, she was rather determined to make a few years of life miserable for herself and for Frank. Long after the fact, she understood that there would be times when situations could be justified and couples should reach an agreement regarding a

"When the philosopher points to the stars, the fool's eyes are fixed on the finger."

conflict; but then, in her case, there was no one else to blame other than her own self. In essence, due to fear of being hurt again from the resentment she held inside; she unconsciously built a *defensive shield* which no one and nothing would penetrate.

Frank might not have been perfect, although, he could have perfectly earned a medal for having the patience and Love he expressed to the being Avon had become. Probably he was able to sense her essence but she wasn't even near to allow herself within, much less anyone else. Frank tried to spend some time with her conveying his Love and in search of hers; however regardless of Frank's efforts to *attract* her, Avon wouldn't accept to be in Love, reacting defensive and she *attacked* Frank back. Without a doubt, Avon was taking Arolf, the young man and everyone who approached her for granted during that phase in life.

Avon was aggressive to Frank and constantly accusing him of infidelity. Their relationship became bitter, to the extent that all they did when together was argue; until the arguments escalated into insults and disrespect. Then, Frank decided to distant from her by sleeping in the guestroom hoping for things to somehow change. On the other hand, Avon was becoming insane of insecurity causing tension and distress for both of them. Yet, after they were intimately separated, Frank was kind to her. Most evenings when Avon was in town and returned from work, she found an aromatic bubble bath tenderly prepared with delicate essences, salts and oils ready for her to immerse. In the mornings Frank prepared a *café latté* bringing it to Avon while she was still in bed. However Avon complained about the bath being too cold or too hot; or the *latté* too sweet or too weak. Frank had no tolerance for Avon's tossing fits and she had no tolerance for his inexperience.

Tossing a reflection to the air...

"While the pole of positivity attracts negativity, the pole of negativity attacks positivity; if magnetized with precision, the merger results in evenness generating the neutral core life-force of all which cannot be created nor destroyed: Energy."

Naturally afterward, contemplating on the lessons learned by experience, Avon realized that inexperience would be a perpetual element in a being; as it was precisely inexperience, her limited knowledge and her great ignorance what allowed her to learn in the path of life. But back then, Avon had made up her mind asserting herself that Frank had no experience and his intention was to take advantage of her. Avon was not thinking at all during that phase, because if she only stopped for a moment and paid attention to the fact that her thoughts had been manifesting all along, she would've considered twice before placing herself as part of the scene she had imagined; since without realizing it, she was generating harmful vibrations through the *defensive shield* she had created based on fear transforming into emotional self-destruction.

Eventually she learned that when creating the defensive shield based on fear, the result rebounded vibrating to its source multiplying extensively with as much force as had been applied while creating it. However, when creating a *protective shield* based on self-confidence, which would be the opposite of fear, the shield would've been built by a higher power source automatically. So, the result would've rebounded vibrating to its source multiplying extensively with as much force as had been applied while creating it as well; but most likely Avon wouldn't have been affected by the bounce, since the source creating the *shield* would've received the

"*When the philosopher points to the stars, the fool's eyes are fixed on the finger.*"

force back. In essence, the *defensive shield* Avon had created based on fear could have defended her, but it didn't protect her from bouncing right back at her.

The certainty of fear was revolving through Avon's emotional mix and the scene ingeniously created by her imagination in her mind's eye manifested in detail one evening when she returned back home from The Hotel de Paris; not located in Paris, France; but in Monte Carlo, Monaco. And it didn't seem to matter that she had just been in one of the most exquisite destinations in the world working for a week; for when Avon arrived from the airport and opened her own condo's door; she heard Frank's voice coming from the guest room. Naturally, she followed his voice and when she approached close enough, she discovered a young lady cuddled up with Frank on his bed. Just like she *knew* it would happen when she imagined the scene in her creative wits; but still, she was surprised, shocked and distressed.

Many years later, Avon realized that after she had declined Frank's marriage proposal leading him on to move-in with her; she was acting out of embarrassment and pride derived from ego. Because by staying with Frank she was pretending to please all their mutual friends who found them a good match as a couple. Obviously Avon would've felt ridiculed declining a marriage proposal, and then, being alone. Therefore, despite of her attempts to conceal her own intention of remaining single and not to commit, the result was total distress. She also recognized that her intentions didn't hide and as much as she wanted to disguise hers from her own mind's eye; her thoughts transformed into decisions becoming actions and bouncing right back at her at the end. She could have been physically attracted to Frank, but she wasn't in Love. Back then Avon wasn't in the position to be in Love with anyone, as she didn't even Love herself.

※

Tossing a reflection to the air...

"The truth that sets one free isn't the truth that one tells or hears from others but the truth that one confronts within."

Totally devastated from the experience, Avon savored what martyrdom tasted like for the first time and being in absolute denial didn't help her either. It seemed as though Avon had forgotten all about discretion by then; because she intentionally contacted everyone who knew her and Frank as a couple and complained. She conveyed to all of their common friends what a terrible and dishonest person her soon to be ex-partner was.

Overflowing of resentment, Avon began searching for sympathy from everyone and she was receiving compassion from the so-called friends who were enabling the woman's self-pity with more drama and supporting every accusation she had against Frank. Consciously or not, every one of those friends concurred with her and went along with everything she said adding more heartbreak to the disturbed emotional state she was experiencing. Not one friend spoke the truth to her and all of them denied that she had been the one who pushed Frank to replace her with a younger woman. Her friends encouraged her to make an expectations list of the qualities she should expect, as well as the flaws she could tolerate in a romantic partner and to start dating again. Her friends were convinced that the expectations list method was the best honest foundation to find the perfect romantic partner; since the list was formulated to place a potential romantic partner through a meticulous indirect test to expose their true selves.

"When the philosopher points to the stars, the fool's eyes are fixed on the finger."

In the mean time, while Avon was dealing with her romantic drama, the same brother who introduced her to Lek called her collect to let her know that the electricity had been disconnected for lack of payment at her mama's. Chet also conveyed to her that a respectful family friend was visiting Arizona looking forward to taking her out and perhaps Avon could show him the area. Knowing where her brother's innuendo would lead, Avon didn't allow Chet to give her any more details regarding the respectful family friend; as she was perfectly capable to send money to her mother for the electricity reconnection not necessarily by selling her company to one of her brother's particular friends and paying no attention to Chet's indecency, Avon sent money to her mama right away.

So, according to Avon's friends, she needed to find a new partner *pronto* demonstrating to her soon to be ex-partner that she had no need to be with him. Years later, Avon realized that her inexpert friends in relationship matters unconsidered the accumulation of ill emotions she would have twisted within had she met someone and acted upon their advice. At the same time, Avon was even more inexpert than her friends were; for she didn't know anything about the dating field either. She ended up learning that opting to date someone to retaliate was called *rebound* making her recognize that such behavior would've caused the cycle of rebound out of fear; which would've bounced vibrating back to its source multiplying extensively with as much energy as it had been applied while creating it. In the midst of her devastation, Avon ignored that the entire drama was damaging her emotions severely. Had she gotten involved with a new person in a rebound motion, she would've caused even more damage to herself than she had already experienced transmitting only harmful vibrations caused by the resentfulness from previous romantic relationships she kept accumulating within. Had Avon met a new partner while in the dating field with her friends, the rebound would have probably turned into a pattern after going through it thrice. Because she had already experienced the rebound cycle twice; from Lek to the individual she divorced, and then, from the divorce to Frank. So after a third time, it could've taken her a lifetime to undo the emotional damage she would've caused to herself if she followed that path. Clearly, the last thing she needed back then was to get romantically involved with a new partner just to show Frank and her friends that she could *attract* someone instead of *attack*; because it seemed that prior to even trying to attract someone humanly, she had to learn to attract herself first and in complete solitude, not needing an audience for her to show off in any way.

Still, Avon did visit restaurants, nightclubs and bars with the group of friends who evidently were not skilled in the matters of Love and romance. Each of them had a list of the qualities and flaws they expected their potential partner to have; there was even a male among them with his list ready to interview potential partners as well and in due course, Avon recognized that she was reacting out of her own frustration by being irresponsible for her thoughts; as she didn't accomplish much, except for spending a lot of money paying for lunches, brunches, dinners, drinks, and whatever her friends managed to extract from her out there while exploring the dating field.

Meanwhile, Avon had been pondering whether to move out of her condo or to ask Frank to move out. However, it didn't take her long to find an opportunity to transfer once more. She had been in Arizona for several years already; so, she applied for a new position in San Francisco, California which seemed to suit her frame of mind at the time. She enjoyed visiting the West coast and by moving to San Fran, she would have the opportunity to explore the Bay-Area to the fullest.

"When the philosopher points to the stars, the fool's eyes are fixed on the finger."

In a matter of weeks, Avon moved on, leaving her acquaintances with their lists of romantic expectations behind and at the end, she didn't agree to make a list of expectations because despite of her denial, frustration and resentment; she seemed to still possess ethics. Understanding that life was meant to be experienced under rules; the rule that Avon associated with the expectations list was the one that everyone in the West referred to as "The Golden Rule." So, since she wouldn't have appreciated being interviewed for a romantic relationship as if she was applying for a job; she wasn't going to do it to someone else. Besides, she was willing to carry on and she decided to start all over again.

Tossing a reflection to the air...

"As high or as low as the expectation, so is the disappointment."

When Avon arrived in San Fran, unsurprisingly, her trusty friend Arolf followed her, and by then, Avon was hoping to find communication between them. Yet, every one of her attempts to contact Arolf failed and energy wasn't flowing much around her. Avon couldn't even distinguish the light at the end of the tunnel anymore; yet, she was pushed by a force that she couldn't explain feeling hope, and as usual, she followed her heart to the unknown. Finally, Avon began to realize that she sought for support and good sense from Arolf only when it was convenient for her and deep in her heart, she became disenchanted with herself. Through the following phase, reconnecting with Arolf was Avon's only hope, and truly, nothing else.

When Avon was a child seemed as if attaining her dreams to travel around the world would take her a lifetime; however at that juncture, she had already experienced trips to just about every glamorous destination in the world she particularly cared for. Therefore, her new position was in a classified division; she no longer traveled through work; and while she was financially able to travel anywhere she liked, she was still in the tourism field having access to complimentary air tickets, fine dining and fine hotels in case she would fancy traveling someday. And as usual, she went through extensive training preparing her to deliver and perform in her new post.

Her new occupation was among a group of consultants solving urgent situations and fulfilling needs that clients encountered during trips. She was working with a team of qualified individuals resolving troubles not many get to learn about. However, from all the cases she solved while working there, Avon couldn't forget a case associated with a minor who was stranded in Mexico with her baby girl becoming one of the memories she treasured in her heart. It was interesting to Avon that being a geographer, so to speak; she had to research the name of the small village in several maps to locate where the girls had been deserted.

It turned out, that the sixteen year old girl had crossed the border with her boyfriend in ground transportation and after getting into an argument; he had left her in the middle of nowhere with her eighteen month old baby who was sick. The girl's father, Avon's client, called desperately trying to obtain translation assistance in relation to what a local police officer in Mexico was telling him in the phone regarding his daughter and her ill baby and despite the fact that the client had reached the wrong department

"When the philosopher points to the stars, the fool's eyes are fixed on the finger."

and the Corporation didn't offer translation services for the clients from that specific team, having the Mexican police officer on an established three way conference call; Avon being fluent in Spanish, immediately took the case instead of transferring him. She had an accent when she spoke Spanish but she was able to understand and communicate efficiently. Most importantly, Avon had learned their negotiating tactics by having been married for some years to one of them, not a Mexican, but the individual she divorced was a Spanish speaking person. Therefore, she made the necessary arrangements and in the minimum time required, the girl and her baby were escorted by the local police officers from the small village to the nearest international airport, which was hours away, and they were ready to board a plane to return to the U. S.

Only prior to attaining the objective, when Avon first took the case, the girl's father conveyed that he intended to fly from New York via Houston to the village where the girls were. However, Avon's job was to avoid discomfort for the client and provide reassurance regarding the situation. So she had to coordinate a plan for the girls to reunite with her client at the Houston airport while he was in between flights saving him the aggravation of translators and uncomfortable hours of driving from one point to the other in his attempt to rescue them.

Avon made arrangements from the distance for the girls to rest in a shelter overnight. She also contacted the local chemist and they provided complimentary medicine to alleviate the baby. The girl had no money and she didn't speak Spanish; money couldn't be wired to her and they couldn't even stay at the only motel in the small village because the establishment didn't accept charge cards. Avon learned many lessons while working with the Corporation and one of them was that at times, people would confront situations when having access to money didn't solve issues. Instead, it was necessary to negotiate with strangers from the other side of the world hoping to find a Good Samaritan willing to assist when no amount of money would buy the solution to an emergency.

So, up till then, Avon's plan was working. The girl and the baby arrived at the airport the next day; yet, they were unable to board the plane. Avon received a call from the police officer in charge conveying that the girl didn't have the proper official identification and that the only identification she had for the baby was an illegible copy of her birth certificate. Then, Avon had to act fast. With the police officer's support, she spoke to the pertinent airline person and they arranged to hold the flight for a while. Then, she needed to speak to an Immigration Officer. Avon wasn't the least surprised to learn that the Security Immigration Officer in duty was eager to speak to her as well, because at that point, everyone's only concern was the baby's health. So, the Immigration Officer requested some information from Avon and she was prepared to send the documents to him right away.

Even though the girl's father assured Avon that the girl had proper ID; focused on doing her job properly, Avon had requested the girl's details and the relevant information from the client anyway, just as a preventive measure because Avon knew that he would be flying and out of reach. Nonetheless, her client never mentioned that the only identification the girl had was a learner driving permit photo ID card. Apparently, there was a time when people could enter Mexico by ground transportation showing any photo ID without objection; yet, showing a learner driving permit as an official ID had never sufficed for anyone to board an international flight from anywhere in the world destined to land in the U.S., and most likely in the particular case, Mexico, wasn't going to be the exception.

However, it was.

"When the philosopher points to the stars, the fool's eyes are fixed on the finger."

Avon and the Security Immigration Officer discussed the situation and since they were most concern about the baby's wellbeing than anything else; as soon as the Immigration Officer received a fax transmit identifying the Corporation's trademark; a statement from Avon stating the girls relevant details and that her client was greeting them on their arrival at the Houston airport as well as Avon's word of honor attesting that the original document was expedited by currier at once; the Immigration Officer granted a temporary permit allowing the girl and the baby to board the plane without an official identification right away.

The only issue that the client had to confront at that point was dealing with the Houston immigration officials which he didn't need translation services for. The case was considered resolved once Avon received a call from her client confirming that he had reunited with his daughter and his grand baby girl at the Houston airport between flights.

Most of the cases were usually solved by making money available to the clients and while the arrangements were in progress; Avon and her peers' job was to provide professional counsel to the affected parties. They resolved issues in any available form of communication through worldwide divisions and clients called from anywhere in the world.

After Avon had settled in San Fran, one day, she was nominated for a prestigious performance award extremely pursued among the Corporation's employees around the world. The client that Avon assisted with the case, providing translation services, turned out to be a high profile professional who wrote letters of gratitude and recommendation to her superiors recognizing her efforts during the ordeal. His letters granted an opportunity for Avon's nomination, and as a result, she was announced among the thoroughly selected winners who performed far and beyond the clients and the Corporation's expectations.

One of the incentives granted to the fortunate award winners was a one week first class tour in Manhattan where the head quarters of the Corporation were located. They were scheduled to stay at the most luxurious hotels beginning at the St-Regis, following by the Waldorf Astoria and ending at The Pierre. The awards were to be presented to each of the employees by the Chief Executive Official of the Corporation in person and Avon was excited looking forward to meeting him, as such summit would represent an honor as well as great reputation in her corporate career. Therefore, she prepared for the trip enthused and with an itinerary on hand making certain that she had suitable clothing for each function and occasion. There were rumors of surprise events planned in Broadway and also private tours including one at Madame Tussauds wax museum organized exclusively for the selected group.

Provided that Avon had been widely trained to perform and deliver, her knowledge of the affluent particular preferences was extensive and when she traveled through work performing her previous job in Arizona, one of her many duties was to fulfill the mystery shopper role evaluating potential vendors' services and amenities internally. Thus while performing other tasks she always traveled discreetly in order to facilitate her anonymous appraisals and reports by pointing out what the vendors should improve, or if the vendor's standards were not suitable for their exclusive clientele preferences and demands; she would not recommend their services to be implemented in the Corporation's travel programs for the clients.

Therefore, when Avon boarded the plane to go to New York to receive her award, the lady sitting next to her noticed the Corporation's emblem on her briefcase and said, "Young lady, as

"When the philosopher points to the stars, the fool's eyes are fixed on the finger."

soon as the flight attendants notice who you work for, the first class service will be flawless." Avon reacted expressing a gracious smile but momentarily disconnected thinking that she should've left the briefcase behind and feeling uncovered from her undercover. Instantly, she realized that she was traveling in leisure time and that she no longer worked in the previous division. Then she sensed relief but she also wondered if she was getting out of practice for lack of travel. After that, she noticed that her thoughts were sort of linking with her senses feeling out of place as if she was detaching from the current events.

Avon didn't give much thought to the lady's approach when they established a conversation, as having met so many passengers through her traveling journey; Avon had encountered people who actually talked the most when they really had nothing to say at all; especially when sitting next to her in an airplane. However the lady's topic captivated Avon's attention during the whole flight.

The lady said that she was returning from a week retreat. So, presuming that the lady attended as a guest Avon asked, "Was it worth the money spent, my lady?"

Then the lady replied, "I am a coordinator of the Sanctuary where the retreat took place and I organize the events, young lady."

Not embarrassed for her mistaken assumption Avon went ahead asking, "Would you share with me the message for those who attended as guests, my lady?" Avon was curious about the worth of such things and she was practically asking for the message that the participants had paid for a week of retreat.

The lady kindly replied, "The message is simple, even though to learn the idea I might have to describe some symbolic examples for you to capture the concept, young lady." They giggled, as they seemed to have bonded with the *lady* term.

Avon keen to learn said, "If it does not take longer than the flight, I am willing to listen."

The lady explained smiling, "The message won't take longer than the flight, but once understood, it would stay within you for a lifetime."

Avon asked, "Is is about dogma, my lady?

The lady replied shaking her head from left to right and looking at Avon directly in the eyes she let out, "Tsk, tsk, tsk."

Avon responded with a big smile adapting an attentive posture and ready to learn, what she ignored at the moment, the foundation of an infinite facet in life.

The lady mentioned details of the Sanctuary's location and she explained her contribution to the retreat. Avon wasn't interested in the lady's activities or the overall particulars; although she treasured in her heart a vivid memory of the essence of the lady's message. The message was about confronting inner-self; as the lady sort of explained to Avon half-way saying, "People that attend our retreats battle with inner- control and manipulation of thoughts; and they seek advice regarding how to leave things up to the Universe. We teach them that they just have to trust and let it be."

"Let what be?" asked Avon intrigued.

"To let it be there is one decision to make, that's it!" Avon was listening attentively trying to figure out what to let be, as the lady eluded her query and the lady added, "Willpower controls the mind and it could get out of control at times because when ego leads, thoughts might end up manipulating and controlling the mind which affects everything in life." Avon looked a bit puzzled. The lady continued, "When understanding the concept the decision becomes clear." Totally puzzled, Avon continued listening and the lady said, "The decision is to give willpower back to the Universe by surrendering within, let ego be, and make a pact." Avon had never

"When the philosopher points to the stars, the fool's eyes are fixed on the finger."

thought about willpower, much less controlling or manipulating thoughts. She didn't say a word ignoring that she looked bewildered though. So, the lady had no option but to explain with a metaphor. The lady labeled the concept a *golden pact* saying, "You surrender willpower and make a pact with your higher-self allowing the Universe to lead and let ego be. Once the pact is made, there is no reverse unless you like to fool around within yourself." They joined in laughter and the lady added, "The process is like purification of gold." Just then, Avon thought *whatever it is that this kind lady has to offer, I doubt that I might need it someday.*

The lady explained the process of gold purification in order to reach higher karats comparing gold purification to a person's purification and she made her point saying that once the *golden pact* was made, people would gradually purify to their purest higher self; just like impure gold would purify over fire from lower into higher karats.

The *golden pact* sounded achy to Avon for being over or under fire wasn't appealing to her at all. During the rest of the flight Avon was querying and the lady was expounding until they arrived in New York; making the flight entertaining and fast, given that Avon felt like while up in the air, time had flown with her.

As Avon walked toward the baggage claim she sensed a signal from her mobile voice mail. She listened immediately thinking that the message was from the person who would greet her at the airport and might have called her while she was flying; however, the message was from her niece Mae conveying that Avon's mother had passed away.

☙❧

Tossing a reflection to the air...

"The higher one flies in the midst of external sources, the more intense descending becomes when distilling emotions through the internal source–the mind."

"When the philosopher points to the stars, the fool's eyes are fixed on the finger."

7

⚮

*T*he other award winners were arriving in New York from all over the world at different airports, flights and times. So, at her arrival, there was a specific greeter and a driver with a car waiting to welcome Avon at the baggage claim; and apart from being highly trained to confront conflicts serenely, Avon did what any other person would've done when learning that her mother had passed away. She approached the greeter explaining the situation and without hesitation; the greeter provided her with comfort becoming the most sympathetic, professional and humanitarian support Avon had ever experienced receiving before. Avon was familiar with the amenities offered to the affluent clients while performing within the guidelines at work; however, she had no idea how priceless those services were until she received the treatment herself. The greeter escorted her to the first accessible airline lounge; an agent from the airline hosting the lounge offered complimentary long distance calls for Avon to contact Mae in Bangkok. Meanwhile, another airline reservations agent from the lounge was checking on available flights for Avon to attend the funeral. The greeter alerted the driver and he was ready to drive them to any of the airports in

"When the philosopher points to the stars, the fool's eyes are fixed on the finger."

the area. Alongside, the greeter had claimed and transferred Avon's luggage to the car waiting and as soon as they found an available flight to Bangkok, the greeter arranged for a complimentary first class air ticket making sure that Avon had the support needed and the greeter also advised every relevant person of the situation organizing all the details.

The last available flight to Bangkok that evening was leaving from another airport and they had to hurry from one point to another. Back then, Airport security wasn't as restricted as safety measures later became; yet, as much as they rushed, when they finally arrived to the check-in desk at the gate; the plane wasn't gone but the gate was already closed.

The greeter and Avon were disillusioned; as they had never experienced what they were about to witness. Sharing an extensive knowledge in the travel industry, neither of them was aware of exceptions from the Federal Aviation Regulations allowing an airline representative to reopen the gate once the doors were already closed; or so was their general understanding. Flying on a regular basis, their knowledge was that passengers who arrived after the gate was closed, mainly if the aircraft doors were closed, most likely should consider their flight missed. But while Avon and the greeter were grasping some air; the airline attendant behind the check-in desk picked up the intercom and spoke inaudibly to someone who authorized to reopen the gate right away. Without much time, Avon walked toward the gateway while expressing gestures of her appreciation to both of them, while the greeter and the airline attendant managed to register Avon's luggage into a passage disguised behind the airline's check-in counter which connected directly into the luggage compartment of the plane for last minute baggage and packages. Avon walked through the gateway rapidly only to find that the airplane's door was closed, and totally disenchanted; she walked back the passage realizing that it had been a misunderstanding. Suddenly, the aircraft's door opened from inside out and a flight attendant greeted her asking her to return and to board the plane. Avon's shocking expression must have been attributed to her mama's demise; because two flight attendants escorted her all the way to reach her assigned seat.

Once Avon had boarded the plane, she just had to relax during an unforeseen flight to Bangkok. Nevertheless, for a moment she felt discomfort because she had always traveled discretely performing her previous job and she wasn't used to attracting attention at all. Also, considering the reason why she had to change course in such a short notice, attracting attention made her feel even more uncomfortable. Then again, when the other passengers witnessed the aircraft reopening the door for her, directing their attention to Avon only made sense. So, surrounded by exclamations of wonder asking who she was, Avon managed to reach her seat while reaffirming her nonentity to every passenger she tried to bypass. The flight attendants assisted explaining that her mother had passed away but it was no reason enough for the passengers' curiosity to be satisfied and after the plane took off; there was a distant murmuring for awhile. As uncomfortable as Avon felt, she was also as surprised as all the passengers were when the aircraft reopened the door just for her. She had never flown spontaneously before and she didn't care to find an explanation or a reason for the event, other than perceiving a magnificent intervention making possible for her to be where she was. She didn't credit any other significance to the experience and she felt what it meant to be where she was supposed to at any given time.

Once seated, Avon wondered if after the lights in the plane went off she would feel like crying for her mama was gone; but instead, she felt a diminishing sensation detecting a gradual void

"When the philosopher points to the stars, the fool's eyes are fixed on the finger."

in her interior. The void wasn't of emptiness but a void of space, increasing and expanding slowly; in and out, back and forth, up and down stretching her inner-self like when a bubble is tenderly blown within its elements allowing the breath of being to pass expanding throughout; to the point where she sensed her heartbeat and she fell asleep with the pace waiting for tears to emerge.

When she woke, the plane was still up in the air and after she freshened up a bit; she traveled into her remembrance path trying to recollect the last time her mama spoke to her. Remembering was in vain, as Avon couldn't recall the last time she had spoken to her mama, but there was a conversation they had in the phone a while back, being the memory that revived in Avon's mind at the time.

She remembered her mama calling her collect one day and requesting thousands of dollars to get her father out of jail. It clearly seemed to Avon as if her mama was taking advantage of the distance on that occasion, for as far as Avon was, she knew that for her father to be released from his offence to the law no more money was required because she had already sent funds; much less the amount her mama was requesting for. During the call, her mama accused Avon's siblings of injustice toward their father. The lady said that Avon's siblings were not cooperating with anything to help and that they would rather see their father rot in jail than doing something him. Avon's tolerance must've been stretched to its limit at that point because she had been in touch with her siblings and they had tried to unite and collaborate together. Avon had sent money to her siblings and they had told her that their father was already out of jail. However, for some reason, her mama wanted to conceal the facts from her.

In any event, Avon responded to her mama defending her siblings speaking like she had never spoken to her before and said,

"As a sister mama, I will not allow my own mother to express about my siblings in such a way and I will support them like a pillar." Her mama was perplexed when perceiving Avon's shift of feelings toward her siblings without her consent and she accused Avon of rather letting her father rot in Jail as well. Avon didn't get trap by her mama's accusations and she confronted her about things which had bothered her for years. She asked her mama to explain why she had never approved her accomplishments. But the lady's responses were vague telling Avon that she always spoke to others about her doing well. Avon insisted demanding to hear her own mama saying it to her, but the lady avoided the subject not giving details bringing up her affirmations of soon dying of a heart attack instead.

As the call went on, Avon asked her mama directly, "Would you tell me that you Love me, mama?" and the lady replied expounding that she loved all her children. Then Avon reminded her, "You dedicated time giving cooking lessons to Kalaya from an early age mama, while besides the cooking book you handed to me when I was packing the very first time I left Bangkok, I grew older and I didn't even get a hint to steam an egg from you." Then, the lady mentioned that despite of so many cooking lessons, Kalaya had never been able to actually cook without injuring herself.

At that point of the phone call, Avon had no option but to settle in agreement with her mama. However the lady went further explaining, "I'm your mother and I know you well Avon. I trust your capacity to cook safely from a recipe book or without it." Avon always managed to end every call reminding her mama of their connection through the sapphire pierced earring and as usual the call ended with loving words between them.

After remembering the phone conversation with her mama, Avon felt enlightened in some way; not only because during that phone call she had heard her mama for the first and last time ever

"When the philosopher points to the stars, the fool's eyes are fixed on the finger."

telling her that she was good at something; but also because she understood that it didn't make a difference who she was, as even siblings didn't seem to be equal. Therefore, no one could expect to be treated exactly the same, or so it was obvious in her case. Avon had just gotten divorced when she had that phone conversation with her mama; being then when Avon shifted into living the now and the moment without being aware that she was momentarily living. Because ever since, Avon had gone through her own unresolved issues learning and accumulating preconceived ideas, concepts and theories which were not going to validate the fact that her mama was dead.

As it turned out, Avon never asked her mama about the alleged student exchange and since her mama was no more, seemed only natural to let the subject go unless her father was willing to open up to her.

Avon felt like her mama's resistance to unite them as siblings was an unconscious protective mechanism caused by fear of not receiving individual attention from each, but instead the attention would've been contained within all her children in harmony, which perhaps her mama felt emotionally unequipped to handle. Avon also felt that she received in person and from the distance, the reflection of her mama's jealousy, martyrdom, resentment and pride through her siblings; because they were always next to their mama. On the other hand, what she received from her mama was extreme suffering and torment bringing Avon to realize that her mama didn't know better and perhaps she never had the will to expand in life; however Avon seriously pondered at that moment, before landing, if it would be in truth feasible at all to expand after death.

When Avon arrived at the airport in Bangkok, no one was waiting for her and she took a taxi to where the wake was being held. When she got there, one of her cousins offered to store her luggage allowing her to spend some time with her father and Mae.

Avon observed her siblings and they seemed to be lost in the midst of death while family and friends gave them hope and support participating in the ceremonies for their mama's transcendence into a better place.

After a while, Avon noticed her garments, shoes and accessories being wore as a display by her sister, her cousins and even some of their friends. She remained serene and didn't express unease or distress intentionally ignoring that they had unpacked her effects as an indication of her not belonging among them. A few days later, the final ceremonies took place and Avon was exhausted. When they returned to her parents' house where some people gathered after the fact, Avon found a cot away from everyone in a corner and she fell asleep.

Avon's sister, Kalaya, walked cautiously and unnoticed toward the cot where Avon profoundly slept. Kalaya was holding a pair of scissors in one hand and she approached the cot carefully for not to wake Avon up. When Kalaya got close enough, she stood right next to the cot and quickly, she covered Avon's mouth forcing her head down. While Avon was suffocating, Kalaya kept pushing Avon's head against the pillow with one hand and with the other hand, using the scissors, Kalaya cut off Avon's left ear.

Avon woke up shacking; as she was only dreaming the same nightmare she always dreamed about Kalaya; only that time she got to see the end. She touched her left ear feeling that her ear was untouched. However to her surprise, Kalaya was sitting on the cot by her feet looking resentfully at her. Avon rubbed her face still trembling a bit from the nightmarish after-effects and she asked Kalaya if everything was well, ignoring Kalaya's intention to be waking her. Instead of responding, Kalaya abruptly reached Avon's

"When the philosopher points to the stars, the fool's eyes are fixed on the finger."

left ear asking, "Why are you wearing only one earring? Where's the other earring?"

Avon didn't realize where the other earring was until that moment and she replied, "The other sapphire earring mama used to have."

Then Kalaya broke into an inconsolable cry and she said sobbing, "After mother died, I purchased the most beautiful set of matching earrings and pendant for her to wear at the wake." Avon listened and Kalaya wept sniffling adding, "When I was dressing mama's corpse, I tried to replace the sapphire earring with the new one, but unless I incised mama's ear, I was unable to take the sapphire earring off."

Then, Avon asked confused, "What do you mean you couldn't take the sapphire earring off unless you incised mama's ear, Kalaya?

Kalaya replied, "Mama must have never taken off the erring for many years Avon, because the earring had ingrown in her ear and I couldn't take it off of her dead and cold flesh."

Then Avon understood where her dream came from, as it wasn't her ear but their mama's ear what Kalaya was attempting to cut off and even though Avon didn't express her emotions, she couldn't help to feel a tad glad in a way; because the whole earring and pendant episode meant only one thing: her mama had departed from life connected to her.

So trusting Kalaya and in an effort to calm her down, Avon shared the nightmare she just had and she explained the connection of the tiny sapphire earring between their mama and her. As a result, Kalaya showed more resentment yet and she threatened Avon telling her that as soon as she went back to sleep again; she was going to cut off her ear for real, just as she had seen in her dream. Not the least surprised, because Kalaya was always mean to her, Avon felt her sister's pain in reverse; as if it wasn't for Kalaya's lack of respect, Avon would've given the sapphire erring at once to her.

Avon spoke to their father about the matter and her father told her not to give the earring to Kalaya; as if she did, the sentimental connection with her mother would be broken just to please her sister, because their mother had died under the impression of a connection through the earring with Avon, not Kalaya. He also mentioned that if Kalaya wanted to be connected with their mother, she should've thought of something to connect with their mother while she was still alive, not after she had died. Bringing Avon to realize the disadvantage her siblings might have had for being next to their parents and taking them for granted perhaps.

Since her mother wasn't in the middle anymore, Avon and her father were able to communicate in ways they never did before. Avon was surprised when she sensed that her father projected protection toward her. He told her to check-in at a nearby hotel for the rest of her stay, maintaining distance between her siblings and her. Avon didn't think that her sister was serious when threatening her. Evidently her father thought different. So having the time, Avon checked-in at a hotel and stayed for a few days getting to know her father better.

During Avon's stay her father and her shared many conversations and one evening while having tea, he spoke to Avon about some of her mother's aspects saying, "Your mother was always afraid to see her children grow and mature further than she had been able to grow and mature in life herself, my child." As Avon listened he expressed, "I understand the endurance you went through and the obstacles you've encountered in life to survive; however, don't allow the memories to block you from carrying on and to continue living life on your own path;" she continued listening to him as he added, "Your mother always meant well, but she never had the

"When the philosopher points to the stars, the fool's eyes are fixed on the finger."

opportunity to fully develop as a great woman; hence she didn't have a great man next to her," meaning himself. Although Avon didn't sense approval from her father but what he gave her was advice; she listened to him with an open heart. Especially when her father told her, "You still have a lifetime ahead of you and you should focus on becoming a great person over anything else my Avon." Her father also tried to explain, "You should not get involved intimately with a partner until after discovering your great heart." However, Avon didn't quite understand what he meant by that, ignoring that apparently as much as her mama knew her, so did her dad.

Her father even shared some personal dreams with her and the reason why he still felt a will to live expressing, "I am a step away from receiving the fortune I had worked for so many years." He confided his most treasured dream to her saying, "Your mother wanted to leave an equal amount of money to each of our children from the fortune I am about to receive and my only drive now, is to fulfill *her will*." He also mentioned his intention to pacify the financial conflicts among them and perhaps his children would unify someday.

Meanwhile, Avon's brother Chet was trying to set her up as an escort with men she didn't care for. Her brother Kyet was demanding an unreasonable amount of money from her in order to claim her share of one of the insurance policies their mother had left, which didn't make sense to her. Therefore Avon renounced to any money generating as a result of their mother's death. Then, her brother Nikom was upset and he didn't even want to talk to her. Because the time when Avon sent money to reconnect the electricity in the house, due to Nikom demands, their mother gave the cash to him for his personal expenses. So the electricity reconnection was delayed and they were living in the dark for several months. After her mother passed away they found the means to reconnect it. In the meantime, Avon was kept in the dark as well ignoring the fact that they had been without electricity for awhile and inevitably, she found out when attending the funeral.

So concerning her siblings, Avon had no reason to stay much longer there and she understood that that might have been the last time she saw her dad alive due to her siblings' rejection toward her. However, she was planning to keep in touch with him from the distance; for the advice he gave her meant much more to her than he could ever imagine in his wildest dreams for the rest of life left in him.

So as awkward as her trip seemed, she still felt that she was where she was supposed to be grasping that in spite of being unable to connect with her own siblings; she found a connection with her father discovering that he also had dreams in life, just as she did. And she had found a perpetual connection through a tiny sapphire erring with her mama resting in peace who indeed must have died pleased; since she had predicted her cause of death for years; because as a matter of fact, her mama not only died in the dark but due to a heart attack.

When Avon was leaving at the airport, her father hissed into her ear, "One day you would appease the curiosity of the arrangements made for your student exchange; for natural explanations of situations come through time and directly from one's heart my Avon."

Tossing a reflection to the air...

"In due course, death comes to one and all; not exactly the same way that one and all rush on the path of life to death."

"When the philosopher points to the stars, the fool's eyes are fixed on the finger."

When Avon returned to San Fran from her mama's funeral, save for her landlord who she hardly knew; she had no one to talk to. After she transferred from Arizona, she didn't socialize much and she didn't know many people in the Bay-Area. Therefore, solitude began spreading through her entire being like granulated sugar dissolving in a cup of steaming hot water. Instinctively, Avon confronted solitude with resignation and kindness which turned out to be the best approach; as resisting solitude's adhesiveness would've brought nothing but sticky misery to her.

Unawares, Avon found herself out of work. She had been granted an indefinite leave of absence from the Corporation giving her the chance to study her position in life profoundly like she had never even considered she would before. She was purely in the mist of entering a natural metamorphosis, just like a butterfly.

Facing the situation, everything seemed to indicate that Avon was an extraordinary performer in the corporate world; yet, she had no idea how to perform in life. While she had been awarded with one of the most pursued recognitions of honor among her peers at work; in life, she had been awarded with solitude, her mama's death and a new connection with a father who always had been a shadow to her.

So, Avon had a fair set of matters to sort out wondering how she should react, mainly, to the fact that her mama was dead. As so far, she didn't feel sad for her mother's demise. Somehow being aware that her mama was no longer lacking of everything and living in a house in the dark granted her some peace of mind. However the anguish, affliction and torment she felt for her siblings was torturing her. Because she felt like each of her siblings had one too many things to regret. After understanding death as the only cause for an action to be too late to generate an effect, Avon's thoughts transformed into mixed emotions bringing her heart to contract pounding all over her inner-self.

Avon had witnessed her siblings' behavior with their mother when she visited them in the past and she felt agony for not being able to provide them with a second opportunity to make amends. She knew that she wouldn't miss their mama as much as her siblings would; for she was afar and she could perfectly carry on living the rest of a lifetime making believe that her mother was only a phone call away. But when she was at her mother's transcendence watch and she observed her siblings being lost in the midst of death; Avon actually sensed that their mother had taken a big portion of each of her siblings to the final resting place with her.

Regardless of her sister's disrespect, Avon admired Kalaya for the qualities no one, but a sister could observe. For instance, Avon couldn't begin to imagine what Kalaya experienced when having to assume the responsibility of dressing a cadaver and putting makeup on a lifeless face, much less her own mother's. She understood Kalaya's jealousy and envy toward her because it was only natural. Since Kalaya had no idea what being fully responsible for her actions and confronting homesick attacks meant in relation to living under the shelter of family and friends. So, Avon understood that Kalaya didn't know better. Avon never had the opportunity to express to her siblings what she actually felt for them; as their mother had divided them. Also, certain cultural practices wouldn't allow it; plus being rejected and envied made the situation even more difficult for her to approach them. In essence, Avon felt so much pain, because they couldn't grieve united as siblings and her sadness intensified when realizing that they didn't seem to be humble. Despite of the traditional spiritual guidance they could resort to, her siblings gave the impression of being violent, insolent and aggressive rejecting every gram of Love residing in their beings and burying it in the deepest areas of their souls.

"When the philosopher points to the stars, the fool's eyes are fixed on the finger."

Avon could hardly sleep wondering in every area of her apartment at all times. She couldn't avoid thinking of the different occasions that she had seen her siblings disrespecting their mama. Her memories played back in her mind like a film. She could only imagine what they were feeling for the unintentional damage they'd caused, and as a result, the regret they must have felt. It took a few weeks of devastated tears and sadness considering her siblings for Avon to begin appreciating the gluey solitude adhering slowly within her.

Lonesome, without a soul to guide her or anyone to follow; not knowing where to go or what to do next; her mama was dead and Avon had no clue about what else could she care for from then on. She didn't know whether to give up by drifting away, or to find the strength to seek for an irreversible comfort zone to appease her torment. Suddenly, a complete sense of deception hit her, when she realized that the world didn't revolve around her and that *she* was the one revolving around the world along with the rest of its inhabitants. Avon sensed for the first time ever what meant to be alone, by her own and isolated from any physical human contact. Still, the world went on, Earth continued revolving and nothing seemed to stop just because she wasn't out and about.

Avon disconnected completely. She felt numbed. She was sad. She descended slowly down. She fell into her own emptiness low, lower, and even lower inside. She began sinking deep and deeper. Her own tears were drowning her. She felt as if a whirlpool was dragging her into the bottom of the ocean. She was inconsolable and ready to renounce. Except, her heart didn't give up; her heart kept beating and didn't stop. In the midst of her numbness; the only thing she sensed was each pound from her core. The strikes were not empty for each beat was full of verve and she noticed that those thumps were not alone. There was oomph behind her heart's throbs and she didn't know where her liveliness came from. The life-force was familiar and brought her relief though. Then suddenly, Avon recognized the force in her heart and, as she ascended to the surface at mind speed, she realized that the energy she felt was neither more nor less than *Her Will* to be.

Then as she began to focus on her heart's activity, she was led to identify within her solitude. Without a specific reason to persevere, Avon found herself narrowing down her awards from life reflecting on each of them in a constructive way. She was exposed to confront solitude, her mama's death and the advice from her father encouraging her to become a great person when he even shared his dreams with her connecting them in ways that her mama never seemed to care. And so, Avon decided to focus on the awards life had presented to her, one by one.

She began by contemplating solitude becoming conscious that, when exploring her heartbeats isolated from the world, allowed her to confront areas within that she had never been aware of sensing before. She spent days, weeks and a few months in solitude. She never realized that she had expertise until she approached them in a diverse way; for in order to appreciate solitude to the fullest as the occasion deserved; she remembered when Lek used to lock her in the apartment and she decided to lock herself indoors by her own self. Then, just like when she ordered her accessories, shoes and clothes; she found a service through the internet which would bring provisions to her door step. And every other responsibility, she managed to carry out online as well.

At that point, she realized that time was not money and that time belonged to her; time was merely free of charge just like air; because from that moment forward, time was abundant for her. Being able to apply as much time as required to extract information to learn about her awards from life, time became unnoticeable.

"When the philosopher points to the stars, the fool's eyes are fixed on the finger."

Solitude forced Avon to think reflecting on Arolf's guidance from the past absorbing and understanding the constructive elements from each of those mysterious awards life held for her in disguise. Progressively, as she willingly studied solitude; she came across general information in books and the internet, combining material which seemed to have been written specifically meant for her to read on the precise moment and her mind opened expanding in extraordinary ways which she had never sensed.

Besides the book she had read so many times; through the years, Avon had acquired some other books that she have not been able to understand, or she didn't get to read farther than the first chapter for lack of interest perhaps; but for some reason she always took those books everywhere she moved. So during her lonely learning, she found company in the words written by authors who had no idea that she would devour their written thoughts like a starving tigress. Amazingly, she understood each and every concept written in those books as if she had just ordered from one of the most prestigious fine cuisine chefs an *à la carte* exclusive gourmet dish served and prepared especially for her. Provided that she cherished every word she learned, she didn't make a list of book names and authors as she read. She only sensed her heart guiding her to each word she was finding and she adhered to each book almost like being another page of their contents. She certainly assimilated that when she was capable to understand; she attracted the information needed at the precise time, because she didn't resort to anyone for a list of books or recommendations as every bit of information seemed to have been following her until she had finally paid attention.

Although Avon wasn't directly communicating with Arolf just yet; she was able to perceive Arolf's presence everywhere. Avon had been immersed into learning and embracing each revelation with an open mind and heart until one day, she noticed that the topics she had been absorbing were Alchemy, Holistic Healing, Hermitic Philosophy, Metaphysics, Quantum Physics, as well as Law and Principles of the Universe in addition to what she understood from Eastern philosophy. So she reacquainted with her early years developing passion of perception, being attracted like the strongest magnet to the intangible through the connection of language, words and thoughts to a person's physical body which captivated her attention merging into Metaphysics; Meta, meaning beyond, and physics defining itself; in other words, the merger of body and soul.

So then, Avon finally granted herself the benefit to approach her landlord intending to discuss the learned topics and discoveries with a wise-minded person. She felt comfortable with him because when she moved-in; he had told her to come to him if she ever felt lonely. Every time they crossed paths by the lobby of the building; she noticed his finesse and kindness. He spoke clearly and he seemed to be in good physical shape for is age. Sometimes his eyes were grayish blue but they turned emerald green now and then; his whiter than gray hair accentuated his wisdom; he always wore casual suits without a tie and his shoes were always shiny matching his trousers' belts.

At any rate, as soon as they acquainted, Avon was fascinated with her landlord; a semi-retired doctor highly regarded in the community. The doctor not only owned the thirty units building where Avon rented her apartment, at the top of Nob Hill, but he also owned another rental edifice with about the same capacity across the street. The doctor had an extraordinary library in the building where Avon lived and he allowed her to help herself throughout it. She was going up and down the old fashioned lift during days and nights, from her apartment on the second floor to the twelfth floor

"When the philosopher points to the stars, the fool's eyes are fixed on the finger."

where the library was. There were plenty of nights when Avon read and researched not even becoming aware of the transition from night to day and back to night.

The doctor and Avon gathered every so often. When she hosted at her place offering a meal, the doctor usually brought a bottle of fine wine. They conversed in depth and he assisted her by clarifying concepts and preconceptions for her to reach her own understanding. Also at times, the doctor hosted at his place for he lived in one of the units of the building where Avon lived as well. And in warmer weather, they enjoyed the freshness of the back garden, where the doctor had a comfy set up with a charming lit fountain and an outdoors fireplace.

Although Avon had spent a few months alone and she had identified pretty well with her solitude, while conversing with the doctor; she enjoyed each and every elucidation she learned. Thanks to the doctor, she understood the differences between motivation and inspiration; creating and manifesting; thinking and remembering; ideas and imagining; understanding and knowing; and among others, attention and awareness. Her mind opened up to learn with passion, willingly. Not learning like when she was in College and she practically had to study a subject in order to pass a test from a curriculum conveniently programmed by leaders of society who imposed their own interests in their teachings. At times, during the College phase, Avon felt forced to learn about a subject regardless of her personal interest in the contents. She considered that no one should be submitted to an educational system which prepared submissive employees rather than preparing great performers in life; but also, she understood that there was a point for all in life, including herself, to reconcile; as many would pay great amounts of money in exchange for learning how to become employed fostering the education system time after time.

So, after experiencing a new approach to gain understanding of her own interests, unaware, Avon was enthused teaching to herself while learning all together and in the midst of her research, she found a quote which intrigued her. Thus one evening she brought the quote to the doctor thinking that he would clarify it for her and when she showed him the quote: "*The lips of wisdom are sealed, except to the ears of understanding.*"

The doctor looked at her profoundly. He nodded assent and articulated kindly, "An axiom, a maxim, a quote, a proverb, and even a metaphor; are the same than painted art, music, sculptures, or ballet, my dear." Then, he went further describing, "All of those I mentioned could be approached with the following intention;" he paused changing pitch and resumed in a low tone, "Allow the quote to glide within for as long as it suits until igniting your senses to activate connecting to the mind its truth." From that point forward, as Avon formulated her reflections; she consciously decided to toss them to the air and whoever captured them, it would be just fine with her.

Avon was fascinated with the method the doctor employed to clarify queries for her; as he rarely provided his own opinion. At times, she felt like the doctor was trying to ignite a symbolic fire within her because she always had to do the thinking in solitude and when she was completely by herself.

Having learned about perseverance from the book she read over and over again; she practiced persistence not getting discourage and she found the doctor's etiquette intriguing and motivating when she learned. Avon continued researching, studying and understanding not giving up until she cleansed her conscious to a certain extent and finally granted herself a reunion with her best friend, Arolf, afresh.

"*When the philosopher points to the stars, the fool's eyes are fixed on the finger.*"

Tossing a reflection to the air...

"Once the mind allies to the core of the Universe; the heartbeat of Love is sensed."

8

❦

$\mathscr{B}$efore precipitating a reencounter with Arolf, Avon focused on accepting, assimilating and appropriating her discoveries. Therefore to continue learning; she locked herself in the apartment one more time and she brought every book she could borrow from the doctor's library with her. She was ready and prepared; except for a major component; as she was unaware that she had to conquer her true intention first, because only then, she would have the proper sense of liberation to confront Arolf again.

The following phase, seemed almost like every topic Avon felt thirsty to learn was an excuse for not to encounter her essence. Because when she reviewed her findings and discoveries; the topics exposed were a bit tedious. But as dreary, colorless and transparent as the steps she followed might have felt when the information ejected to surface; she couldn't escape from revealing her own truth.

Avon found herself in the midst of solitude again and in search for a comfort zone to validate the unwelcome fact that her mama's presence was dead; she reflected with hindsight on the experiences she had lived in life so far. Then in an effort to extract the lessons

"When the philosopher points to the stars, the fool's eyes are fixed on the finger."

learned; she considered her past interactions with people around the world in business as well as in personal levels. Also, she reflected on her personal understanding from her original culture along with the new discoveries she came across when learning from the books in the doctor's library. After that, she was able to think and formulate her own ideas writing down her reflections. And so, she was able to sense her heart connecting to her mind. All of a sudden, her senses revived and the sensation as if her wits were dismaying ceased bringing her to feel alive because she no longer stood like a lifeless cold tree in the midst of life.

Only before feeling alive again, she went through a crucial exploration; for she needed to understand each point clearly and just like peeling an onion layer by layer resisting tears and discomfort; she commenced to distill her ideas one by one thinking *when someone dies, people probably say what they think that the person in grieve would like to hear*, because when she tried to apply certain concepts to her situation; she couldn't help to wonder *even if I want to hear it, the probabilities of applying these concepts to validate mama's death are quite low.* In her dedication to find a comfort zone; she firmly considered the idea that her mama's soul was gliding above; or that her mama was guiding her from a much better place than Earth where she had ascended after death; or that her mama was protecting her and watching over her from the so-called better place. However, in view of her own personal circumstances; Avon felt as if those ideas insulted intelligence itself because she pondered *if mama never told me directly that she loved me when she was alive; mama denied approval of the decisions I made when she was alive; how could mama be guiding me in death? And, if mama didn't protect me when she was alive; how could I consider a person being more truthful dead than alive?* She also reflected on the claim that her mama's soul could be reborn as a baby, or perhaps even as an insect; in any event, if her mama's soul returned to Earth in one form or another the new entity would not actually be the same mama she knew after all; therefore the idea didn't help much.

So, not allowing herself to be fooled by certain interpretations of death; she pondered over information she found in the library; as she had learned through Hermetic Philosophy that every person without exception, one and all, regardless of their personal interests should be capable to develop to their fullest potential at freewill, and during a lifetime, not after death. And so, independently Avon thought, *the very suggestion that a human being should die, so then attain a condition in a better place than Earth in order to expand to their fullest potential is an expression of arrogance and ingratitude in response to the work of art given to humankind by the highest power-of-powers—Energy—in the form of what I recognize as Earth.*

So as to understand her insight; she took the liberty to decipher the word E-art-h creating a new meaning of the word for herself: **E**nergy **Art H**umane—E-art-h.

Then, she also accepted the existing planet Earth in her heart representing the only dreamland for her to expand to the fullest of her potential as a human being and in an everyday life, not necessarily living as a cleric, or a monk, or worse yet after death. Also, she figured out that she couldn't afford to be led by tactless interpretations of her mama's death and she released her mama's physical presence to the midst of the Universe. She kept a treasured memory of her mama deep in her heart without nourishing the idea that her mama was soaring in the clouds; for she was aware that her mama wasn't floating above the sphere. Furthermore, she clearly understood that her mama was no longer her source of life; because she was on her way to discover her only and legitimate source.

"When the philosopher points to the stars, the fool's eyes are fixed on the finger."

It was fundamental for Avon to find a comfort zone; because she was without a doubt, alone. So when in solitude reflecting and contemplating; after validating her mama's physical absence; she became aware that once dead, her mama's presence was completely gone and if she fooled herself trusting invalid interpretations of her mama's death; she could easily mistake Arolf's presence thinking that it was her mama's; except that Arolf's presence was unmistakable for Avon because she was quite familiar with Arolf's presence long prior to her mama's death. Then, as Avon came across written discoveries about living and dying left behind by great minds from earlier generations; she deduced truths within and she learned to endure her own grief appreciating the award that she was studying from life—her mama's death—in her own peace of mind.

Avon's main focus was on returning to work in order to support herself financially; as she had no one else to rely on and she was aware that the Corporation was paying for her to recover; but she wasn't going to abuse the benefits. She was also aware of her demanding job; as her flawless concentration was imperative for her to perform in the professional area without uncertainty or emotional distress. Therefore, she was exploring to attract similar latitude of quality in life attempting to live in perfect harmony in her heart all the time as well; as if she was able to be such a great performer at work; there shouldn't be any obstacles for her to become a great performer in life at all. Then, like aiming for the stars and perhaps ending up hitting a bird, Avon aimed. She understood as clear as the sunshine that possibilities were infinite unless she established a limit and she firmly decided not to go back into the world until she figured out a way to live in complete perfect peace and harmony in her heart combined with being a great performer in life for the rest of existence left in her just like she was expected to perform at work each and every day.

So, in the midst of her thirst to identify the emotions causing her to feel different at her birthplace such as the culture and traditional philosophy; she found a quote that read "*You will be whoever you think I am*" or something to that effect. Hence, she reflected on the combination of words thinking *to be?* And she sensed her natural source; next she thought *I will be whoever I think you are* and she actually became more aware of the concept sensing certain comfort which only she might have been able to perceive, yet in the solitude adhered within her entire being and in an effort to find her own comfort zone, no one else had to agree with her.

Eventually, she accepted E-Art-H as her comfort zone, *Energy* Art H*umane*. However in order to be able to carry on; she came to terms with the aspects of being enclosing her existence and life-force by sensing and reflecting discovering a meaning for her own higher Energy power and source the only way she knew how:

"*When the philosopher points to the stars, the fool's eyes are fixed on the finger.*"

Tossing reflections to the air...

"*The Universe powerful life-force of* **Energy***: perpetual, supreme, indestructible, invincible, omnipotent, inescapable* **presence***. Not one person could describe it, and yet, everyone with no exception could sense it. While some deny it, others cautiously accept its existence granting it no credence unless associated with their kind giving it a name and an image which ought to relate to their form.*

Regardless of the intimidation of Energy's power a low degree supply inspires celestial, divine, angelical and heavenly thoughts. Above and below its core is the source of Love that reveals as a **formless presence beyond gender** *through an intangible oomph within all.*

Energy's power engenders a Universe in which the planet Earth could hardly be distinguished from the distance within its own galaxy through the Hubble telescope; much less a human being could be identified if peeking at the sphere from above the midst of space.

A Universe functioning in continuous, irreversible, mechanical and perfect harmony; synchronizing planets with glowing stars without mistake or delay and providing humankind with days and nights for as long as it has been until today.

Meanwhile, the Universe core empowered by Love vigorously prompts incessant motion maintaining harmony within every element in an ethereal impeccable performance entirely independent from human race contribution at all.

Certainly humankind should be regarded as unique; however, the Universe doesn't appear to exist for humanity's amusement; it would rather seem like humankind was created to amuse the Universe.

Essentially, a human being would be quite arrogant when presuming a free existence divided from the source and yet, attempting to expand **beyond** such a complex Universe disregarding its own realm.

Still, possessing the gift of **freewill** allows human beings the freedom to define their source as pleased:

'To be or not to be?'

The definition could be made influenced by arrogance if freely willed being precisely **'Freedom of will'** what revolves human beings' emotions and the Universe within."

"When the philosopher points to the stars, the fool's eyes are fixed on the finger."

When Avon first identified with her higher Energy power by instinct; she felt rejected, inadequate and out of place. She had ideas perceiving emotions contrary to the philosophy she was supposed to learn. Yet, her will was stronger than anything else driving her to pursue her own childish dreams even if it meant to be alone and far away from those who claimed to Love her. So, when considering that as a child no one validated the oomph she felt inside, as she grew older, after experiencing more and learning some; especially when confronting her mama's death; she became aware of a *powerful Energy presence beyond gender* driving her within—*Her Will*.

As a child, not having identified completely with her will, Avon named it ***Arolf*** meaning nothing to others for she labeled the Energy which she perceived as a presence just like everything else is labeled with words which made sense only to her.

However, despite of her enlightenment; after studying and finding out certain aspects magnetizing her to Arolf's presence and source; Avon only understood that Arolf's presence had been her will force through life. But when she learned that Arolf was much more immense than the greatest her wits could reach to imagine and when acknowledging Energy as the vital presence within her, even beyond gender! Avon was quite intimidated.

There was no direction for Avon to follow so as to confront Arolf again and Avon recognized that her will allowed no external intent except hers to pursue a true path. Therefore not having much to go by and to extract the lessons from the experiences she had been exposed to so far, the only guidance she possessed was following her heart leading her to revisit her memory lane.

Hence she remembered with dread flying to New York to receive her job performance award and what the lady had explained in the plane about surrendering *willpower* and the *golden pact*.

Just then, Avon admitted that she initially divided from Arolf by rejecting her inner-self from the first time she experienced a romantic heartbreak. Then soon after, when she traveled from Bangkok to Montreal; she rejected and refused herself even more. Perhaps it was due to the impact at the airport when finding out that she was going to Canada and not to the U.S.A. causing her the dismaying surprise of having to face Lek; in concert with the alleged arrangement of the student exchange; because as much as Avon tried to ignore the facts it wasn't painless for her to realize that her parents had actually agreed to send her away trading her for money instead.

So in retrospect, Avon clearly recognized being then when she commenced to segregate from her own inner senses; gradually disconnecting her mind from her heart. Not taking her long to adopt misconceptions, preconceptions and all the contamination of thoughts which she was exposed to from then on. After that, she acknowledged that despite of her efforts to keep away from alcoholism, drugs, and certain physical habits; she wasn't absolved from contamination of thoughts.

When she first arrived in Montreal and she disconnected from Arolf; not being able to feel the Energy as she used to when she was a child; she reacted trying to reach Arolf externally making her feel as though Arolf wasn't available for her. Meanwhile Arolf was exactly where Arolf had been all along since the day Avon had been born; Arolf remained in her heart. And then, when Arolf and Avon reunited again; she was pulled away by her mama's demands following the divorce trauma and leaving Avon in despair which once again caused distance between Arolf and her. Yet, Avon distinguished Arolf's presence in each person she met along the way giving her the support needed each step of her path.

Fortunately, Avon was well aware that one of the causes of general depression in an individual is simply lack of attention.

"When the philosopher points to the stars, the fool's eyes are fixed on the finger."

Not attention from others, but attention to one's inner-self and without being under the influence of medical side effects; once she holistically understood by assimilating, appropriating and accepting the potential she possessed, there shouldn't be space for any other emotion but constant joyfulness. Hence giving up and depressing herself was not an option for her.

However, the terror invading her before reuniting with Arolf again was further than description. When she was a child, ignorance was an advantage, for she didn't have fixed ideas; nevertheless at the point where she found herself; after being exposed to as much pollution of thoughts as she had; she literally had to go through a reformation of language from a different perspective than before. At first, the only thing she understood was that she would be making a pact within; the *golden pact* that the lady in the plane spoke about and she would be surrendering *willpower*. Therefore, Avon thought, *things will be just fine, as soon as I figure out how to shift into an inner area that I am quite familiar with.*

Nonetheless, Avon was terrified.

Avon's dread was caused by embarrassment to confront Arolf's powerful presence. A power which in ignorance had possessed her; but by understanding what she had been learning; she was just frightened. Certainly, Avon wasn't fearful of Arolf's power above over there; since admitting and accepting to be part of the power that would generate when recognizing the perpetual merge between Arolf and her was no longer a childish instinct. She was afraid to confront her own inner-self because she had found a quote from a wise man which made her hesitate:

"If the lion knew his own strength, hard were it for any man to rule him."—Sir Thomas More

Avon memories of the course she followed to find a comfort zone were quite vivid. The moments of humiliation she went through causing her to vacillate; being totally conscious of the responsibility she would confront when surrendering within; allowing Arolf's power to possess her again under full awareness and understanding, were solemn.

When Avon realized the meaning of surrendering and what returning *willpower* to the source entailed; she felt more humiliated yet; as she learned through material she read that *willpower* didn't belong to her to begin with, and as a result of contamination thoughts, she seemed to have taken ownership of *willpower* by herself.

Hence her disgrace, for she felt like a thief! When she was a child, she didn't care about control or manipulation of thoughts; because her thoughts were natural and instinctive. Whereas the misconceptions she had selected to acknowledge in her adulthood were clearly leading her through life madly; employing *willpower* as if it was her property thinking that she was capable to attract her inner-self without a drive to direct her. And so, according to Avon, her only option was to become humble and return what she had taken—willpower—by making the *golden pact* with Arolf.

By nature, Avon acknowledged that after making the *golden pact*, Arolf wouldn't be taken for granted ever again. The pact was a personal commitment releasing willpower back to her source and immediately trusting with absolute self-confidence—faith—the will of the Universe to take over and direct her like a driver into her inner-self and life in general. She had to grant herself amalgamation to Energy, the power-of-powers, life-force, the Universe's will, or as Avon called it; Arolf.

Then Avon was able to accept that she had been completely unfair with her inner-self, because she had been blocking her

"When the philosopher points to the stars, the fool's eyes are fixed on the finger."

mind from expanding. She had been learning that everyone has an interconnection and she associated her connection to other human beings through the mind; because she also had been learning that Energy manifested throughout its *Art Humane*–Earth– by transmitting thoughts to humankind. So not until then, Avon finally understood that Energy had been manifesting through the thoughts in her mind all along whether under a pact, or not. As if she came up with her own reflection: *A Universe functioning in continuous, irreversible, mechanical and perfect harmony.* The Universe didn't lack power, and literally, the Universe wouldn't stop its function for no one; let alone for Avon. When understanding that Energy manifested in Earth through thoughts in connection to people's minds; Avon's own reflection became even more clear to her; because to Energy made no difference what Avon was thinking about; or if the thoughts she selected willingly were constructive or not. Given that Avon's thoughts have been manifesting right under her nose from the very beginning and not until her mama passed away Avon stopped to notice and paid attention.

Then the *golden pact* meant for her to make a firm decision which was her vacillation; as she came across the ultimate question: *to be or not to be?* Causing her indecision, because she had ceased *being* long before, from the time when she decided to feel self-important resolving her family's issues and she went on ignoring her inner-self. During that period of time was when Avon obstructed her senses and her thoughts totally; as she decided *not to be* responsible for her own thoughts blocking her own truth and she detached from her own understanding and her instinctive senses all together.

Apparently the topics Avon explored appeared further than closer to find a comfort zone; but she continued her research and as days went by; she was more determined to give in within rather than giving up without.

She carried on researching and she deduced from her learning that if she wanted to formulate her own thoughts at freewill; she had to understand that the art of thinking was composed of thoughts logically formed out of simple words; therefore, her vocabulary in any language had a great deal to do with what she was thinking and what Energy manifested around her at all times and although she had always been an educated communicator; Avon's thoughts were not in the ideal direction for Energy to manifest in her favor; because unlike when she was a child, in her adulthood, Avon had predisposed to focus on remembering and not thinking. Evidently, she had a conflict identifying constructive thoughts and she focused on the opposite. When thinking would allow her to create ideas, and then, Energy would manifest those ideas effectively; remembering manifested through the sensation that she learned to call homesickness.

At that point, Avon had to practice meditation exercises, not like when she was a child and everything was clearer in her mind. In any event, when she tried to meditate visualizing what the lady had told her in the plane about the *golden pact* and she pictured the gold melting transmuting into karats over fire; she panicked just to imagine the intensity of the pain. Then, soon after her visualization failed; she considered the advice that the doctor had given to her about the quotes, metaphors and proverbs *"Allow the metaphor to glide within for as long as it suits, until igniting one's senses to activate connecting to the mind its truth."* And even though Avon would've liked to allow herself some time to understand the *golden pact* metaphor and continue vacillating with excuses; all at once her heart was ready to explode hoping for the contractions to be over; because her ego was making her feel an agony reflecting in pride and embarrassment, a feeling pretty much multiplied in relation to the homesick attacks that she was used to experience.

"When the philosopher points to the stars, the fool's eyes are fixed on the finger."

Therefore, even if the remedy in her heart was to accept deep inside whoever she was releasing *willpower* and surrender within once and for all; Avon's emotional turmoil was intolerable and her heart felt incapable to perform while being trapped and contracted by her weakness and indecision. In her desperation to pacify her heart; she realized that her heart greatest performance was when she allowed her senses to expand by emitting words of reflection into her mind in any language to think, not to remember. Then, her mind transmitted those *words* as thoughts to the Universe in sequence for the Universe to manifest her ideas back to Earth in material form, providing to her physical eyes concrete evidence of the existence of all things which was known to her as creation. Evidently while trapped and contracted with indecision; her heart was unable to perform properly and once again she was being pushed by a force to follow her heart to the unknown.

In her vacillation, Avon was somehow concerned about the actual moment; as she didn't know if she should prepare a ceremony. She didn't know where the event should take place and if her pact should be done at a specific time of the day. Naturally, her heart didn't seem to care because when the moment to confront Arolf finally happened, the whole event took as long as it would take to affirm a simple "Yes."

But in the meantime, Avon took another couple of days thinking of the method she used to communicate with Arolf and she deciphered that a word was pinned to a *silent wave* which transmitted emotions to people amid all the cultures around the world. Once again, what everyone knew at her age; Avon was just learning because not until then she realized that languages had basically been created for the ear-sense and the mind's eye to convey emotions among people, and in general, what a language transmitted was Energy in motion; bringing her to understand that all emotions had been given labels in all languages mainly to convey feelings to someone else.

In any event, she needed to understand because she didn't have much guidance concerning emotions and most of the time she reacted instinctively. But when she communicated with Arolf, Avon always used her intuitive intention as she didn't need to label her own emotions; for only she sensed what she was experiencing within. And then, she search deep inside sensing the *silent wave* and it seemed like the *silent wave* set her senses into motion through thoughts activated by Energy generating what she commonly knew labeled with the word emotion or Energy in motion.

Researching the subject, she came across some information assisting her to relate the *silent wave* she sensed with an emotion known to her by a name and the closest definition she could associate the *silent wave* with was her *pristine awakened intent*. For instance, when Avon was awake she was able to decide in awareness what to think in agreement with the *silent wave* she sensed; as if she didn't determine her own thoughts and allowed other people's thoughts to enter her mind instead; at times those thoughts could become wild. So, when she was in solitude; she experienced peace and harmony because she had no interference from any other thoughts than her own allowing Energy to flow. And when she was with the doctor, Energy flowed smoothly because their attention aimed for the same interest. However, when she was sleeping and she wasn't guarding her thoughts; her mind didn't stop thinking for Energy kept its motion creating dreams through thoughts and without Avon being aware of, once in a while the thoughts Energy created while she slept even became nightmares and affected her emotions.

In other words, she wondered when the mind rested. Because even when she was sleeping her mind was always in motion creating

"When the philosopher points to the stars, the fool's eyes are fixed on the finger."

dreams through her subconscious and her mind seemed to function day and night without ever stopping. The only difference was that when sleeping she had no option to select her thoughts whereas when awakened everyone does.

Essentially, she understood that when she was awake her internal communication was voiceless, silent and soundless; therefore unlabeled. Being the same when she communicated with Arolf; for the alliance between Arolf and Avon had always been through a *silent wave*, hence she always took notes.

At that point everything seemed to indicate that in order to establish a comfort zone to validate her mother's death, the only option for her was to surrender and to unite to the unknown and yet power-of-powers. Because once she united to her true source allowing Energy to guide her thoughts, most likely she would be provided with more constructive ideas than not. Then, she realized that in order to attain her aspiration to be a great performer in life and live in perfect peace and harmony all the time; the simplest way was by uniting to the only thing she knew that was already functioning in perfect harmony—The Universe. Therefore by granting herself the opportunity to function in perfect harmony in accordance with the Universe, in all probabilities thereafter, she wouldn't even have to concern about her dreams while sleeping because the power-of-powers could only provide her with the finest. Just then, the least of Avon's concerns was to prepare a ceremony, as it wasn't necessary to have anyone else's thoughts influencing hers during the pact and the most important was for Avon to trust Arolf to provide what was required for the actual moment.

When the time to make the pact came, Avon allowed a *silent wave* of faith—self-confidence—to immerse into her entire organism while her heart ceased the contractions and pain releasing her from her own ego's trap of embarrassment. Trusting the unknown, Avon accepted the responsibility to let Arolf's presence join her perpetually. The *willpower* Avon surrendered was to be replaced with the will of the Universe instantly, allowing herself to be an integral part of *A Universe continuously working in irreversible, mechanical, and perfect harmony.*

When the pact happened, Arolf was still giving Avon time in space; because Avon sensed as if an arrow warmed with Love had been tossed to the air aiming her core to ignite a symbolic flame and she felt a *silent wave* from Arolf, like requesting her permission to penetrate her heart, which silently sounded close to: "*Yes?*"

Avon's response was affirming with a *silent wave*, "Yes!" and instantly, Avon sensed a flare-up within and she accepted the most profound areas of her soul blindly as Energy activated inside her expanding at mind speed and kindling a flickering flame in her heart.

At the same time, she felt a diminishing sensation detecting a gradual void in her interior. The void wasn't of emptiness but a void of space increasing and expanding slowly; in and out, back and forth, up and down stretching her inner-self like when a bubble is tenderly blown within its elements allowing the breath of being to pass expanding throughout; to the point where she sensed her heartbeat next to a symbolic flame accepting Arolf's presence as a permanent resident in her heart and bonding to the will of the Universe.

Once Avon selected to be and released willpower allowing the will of the Universe to lead; right away, she was brought to absolute peace of mind for she didn't have to hesitate ever again; the perpetual *golden pact* had been made being all it took; because nothing really happened in the surface, the pact was a holistic moment within her.

"*When the philosopher points to the stars, the fool's eyes are fixed on the finger.*"

Tossing a reflection to the air...

"Life-force guides anyone within their own senses to accept the truth to be, needn't ceremonies, spectators nor witnesses."

Making the *golden pact* was only the beginning because Avon seemed to have forgotten her essence. However, by learning some and experiencing more, eventually, she shifted back into her pure self little by little; and then, she began to recognize who she was created to be. Her fear to the unknown would fade away at some point and as soon as Avon reacquainted with Arolf; she would understand that only relying on the power-of-powers—Energy—with blind faith would provide her with what she deserved in life.

Years later, Avon contemplated on her own challenges when she first arrived in America and the rules that she was required to follow in order to obtain a permanent residence in a foreign soil. However, when it was up to her to allow her own inner-self—Arolf—as a resident in her heart; she was ruthless rejecting herself time and again. Meanwhile not even immigration officials were as harsh and ruthless as Avon was toward her own self when accepting a foreigner into their land.

Soon after the pact, Avon faced an inescapable revelation when understanding the reflection: *A Universe continuously working in irreversible, mechanical and perfect harmony;* as it sounded like, truly, to the Universe didn't make a difference if a human being was living or dying. Therefore, she accepted the fact that her mama was gone and dead while she was still alive and living. Avon came to terms with the fact that the only way her mama could expand after death was through her; as she was solely the continuation of a human being—a mama who birthed her. Her mama might have not expanded to the fullest of her potential in life, or perhaps she had; whereas Avon was still in life to explore and fulfill purposes under the will of the Universe not her will or her mama's will at all. Finally, Avon established her own comfort zone validating the fact that her mama had reached the end of only one of the countless paths in life, since each person ought to have one. Avon's comfort zone revealed as an Earth sphere floating deep in her soul symbolizing a peaceful battle field after a war between sources had been resolved. A *silent wave* conveyed Arolf's victory; although regardless of Avon's attempts to ignore it, Arolf's presence seemed to have been dominating the battle field between sources all along.

During those months, Avon was able to discover the awards life had presented to her in a constructive way; she had acquainted with solitude quite well realizing that she had a misconception about being alone; as being in solitude was one of the greatest discoveries she experienced and cherished in life. Because by then, she had clearly understood that generally people sought to extract Energy from her by demanding attention disguising as company, or they searched for her company with the intention to impose their contaminated thoughts to her distracting her from thinking. So, she no longer resisted being alone and she indulged her solitude to the maximum from then on.

After finding a comfort zone; she also understood that her mama wasn't a possession that belonged to her; although there was a familiar relation between them through the birth process, Avon didn't allow pretentious thoughts to possess her making her feel like she had lost someone. On the contrary, Avon had regained her own inner-self and later in life she realized that thanks to her mama's death; she was able to gain strength and expose herself to continue on her own path in life giving her the opportunity to discover her true passion.

"When the philosopher points to the stars, the fool's eyes are fixed on the finger."

Then, she was left with the last award she was studying from life to develop as Arolf allowed; which was the connection to her dad when his encouraging words echoed in her mind *"Focus on becoming a great person"* and she didn't have much of an option regarding her siblings; except for letting each of them reside right next to where Arolf's flame remained, in her heart.

Tossing a reflection to the air...

"Not everything is the way it seems to be or not to be."

9

ears later Avon realized that when she tried to visualize the gold over fire during meditation; her fear had no foundation; because before long, the principle of the *golden pact* metaphor began to unfold through different experiences that she attracted like a magnet purifying her from one aspect of life to another. Unconsciously, Avon was familiar with the manifestation of her childhood dreams and when her adulthood thoughts manifested through *willpower*. However, her wits couldn't even begin to imagine how Arolf would manifest her thoughts in the physical realm once she had surrendered; as the will of the Universe manifesting through Avon's mind with her approval, blessing and consent would certainly surpass in great extent everything she had experienced in life up till then.

After being in recovery for several months, Avon was keen to return to work; meanwhile, she allowed herself to go with Energy's flow trusting Arolf to manifest her thoughts here and there. She reacquainted from the distance with Mae, keeping in touch with her father as well as with her friends Angelina and Jaidee; and she went back to her usual job picking up where she had left off.

"When the philosopher points to the stars, the fool's eyes are fixed on the finger."

At the same time, Avon had to adapt to replace old habits with new ones; because certain things she practiced regularly were simply no more. For instance, every year on her birthday, Avon used to call her mama expressing her gratitude for birthing her on that date. Despite of her mama's protests telling her to send the money of the long distance calls instead; Avon still called her mama every year on her birthday as a gift to herself. However not long after Avon was back in the world; her birthday approached and she didn't have a mama to call, and just like her father had warned her, unwelcomed memories were roaming around her mind as if something from within was luring to divert her attention and trap her in despair. Therefore, for her first birthday without a mama; Avon focused on constructive ideas instead and she found a solution to distract herself by taking a trip. She made the necessary arrangements and calculations to travel to a far enough destination where she wouldn't have to think of her birthday or the date and she prepared. Hence one day prior to her birth date; Avon traveled from San Fran to Japan. She flew high up in the sky bypassing the International Date Line and she arrived in Tokyo one day after her birthday skipping the entire day and date up in the air.

Naturally, Avon had contacts in just about every luxury hotel around the world and when she arrived in Tokyo; greeters who specialized in hosting, dining and wining business prospects and potential partners were waiting for her. Every one of her contacts was aware that she wasn't traveling in business but it didn't make a difference to them for just the same; they had prepared activities to impress her with their finest amenities. Avon spent a few days enjoying the comfort of White-Glove treatment from private drivers to bouquets of flowers and she enjoyed to the utmost every hotel that was in the itinerary for her to experience. After she had been indulging for a week; the evening before she return to San Fran, there was a small private reception offered in her honor at the last hotel where she stayed. During dinner, the hotel general manager approached her to confirm a meeting that they had scheduled the next day after breakfast before she left. Although Avon had received an invitation along with an orchid bouquet and she had already replied accepting; the manager reminded her letting her know that they had a special gift for her and he also mentioned that she might want to wear her boots because it could possibly rain. Avon was a bit surprised with his reminder; as it seemed like they had been observing her footwear.

The following morning when Avon came down to the dining room for breakfast one server was at her service which she found unnecessary; for all she wanted was a plain *latté*. Then, as the server insisted offering biscuits, croissants with marmalade or preserves, mini pastries and anything that could be served with a *latté*; so did Avon conveying that she was pleased with her modest *latté* and she enjoyed the coffee appreciating the view through the glass walls showing a splendid display of the Japanese gardens moisten by the rain.

As soon as she finished the *latté*; the hotel general manager approached greeting her politely by performing a kind and respectful bow and she responded with a gracious nod. The manager pulled her chair allowing her to stand up and he escorted her leading the way to the lobby. The manager continued walking and she followed by his side to the service stairs. Avon went along, as working with the hospitality industry; she was well aware that going through hidden back-paths and service stairs was not really an amenity but a privilege for special guests. The manager led Avon stepping down the stairs pausing briefly between steps and making sure that she was still following him. As they got to the bottom of the stairs; she noticed the scent of the Health Spa inviting her smell-sense and she

"When the philosopher points to the stars, the fool's eyes are fixed on the finger."

wondered if he was taking her to the Spa gift-shop to select some exotic bath oils and salts. Except the minute they stepped down the last set of steps; the manager turned to the opposite side and walked away from the Spa. So not alarming herself, she followed his lead but she sort of wondered where he was taking her. They walked a few feet and the manager stopped in front of a plain door which was clearly closed. Hanging on the door was a sign with a clock indicating the hour as ten and even though Avon wasn't able to read Japanese; she deduced that the door would reopen at ten o'clock. As they waited; she noticed a couple of quality carry bags down on the floor as though they were left there to be found by whoever opened the door. All of the carry bags had whether loose shoes or shoe boxes inside. The manager was quiet and he smiled once in awhile standing by the door and waiting with her. He wasn't telling her much and it seemed as if she was in for a surprise. Perhaps not one of those surprises to get excited about, but something like a *superb prize*, because after a week of wining and dining; Avon never imagined to receive such a wise and kind gift as the one manager was about to impress her with.

A great Shoe Shiner in the world

While they were waiting; an individual approached the door placing a carry bag with shoes inside on the floor and he left. Avon couldn't help to notice that he was a limousine driver unless he was wearing the uniform to disguise his actual occupation. After that a distinguish gentleman approached the door; he spoke Japanese with the manager and their interaction sounded to her like he was looking to pick something up. Avon perceived from whatever they spoke that he would return later on and he left. Next, another gentleman came over with a driver who was carrying the carry bag; the gentleman gave the impression of disappointment when finding the door closed; the driver placed the carry bag with shoes inside on the floor and they left.

At that point, the manager seemed to be hoping that Avon had not figured out what the gift was about; but even if Avon tried to construe what was happening around her there wasn't much that she could actually tell because all she was able to perceive was that the gift had something to do with shoes and considering her special interest in shoes, probably she would've liked it better than exotic bath salts and oils from the Spa gift-shop after all.

Suddenly, another driver and a gentleman showed. They were rushing a bit and totally harmonized, both, performed a kind and respectful bow toward Avon, and then, toward the manager. The gentleman had the key to open the door and as he was unlocking it, the manager spoke to him. Then, they nodded and bowed agreeing with each other; followed by the manager performing kind and respectful bows directing one to Avon and he left her standing by the door next to the driver.

As the gentleman opened the door; shoe smell mixed with some kind of chemical, similar to what a shoe-repair-shop smells like, built up. Except, it didn't seem like a shoe-repair-shop for when the door opened completely, extraordinary intact shoes were displaying on shelves. There were shelves with shoes lined up against each wall. There were also shoe boxes on the floor and on top of something that look like a bench by one of the corners of the room. Shoes were everywhere. Avon was impressed admiring the high quality of the shoes; as those shoes were most certainly custom-made not ordinary shoes brands or styles. *These are indeed refined shoes*, she thought.

While she stood next to the driver by the door; the gentleman spoke English to her acting apologetic for his delay and saying that

"When the philosopher points to the stars, the fool's eyes are fixed on the finger."

he would be ready shortly. Avon noticed that his looks were sort of mixed because he didn't look fully Japanese and even though a mature man; he seemed attractive to her. He was moving shoes from what gave the impression to be a bench putting some of the shoes into boxes and packing others in carry bags. While the gentleman packed; the driver collected some bags and the driver was also holding a designer's dressing hat which clearly belonged to the gentleman because the driver was wearing his own hat. Then, the gentleman took his designer's raincoat off, he handed it to the driver and said with a thick accent, "I don't need it anymore; it's raining outside." In response Avon smiled, but she wondered *why they keep bring up the rain... I hope he does not intend to get my boots wet.*

When the gentleman finished with his movement; he invited Avon inside the room and he dispatched the driver indicating when to return. She entered and what looked like a bench covered by shoes was cleared off and a Shoe Shine Chair was exposed; which was one of those refined pieces of furniture seen only in museums and films or in a luxury hotel semi-baseman as it was in her case.

Although the appearance of the gentleman's hands hidden under an evident coat of grayish tint indicated to her that the gentleman might have been the Shoe Shiner; Avon didn't assume it and she allowed him to lead. He then conveyed to her with gestures to sit on the Shoe Shine Chair and he handed her a pair of disposable slippers pointing to her boots for her to take them off and give them to him. As a female, Avon had never been in the position to sit on a Shoe Shine Chair to shine her shoes before; in fact, she would take her shoes to the shoe-shop to be cleaned and she didn't have the slightest idea of the significance of shining a shoe, let alone her pair of leather combined with suede boots.

At that point, she clearly understood that her boots were about to be shined and cleaned while she witnessed the Shoe Shiner's performance. So then, using the Shoe Shine Stool as a step; she climbed up and sat on the Shoe Shine Chair to wait and observe. Just like she would patiently wait for a pedicure to be done on her feet; except that she was going to miss the amazing massage her boots were about to receive.

The Shoe Shiner intentionally placed the Shoe Shine Stool at her feet; he sat and he positioned himself facing Avon's ankles as if she was wearing the boots during his presentation which seemed strange to her, because he could've carried out his demonstration on a different posture by having the advantage of holding her boots in his hands; but the Shoe Shiner began his performance gently describing his movements and humbly sitting on his Shoe Shine Stool by her feet.

The gentleman who indicated earlier that he would return came back and he looked at Avon in wonder. The Shoe Shiner handed him a package saying something in Japanese which brought the gentleman to bow to Avon a few times and he left. Soon after, another gentleman; another driver; and people were in and out the Shoe Shine Shop bowing and going politely while Avon sat observing the Shoe Shiner's performance.

After a while, a driver who had dropped some shoes not long before returned, but a distinguished gentleman was ahead, leading him. They stood by the door and they looked at Avon amazed. Just like everyone else had been looking at her from the moment that she sat on the Shoe Shine Chair. She thought that their reaction had something to do with the fact that they had never seen a female sitting on a Shoe Shine Chair before. However, the distinguished gentleman was not planning on leaving until enlightening her, for she didn't seem to have the slightest idea regarding the soul sitting at her feet humbly shining her boots on the spot.

"When the philosopher points to the stars, the fool's eyes are fixed on the finger."

The Shoe Shiner glanced at the gentleman saying something in Japanese, they exchanged a few words, and then, the gentleman handed his business card to Avon speaking English and asking who she was. Establishing her nonentity, Avon pulled out from her jacket inner pocket one of her business cards; and handed it to him. He took her card and without even looking at it; his entire body covered with a sophisticated designer's gray leather raincoat turned half circle returning swiftly and he looked at her expressing a smirk on his face asking if she knew who the Shoe Shiner was. Avon smiled back at him a little embarrassed indicating that she didn't know. Then, the Shoe Shiner said something in Japanese; so in a witty tone with his speech accent the gentleman said, "He doesn't care for you to know who he is but he has to at least tell you about the Shoe Shine Chair; otherwise you won't be able to appreciate the gift he claims he's presenting to you." Naturally, Avon wondered about the gift remark, although she got distracted wondering what could possibly be the mystery behind the Shoe Shine Chair; for certainly such a piece seemed to be a bit out of place hidden there and not on display. Therefore, Avon began a short journey with the gentleman and the Shoe Shiner which engraved as a treasured memory in her heart.

Since there were already two people by the door while the Shoe Shiner was performing practically *al fresco* in relation to his customary practice; it didn't take long for people to start gathering when coming and going. Some of them cared and some didn't; but something was indicating to Avon that the Shoe Shiner must have been many things; except an ordinary Shoe Shiner. The gentleman tried to encourage the Shoe Shiner to tell some of the story about the Shoe Shine Chair to her; however, Avon figured out that the Shoe Shiner's modesty was greater than the story behind his humble profession. So, she turned her attention toward the gentleman asking about him and the gentleman gladly commenced talking about himself. He explained about his international affairs at the Asian level saying that he was going to Singapore the following week for a business summit being the reason why his pair of custom-made shoes, which particularly combined with one of his exclusive tailored suits, was brought to the Shoe Shiner. Then, Avon mentioned that she had seen his driver bringing the shoes earlier and she asked if she could sneak a quick look. So, the Shoe Shiner politely took one of the exclusive customized shoes out of the box and showed it to her. In effect, those shoes had to be custom-made for the style was exclusive and well finished looking quite comfortable as well. And she asked, "How could you shine over shine?" Because the shoes looked spotless to her but evidently not to any of them; because everyone who understood what she had just implied looked at her shocked. Then, the Shoe Shiner kindly pointed out the hidden areas which needed his magical touch. After that, everyone continue observing Avon's boots being buffed and buffed.

The gentleman, Avon and the Shoe Shiner felt more comfortable then; so, the gentleman and Avon established a conversation while the Shoe Shiner input a word here and there. They conversed to a point where the gentleman was finally convinced that Avon was a nonentity person compared to the clientele visiting the Shoe Shiner in a regular basis and so she was there, truly, receiving a gift. The gentleman said something to the Shoe Shiner in Japanese and at that stage, the Shoe Shiner reacted indifferent, thus the gentleman conveyed to her that the Shoe Shiner had a driver, he owned his limousine and that he resided in one of the most prestigious areas in Tokyo. Therefore, the Shoe Shiner had not shined shoes right away for anyone in years and he exposed his own example to her. The gentleman explained that he had to wait for his shoes to arrive

"When the philosopher points to the stars, the fool's eyes are fixed on the finger."

in Singapore through especial delivery because the Shoe Shiner wasn't shining his shoes for him then and there. At that moment, Avon understood his earlier remark doubting that she was there receiving a gift.

The gentleman also clarified to her that no one had sat on the Shoe Shine Chair since the last time a prominent personage had sat on it because not even the Shoe Shiner's exclusive clientele had the privilege to sit on the Shoe Shine Chair and he mentioned specific names and details. At the same time, the Shoe Shiner was showing her some of the exquisite manufactured shoes from the shelves which had due dates to deliver, account numbers, locations, and tags with names.

For a slight moment, Avon speculated if she would ever be able to stand from the Shoe Shine Chair just to imagine the personage who sat on it before her. And then, she tried to find out how the Shoe Shiner had managed to get the Shoe Shine Chair from such an admired personage. The Shoe Shiner shared a bit of the story and the gentleman helped asking questions getting the Shoe Shiner to respond and clarify a few points. So, the mystery was out in the open. Avon felt embarrassed after thinking that the Shoe Shiner might have intended to get her boots wet and she was quite impressed. Yet, she didn't feel that she deserved the privilege to be sitting on the Shoe Shine Chair nor for the Shoe Shiner to be shining her inexpensive and ordinary boots then and there.

After enlightening Avon; while performing gentle and flirty bows as well as assuring her that her boots were in the hands of: "*The best Shoe Shiner in the world,*" the distinguished gentleman left followed by his driver.

Then Avon was able to speak from heart to heart with the Shoe Shiner. She sensed deep inside that the gentleman might have helped unwrapping the gift; nevertheless something greater was inside which she would have to open up herself; just like uncovering a box containing a pair of fresh cleaned and shined shoes perhaps.

Avon had read stories about Shoe Shiners who the affluent bypassed indifferently by the corners of the streets. Most of them started to shine shoes as children out of need which profit was worth very little compared to the effort they employed when performing their task thus feeling denigrated to generate an income while facing people's feet. So, she understood the inspirational stories behind those Shoe Shiners who exposed the opportunities they had encountered while shining shoes allowing them to break away from their misery and later on became fairly successful in life.

However, as the Shoe Shiner and Avon were left alone and in silence. She observed the man before her sitting at her feet on a modest Shoe Shine Stool and the manner in which he applied and buffed; applied and buffed; applied and buffed. His extraordinary presentation enclosed certain enthusiasm that Avon had never sensed from anyone before. She perceived the liveliness of his movements rhythmically vibrating tuneful in her ears as her eyes closed for a moment enveloped with the sound generated by the Shoe Shiner's performance. While the Shoe Shiner buffed away, Avon realized in complete amazement that shining shoes was the gentleman's actual vocation which he performed enthused with passion and unquestionable dedication. For a split second; she felt the same sensation that she felt when Clive used to play guitar and at the same time, the words of the gentleman who had just left echoed in her mind "*The best Shoe Shiner in the world.*"

Avon couldn't help to wonder who in their sane mind would aspire to be a *Shoe Shiner*, let alone intend to become *the best Shoe Shiner* in the world. For she understood all about aiming for the stars and aspiring to be the best of the best; however, as far as she

"When the philosopher points to the stars, the fool's eyes are fixed on the finger."

was concerned aspiring to be *the best Shoe Shiner* was an aspiration that her wits were demanding understanding.

She was detecting the purity of the Shoe Shiner's passion because the gentleman before her performed his art not caring that he appeared to be wearing some sort of gloves at all times as a result of the blackish tincture stained in his hands. Evidently he had excelled at his *métier* without ever willing to give it up or feeling miserable about it. He had actually created a fortune by performing his best skill, which was, in effect, shining shoes and he seemed to get pleasure from sitting on a Shoe Shine Stool purposely positioned at an altitude precisely facing people's feet.

Considering that Avon's mind was at full volume lost in thought, the Shoe Shiner broke the exterior silence asking about her flight and if he wasn't delaying her and she replied that there would be no interference from his part. So, under the impression that the manager of the hotel had arranged for the Shoe Shiner to shine her boots, Avon knew that if there was a fee incurred, most likely the Shoe Shiner's services would be included in the incidental charges of her room when checking-out of the hotel. However, she wanted to make sure that the Shoe Shiner received an extra tip and she asked if she could pay out a gratuity for his services directly to him. Then modestly, he replied with his thick accent, "You couldn't afford my services Ms. Avon. I don't intend to receive payment in exchange for my gift to you. It is my pleasure to shine your boots." Avon sort of made a fool out of herself and the Shoe Shiner gave her further details, "My clientele has opened accounts. I charge a monthly rate not for shoe shine. I keep my clients pleased shining their shoes from the distance and in private." She was embarrassed silent.

So then, the Shoe Shiner brought her out of her embarrassment gently by sharing that, certain shoes had silver around them; others had genuine pearls; as well as others were adorned with authentic gems like rubies, emeralds and diamonds embroidered with pure silk and golden threads. At the same time, he was pointing out showing to her the shoes that he had to work on the following few days.

Finally, Avon couldn't contain herself anymore and she asked how he had managed to become such a good Shoe Shiner. He replied trying to find the words saying, "Without passion, there is no inspiration; without inspiration, there is no purpose; and without purpose, there is no sense of success."

Then, he shared with her that when he used to work for the personage who had gifted him the Shoe Shine Chair; he had learned that despite of having all the money in the world what was most important in life was to become great. He also said that being great allowed anyone to generate money from the most insignificant talents just like he did; because once a great heart was developed; money would multiply indefinitely. He mentioned that only few would select insignificant talents, because thanks to greediness, not many people cared to learn how to generate cash inflow; since for most seemed to be easier to pretend possessing things through credit when the creditors actually generated cash flow through others' cash outflow.

As he observed Avon's silence and ignorance regarding his topic he expounded, "After finding passion; regardless of what a person's purpose is; everyone should focus on developing their passion one hundred per cent to reach their highest potential in life with no excuses," and he clarified, "I didn't start shining shoes in the streets like most shoe shiners do." She was listening perplexed and he explained the importance for men particularly in cities like Milan, Paris, London, Rome, Tokyo, and so forth to be presentable being footwear the most important aspect of their entire attire.

"When the philosopher points to the stars, the fool's eyes are fixed on the finger."

Perceiving Avon's eagerness to understand; he simplified, "When I made the conscious decision to shine shoes, I did it out of desire, passion. I used to work as a driver at the personage's palace in Rome. I never aspired to become a Shoe Shiner; however due to unusual circumstances; I became his personal Shoe Shiner." He pause for a moment observing that Avon was enchanted and attentively listening; so he continued, "The personage was unable to find a Shoe Shiner that wouldn't ruin his custom-made shoes. One day, I was still fulfilling the duty of a driver and I witnessed his frustration when he found one of his most valued pair of shoes destroyed by chemicals and his dissatisfaction was such, that as a driver, I offered to perform the task; although I was afraid because I could have been sent back to Tokyo if I failed.

"However, an inner force pushed me to insist and I assured him that I would succeed cleaning and shinning his valuable shoes without damaging them and I was given one opportunity which I successfully seized." The Shoe Shiner also explained that by being able to come up with natural and chemical cleaners, polishers and buffs combined with his technique and magical hand touch; he was able to succeed and the personage was so impressed with his performance; he personally began introducing him to his acquaintances who didn't seem to find a good Shoe Shiner either. Hence eventually, the Shoe Shiner was able to create a clientele developing an art he ignored he possessed. It turned out that the Shoe Shiner discovered passion when shining shoes which he had never sensed while driving through traffic. So as time passed by and his affluent clientele gladly sent their most valuable shoes from anywhere in the world for him to passionately clean and shine for them; he decided to fully dedicate to shine shoes as a profession.

At that point, Avon felt comfortable and asked if he would like to have his own shoe shine shop and the Shoe Shiner said modestly,

"I do not need to because not only my clientele provides prestige to any hotel where I am based, but I do well with a generous percentage from the hotel for showing up now and then." And he winked at her. He also said that at the time; there were three other hotel managers negotiating for him to have his base set up at their hotels and most likely he would stay in the same hotel because they had renewed his contract year after year offering the highest rate.

Then, Avon requested from him to share with her the reason why he was shining her boots; as his performance had gone beyond a gift. But most of all, Avon was intrigued about what had earned her the privilege to sit on the Shoe Shine Chair and for him to shine her boots right there and then. The Shoe Shiner inhaled deeply and exhaled with a loud sigh and asked, "Have you an idea of the many times I've missed flights and as a result missed business meetings just by arriving a few minutes late at the gate after an airplane door has already been closed?" Avon nodded because working in the travel industry she was quite familiar with the experience. Then, he openly disclosed, "I was on the flight from New York to Bangkok the day your mother passed away." Just then, Avon was perplexed and he said, "I was sitting opposite from you in the plane and I observed you during the whole flight Ms. Avon. I noticed your charisma and the manner you carry yourself. I wasn't the least surprised that they reopened the door of the plane just for you. Trust me, considering the caliber of my clientele, I can genuinely tell that not many possess your ingenuous and modest glow which reflects through a spark when you smile inspiring others' hearts in an extraordinary way; that's why everyone in the plane, including myself, wanted to know who you were."

Avon was dumbfounded and he detailed, "So much so that yesterday when you checked-in at this hotel, I couldn't avoid noticing you and I recognized you from the distance. Then I spoke

"When the philosopher points to the stars, the fool's eyes are fixed on the finger."

to the general manager and he informed me that you were in Tokyo bypassing your birthday. I made arrangements to offer my gift to you through the hotel manager and so, I would have the pleasure to meet you."

By then Avon was wordless and the Shoe Shiner looked into her eyes saying, "You have the gift to inspire others but you will find your own inspiration through the reflection of your passion Ms. Avon. Passion is the burning desire everyone feels in their heart but regrettably very few follow. There is no shame to be who you are, once you accept who you are in the heart, where integrity resides, you'll be led to the gateway of greatness." In addition, he told her to go and become a great woman for his words were those of a successful great man. At the same time, he indicated for her to come down the Shoe Shine Chair and to use his Shoe Shine Stool as a step. He held her hand with his helping her down and added; "Do not to concern about the importance of the chair for despite of its splendor, after all, it's simply a chair Ms. Avon."

As Avon had stepped down the Shoe Shine Chair and she had her boots back on her feet; he whispered as though he was unsealing a secret and confessed, "I sat on this Shoe Shine Chair many times after bringing it back to Tokyo from Rome when I announced to my Italian father and my Japanese mother that, I had become *not the best*, but, '*A great Shoe Shiner in the world.*' The best might be for competitors and I am a humble great person who happens to shine shoes as a profession not competitive at all." Avon felt like she was melting inside with his Italian and Japanese culture mixed approach to life.

Then he reached inside a carry bag taking out a package wrapped as a gift and he handed it to her saying, "This is why I arrive late today. I was looking for a specific gift to give you. When you return home, open it and enjoy it for a lifetime not only for your birthday."

Avon accepted his present gratefully and out of instinct; she performed the most gracious curtsy as a response.

The great Shoe Shiner in the world; performed a kind and respectful bow.

Tossing a reflection to the air...

"While success patiently lingers around; many find pretentious excuses to avoid modest occupations and impatiently settle for failure instead."

"When the philosopher points to the stars, the fool's eyes are fixed on the finger."

10

⁊he *silent wave* behind the Shoe Shiner's words revolved in Avon's mind the whole flight from Tokyo to San Fran. Inspiration and passion had just been exposed to her in the most extraordinary way and she contemplated on the sense of accomplishment the Shoe Shiner projected. Yet, regardless of the aspirations and dreams she had attained in life thus far; understanding inspiration and passion was just beginning to unveil for her, and as it seemed; the introduction of those virtues were brought right to her feet. During the flight back home, Avon felt a sense of pure absorption for she achieved to bypass her birthday, and at the same time, she felt as if she had just been born.

The last day in Tokyo emphasized certain personal aspects of Avon's aspirations in life; as the more she contemplated the instance, the more she understood the Shoe Shiner's insight; especially when she realized the difference between attaining a dream out of aspiration and succeeding to attain passion and inspiration.

She grasped then, that when she attained dreams out of aspiration; she practically had reached the end. However, inspiration and passion didn't seem to end when attained; quite the reverse; as

"When the philosopher points to the stars, the fool's eyes are fixed on the finger."

attaining passion and inspiration appeared to be only the beginning of a successful venture she couldn't even imagine. Just then, she had the absolute capacity to assimilate and appropriate the essence of the *silent wave* behind the words of the Shoe Shiner like she had never perceived before; although she had to go through much more prior to practicing what she was learning.

The sensation she felt by meeting the accomplished Shoe Shiner was unfamiliar. The feeling was slowly taking over every inch of her entire being. She felt good. She felt great. As a matter of fact, she felt almost grand. Except, she felt hardly equipped to fully absorb it because it took some contemplation for her to identify the emotion by a name. At the same time as she was feeling a glorious sensation inside; physically, the overexcitement was also causing her dizziness and queasiness simultaneously. It seemed like the more she extracted from the experience, the more those bodily symptoms intensified. So, she considered the contrast between the conversations with the doctor and the intensity enclosed in her recent experience and she realized that when learning with the doctor or by herself; she was introduced to the information gradually whereas the experience in Tokyo was presented to her all at once. Therefore, Avon's trip to Tokyo was the gateway to a new metaphorical territory which she had never dreamed about, bargained for, nor negotiated for when entering life's path and eventually revealed that, anything and everything Avon had been negotiating for all along was meant to be traded for the soilless area where she had stepped in when she made her *golden pact*.

Tossing a reflection to the air...

"On balance, a blessing comes from above as a manifestation of the thoughts that one transmits to Energy in motion from the heart."

The doctor was impressed with Avon's glow as he greeted her at the airport when she returned to San Fran from Japan and he could hardly wait to learn about her adventure. When they arrived home, he had a meal that his housekeeper had prepared and left ready for him to serve. Excited to see Avon, the doctor opened a fine bottle of champagne to celebrate her arrival in honor of her belated birthday and ignoring the details of her recent *voyage;* he raised his glass toasting, "To a bubbly renaissance!" Clicking her glass with his; Avon cheered back radiating of enjoyment.

During the meal, she shared with him about her entire stay in Tokyo and she detailed enthusiastically the last day of her trip explaining what she felt after the Shoe Shiner shined her boots as a gift. "The sensation is extraordinary" she said.

The doctor asked, "Would you search deep and tell me what you feel exactly my dear?"

She hesitated for a moment, "Well–" then she said, "The sensation is slowly taking over every inch of my entire being. The feeling is good. I feel great and I am feeling almost grand. But I am hardly equipped to fully absorb it because evenly, while I am feeling a glorious sensation; I feel sick. It is like a combination of dizziness and queasiness. I sense that if I continue extracting from the experience, the physical symptoms will intensify."

He expressed in wonder, "Really?!" Then he asked, "Not pressuring yourself, would you describe the feeling more in detail my dear?

"When the philosopher points to the stars, the fool's eyes are fixed on the finger."

So she searched deep inside identifying the great sense of consent she felt from the Shoe Shiner, who was a complete stranger, realizing that someone in the other side of the world accepted her as she reflected to be pointing out rewarding remarks of her personality and her propensity to become a great woman. Just like her father had advised her and almost as if the Shoe Shiner was able to see right through her, "Approval, consent—" she paused smiling, "A great feeling!" She exclaimed.

The doctor smiled glowing of joy with her bringing him to push a bit further and he asked, "Would you kindly call out more synonyms my dear?"

Before replying, Avon ran through her mind at the highest speed the synonyms she could think of; *authorization, sanction, permission* and all of a sudden a couple of tears rolled down her face and she identified the emotion calling out calmly, "Blessing!"

Tossing a reflection to the air...

"A blessing is incomplete until the receiver accepts with respect the materialization of their own requests."

Naturally, after many, many, many, years of experiencing rejection from people who were supposed to Love her; that was the very first time Avon had been exposed to identify a blessing. However she didn't know how to respond because at the same time as her *conscious mind* generated a feeling of glorious pleasure; her *subconscious* reacted awkward affecting her physically; as if her body was rejecting the unfamiliar emotion she was experiencing. However she ignored then what later she discovered; because in effect, she wasn't equipped emotionally or physically to assimilate a blessing. Clearly, Avon had not given Arolf a chance to make her aware regarding the purification process in relation to contamination of thoughts just yet; as the method Avon had selected to reencounter with Arolf was through the so-called *golden pact* and Avon had been so busy focusing on the gold melting over the fire; she was disregarding the principle of the metaphor completely. Besides, having made a *golden pact* didn't instantly cleanse the contamination of thoughts that Avon had adopted and accumulated through the years.

Also, ever since Avon commenced learning the connection between her mental vocabulary, thoughts, and emotions; she became aware of an emotion she felt once but she had never been able to experience again. Every so often Avon would revisit her memory lane to revive the moment when she was just a child sensing how she felt right after she gave her only doll to her niece Mae and she longed to experience the same emotion in different circumstances someday. So, when she was experiencing the blessing sensation which was such a feeling of bliss but for some reason she didn't feel the same as she felt when giving the doll to her niece; Avon tried to relate the intensity of her emotions from giving the doll to Mae and receiving a blessing. Then, she realized that the experience she felt with Mae was when she was giving and basically the blessing was the experience of receiving and yet, both experiences encountered mysteriously in the midst of bliss, bringing Avon to wonder how come when she was a child she didn't feel physically sick.

The doctor refilled the glasses offering another toast, "A blessing indeed! And here is a toast for those joyful tears!" he exclaimed raising his glass.

"When the philosopher points to the stars, the fool's eyes are fixed on the finger."

Avon clicked her glass with his and confirmed, "Yes, to joyful tears."

"You do project the glow the Shoe Shiner spoke about, did you know my dear?" he said pausing briefly and adding, "Incidentally, I agree with the Shoe Shiner as you do inspire others in some extraordinary way; for I am profoundly feeling the joy you reflect." Avon modestly smiled giving him a look indicating that the contents of the wine were affecting his judgment and before she said anything he went further, "Except, I don't feel the physical reaction you are experiencing."

When Avon realized what the doctor had just said she queried, "Should I schedule an appointment with a physician? Perhaps is something I ate—"

The doctor interrupted and teased, "Risking side effect symptoms from medication and opting for a quick fix dear?"

"All right; I will search deep inside again, but this time I will focus on the feeling causing my body to reject—" she paused and instantly exclaimed, "I got it!"

"Well—" said the doctor attentively listening.

"Rejection?" she asked herself hesitant and then she tried to clarify saying in a low tone, "*Voices of rejection.*"

"Well, well, well," said the doctor, adding, "It seems like the contents of the wine might be affecting our wits after all. Are you hearing *voices* my dear?" He got up taking the bottle of wine away from the table and he prepared to serve dessert. "Would you mind elaborating about these *voices of rejection* dear?" He asked from the kitchen where he was blazing the *Crème Brûlée* that was left by the housekeeper for him to serve.

Avon was standing by the table pacing around holding her glass sipping wine and observing him without replying. She was trying to identify what she felt and as he was bringing dessert to the table he asked again, "What do you mean by *voices of rejection* dear?"

Still thinking, Avon went to the kitchen and she poured more wine in her glass; she leaned against the kitchen counter sipping wine while she continued observing him. The doctor opened a different bottle of wine to go with dessert and he replaced the wine glasses with clean ones. Just then, something clicked inside Avon's heart; as she began to understand the principal of the *golden pact*. Only that time, she seemed to have seen the purification process more clearly through the crystal glasses than by trying to imagine the metal over fire that she had been failing to visualize.

"Mmmmm, *Crème Brûlée*, looks great!" she exclaimed going back to sit at the table for dessert and she began to explain, "Correction" she said in an apologetic manner adding, "I do not hear voices. I feel the symptoms because my body is rejecting the joy I feel. It is like my body is not used to receiving approval. There are no voices; it is more like words, statements, something like— I have heard it so many times; I could not tell who said it to me first or who said it to me last. However, something inside is not allowing me to fully enjoy. It is almost as if the statements of rejection are so ingrained in me that my body's only role is rejecting. Does it make sense?"

"No" said the doctor, "Would you kindly rephrase the last part, my dear?"

"Certainly; I have heard so many statements from people rejecting who I am that apparently those statements convinced something inside me as well. Because, I feel comfortable with myself but now that the Shoe Shiner has brought it to my attention something inside me is predisposed to reject acceptance. Is that a defensive mechanism?"

"No and yes" he replied. Avon's eyebrows rose. He asked, "Are you aware that you can reprogram your thoughts dear?"

"When the philosopher points to the stars, the fool's eyes are fixed on the finger."

Avon thought at the highest speed *The Greatest Salesman in the World*, "Yes" she replied instantly.

"Well, what the solution entails is to reverse the statements ingrained in your *subconscious*. Your body reacts to your thoughts and all those statements of rejection are ingrained in your subconscious. Your physical symptoms are the result of your unconscious thoughts which connected to your body through others' emotion of rejection; so, you might want to deprogram and reprogram those thoughts; or if you are able to reprogram without deprogramming the results will be just as good" he paused and Avon assimilated attentively. Then he asked, "Dessert wine my dear?"

"Yes, thank you" she replied smiling and added, "Same glasses, but cleaned; the glasses are refilled with different wine to go with the flow of our meal. Just like reprogramming the mind by refilling constructive thoughts into the *subconscious* to go with the flow of life, eh?" They clicked their glasses cheerfully toasting and the doctor winked.

Tossing a reflection to the air...

"Physical health is the result of healthy thoughts connecting to the body through emotions. If the feelings caused by a blessing combined with contaminated thoughts could be mistaken for an illness; emotions caused by ill thoughts would naturally destroy."

Stepping into a new soilless area by making a *golden pact* and having enlightenment and awareness; didn't exempt Avon from exposure to challenges. Because Avon found herself in situations when she had to be firm without bending a bit maintaining full awareness and respecting her decision to trust Arolf's path and will. For as much as anyone else; she was exposed to society's temptations in the least anticipated way.

Before the New York trip when Avon was getting acquainted to the Bay-Area; she had attended a few parties organized by some of her peers from work and those parties reminded her about many years earlier when she was around Lek. Then, once she had been recognized in a world-wide level as one of the best performers in the Corporation; her peers were anxious to socialize with her again and when she returned to work from her leave of absence after her mama died, her co-workers even showed some admiration toward her. So, few days after Avon retuned from Tokyo; they organized a gathering to celebrate her belated birthday. Naturally, she attended as the guest of honor and they welcomed her as such.

At her belated birthday party, they were offering an assortment of beverages and they set up a Martini bar. There were also gifts, party favors, and what seemed to Avon the cutest party ornamental straws which would have been inappropriate to use for Champagne but could be used to sip a chocolatini perchance. Although, when she sipped a chocolatini using one of the ornamental straws everyone laughed at her and she realized that the straws were a bit too short to sip from any beverage which left her in wonder, as she didn't realize that she had no birthday cake.

There was a thoughtfully decorated table with birthday cards, fresh flowers, balloons, and a chocolate fountain for various fruits to be deepened in delight. At the center of the table laid a rather large mirrored tray with an inscription made out of a sort of confectioners' sugar that read: *Happy Belated Birthday Avon!* And as Avon had seen in the previous parties; everyone was enjoying

"When the philosopher points to the stars, the fool's eyes are fixed on the finger."

colored tiny candies which they had spread out on the surface of the table as a decoration for the particular occasion.

As it turned out when the traditional moment to blow the candles and cutting the cake arrived; the mirrored tray with the birthday wishes inscription was brought to her. Then, she discovered that she had to actually do the honors of cutting; not cake but distributing lines to everyone; as the inscription on the mirrored tray wasn't designed out of confectioners' sugar but cocaine.

So, the purpose for the party ornamental straws became obvious to her and not surprised; she kindly declined to participate followed by taunting remarks from everyone. She was dared, ridiculed and teased to do what about thirty people were expecting her to deliver and in spite of their offensive remarks and negligent behavior, Avon kindly expressed for the second time a firm, "No."

Her friends insisted trying to push her saying that as the guest of honor it was her place to be the first one to consume, and then, distribute the inscription to the rest which made everyone wonder if Avon wasn't toying around; what did she ever mean when saying "No." Because they had put so much effort into her surprise party; they were definitely disappointed for not receiving the expected response. So she expressed her seriousness conveying, "So far, I have managed to keep away from drugs by simply refusing. Even when I was exposed to physical abuse for not participating, I always said 'No.'" Everyone laughed at her, "I would rather receive a beating than falling into the trap of drugs at this stage in life my friends. You may continue insulting me if you wish; as the same insults from different voices won't diminish me."

One of the voices in the room asked, "If you do not do drugs; why did you come to our parties then?"

Apparently, her peers have been assuming that she attended the parties with the same intention they did and even though Avon knew that they were doing drugs; she didn't care to find out the particulars of how they were actually consumed or employed. So she openly shared with them, "I came to the first party because I didn't have anything else to do; but I had no clue of the kind of party I had been invited to. I observed all of you through the evening and when I was invited to the next party, I didn't think it would affect me to attend again; as it made no difference to any of you if I was there or not anyway."

Everyone in the room was intrigued to learn what motivated Avon to be at the parties if not drugs and Avon expressed curiosity as well, as she didn't quite understand what made them consume the drugs they did. For these were not people in limbo like Lek and his friends; these people were her co-workers. People who worked with her solving serious issues and cases around the world; people who seemed to be decent members of society; yet, something drove them to consume drugs.

Then taking turns, some of them voiced from a close distance and others from where they were explaining the different sensations they experienced when consuming drugs saying that drugs provided them with something that they didn't have; as only drugs would transport them into different dimensions.

"I feel high" said one voice.

"I feel mellow" said another.

"I feel like talking" say the other.

"I want to dance" said one jumping.

"I am hungry" said one eating and so forth.

Then Avon realized that their different cravings came from the levels of Energy impelled by the drugs they had been consuming and she thought, *ultimately they consume drugs to explore the intensity of Energy.*

However, while she was ignorant about the use and employment of drugs despite of her age; her peers seemed to

"When the philosopher points to the stars, the fool's eyes are fixed on the finger."

have been ignoring the fact that they could explore the intensity of Energy naturally without the need of drugs. Then, it was Avon's turn and she exposed her motive to attend the parties saying, "Well, I attended the second party just to make sure that you returned home safe at the end of the night; as I didn't mind fetching taxis for you at dawn."

Bringing some of them to mock her again; because they were wondering how did she manage to stay awake longer than they did without consuming some kind of drug; since at the end of the parties, Avon was indeed the only one alert while none of them made it through the night without passing out or being very close to it. In addition, Avon seemed to have some sort of protective charm toward the ones that totally passed out who she took to rest at her own place while the effect of the drugs faded away.

In the end, only few of them were involved in the conversation; as most of the guests' attention was on dispersing the inscription of the tray. The emotional mix and different interests among the group impeded for them to focus, blocking Energy from flowing and Avon quietly noticed that the method they employed to explore Energy was quite pricey. Meanwhile exploring Energy lucidly through her studies was priceless and best of all free of any physical harm or lawful charges.

After the belated birthday party with her peers; Avon's physical symptoms intensified, the happiness from the experience in Tokyo vanished and so did her blissful sensation. Because by then, it was clear to her that her co-workers weren't going to invite her to parties again and she sensed several *silent waves* of rejection from them. Bringing her to understand that she wasn't exempt to be exposed to the influence of other peoples' thoughts, contaminated or not.

Then she was able to contemplate the bliss she felt after Tokyo in contrast to the inadequate sensation she was experiencing by her peers' rejection and she perceived a clearer revelation in relation to the principle of the *golden pact*. After returning from Tokyo she felt like gold, while after her belated birthday party; she felt like *Crème Brûlée* being slowly blazed with a torch symbolizing the gold and fire concept of purification process in the metaphor.

Therefore, she realized that if she opted to wait for a blessing to come her way and continued confronting society temptations out there; it would practically take her a lifetime to attain purification through the gold transmutation concept. So instead, she began to focus on reprogramming her thoughts starting by cleansing the statements of rejection that were ingrained in her subconscious.

Also, she reflected on the glorious sensation she felt with the Shoe Shiner's acceptance who was a total stranger making her feel like gold and she wondered *what would I feel like if I approve with authority not only who I am but who I have been as well as whoever I become without waiting for anyone's blessing and instead, bless myself?* Simultaneously, the granny's words echoed in her mind saying, "*I have lived a lifetime without knowing you Avon. I could live the rest of life left in me without seeing you again.*" Or something to the effect; so, Avon recognized that if she could live the rest of a lifetime without a mama; she could live without friends whose intention was to manipulate her thoughts bringing the worst and not the greatest out of her. And since she enjoyed solitude; she thought that she would be better off not socializing at all. Therefore, she decided not to socialize anymore; except with friends who were genuine with her like the doctor in person, as well as Angelina and Jaidee from the distance.

Tossing a reflection to the air...

"*When the philosopher points to the stars, the fool's eyes are fixed on the finger.*"

"Decisions invested in life are matched with one hundred percent blessings earning inner wealth from purified thoughts as the highest dividends."

11

On the interim when Avon had just returned to work; she noticed that her financial statement from the bank reflected a greater amount than what she was used to keep in the past. And although at that point Avon's salary was close to six figures; she had never seen so much money in her bank account before, leading her to realize that during the time that she had been recovering from grief; she had spent in basic needs leaving the rest of the money untouched. So, for the very first time ever, Avon grasped the concept of saving money; and as usual, she was behind everyone else regarding common knowledge for she was just discovering a fundamental principal of economics.

Avon knew that even if she spent here and there; she had managed to gather an amount of money that would take many people a couple of years of labor to generate so as to support a whole family. Yet there she was after fulfilling her financial responsibilities; and she had plenty of money in the bank. She couldn't help to feel certain pleasure from having money saved and she also felt a sense of security in some way. Then, she distinguished the difference between financial security and social insecurity leaving her with a

"When the philosopher points to the stars, the fool's eyes are fixed on the finger."

much better sense of satisfaction; for as long as she was capable of supporting herself financially, most likely social acceptance would ensue. Revealing a new discovery for her because even if everyone knew those things at her age; Avon was just being introduced to Financial Independence which was something she had never considered in her wildest dreams.

At the same time, in order to reprogram her thoughts; Avon began to create a customized process that generated results for her to assimilate, appropriate and practice personally. She employed a combination of information from her limited knowledge and what she had learned in life so far. Then, she figured out that the best effect would materialize by using the only method she knew which was writing her ideas; and just like when tossing reflections to the air, she wrote; except at the time she was tossing those thoughts of reflection directly into her mind and not to the air. Every idea she wrote was affirmative, solid and a confirmation of what her heart dictated for her individual wellbeing.

So, in her effort to isolate herself from polluted socializing; she longed being back in Tokyo again. And then, she remembered that the Shoe Shiner had given to her another gift that she hadn't fully accepted just yet; because she opened the present that the Shoe Shiner gave her at the end but she didn't actually get to appreciate it. The gift was a compact disc of some classical melodies which might have not been her cup of tea and she hadn't even paid attention to it. Thus in view of her silent solitude and desire to be back in Tokyo; she thought that while reprogramming her thoughts; classical music from there would be suitable for her to play as company in the background. In any event, as soon as Avon played the compact disc; she wasn't taken back to Tokyo at all, as she was taken to a totally new area. The melodies were a version of *Vivaldi's* very best compositions reverberating neither more nor less than brilliant. Avon's ears of understanding captured for the first time what the seasons of the year meant in musical notes. Up till then, the only other link to the *Four Seasons* Avon had explored besides the weather was *Le Manoir aux Quat' Saisons in the U.K* and the *Four Seasons* hotel chain. However, the melodies her ear-sense was absorbing indulged her heart opening her every sense and feeling the intensity of bliss allowing her to experience almost the same sensation that she felt when giving the doll to her niece. The concertmaster of the ensemble and soloist violinist playing was *Federico Agostini* executing and transmitting the *Four Seasons* from *Vivaldi's* masterpiece through his own immaculate perception.

From that moment forward; Avon had a new and loyal friend that didn't expect anything in exchange from her. Although the talented renowned violinist had no clue of Avon's existence; *Federico Agostini* became a great friend to her. Therefore, slowly but surely Avon was reprogramming her thoughts by writing affirmations along with the companionship of *Vivaldi's Four Seasons* harmonious vibrant rhythmic notes playing in the background and expanding through her whole being echoing waves of true Love.

An uneventful evening, while gathering her recent experiences and trying to adapt to her new approach to life; Avon thought that she had seized the concept of Financial Independence and learning to request through gratitude in advanced; she wrote an affirmation on her *affirmations journal*:

In accordance to the will of the Universe; expressing intention of peace and harmony to the entire world; under the grace of a perfect path; I am grateful for being financially independent. Thank you for listening to my request and for giving the order for my intention to manifest.

Little did Avon know, as her great ignorance and limited knowledge couldn't differentiate between her several thousands of dollars saved in the bank compared to what financial independence

"When the philosopher points to the stars, the fool's eyes are fixed on the finger."

really meant. Certainly, she required much more than the amount reflected in her bank account at the time to become financially independent. However, she wrote her affirmation with the most honest and genuine conviction thinking that she was already financially independent.

Months passed by and during the phase that Avon was grieving and totally captivated by being revived; her *sunshine* friend Angelina had gotten married. So, Avon was unable to attend her wedding; but having an upcoming vacation from work and plenty of money in the bank; Avon decided to go to Florida and visit her *sunshine*.

Angelina and Avon were looking forward to seeing each other again and Avon was quite excited to meet her husband as well. When Avon arrived at the Daytona airport; Angelina was waiting for her allowing Avon to sense the glow of a sunshine illuminating her soul just like she had always sensed from Angelina years before.

Angelina wasn't working with the Corporation anymore and they owned a real estate business in St-Augustine with her husband. They also refurbished old houses along with appraising properties; or so was Avon's perception of their occupation.

When they arrived at the house from the airport; Avon met Angelina's husband confirming her *sunshine*'s description as accurate as if she was actually looking at him when Angelina describe him to her. Handsome Gabe was educated, respectful, elegant, and smart. His eyes were a pair of blue bright stars and his slight baldness accentuated his middle-aged wise-minded character. Precisely like Angelina had described him. Avon and Gabe's personalities connected at once and everyone felt comfortable and fine.

Their house was sitting along the Intracoastal Waterway with the most dazzling view of sunrises and sunsets. In the center of the yard was a Tiki bar surrounded by a breathtaking landscape. A Jacuzzi sat in a hidden corner of the garden and nearby was an exterior shower. At one side of the backyard a deck extended into a pier, and at the end, a sailing boat seemed to linger patiently waiting to be blown away by a puff of air welcoming the waves when rocking its massive weight splashing gently once and again and forming ripples on the water echoing everywhere.

The interior of the house was converted into a manifestation of the couple's personalities. Angelina's tasteful touch and Gabe's configuration seemed to be the perfect match. Their grace resonated in silence through the reflection of a gorgeous grand piano and a collection of diverse instruments displayed in the living area. The massive two sided aged fireplace resting in the middle of the structure facing both, dining and living areas, was the only thing they had not changed in the whole house, as they bought it in ruins and rebuilt it from scratch.

Angelina, Avon and Gabe enjoyed conversations, they looked at pictures, watched a video of the wedding, and they shared their romantic encounter with her. Then, the couple allowed Avon to share her adventures and international experiences with them. Avon and Angelina comprehended each other as clearly as the sunshine and although Avon had experienced a major inner shift; Angelina and Gabe supported her projecting to be a true and natural merge.

Gabe possessed distinguishing gifts and one of them was collecting old-fashioned automobiles. Therefore, the couple was driving Avon in a 1960's convertible Corvette to dinners and a 1959's Cadillac around town during the day, with the top down as well. Avon didn't have much interest in cars and she didn't observe the other cars' brands or details. Although, she could tell that those cars were amazingly well preserved and as much as she enjoyed riding around in such gems, it didn't compare with the joy she felt seeing the couple working, having fun and loving each other like no other.

"When the philosopher points to the stars, the fool's eyes are fixed on the finger."

One evening after dinner while Avon read by the fireplace, Gabe approached holding a bottle of wine and glasses in his hands inviting her to come with them by the pier. Gabe had kindled a cast-iron fire-pit which sat in the middle of the deck surrounded by lounging chairs and Angelina was already there lighting some mosquito-repellent candles and waiting for them. As Avon and Gabe joined Angelina; the ladies delighted themselves with the beauty of the sunset; meanwhile Gabe grilled some marshmallows in a stick over the fire-pit. The water was calm and as the sun beams hesitated to set; the couple shared funny stories and they spoke about some current events. The conversation led to an extent that Gabe expressed some of his emotions to Avon; as he was aware of Avon's interests and explorations in the matter. Thus Avon listened to his insight asking to clarify some points and perceiving others, and suddenly, an unfamiliar instinct possessed Gabe and he reached Avon's left hand. She reciprocated connecting within and trusting Gabe, Avon closed her eyes giving in and they followed a flowing force while Angelina held Avon's right arm crawled up next to her.

Shortly after, Gabe let Avon's hand go stopping the flow, and right away, she sensed a force of Energy being released directly to Gabe. Gabe opened his eyes calmly and Avon instantly opened hers unleashing the force. The three of them reacted naturally joking about having drunk too much wine. Then, Avon and Gabe played a game of Chess while taking turns looking at the full moon, *Dark Matter,* and the glowing stars through Angelina's telescope that was placed on a corner of the deck.

Evidently Gabe possessed a gift that he didn't disclose to many; back then, Avon ignored what she later discovered for whatever it was that Gabe had perceived from her developed gradually as years went by. Ignoring what he had done, Avon didn't make much out of Gabe's approach. On the other hand, Gabe had perceived

Avon's fate in a matter of seconds; because he was able to see other people's future and he couldn't resist checking hers out.

Afterward, Gabe told Avon discretely that, one day, she was going to be surrounded by abundance and Love. Avon received his words with an open heart and as a sign of hope.

The couple and Avon spent a fabulous week together learning about each other and sharing different ideas about their business allowing Avon to understand better what they did for a living. Gabe had initiated Angelina into generating cash flow and passive revenue which provided them with the means to satisfy their needs and pleasures. Albeit they didn't consider their occupation to be what they did for a living; or to identify them for whom they were. One afternoon while admiring Gabe's musical instruments in the living area; Avon was captivated when Gabe expressed, "Angelina and I accept the simplicity of breathing to define what we do for a living Avon."

Angelina concurred exclaiming, "Yes, we breathe for a living! That's what we do for a living, breathe!" Then Avon mentioned the fact that thinking was as important as breathing to live a healthy life and they seemed to agree with her. So, the three of them settled that breathing and thinking would defined perfectly what they did for a living while producing an income when working in between. After that, Angelina suggested to Avon in an informal way, "Avon, would you write your memoirs someday?"

Avon perceived Angelina's suggestion as casual because Avon had never considered herself entering the art of writing at all; as she had always been under the impression that a writer should begin writing at a young age, pursuing literature studies to be prepared and writing wasn't a field that she ever aspired to explore due to the variety of languages she had to keep in mind. So Avon replied, "Well, I do write in a regular basis *sunshine*; however, I do not write

"When the philosopher points to the stars, the fool's eyes are fixed on the finger."

keeping a diary like many do. So, I don't know much about writing memoirs."

"I suggested it because you have amazing stories to share and what I enjoy the most is the way you always manage to extract a lessons from your experiences; good or bad." Angelina said.

"Are you serious?"

"Yes!"

Avon added chuckling, "I am still learning to extract lessons from every experience my *sunshine,* thank you for your encouraging words. Although there is slight detail; if you would like to read my memoirs, how could I write in English with my speech accent?"

Then Angelina expressed giggling, "Oh, your accent is the best part, it would be great if you could manage to convey your accent in writing somehow but I meant for you to write, don't you worry about the accent, if you decide to write, just write." Then Angelina didn't let go Avon's previous comment and she asked, "What do you mean you don't write a diary like others do?" Just then, Gabe left the living area allowing them to chitchat like only ladies seem to interact.

Avon's reply was hesitant, "Well, I do not know exactly what I mean. I am just getting familiar with the concept myself and I would not know where to begin."

"Did you know that the best way to learn is when teaching?" Angelina asked.

Avon looked at her smiling and said interested, "No. However, I am listening."

"I saw it online and as soon as I find it, I'll e-mail it to you. I remember the last part said that when people teach is when they learn the most," said Angelina.

Avon insisted intrigued, "I am still listening *sunshine.*"

"So, if you're learning the concept and you explain it to someone; it'll be as if you're teaching it. If you like you could explain it to me. We'll understand it together; don't you agree?" Angelina suggested.

"I see..." said Avon, exclaiming, "You are truly my *sunshine!*" And she added, "I warn you, I might get carried away, eh?"

"I don't have anything else to do, do you?" Angelina replied anxious to learn what Avon had to say.

Avon began describing what she had learned about writing so far, stressing the difference between written words and the meaning behind them; and not precisely referring to the art of writing literature which Avon didn't know much about. But according to Avon written words carried a different wave, not the *silent wave* that she perceived when communicating verbally but a *sealed wave*. Meaning, a written word would have a final, established and sealed gist and once written, a word would carry the power of materializing just like predictions do. Then, Avon explained that she was learning how to fully understand, because up till then, she had been practicing to reprogram her thoughts and she wasn't certain of the process. "Give me an example" Angelina requested.

"Well, I write affirmations and it seems like while I am sleeping there is a part of me thinking of the affirmations I wrote during the day," Avon responded.

"Do you dream about it?" asked Gabe returning to join them.

"No," said Avon clarifying, "It is different than dreaming. It is just like I said, some part of me thinks of the affirmations. Wait! Now that I think about it, it is not only when I am sleeping. It happens when I am awake also. Let me think, yes! It happens when I am awake as well. I guess I didn't mean to say that it happens when I am sleeping. What I actually meant is that I think of the affirmations *unconsciously*. See? I don't know what I am talking about."

"When the philosopher points to the stars, the fool's eyes are fixed on the finger."

"No, you don't seem to know what you're talking about Avon, but if you focus, it would be simple," said Gabe. Angelina turned her head looking at Avon in wonder, and then she turned her head, still in wonder, looking at Gabe.

While Avon reflected for a moment, Gabe asked, "Are you familiar with manifestation of thoughts, Avon?"

"Yes." She replied without hesitation.

Then Gabe asked, "What creates your dreams, Avon?"

Avon thought at the highest speed *The Greatest Salesman in the World*, and she replied instantly, "My subconscious."

"It makes sense" said Angelina adding, "It's like when taking notes at school. If not, we wouldn't '*unconsciously*' learn whatever they teach us. Everything we see, hear, read or write goes to our *subconscious*. Then we end up thinking about it *unconsciously* and automatically manifesting it."

Avon added, "So, the point seems to be that written words have power behind them and we could manifest our own thoughts through writing." Angelina and Gabe looked at each other allowing Avon to continue, "Talking with you I realize that writing affirmations reprograms my thoughts by sending the message to the *subconscious* and when thinking of those affirmations *unconsciously*, I am attracting everything that manifest around me—"

Gabe interrupted, "So, if you write a diary about the events that happened during the day, daily; the message stores in your *subconscious* and you would be thinking about those events *unconsciously* as well. And being aware that thoughts manifest, the thoughts stored in your *subconscious* would attract what manifests around you day after day and situations would reoccur. The only difference is the people and the places, but *unconsciously*, you would approach situations the same way."

So Angelina exclaimed, "No wonder we blame life for having to deal with the same circumstances over and over again! From now on, I better think before writing on my diary."

Then, Avon realized that Angelina's suggestion was good because she was able to actually learn while she was trying to explain the concept to them and she said, "Thank you for your suggestion *sunshine*, would you really e-mail me the information about *learning when teaching?*"

"Sure, but I still think that you should write your memoirs," Angelina insisted and beckoned her. Avon followed her down stairs. Angelina opened a door and beyond the darkness was her painting studio facing a gorgeous view through glassed French doors into the garden. Angelina turned on the lights and said "I discovered that painting is my passion."

Avon excitedly asked, "Have you painted the ones displaying on the walls upstairs?"

"Most of them," Angelina replied nodding and added, "I thought you'll appreciate learning about my still developing passion because when talking about manifestation of thoughts, I wanted to show you my way to manifest my thoughts." Angelina uncovered a set of unframed paintings which appeared unqualified for display. Then, she lined them up on a bench allowing Avon to appreciate her painting art. Avon was able to perceive from the paintings some kind of melancholic mix of emotions understanding why they were not on display. However, she absorbed the purity of her *sunshine*'s creativity. After Avon observed the paintings for a while, Angelina beckoned her again to go back upstairs where Gabe sat on an armchair enjoying a Brandy, smoking a cigar and contemplating a painted portrait of his late dog June hanging on the wall while petting Otis, although a deaf dog, Gabe's loyal friend.

"When the philosopher points to the stars, the fool's eyes are fixed on the finger."

As they entered the living area Angelina stretched up her arms swiftly twirling around showing the paintings on the walls, "These are the manifestation of my thoughts too!" She exclaimed landing on a sofa with her feet up next to her cat George.

Avon admired each painting and she asked, "How do you manifest your thoughts Gabe?"

Then not replying right away, Gabe got up and he walked toward the piano. He sat, he positioned himself to play and he said, "Even though I compose music Avon, at times, I manifest other people's thoughts that are not even alive anymore and their thoughts are not necessarily written in words but written in musical notes; would you fancy some *Beethoven?*"

Gabe delighted them playing *Moonlight Sonata*.

Tossing a reflection to the air...

"Energy manifests through thoughts one generation after the other consistently, whether people are alive, blind, awake, deaf, mute, sleeping, or dead."

During the flight back from Florida to San Fran Avon was already missing her well appreciated friends Angelina and Gabe. She returned to her working routine and a few uneventful months passed by.

Meanwhile, she kept reprogramming her thoughts; she spent most of the evenings in the library learning and she got together with the doctor usually on weekends. Sometimes they played Chess and other times they simply enjoyed a good meal. One evening, they were playing a Chess game in the garden and the doctor shared some of his plans with her. After Avon was facing Checkmate he said, "My dear, I am placing this building in the market for sale"

"Is this double Checkmate?" Avon asked a bit disillusioned by the news.

Then he explained, "Do not concern about having a place to live dear. This will always be a rental building and I am planning to live here until I sell the other building in a few years. I am just preparing to retire completely and it seems like the right time to sell; besides, have you any idea of how long it would take to sell a building of this scale?"

"No, but I could ask my friends. They might know someone interested to purchase it," Avon said.

"Your friends in Florida dear?" He asked and she nodded. Then, they engaged in a conversation about what Angelina and Gabe did to generate an income and the evening went on.

The following phase sealed Avon's fate; as she was tenderly showered with sprinkling glowing sunbeams from above and below like a fresh blooming flower.

As soon as Angelina and Gabe learned about the opportunity to purchase the building which conserved the library where their friend Avon spent most of the time thinking, breathing and learning; they didn't think of the investment for themselves. As a matter of fact, *they did know* the ideal person to purchase the building.

Angelina and Gabe flew to San Fran. They checked out the property's potential and since they owned real estate on a national level; they were familiar with every aspect to be considered. After meeting the doctor and learning the building details; they were satisfied and they confirmed a fair and productive business prospect. Then, Angelina and Gabe took Avon out for dinner

"When the philosopher points to the stars, the fool's eyes are fixed on the finger."

with the intention to present a once in a lifetime opportunity and business proposition to her.

They already had an idea regarding Avon's financial status; therefore, the first thing they suggested was for Avon to keep her personal account as a reserve followed by a proposal that not many would reject. The couple offered the down payment as a loan for Avon to purchase the building that held the library where she spent most of her productive time learning about life. Taking into consideration that the building was a rental investment; the couple's cash flow projections indicated that as long as Avon had an income from work, the revenue produced by the rentals would allow her to cover expenses, mortgage and the installments that they would collect from her to repay the down payment. They had calculated the worst case scenario and even if the building was twenty percent vacant; she could produce a reasonable profit after paying all the expenses. Additionally, by living in the building Avon would be able to claim homestead and she wouldn't have to pay rent. It seemed that Avon found herself flowing into the path of Financial Independence. When she understood what her *sunshine* and Gabe were proposing to her, apart from being amazed; Avon wondered about her written affirmations and the way they really worked.

Then, Avon also had to consider the opportunity as business; because what was a blessing to her, for her friends wasn't only a blessing but an investment plan as well. Evidently they had money in need of circulation and instead of keeping it in a semi-dormant account accumulating low rate dividends, or exposing the funds to high-risk in any other investment; they would invest their funds by processing an "*I owe you note*" which would generate a greater surplus return from what any financial institution would pay. Hence considering that not many could be entrusted with an "*I owe you note*" of such a sum of money, the opportunity was beneficial for all the parties involved, including the doctor.

In addition, Angelina and Gabe would share their knowledge with Avon allowing them the pleasure of giving her a chance to enter into a different dimension regarding responsibility, rather than limiting herself to the social responsibility of chasing a career. The trust they established in Avon brought her to shed tears of joy and as unreal as the acquisition of the building seemed to her, Avon accepted the proposal on the spot.

With the doctor's guidance and the couple's advice; Avon was confident to continue working and managing the rentals at the same time. She was also encouraged by the doctor; especially when Angelina and Gabe negotiated a sell by owner deal with him omitting the fee that a real estate agent would charge which allowed the doctor to lower a generous percentage of the property's sale price. Angelina and Gabe were used to handle business long distance, and after they left, they were able to provide Avon with assistance. On the other hand, the doctor was with her in every step of the way concerning the red tape.

In a matter of weeks, Avon got approval from a financial institution for the mortgage loan and a few months later; the doctor was pleased to sign the property over to her, making Avon the new owner and landlady of the rental building. Everything had happened so fast; Avon hardly had time to reflect on the enormous mountain she had just leaped.

Days, weeks, and months went rather quick and Avon was enjoying every minute of it. The doctor continued living in the building; except their roles were reversed given that the doctor became Avon's tenant. Therefore, Avon had the comfort to continue visiting the library at her leisure and in the process, she focused on thinking, breathing and listening to her violinist friend while

"When the philosopher points to the stars, the fool's eyes are fixed on the finger."

becoming acquainted with finances learning from the books in the library and any information she found regarding currency on the internet.

As months went by, Angelina and Gabe introduced Avon to real estate revenue in order to circulate some of the money she had in reserve and she started with moderate investments. Even if Avon's return was low, slowly but surely she learned the concept, and gradually, she became comfortable directing money toward its own natural curse of flowing. Avon instinctively followed Angelina and Gabe's advice trusting them as they had trusted her and she adapted to live under her means but comfortably. She paid attention to her indispensable needs and the extra money was turned into purchasing and reselling single homes with Angelina and Gabe's lead.

One day, Avon actually understood how long was going to take for her to be able to repay the down payment to her friends and to pay off the mortgage. So, she finally grasped the real meaning of Financial Independence. However, after managing the rental business for over a year; she realized that the occupancy had been above ninety-five percent making her feel that life couldn't get better than it was. Except deep in her heart; she wondered if she would ever encounter an intimate ally for her to share her experiences with; bringing her to request in advance gratitude again and she wrote on her *affirmations journal*:

In accordance to the will of the Universe; expressing intention of peace and harmony to the entire world; under the grace of a perfect path; I am grateful for the person created to be my intimate companion in life. Thank you for listening to my request and for giving the order for my intention to manifest.

※

Tossing a reflection to the air...

"Riches usually reveals to those who need the least disguising from those who seek having the most."

"When the philosopher points to the stars, the fool's eyes are fixed on the finger."

12

As Avon continued spending time in solitude at the library; she had already acquired a complete collection of *Vivaldi's Four Seasons* melodies from different violinists. So, she was constantly accompanied by the pure manifestation of vibrating Energy in motion, and more often than not, she became engrossed listening to her new favorite harmonious selection.

An uneventful evening while continually enjoying one melody after the other; Avon was breathing and thinking learning about her inner-self, and suddenly, she began to recognize her own presence for a change.

Avon perceived her own reflection rather than relating to being present in the physical realm and her senses. Thus far, she had learned about concepts of being present in the moment, being present when thinking in the now, or definitions applying to an individual being present by sensing nature within through meditation. But personally, Avon didn't enjoy momentarily living that much, because her senses; meaning, eye, ear, taste, smell and touch, didn't relate to the presence she had just encountered.

"When the philosopher points to the stars, the fool's eyes are fixed on the finger."

Avon's personal experience of meditation when immersing within, savoring each and every emotion she felt, entering a different dimension of space deep inside granting her access into a soilless area of satisfaction; allowed her to understand situations in order to confront the physical world. However, the presence she had just perceived was alertness and awareness like being connected to Arolf's Energy source at all times and within herself all at once.

On that particular evening Avon wasn't even meditating; she was thinking. She was simply writing affirmations and she felt pleased. She felt delight. She felt joy. She felt content. She felt happy. She felt glad. For the first time ever, Avon realized that she was *in* Love.

Then, she embraced her feeling contemplating that she had finally accepted being within Arolf; because when she had made her pact; she thought that she had surrendered by accepting Arolf to be within her. However, she was far from surrendering until she actually gave-in and acknowledged to be *in* Love with the Universe herself.

Arolf was Avon's source of Love and the Universe had always been *in* Love patiently waiting for Avon to join. Thus suddenly, everything felt like a romance to her; except that it wasn't a romance when the interested party brought flowers; a delicate sophisticated scent; or an exquisite gold ring embracing a gem. Arolf and Avon seemed to have been romancing each another for longer than a physical couple would tolerate and even though they were within the other and one all together; Avon felt like *that* was the first time she had recognized her essence reflecting on an inner mirror which she had just discovered deep inside—Love.

After her instant of delight; she also realized that she hadn't felt homesick attacks for a long time and instead, she had been experiencing a diminishing sensation detecting a gradual void in her interior and not a void of emptiness but a void of space increasing and expanding slowly; in and out, back and forth, up and down stretching her inner-self like when a bubble is tenderly blown within its elements allowing the breath of being to pass expanding throughout to the point where she sensed her heartbeat. And she had first noticed feeling such sensation after boarding the plane on her way to her mother's funeral. However back then, she didn't understand what was happening to her.

Avon finally admitted that she had been torturing herself by manifesting her family's thoughts suggesting disapproval and denial of Love. Consequently through her *subconscious*, Avon didn't approve of herself either. *Unconsciously*, Avon rejected herself. She wasn't attracted to who she was. She went on denying Love to herself and as a result the whole ordeal caused her what she learned to call homesick attacks.

Precisely then, Avon sensed the greatness of all; she earnestly blessed, accepted and admitted with the same certainty as when she was a child, almost arrogant, the revelation to be great. Being a great person, she couldn't expect anyone's approval; as only Arolf knew who Avon was; since not even Avon knew who she was deep inside. Avon had to trust Arolf with her entity by falling *in* Love and accept the Universe presence in her heart at all times as her essence, because as far as Avon was concerned, she had always been a nonentity person. Then, she began understanding the magnitude of her connection to the unknown and yet, one Energy source as her exposure to greatness and her propensity to become a great woman one day. Right then, Avon decided to accept with grace and faith being an integral part of the greatest power-of-powers by blessing herself and fusing with the realm of Love as one.

From then on, Avon was *in* Love with her essence; not as an insane narcissist but as an insane romantic! She felt Love toward

"When the philosopher points to the stars, the fool's eyes are fixed on the finger."

anything and everything that emerged from her inner-source. She was particularly *in* Love with her emotions and totally enraptured with her thoughts. She would think for hours in the library while breathing simultaneously which defined what she did for a living. She understood the concept as Angelina and Gabe described it to her and basically; she breathed at all times and after she retired from her daily activities, she employed the art of thinking when going to the library every evening. While the simplicity of breathing and thinking allowed Avon to live a lifetime in one minute; she realized that many would live a lifetime holding their breaths without actually living one minute of it.

So far, everything indicated that Avon had to learn to Love herself prior to sharing Love with an intimate ally. And then, she understood what her father had advised her the last time she had seen him when he said, "*You should not get involved intimately with a partner until after discovering your great heart my child.*" The experience seemed as if she had to break through Love's realm like inflowing a bubble without bursting it in order to be able to share Love with someone else who hopefully was already *in* the bubble of Love as well. Finally she grasped what being *in* Love was all about and she understood as clear as the sunshine that, she didn't have to find someone to Love her externally to be *in* Love.

Eventually she learned that self-Love was not about being loved by another or Loving herself like an insane narcissist allowing ego to turn Love into vanity. Over the years, Avon finally grasped that loving herself meant to accept with grace what she really was; her essence; her true source. Then, she clearly understood that she couldn't give away or take-in Love from others, but instead, she had to Love who she was inside and loving another meant sharing the Love residing in the deepest areas of her soul from heart to heart.

Once Avon made her pact, she had surrendered *to be*, and *not to be* just another being going through life simply existing. From the moment when she made her pact; she was positioned wherever needed to perform in perfect harmony in accordance with the Universe. And although Avon understood many things; she understood very little in relation to what Arolf had in reserve for her, if Avon was willing to accept, that was; as Avon was still learning and she had to absorb, appropriate, and practice her discoveries prior to actually cleanse her subconscious and expand within the Love realm; because she would never be absolved from alluring emotions.

Tossing a reflection to the air...

"The magical trick is falling *in* Love with the Universe's core, Love itself. Only then, Love may be spread and shared above, below and even beyond all."

In the meantime, Avon continued socializing with the doctor and learning lessons from him which later on defined some of her humanitarian tendencies in life.

"What would be of a life without amusement, my dear?" The doctor asked after making his move and placing Avon in Checkmate once more.

Glancing around the garden, Avon replied with a grin on her face and in a teasing tone she said, "I can hardly wait for *you* to amuse *me*."

"When the philosopher points to the stars, the fool's eyes are fixed on the finger."

"I will initiate you to develop a virtue not many encounter during an entire lifetime my dear" said the doctor enthused.

Unable to resist another of those once in a lifetime opportunities that kept coming her way and ignoring what the doctor was proposing to her, "Whatever it is, I will accept." Avon replied.

The doctor was planning to take Avon by the hand leading her to explore her goodwill intentions along with maintaining boredom away by cultivating a new truth in her heart.

Avon listened attentively as the doctor conveyed to her that certain evening of the week he dressed completely down to attain an appearance not many would make the effort to appear like. He also said that he even wore heavy makeup over a latex mask to transform his face and disguise. What's more, the doctor would leave sporadically staying out most of the night and returning at dawn. Where would the doctor go looking like a vagabond? Remained a mystery to Avon; but in addition, he confessed that he had been living a double secret life for some time. Avon waited patiently until the doctor was ready to share more about his double life with her, for she was aware of his wisdom and she respected his privacy.

The day arrived when the doctor invited Avon to go out with him and he had two requests for her: to disguise her appearance and to conceal her identity. After accepting the invite, Avon developed an opposite dressing look from what others were familiar to see as well as disguising her face just like the doctor did and she was ready to experience the doctor's mysterious evening outing for the first time.

As the doctor and Avon left the building the fog was beginning to lift in the distance. They walked at a quick pace for couple of blocks in silence welcoming the coldness of the crisp night ahead.

All of a sudden, the doctor stopped walking and looking aimlessly up and around; he took a couple of steps back. Meanwhile, Avon had also stopped and she stood on the spot observing. She was shivering a bit keeping her hands warm inside the pockets of the outworn coat she wore. Then out of the blue, a Good Samaritan passing by handed something to her. It happened so fast; Avon actually received it and to her surprise; she found herself holding a handful of change. Avon looked at the doctor with an expression of uncertainty in her face and at the same time, the doctor exchanged a profound stare, instantly, bringing Avon to look around and to understand.

They stood where the famous Union Square indifferently hosted a fraction of the population that had selected not to have a roof over their heads, or have entirely forgot the concept of such comfort for all Avon could tell.

Near the time the distinguished shops, *cafés*, and restaurants opened their prestigious doors visited by numerous people from around the world; the homeless people would be forced to bashfully pick up their insignificant, but only possessions, leaving behind during the day the spot they had warmed during the night. Some of them would roam adrift. Others would roam around. Either way they would patiently wait with a sense of hope for the prestigious doors to close again or until the visitors went away anticipating the moment when the territory could be reclaimed to readjust in their preferred area and anxiously restart their spot warming cycle afresh.

The doctor and Avon had not been homeless for long, as only a couple of hours had passed when they found themselves immersed into the homeless cycle. They had already received few handfuls of loose change from Good Samaritans passing by and even a few dollar bills were gathered in their piles. Avon was afflicted because

"When the philosopher points to the stars, the fool's eyes are fixed on the finger."

she felt as if she was taking away from the genuine homeless and she didn't know how to approach the doctor to convey; but at the same time, she sensed that the doctor's intentions were valid; so, she didn't allow her wits to misdirect her and instead; she followed her heart absorbing her new lesson to learn.

On the other hand, the doctor seemed quite cheerful counting his coins and he expressed even more excitement counting the dollar bills that he had collected in his pile. After awhile, the doctor beckoned her discretely with his head leading toward an alley. Avon went along and when they were in a hidden corner he asked, "My dear, are you ready for a *high tea* party? Avon's sole familiarity with a *high tea* party was somehow associated with *The Ritz*; therefore she was speechless and not having a response; she handed her pile of alms to him nodding and indicating that she would follow his lead.

After being in the alley for a few minutes, one of the restaurants' service doors opened and the doctor approached excited with their combined piles of alms in hand. While Avon caught up with him; he had met a gentleman behind the door and was reporting the pile of change to the penny. Then, the doctor pointed out for her to only observe leaving Avon in wonder again; but still, following his lead. The gentleman was dressed as a chef and he allowed them to step into the kitchen. Next, the chef showed the doctor the goodies available for the evening. The doctor knew how much they could afford with the stack of change they had, and yet, he selected two gallons of water and one gallon of milk spending most of their alms right then and there. After that, he got two electric kettles to boil the water in; as many tea bags, sugar, and paper cups, as they could gather; and a tray of pastry which was offered as a bonus for if the doctor didn't take it, most likely it would've been found in the trash. The chef seemed to be under the impression that the doctor was a genuine homeless person; with the difference of being the most generous homeless person he had met so far perhaps. Also, every time the doctor came by, the chef trusted him with the electric kettles and a small portable table with strict conditions to bring them back. And most of the time, the doctor's outings seemed to coincide with the chef's shift schedule when working overnight.

Avon had never seen the doctor as excited as he appeared to be that night. She was impressed for what she was witnessing and she was absorbing it to the fullest. She could hardly wait for what was coming next. The doctor had everything managed and he indicated for her to go back to their spot and observe. Few minutes after Avon had gone back to the area where they were; the doctor joined her. Afterward, the doctor asked discretely among the homeless who would like to go and check if the goodies were out yet. One of them volunteered walking slowly to the alley. Then, from the distance the volunteer indicated with gestures that the *high tea* party was set up for them. Avon was amazed with the gratification the faces of the homeless people expressed. They moved slowly not crowding the area; as the tea was indeed as high as *high tea* could be.

Since they were without doubt out in the street, the doctor had placed the tea table high up at the end of a set of steps so that the electric kettles cords reached the only accessible exterior electric outlet out there. But what impressed Avon the most was the huge relief the homeless people expressed after they warmed up a bit with a hot tea sip.

The homeless people were so distracted; they assumed that the tea was put out by the employees from one of the restaurants at random; which was best for the doctor to protect his disguise, because the doctor couldn't allow them to take the *high tea* party

"*When the philosopher points to the stars, the fool's eyes are fixed on the finger.*"

for granted. Otherwise, they would've expected it at any time, even when he was unable to come by.

The doctor had been observing the homeless for some time and it appeared that they misused the alms they obtained from the Good Samaritans. Thus the doctor found different ways to provide what they seem to need in an inconspicuous way. At the same time, he was enthralled studying their behavior. He talked to them for long periods of time casually and individually learning about the circumstances which brought them where they were. Hardly ever the doctor met the same people when hanging out at Union Square, being part of the homeless world, because if they didn't feel like doing so, they didn't have to return to the same spot.

Avon noticed that some of them were more equipped than others; for there were homeless with thermoses, having hot beverages and eating from what look like lunch bags. And some of them even had portable heaters while others were hardly keeping warm with undone carton boxes, outworn tarpaulins, or overused garbage plastic bags.

Although, Avon wasn't able to see the doctor's facial reaction; she could perceive from him an immense sense of satisfaction; bringing her to deeply appreciate what the doctor meant when cordially inviting her to a *high tea* party; so high, she wondered if she would ever come down. The doctor knew that not all homeless people were actually baggers and not all baggers were actually homeless. Avon didn't know a thing about it though. And so, the *high tea* party that the doctor shared with her during the first outing was engraved as a treasured memory in her heart and it was worth to attend many more outings, becoming the beginning of a lesson for her to learn. And since Avon wasn't wise enough to realize many things as the doctor did; she was able to appreciate the experience and perceive her own notion of the homeless people.

However, she had no clue of the ideas and creativity she would explore in the future by hanging out in the homeless world.

As Avon learned more about living on the streets; she couldn't help to evaluate the differences between some and others. Some of the people who gathered at Union Square were actually homeless and they had been through some sort of trauma leaving them out of a home and unable to recover strength to simply start all over again. They disguised their evasion to confront the situation with alcoholism, drugs, procrastination, or even through prostitution which prolonged day-in and day-out their languish in the streets.

Others were not even genuine homeless; they just acted as if they were. They had not lost their homes and they even had vehicles parked around the corners. They performed being homeless to obtain an extra income and those were the shameless well equipped homeless which only someone attentively observing noticed their deception. And then, there were the Good Samaritans who nourished and enabled all of those lingering at Union Square, including the doctor and her.

As the doctor and Avon continued their mysterious outings; several times they found homeless people in need of a clinic or a hospital. They faced emergencies managing to take some of them to immediate medical care; especially the ones with children. However, when mingling among the homeless; the doctor and Avon had to maintain their disguise firmly; as they were exposing themselves to tragic risk; since the genuine homeless people were seriously in a different dimension of society and they would have resented deeply if they realized that they had been confiding in the doctor and around Avon who were not genuine beggars nor genuine homeless. Because the genuine homeless were a tad defensive toward the ones who begged for extra income; so, Avon

"When the philosopher points to the stars, the fool's eyes are fixed on the finger."

and the doctor couldn't even begin to understand the daily torment and torturing thoughts going through the homeless people's minds.

Avon had learned that the doctor was a posh from the North East coast who had been born within riches. He didn't know and couldn't experience the sensation of lacking material possessions; as he had always had access to resources and most certainly money acquisition had never been one of his issues. Therefore, when the doctor disguised as a homeless person trying to find out what would be like not having anything, not even a home; his whole experience was an adventure whereas for Avon was another lesson. As a result, when they gathered and spoke about the matter, in the midst of the doctor's adventure and Avon's learning lesson; they ended up creating projects with good willing motivation.

Some time had passed since the first time the doctor had invited Avon to the *high tea* party and together they had been learning about many different aspects of the homeless world. He was fascinated with the genuine homeless people's behavior, reactions to situations and circumstances in general; and so was Avon. However, after many outings the doctor was curious about *Avon's behavior* around the homeless and he decided to invite her to dinner with the intention to satisfy his curiosity.

The doctor's prestige allowed him to enjoy certain advantages not everyone had the benefit to experience; given that when he dined out, reputable restaurants in the Bay-Area complemented him with amenities including sending bottles of the finest wines to his table. Especially when he crossed the entrance threshold of establishments to be seen; as usually when he felt like indulging a fine meal, he reserved a private table.

Avon gladly accepted the invitation and after they had dinner at one of the most exclusive restaurants in the area, while waiting for dessert, they were enjoying a complementary bottle of *Dom*

Pérignon and the doctor found the appropriate moment to ask, "Do you feel uncomfortable around the homeless dear?"

Avon replied, "No, not at all. On the contrary, I actually look forward to our outing every week." Instinctively, Avon didn't express curiosity about the doctor's query making it a bit challenging for him to approach her.

Then, he couldn't contain himself anymore and he asked openly, "My dear, you do not talk to our acquaintances at Union Square. I have noticed, and you have not talked to any of them. You are always observing, but if you only spoke to one of them, I am certain that you would enjoy our outings even more."

Then, Avon stretched her full lips expressing a bright smile and she replied, "As you requested, I am protecting my identity. When I express verbally, I have a distinctive accent and if under any circumstances I cross paths with one of them during the day, I'll be exposed, doctor." She paused for a moment appreciating the doctor's expression of relief. However, he was absolutely impressed by Avon's perspicacity. Then, she added, "As a matter of fact, when they brought the *Dom* by the table, I was hoping to enjoy it while exposing some ideas I have to aid at least some of our friends from Union Square, because something tells me that they might be homeless, but not hopeless, doctor."

As eager as they were to assist the homeless, they discussed briefly the challenges that they would encounter as a result of their humble intention; which was simple, as their sole intent was to aid the homeless to reacquaint with society again. However, little did they know, for their genuine intention to help had absolutely nothing to do with what each genuine homeless person actually wanted while hanging out at Union Square.

Avon grabbed her handbag and she took out a small notepad showing the doctor a couple of reflections that she had written

"When the philosopher points to the stars, the fool's eyes are fixed on the finger."

regarding the matter and speaking softly he read, "'*The disguise of a being's emotions could be the greatest disguise there is; or else, truth would be homeless lacking the shelter of deceit.*'

"'*Promenading through life on a truthful path brings dishonesty to homeless exposure.*'

"My dear, do you think that our friends have been without a roof for so long that the only shelter they have is an umbrella of deceit covering their truth?"The doctor asked.

"Well also, if they have sheltered their truth under a torment of lies for so long, they could be physically manifesting it. I guess it is the beauty of written words, one can read them back and forth and every mind perceives a different meaning which could be assimilated at freewill. Although this is only a start for perspective, just in case I do arrange verbal individual meetings with our friends at some point" she said.

"You are serious and not just thinking about it then!" the doctor exclaimed.

"Correct. I do get quite encouraged by them." She confirmed.

Eager, the doctor looked into Avon's eyes intensely and affirmed, "My dear, we will focus on revealing lies until truth emerges homeless."

By then, it was time for dessert which was delicately served along with recently grinded roasted coffee grains seeping into a see through glass espresso percolator and prepared right there next to their table; Then the coffee was slowly poured into fresh hand frothed milk and presented to them after having been converted into a delicious *latté*.

The doctor was quite excited and asked, "How would we approach them; where to begin, my dear?"

"Let us begin anywhere, except compassion," she replied.

"I beg your pardon, my dear"

"Would you like me to actually repeat?"

"No, of course not; however, I wouldn't mind if you clarify your point"

"Well, my humble opinion of what I have observed in silence around our homeless friends is that they are already in a sea of martyrdom; thus enabling their suffering with compassion would sink them into self-pity. I find that there is a fine line between receiving compassion and feeling self-pity; therefore to avoid imprecision, I do not practice compassion at all."

"I understand what you mean, but not practicing compassion dear," the doctor said in a doubtful tone.

Avon looked at him firmly saying, "I mentioned that I sense a fine line and it is such a fine line doctor, I cannot detect it. So if I cannot manage compassion, why practice it? Giving compassion won't affect me, but it would affect them." He smiled while nodding and encouraged her to continue. "As far as our homeless friends are concerned they are worthless; while for us they are worthy. I put myself in their situation and I do not have the courage that they do. Our homeless friends are the bravest people in society, but no one is paying attention. I vaguely remember, although I am pretty certain that what taught me to learn social responsibility was to pay my rent on the due date, because apparently I was brave; however not brave enough to survive lacking of a roof over my head, they don't need compassion." She concluded.

Then the server approached offering to open another complementary bottle of *Dom Pérignon* which brought them to appreciate the end of dinner. So, declining the glamorous offer of more delightful *Dom*; they realized that their original intention was going to unfold many other issues prior to accomplishing any results and since they seemed to have a new project; they decided to work in private from then on.

⸙

"When the philosopher points to the stars, the fool's eyes are fixed on the finger."

Tossing a reflection to the air...

"At times one ought to be unkind only to be genuinely kind all the time."

13

ears earlier when Avon was living in Arizona after being
exposed to the deceiving experience with Frank; she went out and
about with her friends exploring the dating field. As a result, they
visited nightclubs; they visited bars; they had brunches, lunches,
and dinners. They went on long road trips, short trips and picnics.
They played golf and they even hiked Camelback Mountain;
however once, Avon was enticed to go on a hot air balloon ride.

Back then, in the midst of martyrdom and suffering her
torment; Avon felt like she deserved a treat and off she went up
in the air. For a change, she didn't bring any of her friends with
her and she took the hot air balloon ride by herself. Perhaps she
hoped that she would attract someone romantically, or maybe she
went alone out of pure instinct because she ended up not meeting
anyone after all.

At any rate, when considering that the closest she had been to
martyrdom was the experience with Frank; when she was thinking
of ideas to aid the homeless; she remembered exploring the hot
air balloon ride and while she was up in the air appreciating the
immensity from above and below; she had regained some senses

"When the philosopher points to the stars, the fool's eyes are fixed on the finger."

and she reclaimed confidence to start all over again. Hence, she found the strength to relocate from Phoenix to San Fran.

So, Avon decided to begin her goodwill project with a simple plan. She designed flyers targeting the homeless that could read as well as those that didn't by inviting them to a *complimentary hot air balloon ride* with no conditions attached. Although according to Avon, whoever showed up replying to her invite would reveal admitting to deserve a treat and their desire to explore life; which would allow her the opportunity to give them a chance to reintegrate into society.

"Brilliant idea and simple enough" said the doctor once Avon explained the plan and he asked, "Are we prepared in case our friends show up all at once for the hot air balloon ride my dear?"

Avon thought of every detail because she replied, "I find reasonable to make a reservation for a group of ten to start, do you agree?" And the doctor agreed with her.

So, the doctor and Avon distributed the flyers discretely sticking them inside empty carton boxes or in strategic places where the homeless would find them and they waited for the anticipated day.

On the projected day at half past eight in the morning; Avon set up a coffeemaker along with a tea maker on a console table in the lobby of her building. She had fresh-baked cookies, cream, milk, sugar, and even some cocoa to welcome her guests with hot beverages as they arrived for the hot air balloon ride. The homeless were supposed to arrive between nine and ten that morning.

As Avon read a book sitting on a bench next to the console table with the beverages; she heard the chime coming from the end of the lobby when the grandfather clock pendulum marked three in the afternoon and not one guest had shown up. She had been sitting all day reading, waiting and calling the hot air balloon ride operations office every hour to delay the reservation, and just then, Avon called the operations office again; not to postpone but to cancel the reservation instead. Yet Avon didn't give up, she made a new reservation for the following week changing the number of guests from a group of ten to a group of five and she also changed the flyers promoting the complimentary hot air balloon ride as weekly and not as an event just the once.

The following week, Avon called to cancel the reservation around one in the afternoon as she didn't find necessary to wait until three; for not one guest had shown up again. However she didn't give up, she made a reservation for the following week changing the number of guests from a group of five to a group of three.

About six weeks had passed and it was around midday when Avon called to cancel the reservation once more. Her plan didn't seem to be working for up till then, not one homeless had shown up accepting her invite. But not giving up; she kept the reservation for a group of three for the following week like she had been doing the previous weeks.

In the meantime, a couple of months must have gone by. Avon and the doctor continued their daily activities, their Union Square outings and distributing the flyers discreetly. Also, Avon had been exchanging some e-mails with her friend Jaidee, who was still living in France with her husband and children. The holidays had just passed and Avon mentioned to Jaidee that she had spent Christmas alone; because the doctor spent holidays in the East coast with his relatives. So, Jaidee invited Avon to come to France to celebrate the following Christmas with her family and her, and Since Avon hadn't seen her friend Jaidee for many years; she considered only sensible to accept the invitation and she agreed to celebrate the following Christmas with them. Therefore, Avon made arrangements booking

"When the philosopher points to the stars, the fool's eyes are fixed on the finger."

a trip far enough in advanced sealing the deal to be in France during the holiday season that year. Furthermore, Avon's Citizenship was under process and she was excited planning to travel internationally with a passport from the U.S.

On the eighteenth week, it was about half past nine in the morning when Jimmy showed up for the first time. "You are early!" Avon exclaimed, adding, "Welcome to our *complimentary hot air balloon ride* of the week, would you like a coffee or a tea before we live?"

"Thank you ma'am" Jimmy spoke soft and timidly.

Whatever Jimmy meant, didn't seem to make much of a difference to Avon for she prepared both beverages in a flash for him to pick either one. Then, Jimmy accepted the coffee and Avon indicated that he could sit on the bench next to the console table; where she sat for hours waiting week after week prior to his appearance. After he sat, Avon handed him a paper napkin with some fresh-baked cookies in between which Jimmy humbly received.

Jimmy looked up at the gorgeous chandelier hanging down from the center of the high ceiling. His eyes lowered slowly as he admired the French colonial giant mirrors resting on the walls as well as the matching antique console tables holding huge bouquets of fresh flowers. Jimmy sipped his coffee gradually and he turned his head to the left, admiring the grandfather clock at the end of the lobby. "Do you mind if I sit next to you?" Avon asked holding a paper cup with coffee in one hand and a cookie in the other.

"Ma'am" said Jimmy moving a bit to the side and allowing her to sit next to him. Avon was dressed simple wearing jeans, a plain top and running shoes.

Sitting next to Jimmy; Avon sensed his anticipation and excitement; although he looked as if he had not ate a decent meal in years and she wondered how many Jimmys would fit lined up in the two-seater bench, three or four perhaps.

They didn't speak. They sat sipping coffee and eating cookies while admiring the lustrous faux-marble floors and the emptiness of the ample lobby in silence. Until the grandfather clock chime indicated ten in the morning. Then Avon stood up, she reached for her jacket which was resting on one of the arms of the bench and she asked, "Are you ready?"

"No one else is coming?" asked Jimmy in wonder.

If Avon didn't know better, her certainty sounded almost arrogant as she looked at him firmly shaking her head and she winked replying, "No, it is going to be you and me, my friend."

They walked out of the building and all of a sudden, attentively, Avon looked up at Jimmy. He lowered his eyes looking at hers and listening; a bell dinging approached closer and closer. Perceiving their senses; they started to run amid pedestrians to the corner. They arrived at the trolley stop catching their breaths and they jumped inside the trolley just in time before it left. Then Avon looked at Jimmy directly in the eyes while conveying to the conductor, who was approaching Jimmy from behind, "I have my friend's ticket Sr." And she handed out two tickets to him. At that moment, Jimmy got to appreciate one of Avon's grandest smiles. While they were in the trolley, Avon called to confirm the reservation from her mobile and having rescheduled over and over for many weeks the operator seemed to be more excited than Avon was; for she would finally take the hot air balloon ride after cancelling the anticipated expedition seventeen times.

When they got off the trolley they began walking and Avon was explaining to Jimmy that a minivan would pick them up a few blocks away and that the minivan would take them to the area where the hot air balloon ride would start. Then Jimmy asked if

"When the philosopher points to the stars, the fool's eyes are fixed on the finger."

they could stop walking for a moment. Avon agreed and she stood
next to him while she observed; Jimmy took an old bandana off
his head letting loose about one hundred long mini-braids which
he pulled back into a ponytail. Next, he pushed his top-wear into
his pants, pulling them up a bit, as his pants seemed to be falling
down his hips. Avon waited patiently for they had plenty of time.
Then, the outworn scarf that he was wearing on his head; Jimmy
rearranged on his neck pulling the end corners down and adjusting
them to exact match. After that, he crossed the scarf by his collar
tossing the ends over his shoulders and out of the blue he exclaimed
out loud, "I am ready to fly! Yeaaaah ma'am!" or perhaps he said
"Yeaaaah man!" Avon couldn't tell.

In any event, as a sign of encouragement Avon agreed
exclaiming "Yes!" right after him and they continued walking
enthused.

They arrived where the minivan was scheduled to pick them up
and they sat on a public bench to wait. Avon noticed that Jimmy's left
hand didn't move the same as his right hand did and he wore an old
glove covering it. They had been waiting for awhile, and suddenly,
Avon got a phone call. But at the same time, a black shiny sedan
pulled up. As she took the call, the driver of the sedan got off holding
a sign reading: *Ms. Avon*. The phone call was from the hot air balloon
ride operator letting Avon know that the minivan wasn't going
to pick her up and that they had sent an alternate complimentary
vehicle for her. Even though Avon was flattered; she didn't want to
scare Jimmy away. So she kindly conveyed to him that there was an
issue with the minivan and that they had replaced it with the sedan.
Then she asked, "Would you mind riding in this car?"

"It will be just fine Ms. Avon," Jimmy replied. Just then, Avon
realized that Jimmy could read her name on the sign that the driver
was holding in his hands.

When they arrived, the hot air balloon was ready. Avon found it a bit strange for it was quarter past eleven and the reservation was for midday. But still, she didn't make much out of it as the hot air balloon ride meant much more than the clock time to her.

To best describe her own experience when taking a hot air balloon ride; Avon related it with her birth. Because except for the stories she had heard; she had no recollection of entering the realm of life and figuratively speaking; she felt that ever since she was born she had been in life sort of taking a ride. So, since she couldn't tell exactly how she found herself in the midst of space floating around after a hot air balloon had been released from Earth; she just took the ride as well. In essence, the whole experience appeared like a miracle to her.

Avon would get totally enthralled while being up in the air; as she appreciated in complete awareness that the only support between her feet and the open space was sturdy interwoven wicker crated by men. Then once up there she did nothing; except to stand and absorb to the fullest the magnitude of Earth. Being inside a basket; gliding on top of mountains, fields, valleys, water, and everything there is under from aloft; feeling the wind from above and below touching her skin; soaring with the breeze's flow not forcing the situation and following the wind in the course of nature; engrossed Avon completely.

Furthermore, when feeling her entire being floating all over in the air inside a gondola triggered by the simple heat of a flame; Avon's personal experience became even more intense.

Tossing a reflection to the air...

"When the philosopher points to the stars, the fool's eyes are fixed on the finger."

"A hot air balloon ride either diminishes one to understand the insignificance of humankind in relation to the Universe, or releases one's potential sheltered in the heart toward roofless greatness."

After gliding high up in the air for a couple of hours, which was way longer than a regular hot air balloon ride would last, Avon and Jimmy were descending by Napa Valley on top of some grassland. From the distance; they could distinguish a table covered with a white cloth being caressed by the breeze and displaying a lunch feast. Not far from the table was parked a stretch limousine which seemed to be waiting for them and on the opposite end was a minivan where a server stood by and attentively observed.

When they landed and got off the gondola; a greeter escorted them to the table and at the same time, the server began walking toward them. Avon was a bit uncomfortable as she didn't request any of those extravagant arrangements for not to scare her homeless friend away. However she followed their lead thinking that she would find the appropriate moment to talk to the greeter or perhaps the server. Then, as soon as the greeter pulled their chairs and they were seated; the server approached the table and handed an envelope with a note inside to Avon.

The note said for her and her companion to enjoy a complimentary lunch. Also, the note encouraged them to enjoy a complimentary stretch limo ride back to San Fran. On top of the well appreciated amenities, the note also said, "We hope you enjoyed your *complimentary hot air balloon ride*."

Avon was flattered again, but she excused herself for a moment leaving Jimmy sitting by the table. While she walked away; she called the hot air balloon ride operations expressing her surprise and puzzlement and the operator said, "Ms. Avon, you paid so many cancellation fees; you really deserve to have a complimentary treat. Therefore, the hot air balloon ride was not charged to your account."

When finishing the phone call, Avon stood in the middle of the greenery thinking, *complimentary hot air balloon ride, why does it sound familiar?* Then she realized that she had made so many flyers promoting the *complimentary hot air balloon ride*, after eighteen weeks of focusing on the same goal, her actual hot air balloon ride was, in effect, complimentary. She felt like jumping up and down and yelling out, *we got a complimentary hot air balloon ride!* But of course she didn't; as she had to be considerate to her homeless friend for she didn't want to scare him away. Still, she couldn't help noticing how the Universe works in mysterious ways when manifesting one's intentions; since the Universe provided her with a *complimentary* hot air balloon ride just as she intended it to be. Yet, had she been more specific and focused on the homeless joy *to receive* and not on her ego's good deed *to give*, perhaps more of her Union Square friends would've accepted her invite and enjoyed the ride.

So, after realizing how specific her intentions should be with the Universe; she walked to join Jimmy who was gratefully enjoying the lunch feast.

Afterward, Avon and Jimmy took pleasure in the stretch limo ride from Napa Valley to San Fran and as the limousine pulled in front of her building; Avon reached a card from her jacket inner pocket and handed it to him. Her name and her contact numbers were hand-written on the card and she said, "Whenever you want to talk, call me. I will come wherever you are."Then, she expressed her appreciation to the driver while he held the limo door opened for her.

"When the philosopher points to the stars, the fool's eyes are fixed on the finger."

Unexpectedly Jimmy said, "I'll get off here too Ms. Avon." The driver rushed to open his door but Jimmy was already standing on the sidewalk. Avon and Jimmy stood in front of the building looking at the limo drive away and as she was taking her keys out of her jeans pocket, Jimmy lowered his eyes looking at hers. He put his right hand on his chest and lowering his head he said, "Ms. Avon, my name is James and I am at your service."

Avon replied, "So am I, James, so am I." As a response while his head was still low; Jimmy moved his eyes up looking at her surprised and smiling. Then she asked, "May I call you Jimmy, James?"

Jimmy's smile intensified nodding as he replied, "You may, Ms. Avon. By all means, you may."

She smiled looking firmly at him and she entered the building allowing him to take the initiative after that.

Jimmy walked backward in between pedestrians with his hand still on his chest until he lost sight of Avon's building entrance door from faraway.

Tossing a reflection to the air...

"Up in the air or down in Earth the best approach to an aim is romancing the target."

The doctor was waiting for Avon in the back garden and anxious to learn about the hot air balloon ride adventure. It was early evening and as Avon came down the steps into the backyard;

her glow combined with the sunset beams illuminated the whole area and the doctor looked at her for a moment in wonder.

Avon sat at the table radiating of enjoyment. "Well, my dear?" said the doctor making his first move on the Chessboard.

"His name is James but we established that we will call him Jimmy" Avon said. The doctor patiently waited for her to make her move and to regain some senses; because Avon seemed to be still up in the air and after a couple of moves she expressed, "He knows how to read."

"Does he my dear? Good!" said the doctor pausing and saying again, "Good!"

Then Avon said, "I think he likes photography."

"How can you tell?

"He took pictures." She replied making her move.

"Does he own a camera, my dear?"

"I do not know, but he certainly took loads of pictures" she replied.

Then, the doctor looked at her intrigued. So, having the doctor's full attention; Avon mimicked holding a camera with both of her hands in front of her face and eyes; and as she moved her right index up and down; she let out, "Click" capturing different areas, "Click" around the garden, "Click." She was kind of photocopying Jimmy's way of taking pictures. Then, the doctor couldn't help himself letting out the longest laughter he had ever shared with her.

The conclusion of Jimmy's first visit was to wait as he seemed to be discrete and quiet. The only thing Avon was able to perceive from him was his desire to explore life and Jimmy projected certain sense of confidence being humble at the same time, thus Avon was positive that sooner or later Jimmy would be back.

As it turned out, Jimmy's return happened sooner than later, because the next day at half past nine; he was calling Avon from

"When the philosopher points to the stars, the fool's eyes are fixed on the finger."

the intercom outside the building. When Avon realized that Jimmy was back; she didn't even buzz the door to open. She was excited and she rushed downstairs to greet him at once. In the meantime, the doctor set up a tripod with a camera in the library to see Jimmy's reaction when he saw it, so as to find out if he was, in fact, interested in photography. However, when Avon brought Jimmy to the library; he stood by the door and he didn't enter right away.

Jimmy's big brown eyes moved slowly as he looked to the right side of the room where three columns of bookcases were lined up and filled with books from the ceiling to the floor. Then his eyebrows rose as his slow motion continued looking ahead and he observed the oversized French doors opened out to a terrace exposing a gorgeous view of the bay from the elevated level where the library was. Next, he looked down to his left in direction to a set of steps which split the level of the glossy hardwood floors going down to the seating area. Jimmy was impressed with the lighting features. He stared at the chandeliers hanging from the high ceilings. He looked at the lamps on the tables as well as the spotlights by the huge bookcases resting against the walls. His eyes' slow motion continued observing toward the front left corner and he looked at a spiral staircase one step at the time, going up gradually, as if he was climbing each step with his eyes to the interior balcony where more books were displayed in a high opened section. He was overwhelmed looking at the oval glassed tables which rested on stands appearing as part of the flooring. The matching wood tone combined with the design gave the impression that the tables' stands grew out like branches from the floor and vice versa. Yet, Jimmy didn't notice the camera placed on the tripod right in the middle of the room facing him.

"Doctor, allow me to introduce Jimmy" said Avon adding "Jimmy this is—"

Jimmy had his right hand on his chest and lowering his head he said, "The doctor" finishing Avon's sentence.

Then the doctor said, "It is my pleasure Jimmy. Would you like to come in? This used to be my library. Now, only the books belong to me."

Jimmy expressed amazement stating, "You seem to own the essential element in this room doctor," and he spotted a book.

"Which reminds me to go back to our project," said Avon.

"Certainly, I will catalog this section," input the doctor.

By then, Jimmy was holding the book that he had spotted between his hands and he asked, "Is the new owner looking to duplicate each of the books in this library?" Avon and the doctor couldn't look at each other from where they were, but that moment was significant to both of them; for Jimmy's perception was sharp and they began to realize that Jimmy's grays reflected wisdom and not neglect.

"As a matter of fact I am," said Avon peeking at him from behind a bookshelf and smiling.

"Ms. Avon, is this library yours?" Jimmy asked looking up and down referring to the whole building.

Then Avon exclaimed, "Yes, the books were not for sale; so, I purchase the whole building instead!"

They expressed laughter briefly and the doctor suggested, "Jimmy would you like to join us for brunch? On Sundays, we usually enjoy it in the garden."

"Yes, thank you. It will be an honor." Jimmy replied.

Before long, the doctor's housekeeper had brunch ready and called them through the intercom to come down to the garden. The doctor conveyed to Avon with a hinted look to go ahead and that he would catch up with them. Then, the doctor took the camera off the tripod and when he joined them in the courtyard; he discretely

"When the philosopher points to the stars, the fool's eyes are fixed on the finger."

placed the camera on a nearby garden bench and he sat with them. They were enjoying the meal and unexpectedly, Jimmy asked, "Doctor, do you always carry a camera around the building?"

"No Jimmy not always. Only today," said the doctor not having a valid response.

Then, Avon changed the subject asking, "Jimmy would you mind sharing with us about your hot air balloon ride experience?"

"Well–" said Jimmy and he paused. The doctor and Avon waited attentively and he continued, "The balloon ride was rejuvenating. I really felt like I was being born again, but today I feel the same." They expressed amusement and he added, "I don't know, but there is no much difference between the hot air balloon ride and this young lady's smile."

"What do you mean? Avon asked bashfully.

"Well, I have been feeling this way ever since I saw your smile in the trolley, Ms. Avon." Jimmy replied.

"If you do not mind me prying, what do you feel exactly, Jimmy?" The doctor asked.

Jimmy replied, "I don't mind doctor and you are not prying at all. I'll recapitulate in one word, I feel…" he paused and expressing a satisfying smile, "Inspired!" He exclaimed. The doctor and Avon looked at each other wondering and Jimmy added, "So much so that after I saw Ms. Avon smiling once, I had to find a way to see her smile again. That's why, despite the fact that at the present time I have no interest in photography whatsoever, yesterday I took imaginary pictures most of the day; but my intention was to see Ms. Avon smile time and again." They joined in laughter and from that point forward; Avon, the doctor and Jimmy became inseparable. Jimmy had many attributes and one of them was his sense of humor.

The doctor and Avon decided to cease the Union Square outings for a few weeks, or at least until they figured out the outcome regarding Jimmy. Therefore, they dedicated their attention to Jimmy's periodic visits. The doctor found a new Chess partner and Avon spent hours talking with Jimmy in the library. The doctor encouraged Avon to expand her learning in Jimmy's company and he assisted Jimmy through the same method he used when Avon looked-for his insight. None of them spoke of the past. They usually discussed ideas and gave each other motivation to look forward in life and not back.

An uneventful evening after a few weeks had passed; while the doctor and Jimmy played Chess in the garden, Avon observed and she noticed that Jimmy's left hand was swelled. "Is your hand all right Jimmy?" She asked.

"Not really." Jimmy replied.

Then, the doctor asked, "If you do not mind me prying, what happened to your hand, Jimmy?"

"It's a long story, but I'll recapitulate." Jimmy said and he added shaking his head, "You are not prying doctor; on the contrary, I am grateful for your concern," and he explained, "I used to be left-handed and also an accountant. I worked for many years at the Financial District in Chicago and one day, I got myself in trouble. Accounting is part of such a competitive trade; I wanted to blend-in among peers and alleged friends but I lost my senses and I ended up getting involved in a bad deal. The next thing I knew; I was in a dark room being interrogated and tormented by some people who were looking for answers. They had been tracking each transaction and I was the key suspect. In desperate seek of information, when I didn't give out any names, someone smashed my hand. I guess they did it as punishment for me not to be able to use a calculator ever again. On top of it I lost my credentials. I served my prison term for over a decade and ever since I was released I've been out on the streets for nearly ten years. Winters can be torturous in

"When the philosopher points to the stars, the fool's eyes are fixed on the finger."

Chicago for a person who lives on the streets and my hand never really healed, usually the weather affects it and although I've been in the Bay-Area for about nine weeks, my hand is still reacting to the climate it seems."

"Nine weeks?" said Avon surprised. Jimmy nodded assent and she exclaimed, "It has been about that long since our hot air balloon ride, Jimmy!"

"Yes, I had just arrived the previous evening when we went on the ride, Ms. Avon." Jimmy confirmed.

"How did you manage to find out about the hot air balloon ride so fast Jimmy?" the doctor asked.

"Oh well, I learned about the hot air balloon ride roughly two months before I came here doctor." Avon and the doctor listened and Jimmy explained, "One night, I was shivering under pieces of undone carton boxes in an alley by Rush Street and I felt the winter wind trying to keep me awake. When I was trying to rearrange my shelter, I could avow that the hot air balloon ride flyer drop down from above; but seriously, I couldn't tell where it came from."

Avon and the doctor were wordless; but Avon found the words to ask, "Did you come to San Francisco from Chicago specifically to go on the hot air balloon ride Jimmy?"

"Yes, Ms. Avon, I browsed California Street in the internet at the public library and San Francisco was the only destination coming up as a result." Jimmy replied. Then, Jimmy noticed their curious expression. So, he detailed a bit more, "Back then, I was almost at the end of the rope; as I mentioned before, winters can be torturous for a person who lives on the streets and I had put up with those winter storms long enough. But just by the idea of going on a hot air balloon ride, I revived!" Avon and the doctor were listening in amazement and Jimmy continued, "Then, as soon as I was able to gain some strength; I started to hitchhike South-West.

Eventually, I managed to collect enough money for a bus fare from Vegas and I made it."

Tears rolled down Avon's face. She got up to hug Jimmy from behind and as she sneaked a peck on his right cheek; she hissed by his ear, "Jimmy, call me Avon without the Ms., would you?" Jimmy agreed nodding and smiling.

"What would you like to do Jimmy?"The doctor asked directly.

"I gave up my passion and I do not seem to be able to replace it doctor." Jimmy replied.

"Jimmy, since you haven't replaced your passion with another passion, seems to me that you haven't given up your passion to begin with," said the doctor and he asked, "Is accounting your passion?"

Jimmy nodded and said, "I did mention that I lost my credentials. I cannot practice without credentials doctor."

"Well, we would have to remedy that, won't we?"The doctor added.

"I do not mean to interrupt gentlemen but talking about remedies, should Jimmy have his hand checked? I know you do not practice anymore doctor; however, would you mind checking Jimmy's hand?"Avon asked.

Then, wishing to fulfill Avon's request the doctor hesitated as he replied, "He– He should go to the clinic and have his hand checked my dear."

"I apologize. I didn't mean to be imprudent." Avon said embarrassed. Jimmy was quiet and observing.

Then, the doctor realized that he had never shared much about his occupation with Avon. He had a clear understanding of what Avon did to earn an income; yet, she could perfectly be under the impression that he was a medical doctor when he wasn't. Then, the doctor said, "My dear Avon, being prudent is one of your greatest attributes; but at times, it might lead you to presume and

"When the philosopher points to the stars, the fool's eyes are fixed on the finger."

my discretion could have influenced for you to assume that I am a medical doctor."

"Are you not?" Avon asked totally amazed and he shook his head confirming. At that stage, Jimmy was perplexed because he had presumed that the doctor was a medical doctor as well.

Then, the doctor explained, "Permit me to enlighten you my friends; I am a *Juris Doctor*. At first I practiced in a firm; later on, I discovered my passion to teach and eventually, I became a professor which granted me the title of 'The Doctor' among my University students and the label has followed me ever since." Both, Avon and Jimmy looked puzzled. So the doctor went further explaining, "Although currently I am semi-retired, most of my activities in the field are consulting, seminar appearances, assessments, and lectures." Avon and Jimmy were not reacting at all and the doctor added, "Let us say that I might heal people from a different approach; but, I have never healed anyone physically my friends." Jimmy and Avon were totally dazed by the doctor's revelation. Then, the doctor suggested, "Would you like me to take you to the clinic Jimmy? Let us discuss your credentials on the way." And even though Jimmy was practically in shock; he humbly accepted and they left. Avon stayed sitting in the garden and baffled for a long while.

With Avon's research skills and the doctor's influence, Jimmy was able to acquire new credentials. Provided that so many years had passed and that he was in a different State; Jimmy just had to reacquaint with his passion and the day that he received his permits he was the happiest man in the world. Jimmy didn't know how to express his gratitude, but the doctor explained, "Law does not bend because law is not flexible Jimmy; however, law is a science of pardon for it was designed to rectify mistakes. What really matters in law is research and being always aware." Then, the three of them went out to celebrate.

As time went by, Jimmy became their personal accountant and administrator. Eventually, Jimmy rented one of the doctor's units in the other building and slowly but surely; he was reacquainting within society, earning a salary, he lived under a roof, and he had encountered two new friends.

Tossing a reflection to the air...

"When admitting mistakes; the lessons learned open a gateway to a trail of endless possibilities."

"When the philosopher points to the stars, the fool's eyes are fixed on the finger."

14

With the doctor's guidance; Avon researched corroborating Jimmy's story and it turned out that Jimmy was, in effect, part guilty of the fraud he had committed. However, he had already served his sentence and he had lingered long enough on the streets dealing with his guilt. So, since Jimmy seemed eager to reintegrate into society; Avon and the doctor discussed the probabilities to give him an opportunity. They considered giving Jimmy hope to become a responsible member within society again and even if in the surface appeared like Jimmy could take advantage of their kindness due to his past record, it was Jimmy's option to accept the chance and decide if abusing the opportunity would be worth at all. The doctor and Avon sheltered each other above anyone else and given that Jimmy was about his age; the doctor decided to approach Jimmy with a proposal himself. Avon and the doctor had nothing to lose because their intention was for Jimmy to take a chance; not to take a chance with Jimmy themselves.

Few days after Jimmy had obtained his credentials, while Avon was in the library, the doctor and Jimmy were in the garden playing Chess and the doctor asked openly, "Jimmy, would you like to stay overnight instead of taking naps here and there during the day?"

"When the philosopher points to the stars, the fool's eyes are fixed on the finger."

Jimmy looked at the doctor a bit hesitant and replied, "Doctor, living in your property is one of my most desirable dreams but it's a responsibility that I am not able to comply with."

Then the doctor said, "One issue at the time Jimmy, you are getting ahead."

"Doctor, I would like it very much! Yes indeed!" Jimmy clarified.

"Great!" Said the doctor reaching a notepad that he had nearby and he asked, "Would you like to calculate what would be required for your dream to become true?" Jimmy agreed with a pleasant smile. After they settled an amount for rent, expenses and enough money for Jimmy to be able to satisfy his basic needs and extras; the doctor said, "Well, having this information, the next step would be to find an income source, Jimmy."

Jimmy's eyes lit up with a glow of hope. For Jimmy knew that the doctor had reputable associations and he asked, "Do you think that someone would employ me out there, doctor? I'll be the happiest man working as an accountant again."

The doctor looked at Jimmy sincerely and replied, "No, Jimmy. You are fifty-eight-years-old and I am sixty; at our age, going out there looking for a job would be like jumping into a pool of sharks. Do not take me wrong as I am certain that with your determination you will succeed. However, the effort employed in the process will extract every gram of vitality left in you my friend. Permit me a moment, would you?" The doctor went to the library to join Avon and left Jimmy in the garden thinking by himself.

Before long, the doctor called Jimmy into the library. Avon had prepared a management position offer for him. Evidently, when facing such a chance Jimmy was the happiest Jimmy they had ever seen. He decided to commit to the responsibility of a new job going back into society and he agreed to sign the required paperwork. They presented Jimmy a schedule, detailed duties and

Avon assigned the front office at the entrance of her building for him to perform his tasks. They hired Jimmy legally and he was added to the payroll as part of the small group of employees that they had been managing so far. So, besides being their accountant; Jimmy was also going to be responsible of managing their staff. Naturally, Avon and the doctor were accountable for their staff's salaries and Jimmy's salary cost was divided in equal parts.

From then on, Jimmy's days were filled with joy and it didn't take him long to adjust to hygiene, a routine and a daily change of clothes. Months went by and as far as everyone was concerned; Jimmy had demonstrated gratitude, responsibility and respect. Avon, the doctor and Jimmy were able to maintain a professional relationship as well as continue socializing as friends.

Some time passed and when the holidays came, Avon went to France to spend Christmas with her friend Jaidee and the doctor went to spend the holidays with his relatives in the East-coast. The plan was for Avon to return before the beginning of the year to help collecting the rents and the doctor would return after the holidays. Jimmy was excited to spend Christmas with some tenants and Avon was quite excited to travel to France with her new passport from the U.S.

Tossing a reflection to the air...

"The most sublime expression of gratitude after one accepts a good deed from another is being loyal to self-accountability by upholding liberation of guilt."

"When the philosopher points to the stars, the fool's eyes are fixed on the finger."

As Avon was in the plane ready to land in the South of France where Jaidee and her family lived; she look through the window appreciating the moon beams and the sparkling stars reflecting against the rippling waves of the Mediterranean Sea. The view was splendid as the flickering peachy-turquoise lights glowed in the city welcoming planes landing form East, North, South, and West. Then as the plane descended immersing into such a glorious illumination and colors blend; she felt as if she was entering a dimension into outer space.

When Avon arrived in Marseille it was late evening and although she had been in France working many times; she had never been in Marseille in the past. So, she was absolutely charmed absorbing every minute of it. At the airport, Avon was able to recognize Xavier from the distance waiting for her by the baggage claim. They reacquainted as if they had been seeing each other regularly in the years gone by and even though he looked aged; he seemed as gentleman as ever to her.

When they arrived at the house her friend Jaidee and four lovely girls more or less in the ages of seventeen, twelve, ten, and eight were anxiously waiting to welcome her. They had prepared an appetizing dinner to celebrate her arrival and the evening was filled with good memories and updates from the years that they had been distanced.

The following morning when Avon woke up, the girls had prepared breakfast, along with Christmas carols playing in the background arousing the spirit of a season that Avon had never sensed. Jaidee explained that celebrating the holidays around children was different and she also mentioned that when she first arrived in France; she had to learn to adapt to the Western holidays enjoying them as part of the culture. Xavier had breakfast with them taking part with a word here and there; but he had affairs to attend and he left the ladies with the girls to enjoy the rest of the day. Jaidee and the girls had prepared the menu for Christmas dinner. They seemed to have everything organized and they spent the day out and about preparing for the holiday.

Later in the evening, Xavier brought a gorgeous natural Christmas tree into the house with the assistance of a neighbor. Avon noticed that Jaidee and Xavier were speaking inaudibly for a moment and Jaidee seemed a bit upset; however, Avon didn't pry for she wasn't there to rearrange a family which had been solid for many years without her help. Therefore, Avon only hoped for them to solve whatever they were discussing and she carried on getting out of their way. Although, Avon sensed a *silent wave* echoing the granny's words saying *I have lived a lifetime without you, I can perfectly live another lifetime without your help, Avon;* or something to that effect.

When Xavier and the neighbor finished setting up the Christmas tree; they sat in the living room to enjoy a cup of tea. Avon was in their studio checking e-mails. The girls were getting the Christmas tree decorations running up and down the stairs and Jaidee was in the kitchen preparing dinner. Avon had not seen the neighbor at all and when she finished her affairs in the studio to avoid interrupting the gentlemen tea gathering; she went to the kitchen to help Jaidee. As they were preparing dinner Jaidee said, "I feel uncomfortable because we may have an unexpected guest for Christmas dinner." Avon was peeling some potatoes and she listened as Jaidee continued, "Our neighbor is an abandoned farmer. Many years ago, his wife left him to wed another man and his two children grew up in London. He just sees them during the holidays." Avon looked at Jaidee listening and peeling potatoes. Jaidee added, "Xavier mentioned that the children were supposed to spend Christmas with him, but now that they are teenagers, seems

"When the philosopher points to the stars, the fool's eyes are fixed on the finger."

like they didn't want to be around him because they didn't come."
Avon continued listening and doing her chore. Jaidee carried on, "I
feel bad for him because he's responsible and a hard working man."
Then, Jaidee showed Avon some things that the neighbor repaired
in their kitchen explaining that he fixed stuff around their house to
generate extra income so as to send child support and apparently
he worked as a handyman for them. Furthermore Jaidee said, "I
admire his determination, because he works so hard in the farm
to be able to provide for his children that he even lives in a small
caravan."

Suddenly, Avon seemed interested in the subject asking,
"What is a caravan, Jaidee?"

So, Jaidee explained that a caravan was sort of a trailer; like
a campervan; or like a motorhome and she said, "Although his
caravan is tiny Avon. I'll show it to you sometime and you'll be
surprised to see where the man lives."

Avon asked, "Why are you uncomfortable then?"

So Jaidee explained, "Well, Xavier says that you should be
the guest of honor and that we shouldn't share our attention with
anyone else."

Avon responded with a big smile on her face, "I appreciate
your kindness but it is my honor to be your guest. I felt privileged
from the moment you invited me to spend the holidays with your
lovely family Jaidee. I don't mind sharing attention at all." Then,
Jaidee approached Avon showing affection and they hugged.

After that, Avon asked for an apron and Jaidee told her to
get one from a rack behind the door. So, as Avon was getting the
apron; Xavier and the neighbor entered the kitchen. The neighbor
was holding the cups of finished tea and brought them into the sink.
Then, Jaidee asked him, "Are you coming for Christmas dinner?"

The neighbor politely replied, "I have other plans Jaidee."

The neighbor's soiled look was the obvious result of hard labor and Avon perceived a strange aroma from him. The scent wasn't offensive; it was just an unfamiliar smell for her. Then, Avon noticed that they didn't honor the insignificant farmer an introduction to her. So, since she was returning to America before the end of the year and the neighbor declined the invite, Avon thought that most likely she wouldn't see the soiled farmer again and while tying the apron on her back-waist she asked, "What are your plans?" Not realizing that she was putting the farmer on the spot.

Then, while the soiled humble farmer washed the tea cups facing a window above the sink; he gazed out into the infinite and addressing Avon as *my lady* with a thick accent and a firm tone he replied, "My lady, I plan to spend some time with *Dark Matter* and while I'm at it; I could toss some stars from above for you if you'd like me to." Avon instantly felt like her entire body blushed and her heart had been set on fire. Electric shivers traveled from the tip of her toes to her crown spreading slowly through every inch of her body and gradually burning from inside out each of her pores. Her heart throbbed fast and she was standing right in the middle of the kitchen. Clearly, she had embarrassed herself and in the surface she reacted bashfully smiling; although the farmer didn't even see her because he was facing the sink the whole time. Then Xavier broke the Energy asking what were they cooking for dinner and Jaidee replied that they were preparing *Pot au Feu*. Jaidee and Xavier didn't make much out of the farmer's response because they didn't seem interested in *Dark Matter*. However, while Avon didn't know what a caravan was; she was well aware of the affinity between her Arolf and the farmer's *Dark Matter* remark. On the other hand, Avon's embarrassment was a moment of perplexity; as she couldn't figure out what the farmer meant when proposing to toss stars from above to her other than feeling as if she had just been romanced. After

"When the philosopher points to the stars, the fool's eyes are fixed on the finger."

the insignificant farmer finished washing the tea cups; he nodded once politely and without saying another word, he left. By then, after the farmer had been exposed; Jaidee was obviously aware of his unjustifiable plans for Christmas. To Avon made no difference if the farmer declined the dinner invitation thinking that he might have liked to be by himself; because she had spent so many holidays alone; the whole drama meant nothing to her. However, she couldn't avoid wondering what the Energy she absorbed standing in the middle of the kitchen was all about.

The following day was Christmas Eve. Avon, the girls and Jaidee promenaded through the streets of the nearest town, Martigues. They were looking to buy the freshest produce, ingredients, and condiments needed for Christmas dinner. Avon was taking pleasure going in and out of the stores and although she didn't enjoy shopping much; she was pleased sharing with Jaidee and the girls at the market and the shops. Also, she enjoyed delivering the last minute Christmas cards in the neighborhood because they actually delivered each card in person. Xavier and Jaidee lived far-off town in a farmhouse that his parents had left him after they passed away. So, the vicinity houses were rather distant from one another, not like Avon was used to see in the city; one apartment building next to the other.

After shopping, when they were delivering the last minute Christmas cards, Jaidee showed to Avon where the neighbor farmer lived and she pointed out the small caravan; except they didn't deliver a card to the farmer. They delivered a card in the main house of the farm and in a cottage on the other end. So, when Avon saw the tiny caravan from the distance; she was able to confirm what Jaidee had said. Avon couldn't imagine a person living permanently in there and despite the small size; she thought that it was cute because the landscape looked like a miniature area in a fairytale.

The rest of Christmas Eve the girls were great hostesses to Avon. They treated her like a special guest giving her a foot massage, polishing her hand and toe nails and they even practiced new hair styles on her. Also, the girls were getting along with Avon as if she was their age because one of the girls even confided her new school romance to her. Overall the girls showered Avon with attention and their most genuine intention.

The following morning was Christmas day and everyone was so excited unwrapping gifts, dinner was almost neglected. So, when the time to cook the meal came, Avon helped Jaidee with the sophisticated menu and preparations while the girls were wrapped up joining their father in celebration. And, albeit their activities indicated that every year Xavier took care of the traditional events while Jaidee took care of the meal, Jaidee kept apologizing to Avon insisting that the girls were supposed to help. Avon didn't care as she just enjoyed preparing such a fancy feast.

As dinner time approached and the ladies finished garnishing the dishes; one girl played the piano with her father while the other three sang trying to keep the tune of festive Christmas carols. Suddenly, a knock echoed from the entrance door and Xavier and the girls greeted a guest. Jaidee was ready to serve and Avon ran upstairs to freshen up. However Avon was a bit surprised as she wasn't aware that the farmer ended up accepting the Christmas dinner invite.

By the time Avon came down; everyone was already sitting at the table. The first course was ready to be served and they were all set just waiting for her. Xavier was sitting at one end of the table, Jaidee sat to his right and the four girls sat to his left. At the other end of the table sat the farmer leaving the seat to his left assigned to Avon. When Avon approached the table; the farmer stood up right away and he introduced himself saying politely, "My name

"When the philosopher points to the stars, the fool's eyes are fixed on the finger."

is Valentin, would you allow me?" Then expressing appreciation, Avon said her name and he repeated it to pronounce it well. At the same time, Valentin pulled the chair out for Avon to sit, but he rearranged it closer to his end of the table. Once everyone was in place, the toasts and celebration began.

Revealing the obvious any French meal could be a ceremonial celebration. Therefore, Christmas dinner on the occasion wasn't going to be the exception. The meal courses were served harmonized with the china, glasses and silverware. Every wine was perfectly combined with each dish zest and everyone ate enjoying the meal at a slow pace.

The conversation was casual and the girls helped to serve participating in the festivity but not demanding too much attention and allowing Avon to enjoy as a guest. While everyone was distracted serving; Valentin found an opportunity to approach Avon asking in a soft tone, "Do you feel my heartbeat Avon?" Avon bashfully smiled and before she said anything he added, "I thought you might have, because you've been right next to my heart for awhile." Then, Avon felt the entire body blushing sensation again while Valentin softly explained, "I just tossed a star from above to you." He mimicked catching a star forming a fist with his hand in the air and he brought it to her. Then, Avon confirmed what he meant in the kitchen a couple of days earlier. As he was indeed, romancing her; and not knowing how to react she blushed. After that, he assigned a corner next to her chair to place the imaginary stars he was catching in the air for her. Valentin noticed how bashful Avon was and trying to break the ice, he said, "Your innocence strikes me like an arrow from above directly into my heart Avon." And at the same time; he placed his hand on his chest imitating with his face as if an arrow had just hit him in the heart which brought Avon to giggle. So far, Avon and Valentin's eyes had not encountered yet, because Avon was shy and she was avoiding eye contact with him.

Then distracting her eyes with the food in her plate Avon asked, "Would you tell me about *Dark Matter*, Valentin."

"Certainly" he said and he explained, "In Science, *Dark Matter* is considered as the unknown and to me *God Almighty* is as unknown as *Dark Matter*, so when I refer to *Dark Matter* is not from the scientific approach." Avon had learned about *Dark Matter* in her studies and being such an atypical topic; she was interested in Valentin's opinion. He added, "*Dark Matter* is important to me because I sense it in my heart all the time."

"Would not be simpler to say *God* like everyone else says in the West?" Avon asked wondering his perception of a higher power.

"Well–" he hesitated and then he said, "*Dark Matter* is neuter; *God* implies masculinity and what I feel in my heart identifies more with *Dark Matter*." She smiled expressing agreement and Valentin added, "You have the most beautiful smile I have ever seen before Avon." She responded with another smile but she was far-off thinking of his words about *Dark Matter* while distracting her eyes and avoiding his, spreading butter all over a piece of bread.

Avon and Valentin continued celebrating with the family; although both of them were anxious to find a private moment to share more about *Dark Matter*, stars and the war of romantic arrows flying from above and below they were having. Christmas dinner must have been just about the third course at that stage challenging them with very little opportunity to talk and time seemed eternal to them. The next chance Valentin had he asked openly, "Avon, how are you getting to the airport when you go back to America?" Then she glimpsed at Xavier looking for an answer but Valentin kept talking, "If you'd like, I'll be pleased to drive you." Clearly, she

"When the philosopher points to the stars, the fool's eyes are fixed on the finger."

couldn't decline his chivalrous propose and she accepted his offer on the spot.

As the meal took course after course and yet, another course; they ate, drank, laughed and enjoyed with everyone. Unawares, Avon was entering into another dimension gradually pulling her away from everything she appeared to know as a normal life up till then. Every minute passing by was increasingly stirring up her senses and she was feeling a rare attraction toward Valentin the farmer which was bouncing her heart back and forth in wonder; because she could've been setting herself up for disenchantment being that she was there just for the Christmas celebration going back to America shortly after. On the other hand, the farmer didn't seem to be wondering at all for his connection to *Dark Matter* defined his naked truth, gallant rareness and genuineness; being that he had no intention to hide his source from anyone, in particular from himself.

While dessert was being served, the girls brought a Chess game to the table to play with Avon. They had been looking for the Chessboard since Avon's arrival; because they had tried to persuade her playing other games with them and Avon had told them that the only game she played was Chess. So, they were ready to play Chess during dessert with her. However, there was a slight inconvenience, as the girls couldn't decide which of the four should play first. Then, they began behaving their ages, demanding attention, tossing fits and pulling the Chessboard from each other's hands. They were disputing who should play before the other and suddenly, Valentin managed the moment saying, "Girls! Girls! I am going first and I play quick. In the meantime, you might want to unite and settle who plays next; what about it, eh?" He gave the girls no option, but to hand the Chessboard to him and they stopped debating. Evidently, Avon wasn't even aware that the humble farmer played Chess.

Meanwhile, when Valentin was talking to the girls, Avon perceived a glow spreading-out over him; a magical presence allowing her to appreciate the correlation between her Arolf and what Valentin called *Dark Matter*—the unknown Energy source.

Also, when observing Valentin's kindness to the girls; Avon felt charmingly more attracted to him. Probably because the girls were familiar with him they felt comfortable; but when the girls accepted Valentin's suggestion without objection everyone felt a moment of peace.

Tossing a reflection to the air...

"Apparently in war; the loser is the one that runs out of expendable people to expose to death sooner. However, the audacity of victory rests in the wits and has nothing to do with killing."

Avon had learned to play Chess from the doctor's approach which was a bit different than the norm; he taught her that competing was for fools and as she was getting ready to play Chess with Valentin; she remembered the doctor's words *"The essence of the game is to develop a strategy to corner the king. Neither of the players is looking out to destroy the king. Bear in mind my dear, the king cannot be held captive, once the king is cornered, the game is over. Every piece is a symbolic member of a kingdom and in course to the objective each piece risks to be held captive; however never destroyed. There would be a tragic situation for a Chess player if a piece belonging to a specific Chessboard is misplaced, much less destroyed. The game of Chess cultivates not destruction*

"When the philosopher points to the stars, the fool's eyes are fixed on the finger."

but honorable warriors instead. There is a difference between surviving in
battle for a humanitarian cause and competing to win for gold or fame."

Therefore, Avon had developed her own personal approach
when playing Chess and she noticed that once the opponent revealed
their strategy in the game; she could perceive the player's essence,
true intention and approach to life. She also noticed that any game
could be played with honor; without diminishing the opponent's
hope, or aggressively destroying the very spirit of a being; because
as a winner, she wouldn't be much better in the midst of tomorrow
when facing a different opponent anyway.

The doctor also shared words of wisdom teaching Avon what
competition was all about saying *"Competition nourishes the incapacity*
of a human being. While in competition there is only one winner, at the
heart of creativity, anyone is capable of excelling allowing ideas to emerge
by thinking and generating many great minds instead. Some might kill one
person out of greed in order to win in competition and as a result they become
murderers; whereas great creative warriors kill hundreds united in battle for a
humanitarian cause to defend the weak and as a result, they become heroes."

At any rate, when Avon played Chess, she exposed herself
revealing to the opponent her true intention, her approach to life and
her essence as well. Therefore, Avon and Valentin the farmer were
about to confront a Christmas surprise that they didn't anticipate.

Tossing a reflection to the air…

"The winning joy is the shortest joy there is; for the 'best' is
only the 'one best' until the next 'best one' appears."

15

Her eyes were fixed as if she was looking through a passage into the heavens while his sparkling lucid azure eyes were gently opened looking back at hers inviting her into the vastness of the infinite. She observed the long, thick and abundant golden eyelashes around the intense indigo eyes she was profoundly staring at, and all of a sudden, Avon and Valentin realized that their eyes had met for first time.

His eyes reflected a rapture of fervor in her heart and she didn't know how to react. Avon gazed at his eyes with such intensity; Valentin felt like he was being set on fire inside. At least by getting ready to play Chess; she had an excuse to stare at his eyes as far as others were concerned, because Avon couldn't take her eyes away from Valentin's. They were immersing in the same dimension together. The Energy surrounding them was such; they were able to sense their hearts' throbs in between the space, about the scope of a Chessboard, separating them. Valentin gentleness combined with certain natural seductive rareness that some Europeans flirt with; magnetized Avon toward a new area. His consideration projected modesty and at the same time a romantic craziness when in a soft

"When the philosopher points to the stars, the fool's eyes are fixed on the finger."

tone he addressed her as precious and he asked, "Would you mind if your new set of eyes look away to place the Chess pieces on the board precious? I'll place yours as well." And he ardently winked at her. Since she didn't seem to be able to look away; he blindly gave his eyes to her letting her know in a considerate manner that he would not look away impolitely and that they should begin the game; which in fact allowed Avon to regain sanity, because for all she could tell his eyes were turning her romantically insane.

Then Valentin mentioned that he wasn't going to be able to concentrate on the game and he suggested, "I feel a bit distracted. Would you mind playing to learn about each other precious?" Avon was melting inside and not knowing how to react; she asked if he didn't play to win and he kindly replied addressing her as Queen, "There might not be an actual winner in the game of Chess other than a great warrior figuring out a strategy to endure through wits and not through force, Queen."

As they began playing, they felt slowly dragged into each other submerging in a realm where once inside it, not many would want to escape. The game lasted long enough and both of them played well.

Out of courtesy, Valentin took the liberty of making the first move and whispered, "The more Chess is played, the better the player," and he looked at her as if he wanted to penetrate her through her eyes. She was static and she remained quiet. After she made her move, making his next move he added saying tenderly, "Just like life my Queen; the more life is experienced, the greater the person." Avon made her move erupting of Energy in her heart and sensing how he made her feel.

Then she asked, "How could life be like a Chess game Valentin?"

He replied saying softly, "When stumbling upon life barriers, at times, it feels like when a piece is captured by the opponent in the game," and he captured one of her horses adding, "Isn't the feeling of losing a piece quite the same gorgeous?" Avon didn't reply trying concentrate on the game.

As they continue moving pieces she said, "Life would be a very long Chess game."

He looked intensely into her eyes saying, "Well, life might be just a game, but not to be taken as serious as a Checkmate lovely." After making his move, he went further saying, "I don't really have a point but I would say this: most Chess players would pay more attention to the game than life itself." He tossed her another passionate wink. Just then, Avon was facing Check and when she defended her King drawing his attention toward his Queen; he instantly captured her Queen in exchange for his. At that moment, Avon was able to perceive the essence Valentin held within.

The man before her projected self confidence, courtesy, integrity, kindness, principles, respect, and a mix of rare attributes along with some unaltered characteristics not indicating that he was just an abandoned insignificant farmer as Jaidee had said. Also, Valentin reflected an uncommon sagacity; feeling like safeguard to Avon. She had not perceived it from anyone in the past and she wondered if he was reflecting protection toward the children. In any case, she had never encountered a man who behaved like Valentin did, as not far from them was the man Avon once considered to be a *Prince Charming*–Xavier. However for all she could tell, Xavier was practically fading away in contrast to Valentin that evening. Then again, Valentin couldn't help noticing Avon's innocent fascination toward him which he had never experienced with anyone before but he didn't mind to entertain at all.

At the end, Valentin honorably demonstrated to be quite a warrior by defeating Avon on the Chess game.

"When the philosopher points to the stars, the fool's eyes are fixed on the finger."

While they were playing Chess Xavier and the girls stepped away, and being Christmas, Jaidee had taken the liberty of enjoying a bit. So, right after they finished the game Jaidee asked Valentin to dance with her. Valentin politely accepted and stood up taking his suit jacket off following the fast pace music that Jaidee had selected to play. Then Avon slowly noticed what she had never neglected when being attracted to someone before. The insignificant farmer, Valentin, had a shape and a form.

Avon had not even noticed his gorgeous golden locks pulled back and tied up in a ponytail. She had not noticed that he was quite well shaped revealing a straight backbone and a robust figure through the shirt and trousers that he wore. When Avon observed him while he danced with Jaidee, Valentin's physique attracted her even more. She thought that those curves were the reflection of perfection, at least from the angle where she was looking at him. Then the Energy Avon had felt standing in the middle of the kitchen intensified as seconds went by. Valentin seemed to enjoy being admired and while he danced; he tossed quick winks to her. He was experiencing the revolving romantic emotions as well; he danced looking at Avon and she sat observing him while he danced with her friend.

By the romantic winks, arrows, and stars being tossed around the midst of *Dark Matter* during dinner, Jaidee had already noticed a couple of loving seeds sort of planted right in the middle of her dining room. So, intending to fertilize the seeds to flourish; she had arranged for Xavier to retire for the night, and at that stage; the girls were in their respective rooms resting as well. Then, the last thing Jaidee had planned before retiring for the night herself was to invite Valentin for dinner the next evening which he accepted right away. As Jaidee left them alone to dance the rest of the night off; Valentin performed a sort of knightly reverence bow bending a knee and inclining his head toward Avon soliciting the next dance.

Then, as soon as Avon stood up accepting to dance; he approached her but he didn't touch her. From a very close distance; he observed her every curve as she danced slowly following his lead. There must have been some music playing in their ears, because the music Jaidee had left playing was rather quick.

At the heart of the Energy built up between their two bodies; Valentin touched Avon's back, so tenderly, it almost hurt her. Desperately driven by an agonizing desire of his touch; she turned around and she embraced him. When Valentin sensed Avon's entire body shaking like a lost feather gliding in the air; he embraced her back strongly; he carried her holding her tight and sat cuddling her on his lap.

Since Avon didn't seem to be ready to let him go; Valentin gently reclaimed his neck back with his rough hands tender touch. Just then, Avon perceived Arolf's safe haven and she surrendered her entire body into Valentin's firm and strong muscular arms. He held her sturdy supporting her firmly and they looked at each other without saying a word for a long while sensing their ardent beings infuse into one Energy source.

After awhile, Valentin stood up allowing Avon to take the seat and he knelt on one knee facing her. His eyes were fixed on hers. He held her hands softly with his rough but gentle touch and he asked, "Would you allow me to kiss you gorgeous?" By then Avon was ready to allow him to kiss any part of her body if he wished; however, Valentin expressed calmness bringing an air of insane romance into the intriguing passion between them. He was experiencing emotions he had never felt and he was wondering about his previous romances; for at that moment he questioned in his mind if he had ever experienced any romance at all. When he found himself facing Avon; he reacted natural but restraining his instincts as in different circumstances he would have crossed

"When the philosopher points to the stars, the fool's eyes are fixed on the finger."

the intimacy boundaries long before. He felt like exploring and expanding into a more intense depth within the adventure of their connection. He was enjoying the anticipation of discovering what Avon held within especially for him. Even though, he had already learned about Avon's essence while playing Chess; he perceived worth waiting to disclose her mysterious innocent soul slowly and when Avon nodded assent submissively allowing him to kiss her; he tenderly placed his thin, warm and slightly moist lips on the back of her trembling left hand.

Valentin was stirred by Avon and his thirst to learn about her felt almost insatiable. After kissing her hand tenderly; he stayed in the same posture and asked, "My loving Avon do you have a connection with *Dark Matter?*"

Avon felt such an intense Energy bond at that moment; she expressed instinctively, "Yes Valentin, *Dark Matter* is my source and my only priority." Then she conveyed the emotions she was experiencing toward him feeling completely exposed and vulnerable. In response; he listened to her attentively as if he had not yet noticed what she was verbalizing. She also said in wonder, "Shall we live the moment and move on as we were before we met? I will be going back to America in a few days and we will be separated by land and ocean Valentin." He felt like the more Avon spoke, the more her glow reflected into him. However, he didn't even want to think to separate from her. Little by little, Avon calmed down regaining serenity and she continued talking and expressing facts of life. But to Valentin, her words began echoing soundless inside his mind just like the reflection of an immense shooting star and he didn't seem to need ears to hear what she was saying. The radiance he was progressively absorbing from Avon when she spoke to him was penetrating the core of his being. Then she finally ceased trembling saying, "Everything happens for a reason Valentin, we were meant to meet and there would be a future explanation for this occasion." They both felt like their entire bodies were extracting the Energy from one another attracting each other like magnets. So, as intense as the moment was for both of them; they agreed that their encounter wasn't a common romance, much less a one night stand. They had stepped into an entire new realm which they were hardly equipped to understand.

Avon spoke about confronting solitude and when they realized that they had similar concepts regarding faith based on the same source, the two were mesmerized. Valentin stood up finding himself in the midst of vast space; as Avon's words seemed to have an effect of comprehension in him that he couldn't explain. He felt like his brain had been pierced allowing an interconnection of ideas to expand at the highest speed which after many years of trying to discern, suddenly by listening to her everything made sense as cohesive thoughts within his wits.

After having such an intense encounter; they sat side by side on a swing in the back porch of the house sharing more thoughts and conversation. The more they spoke, the more companionable they felt. They prepared some herbal tea and they relaxed surrounded by the serenity of the stars crowning the moon while sipping hot tea and talking. They spoke about intimacy and they felt good for not trespassing to that phase right away. They both agreed that it would've been traumatic being intimate with each other in such an intense emotional state. Valentin thought that if he had been intimate with Avon right then and there just to satisfy his desires without considering the consequences; he would've felt dishonored afterward. Because she was trembling like a defenseless bird and although she expressed her desire for him; she was only looking for his touch nothing else, as she wasn't thinking of intimacy just yet; contrary to what Valentin's instinctive reaction was as a male.

"When the philosopher points to the stars, the fool's eyes are fixed on the finger."

Next morning, Avon had hardly slept. Valentin had left at dawn separating from her with an immense desire to meet her in the evening for dinner. Avon couldn't sleep because her entire being was revolving from continent to continent wondering what would be like when departing and leaving behind the Energy she had exchanged with Valentin.

During breakfast, brief comments and quips about the romantic sparkles between Avon and Valentin were made. While Jaidee was excited for them, Xavier comments seemed derisive and Avon wondered if Xavier's reaction was due to Jaidee's excitement.

Around midday, Avon received a call from Valentin on her mobile. He asked if she had slept well and if she was in disposition to meet him again; and if so, he requested for her to prepare to spend the night with him after having dinner with Jaidee and Xavier. Avon was hesitant about spending the night with him but Valentin said, "I'll drive you back at any time during the night if you are not comfortable. I just want to be with you in private princess." Then, he mentioned that Xavier had already told him not to bring her back later than ten the following morning and Avon sensed the same feeling she did during breakfast when Xavier made a couple of sarcastic remarks about her and Valentin. Naturally, she didn't feel comfortable with Xavier and Valentin making plans for her behind her back.

So in response Avon asked "Does Xavier tell you what to do Valentin?"

Then, Valentin clarified his intentions explaining, "Precious, you are Xavier's guest and it's only proper for me to follow certain etiquette. Don't get upset, I only want to be with you and my intentions are pure."

"I am sorry. I am genuine as well Valentin" she apologized for overreacting.

Then he said "It isn't a curfew lovely, it's just that Xavier has plans for tomorrow."

"I want to be with you as well and every minute that passes by, I feel like time is wasted if we are not together while I am around," she said. Then, they ended the phone call agreeing to spend the night together.

Avon prepared an overnight bag enthused as she could hardly wait to see Valentin's eyes again. However, Xavier plans were not in Avon or Valentin's favor at all. Before going out for dinner, Xavier beckoned Avon to join him in the living area for a private talk. Then, he told her to reconsider her attraction toward Valentin saying, "You must realize that pursuing a long distance relationship between you two is impossible. Enjoy your fling and afterward, I advise you to forget about Valentin." Avon listened with composure and alertness. She knew that when socializing she would confront challenges but she never anticipated that Xavier, a man who she had high regards for, would become the challenge between her and Valentin.

During the time Avon had been there, Xavier didn't speak much with her as he evaluated her like he would his wife; being that they were born in the same country. So Xavier assumed that Avon was the same girl that when he had last seen her and that she would follow his lead. However, Avon instantly realized that Xavier's advice was useless to her. Xavier had no basis to evaluate her, let alone advise her about how to feel toward Valentin, unless he had something terrible to disclose about him but it wasn't the case. Avon sensed Xavier's disguise at once; his actual intent was far from concern regarding her or Valentin for she felt like Xavier was more like protecting himself. Avon listened to him serenely and well aware as the granny's words echoed in her mind like a *silent wave* but then, the words were in reverse saying *Avon you have lived*

"When the philosopher points to the stars, the fool's eyes are fixed on the finger."

forty years without Xavier's advice, you can perfectly live another forty years without Xavier's advice as well. Also, when Xavier challenged the possibility to pursue a long distance relationship with Valentin; Xavier awakened Avon's senses from a different approach, since he was speaking about impossibilities to a great supporter of possibilities. Then again, Xavier ignored the strengths Avon possessed because after she had learned some and experienced more; she was aware that encountering a challenge on her path meant only one thing; an opportunity to expand into purification, and usually, every challenge brought a blessing attached to it. So, Xavier ignored that Avon didn't approach challenges as threats but as opportunities to purify her inner-self.

Then, Avon asked, "Anything else you might have in mind Xavier?"

Xavier replied, "I'm uncomfortable, because Valentin is clearly out of your league Avon. I'm sure that as soon as you go back to America and run into men dressed in suits and wearing shiny shoes; you will forget about this insignificant farmer." Avon didn't say much after Xavier's remark; as she didn't care to understand what "*Being out of a league*" meant in the dating field. Thus she relaxed allowing the situation to develop naturally; as if it wasn't for Arolf and their connection through *Dark Matter*, Valentin and her wouldn't have met to begin with and she just hoped to enjoy the rest of her stay.

Shortly after the interaction between Avon and Xavier, Valentin arrived and Xavier seemed annoyed. However, when Avon said in the phone that she wanted to spend as much time as possible with him; Valentin's intention was to please her by going to dinner in his car together instead of meeting in the restaurant as Xavier had instructed.

Valentin looked smart in casual wear and Avon noticed more and more his gorgeous shape. He was a couple of years older and at least half a head taller than her. His bronzed skin tone enhanced his azure eyes. His golden locks pulled back in a ponytail glowed with the evening sunbeams while the sun was fixing to set.

Valentine was polite; although, he didn't get carried away. His conduct was part of his natural rareness. He brought no bouquet of flowers, no chocolates and no candies. Valentin was there to take Avon to a dinner organized by Jaidee and Xavier, as going to dinner wasn't his idea but theirs.

At the restaurant, Avon and Valentin learned that they were celebrating Jaidee and Xavier's upcoming wedding anniversary and since Avon would be gone by the actual date, Jaidee wanted to celebrate while she was still there. They enjoyed dinner and at the end of the evening; after kissing Jaidee and Xavier goodnight, Avon walked with Valentin to his car. Yet, Xavier was unkind; he reminded the curfew time in a commanding tone to Valentin from the distance and Jaidee interfered telling him to let them go. Avon sensed Xavier's controlling intent, while Valentin disregarded his imposition because he knew that Xavier was just trying to embarrass him. However, Avon ignored that if something was a challenge for Xavier was to embarrass Valentin. At any rate, once Avon and Valentin got into the car; he held her hand kissing it and said, "Everything is fine lovely. Let's enjoy our valued time together." She smiled agreeing with him and while driving; Valentin explained, "I wanted to bring you to a proper place princess, but most of the lodgings in town are booked during the holidays. I hope you don't mind me bringing you to my humble home."

Avon asked excited, "Are you taking me to the caravan?"

"Yes, I am" he confirmed. Valentin was a bit surprised by her reaction but he didn't care to question how she had learned about his caravan.

"When the philosopher points to the stars, the fool's eyes are fixed on the finger."

Tossing a reflection to the air...

"Not everyone expressing attention approaches with a good intention."

16

⚬⚬

When they arrived at the caravan, Valentin politely opened the car passenger's door for Avon, making her feel like she was about to step on the red carpet; except that she was about to walk on a path that he had improvised with old pieces of plywood covering the sludge on the ground for her not to get her shoes dirty. As they walked to the caravan's entry, Avon noticed that the path continued further but she didn't pay much attention where it led. Valentin opened the caravan's door and turned around facing her. Next, he stepped backward inviting her in and she stepped forward following his lead. Once inside he said, "Welcome to my nest, it's small, but here is where I live; would you like to seat?" Indicating for her to sit in the only place at hand, his bed.

Avon was amazed because the tiny caravan seemed smaller from outside than what it was being inside. The small area was well organized. Valentin seemed to have the basics. He had a TV, a tiny kitchenette and it felt certainly warmer than the restaurant they had just left.

As soon as she sat on his bed; he sat crossed-legged on the floor facing her. Then, he showed her a kettle to boil water so that they

"When the philosopher points to the stars, the fool's eyes are fixed on the finger."

could prepare an assortment of herbal teas. He also had chocolates, cookies, and sweets to enjoy with their tea. After that, he reached into the fridge taking out a bunch of wild flowers and he tenderly expressed, "I picked these flowers myself for you princess. Every shop was closed today." Avon received the flowers with her heart feeling like all the bouquets she had received in the past weren't as wonderful as Valentin's bunch of wild flowers were and tears rolled down her face when he handed them to her. Valentin never thought that the insignificant flowers would impress her so and gently touched her tears with his rough hands saying, "My intention was to see your smile precious, not to make you cry."

Avon replied, "These are tears of joy Valentin, I cannot possibly be crying because at this moment I am the happiest woman in the world." Then, he took the same posture from the prior night; except, he knelt in both knees while facing her. His strong arms embraced her tenderly allowing her to feel his chest against hers. He smelled her neck moving slowly and after briefly touching her left ear with his thin soft lips; he kissed her cheek. Their lips were almost touching. He slid his hands behind her neck and softly passed his fingers through her hair holding the back of her head gently. His eyes looked at hers. Then, he approached slowly closer and closer for their lips to meet for the first time and they kissed.

Their kiss was patient and tasty, passionate but not desperate. They kissed gently wild like the flowers were increasing into a moderate interchange of breaths. They knew there would be time to kiss again; it wasn't the last kiss but the first one; the kiss was special and they enjoyed it to the fullest. Although, Avon didn't know what she enjoyed the most if the kiss, or when they stopped kissing and he hissed in her ear, "Princess, I am *in* Love with you."

The feeling as if she was melting inside intensified as seconds went by and they both allowed Energy to flow. The surroundings were peaceful, harmonic and calm. The time to surrender to each other had finally arrived; with the exception of a last decision pending for Avon to make; as when she surrendered to Arolf, her hesitation was within; however, surrendering physically to another being entailed to depend. She was faithfully committed to depend on *Dark Matter* intangibly, but she had to be ready to commit physically to Valentin.

In a matter of seconds, Avon was as ready as Valentin was to immerse into the bubble of Love not caring if they fell *in* without ever finding the bottom. She reacted instinctively and she decided to commit. She had already taken her shoes off by the entry door and after he said that he was *in* Love with her with no reservations or expecting a response; she felt unleashed. So, she pulled her legs up on the bed and she invited him to join her.

He slid into the bed approaching her delicately and he supported her with one arm strongly bringing her body close to him. Then, she was able to feel every inch of his and he was feeling every curve of hers. The time they were making-out was a short eternity. They traveled to the infinite and returned unified. By then, there were fairly ready to merge into the unknown midst of space where they were to discover their properness to unite, as *Dark Matter*'s presence was sensed by both of them. Except that surrendering moments were special to Avon and regardless of the arousal; she couldn't help to wonder if they should have a ceremony. However, she realized that during the course of intimate unity the involvement entailed two physical bodies and one life-force. Thus, as long as Arolf was present in their hearts; no other presence was required when having the blessing from the greatest romantic match maker of all times—Love.

Avon and Valentin's hearts were throbbing at the same pace anticipating a merger into one another in perfect harmony.

"When the philosopher points to the stars, the fool's eyes are fixed on the finger."

They discovered being equipped to implement complete Energy absorption and in the middle of their intense passion, desire, kissing, and touching each other; they became aware of their warm undressed bodies.

Valentin gently laid Avon on her back while his body naturally took place above hers immersing themselves into the midst of as above so below; as below so above corresponding to each other and reaching amalgamation of two souls into expansion of the all.

Tossing a reflection to the air...

"The trust of commitment uniting two has nothing to do with the physical presence of three but with one powerful Energy of Love fusion of two souls which defeats any public ceremony."

After they reached rapture several times; Avon found herself in a rather embarrassing moment for she couldn't find the restroom door in the tiny caravan. There was only one door leading outside but that was it. There were no other doors. Valentin was amusing himself as she gave up looking for doors and she was completely lost trying to figure out which crack in the little place led to the restroom. So, covering her with a fluffy fresh bath robe; he opened the door for her and politely pointed out the way to the outhouse. She must have really thought that she was in a fairytale where restrooms hid behind walls inside small caravans. Then, she figured out where the improvised plywood path continued leading and she had no option but to leave the cozy caravan and walk out to the privy.

The outhouse was lit with big aromatic candles set on a shelf; there were fresh towels and the necessary basics. A portable heater kept the area warm and there was also a shower in a corner. Avon was impressed by Valentin's sense of consideration as he had followed her with a bowl of warm water in case she'd like to use it as a bidet. Observing the surroundings, a new discovery revealed when she realized that the odor she sensed from Valentin a few days earlier was the scent of a hard working man who feared not to dirty his hands which she had never been exposed to in the past. At the same time as she was using the things that were placed for her comfort in the outhouse; she felt the safeguard sensation from Valentin again. The same feeling that she felt when they were about to play Chess the previous night and she realized that what she was sensing from him was his vigorous sense of survival. Being in the outhouse; Avon was able to appreciate that in such a short period of time Valentin had come up with spontaneous ideas and he had improvised. Then, she felt his endurance and sagacity sheltering her understanding that regardless of any situation she could encounter while being next to Valentin; he wouldn't hesitate to build a shack and he would probably hunt for food if necessary to survive and stay alive. She absorbed the drive of determination in him; as his stamina would allow him to protect her and endure every circumstance. Unlike most who would offer to die for their Love one, Valentin was not indicating that he was ready to die for her in any way; on the contrary, he was a man that was utterly equipped to survive by her side for Love, not to die. All of a sudden, while in the outhouse; Avon sensed trust, refuge, safekeeping, wellbeing, and total peace of mind.

Afterward, while having some tea, they spoke of many subjects; existence, life-force, and topics which not many would opt to speak about on the first romantic night; however after satiating each

"When the philosopher points to the stars, the fool's eyes are fixed on the finger."

other physically, sharing their individual perspective about being seemed to bring as much satisfaction as physical sexual pleasure to them; even though sensuality was sensed in every conversation. The more she spoke, the more fascinated Valentin was with her and she was strongly attracted to him as well, especially when he merged Physics with her Meta approach, sort of materializing her ideas.

They were yet to encounter challenges as the first night together was just a taste of what could be the greatest Christmas gift they had ever received. Still, they had to make conscious decisions to surpass the barriers found along the way to claim each other as gifts. When merging willingly, their intention was to entrust each other without aiming to distract one another from their individual passion and purposes in life. Their intent was not to change one or the other; as they were to remain genuinely respectful, honest and truthful in every aspect of their union as a couple allowing themselves to expand in life individually. Their habits, hobbies, dislikes, likes; favorite films, colors, food, and songs were minor concerns in contrast to the challenges they were about to confront in order to have more of what they had just savored; because up till then, they didn't seem to have anything in common apart from being blindly faithful to the same source of Love.

Then, they rested a couple of hours and when they woke up; it was time for Avon to return to their friends' home which didn't make sense; as even Jaidee disagreed with the fact that they had to be back when Xavier told them so. At any rate, thanks to social protocol, it would have been inappropriate for Avon to spend the rest of her visit in Provence only with Valentin. So, they just had to be prudent regarding Xavier's manipulative ways.

When they returned to their friends' home, Xavier told Valentin to leave because the family had plans with Avon and referring to her as their guest he said, "We have plans to enjoy our guest and you should leave Valentin. Avon won't be seeing you again." Upset with Xavier's imposition; Jaidee intervened suggesting for Valentin to return later in the evening and if they wanted to spend some time together; they certainly should see each other any time they wanted. Avon was tired and she found Jaidee's suggestion reasonable; so, Avon walked Valentin out to his car settling to meet later that night.

Xavier had plans for the family, including Avon but excluding Valentin, to visit relatives out of town who they had only visited once in the past. Jaidee was annoyed because they had not been invited and she didn't want to visit practically strangers without an invitation. Yet, the family had to follow Xavier's lead and off they went visiting relatives out of town for the rest of the day.

Xavier extended the visit as much as he could to prolong their return. When driving back; he expressed resentment in relation to Avon and Valentin's romance. Essentially, Xavier's intention seemed to be to separate them. Little did Xavier know, because Avon and Valentin's unrest during the hours Xavier impeded for them to be together, instead of driving them away from each other, purely solidified their merger.

When the family returned late in the evening; Valentin was waiting outside their house. Avon got off Xavier's car and desperately ran looking to embrace Valentin. They met in the middle of the road like she had been captive for days and after having a quick chat with Jaidee; Avon left to spend the night with Valentin.

By then, he had found an available room at a guest-house for them to spend the night comfortably, and when they arrived; somehow he had managed to arrange total privacy for them at the lodge's lounge. So before going up to the room; they sat by the fireplace enjoying a bottle of bubbly and the lounge all to

"When the philosopher points to the stars, the fool's eyes are fixed on the finger."

themselves. And even if they didn't want to misuse time talking about Xavier; they couldn't escape from doing so.

Valentin was plain when he explained the situation to Avon which might have not been what seemed to be. He clearly said, "Don't pay attention to Xavier. He disguises pretending to protect Jaidee and the girls. Since you're a woman; he might want to control you. Xavier doesn't occupy his mind constructively, princess."

"What do you mean luv?" Avon asked.

"Well, when his parents were living, he seldom came to visit and he never did much for them. All I know is that I was the one taking them to doctor's appointments when they were ill and most of the time I fixed things around their house. Sometimes Xavier shows resentment for my kindness to his parents and other times he seems to regret not being there for them." She listened to him sipping wine and Valentin continued, "For the most part Xavier acts as an inept. He doesn't like to think. He cannot figure out how to fix a leak in his own kitchen sink; or how to fix the toilet for his own wife and for his own girls. He doesn't like to dirty his hands while his thoughts are filthy."

"Is that so?" Avon asked surprised.

"What?!" he exclaimed.

"Jaidee said that you do small jobs in their house for extra income" she said.

He guffawed and added, "I have been doing repairs in that old house for many years and after Xavier's father passed; it was harder for his mother to keep up with the stuff. Still, I do not charge money for my kindness precious." Avon kept sipping wine and listening, he kept talking, "Xavier claims he's unemployable, so he doesn't work. They have means to live well, I suppose; but he never paid for my kindness princess."

Avon was wordless, but she found words to ask, "Do you know why Jaidee was upset when you helped bringing the Christmas tree into the house, luv?"

"I didn't notice much as I was busy with the tree; she asked me if the children were in town and when I said that they were not coming this year, she invited me for Christmas dinner. I didn't answer because I was sure that Xavier wouldn't want me around."

"Xavier claims that you are friends. Was he using you just to help with the tree then?"

"Friendship has nothing to do with being humane princess. Xavier's prejudice wouldn't let him be kind to me. Being that I am from Eastern Europe and not French; before Xavier's eyes I am an insignificant second class citizen. I won't say much, except that I've noticed that Xavier makes Jaidee take the train to the airport when she travels abroad and I wouldn't have been the least surprised if after a couple of days, Xavier decided to send you by train to the airport as well." Then, Avon understood why Valentin offered and secured a ride to the Airport for her. Valentin said that Xavier and Jaidee had not lived in the farmhouse for long and that they had been neighbors just for a few years. He also clarified that he and his ex-wife were closer to Xavier's parents than Xavier ever was and that Valentin had been living and working in the farm since his arrival in France. So, Avon deduced that Xavier knew about Valentin through his parents who were Valentin's original neighbors and what Valentin knew about Xavier was that he was biased and he didn't enjoy repairing things around the house.

Avon and Valentin went up to their room and every time they experienced immersion into one; their merge was intensively vast. They integrated into the oneness of all and their souls expanded beyond the reproduction of a being.

At the guest house, having Valentin sleeping next to her, Avon considered how Jaidee reacted to see her again; because the evening Avon arrived Xavier said, "I haven't seen my wife express laughter for many years, your presence makes her happy Avon!"

"When the philosopher points to the stars, the fool's eyes are fixed on the finger."

And then her presence seemed to have also absorbed Xavier's daughter's attention when on Christmas Eve he mentioned, "Avon, you get along with my girls better than I do." In addition, she was captivating the attention and heart of Xavier's handy man and friend Valentin. So according to Avon, it was only natural for Xavier to feel helpless expressing his frustration with aggression while as a response of his conflict; he received kindness and respect from her. It was easy for her to suppose that out of irritation, Xavier's controlling manipulative thoughts were openly exposed. Avon admitted then that her presence must have been annoying to him. Not because she was unpleasant but something like too good to be true, almost nauseating; as her presence seemed to annoy some people to the point that they felt sick; just like she felt for not being well equipped when receiving a blessing and she decided to use that analogy to excuse Xavier for his conduct accepting that not many tolerated her presence. So, thanks to Xavier's rejection; she sort of figured out the reason why she felt out of place when she did; especially around her siblings. She also realized that if when she was alone, she had been challenged by others due to the glow the Shoe Shiner pointed out to her. Naturally, after the merger between Valentin and her, the glow must've have multiplied and seeing two people projecting so much Love must have bother Xavier and he might have felt out of his element. Besides, since she was practically immune to rejection at that point and truly accepted that not everyone had to be pleased with her presence; she decided to continue expressing kindness and respect to Xavier during the time she had left in Provence.

Back then, Avon was unaware that her purpose was no longer pursuing her childish dreams, as her childhood dreams were just about to be fulfilled. From then on, she was to reach full potential by extracting creativity from Energy. The combination of emotions she developed when joining Valentin where the precise dose of bliss she required to engage her natural emotional state in order to perform in perfect harmony and in accordance with the rest of the Universe. When meeting Valentin, Avon was at the verge of experiencing a true inner expansion and transformation. Thus she was better off making up her own assumptions, because the unknown was a step away from revolving her existence in the most unanticipated way.

The few days Avon remained in Provence went rather quick. She got to spend time with Valentin as well as with the girls and Jaidee and on New Year's Eve, when Valentin dropped her off at the airport, the moment was mostly difficult for their hearts.

Tossing a reflection to the air...

"The more one learns, the better understanding one attains; as long as one allows great ignorance and limited knowledge to be a reminder of how soon one forgets."

"When the philosopher points to the stars, the fool's eyes are fixed on the finger."

17

⬥

Avon's childhood ultimate dream was about to be fulfilled, but she didn't even remember. And although she felt like she was distilling throughout when thinking; she didn't have to think for long because she was no longer alone. For the first time ever there was a heart communicating with hers from other side of the world, Valentin's. She had the support of an intimate ally assisting her to make decisions without an agenda; not requesting anything in return; someone who was looking after her heart's wellbeing and embracing her with genuine Love.

Avon returned to San Fran from Provence trying to adapt to her daily routine; however deep in her heart she suspected what was coming her way. A few days after she arrived from France, while she was at work, Jimmy accidently locked up the payroll paperwork in the car when he was returning from the bank. The doctor was still in the East Coast and Jimmy didn't have much time. The staff was going to be looking for their paychecks soon and not knowing what to do; Jimmy called Avon at work to let her know. After Avon learned what was going on; she said on the phone, "I will send the auto-locksmith to open the car for you at once Jimmy."

"When the philosopher points to the stars, the fool's eyes are fixed on the finger."

"It wouldn't be a good idea Avon" said Jimmy. So, Avon suggested breaking the car window if necessary to get the paperwork to be able to pay the employees and that they could deal with the car repairs later.

However, Jimmy was not comfortable and he said, "Avon, the car is parked in front of your building and as you know this isn't the most quiet neighborhood in Nob Hill. There are people out and about everywhere and it's the same reason why I don't want a locksmith. If anyone sees me trying to break into the car; the cops will show up in a flash."

"Well, if the police show up explain that the car is in your custody and everything would be fine. Do not be paranoid about the police Jimmy. You are a great man." Avon said.

Then, Jimmy got a bit annoyed and he retorted, "Avon in case you haven't noticed my color and with my background; while I explain to the police that the car is in my custody, I'll be back in jail in no time."

"What do you mean *your* color? What color is that, Jimmy?" Avon asked in wonder.

So, raising his voice in an angry tone and stressing on the Ms., Jimmy said, "*Ms.* Avon I am an African American and—"

Then Avon interrupted him saying, "I do apologize, Jimmy; as a matter of fact, I had not noticed *your* color. I use glasses to enhance my sight for not to stumble around things; however opposite than most, *I do not feel what I see.* I perceive people as they intend to be through my blind heart Jimmy. I'll be right there with the auto-locksmith and if the police show up, just allow me to deal with them; calm down Jimmy, everything is fine."

At the same time, Avon realized that not long before there was a scandal in the news about a respectful professional who had been arrested when entering his home and the facts indicated that they had accused him of burglary for braking into his own house just because he fit the profile of African American suspects which clearly justified Jimmy's paranoia.

As a result, Avon walked away from a rather important meeting and although she explained that she had an emergency before she left work that day; the fact that she was such a great performer didn't seem to matter for Avon failed to notice that her emergency excuse would be taken as a conflict of *personal business* interest, hence improper. Clearly the Corporation's concern wasn't Avon's individual growth and due to that incident she was fired and terminated from her post.

At that point, the career was the only thing stopping Avon from attaining her ultimate childhood dream and to be with her loving Valentin. Because even though Avon's well appreciated career had reached the end and had served its purpose; Avon wouldn't have resigned from her job by herself. Her heart was too blind to understand that another purpose was waiting for her to disentangle from the social responsibility of chasing a career in order to manifest. Therefore, once she didn't have a job anymore; the Universe continued working in perfect harmony and around matters in sequence to place Avon where she was supposed to be.

Angelina and Gabe supported Avon and Valentin's romance completely and after losing her job; Avon expressed her anxiety and that she could hardly cope without Valentin. So, Angelina and Gabe encouraged Avon to go back to Europe and not to return until she was able to bring Valentin back to America with her. They couldn't do much for Avon from the opposite coast; except for *for-giving* the installments toward the down payment of the rental building during her absence. They settled to wait for the payments until Avon and Valentin returned from Europe together, and on top, not charging her an extra single penny on penalties. Avon gratefully accepted,

"When the philosopher points to the stars, the fool's eyes are fixed on the finger."

but she was amazed by her *sunshine* and Gabe's extreme generosity and confidence on her. Given that Avon wasn't going around the block for a promenade; she was actually leaving the country not knowing when she would return from another continent, and yet, Angelina and Gabe gave her a great sense of fulfillment by trusting her and encouraging her to go despite the fact that she owed them a significant amount of money. However, Angelina had worked with Avon and she admired her integrity; on the other hand, thanks to his "Gift," Gabe was more than confident to trust that Avon would return one day to repay her debt.

Once again, Avon was following her heart going after an unknown farmer that time; except that she knew that the unknown farmer was also *in* Love.

Meanwhile, the doctor and Jimmy were excited that Avon had found an intimate companion and they didn't hesitate to give their support. So, the doctor offered to look after the rental building as he used to do before selling it to her and having Jimmy's assistance made things even simpler for them. The doctor and Jimmy were under the impression that Avon had resigned from her job because she was *in* Love and with her discretion; she allowed them to perceive things as they seemed to be. Avon recognized that if there was anyone to blame for losing her job; she would figure out who was responsible eventually, as Jimmy had nothing to do with the situation for it wasn't Jimmy's fault to be part of a discriminatory and biased civilization in progress to expand into the transparency of truth at a snail's pace. So, Avon didn't even consider talking about the matter. She understood that at that point, explanations were useless. Besides, Avon sensed from heart to heart that Jimmy was, in fact, a transparent great man.

Once more, Avon prepared a couple of suitcases to move away. She didn't feel the same as she did in the past though; as she wasn't going somewhere just bouncing adrift. By then, she had nothing to seek anymore but someone to join. She prepared to manage most of her responsibilities through the internet from abroad while the doctor and Jimmy would look after the rental business for her. However, Avon also had a personal request for the doctor before she left. She had been unable to reach her father openly for some time due to her siblings' financial disputes claiming to protect their father's interests which resulted only on advantages for themselves. So, Avon requested from the doctor to keep in touch with her niece Mae passing messages between them. It was vital for everyone to keep her siblings unaware of Avon's whereabouts; as her siblings antagonism could have interfered with her intention to return to America in peace of mind.

⚃

Tossing a reflection to the air…

"No mind could conceive being part of a Universe functioning in Perfect Harmony unless blindly allowing life-force to provide what is deserved in life. After that, everything falls into perfect place and so does one."

⚃

From America to Europe

Valentin was waiting for Avon on her arrival at the airport in Marseille and they greeted each other excitedly by the baggage claim. While Avon excused herself to go to the restroom, Valentin ordered *lattés* at one of the airport's *cafés*. When Avon came back

"When the philosopher points to the stars, the fool's eyes are fixed on the finger."

and approached the table where Valentin was sitting with a fresh *latté* for her; he pulled a chair out inviting her to join him. After she sat, he remained seated as well. He held her left hand and tenderly kissed it. He reached inside his jacket pocket taking a ring out followed by a placid marriage proposal and in a teasing tone he said, "If you marry me princess, this ring will be yours. If not, you might as well take a flight back to America." Naturally Avon accepted the bribe and proposal on the spot, although she couldn't help to laugh. Everyone around them noticed that they had just gotten engaged and congratulated them; however no one could tell why the occasion seemed funny for the bribed bride-to-be.

Obviously Valentin couldn't wait to propose to his soon-to-be bride and he found a humorous excuse to pop-up the question right at the airport. However, when Avon was still in San Fran; they spoke about her engagement ring and he asked in the phone, "What is your favorite gem precious?"

Avon replied, "When I look at the ring I would like to think of you and your taste luv, would you mind selecting the gem for me?" Therefore, he selected a gorgeous sapphire cut adorned with diamonds around it which matched the only earring she wore and Avon absolutely adored when Valentin devotedly slid the gems mounted in the highest karat gold ring through her delicate ring finger.

During the short period of time that Avon was in San Fran, after she had returned from Provence, Valentin and she had exhausted every resource of information regarding immigration laws related to their situation. After she lost her job and being separated for a few weeks; their hearts were sad and about to explode. So, they realized that in order to be physically together, in the same country, not separating ever again, avoiding dealing with visas expirations and renewing immigration permits; they were better off getting married.

Following their conclusion, Valentin proposed for Avon to come to France and live with him so they could get married. She didn't have a job holding her back anymore and if he entered America as a tourist; they could've enjoy some time together, but it would have complicated matters in the future being that their aim was to reside in America not in Europe. So, Avon entered France as a visitor allowing her the maximum time granted for tourists to stay on a year period and they were hoping that that time was going to be enough to get all the paperwork required for their marriage, organized. Their intention was to be together not necessarily married, but in view of the circumstances before applying for any other visa or permits; Avon had to learn every legal detail about international marriage. She knew about cases that turned out rather complicated for couples not paying attention to details when requesting a fiancée visa, a marriage entry permit, or when hiring a third party to represent them.

The very first thing Avon learned was that getting a marriage certificate, or a marriage license as the document was known to her in America, was going to be their biggest challenge; because as an interracial couple they basically had to request permission from the authorities to unite in matrimony. Then she learned that after getting married, once a petition was submitted from one of the two *in* Love to sponsor the other as a permanent resident in the country where they were planning to reside together; the request would be at the mercy of immigration officials to determine the conditions for the two people *in* Love to finally unify in person; even if they paid fees to a third party like an immigrations attorney. If the circumstances reached a point where immigrations ordered for the petitioners to wait for sponsorship and the officials instructed one of the parties *in* Love to remain at their individual country of residence; nothing could be done except for the two *in*

"When the philosopher points to the stars, the fool's eyes are fixed on the finger."

Love to wait and most likely separated; until immigration officials approved or denied their union. Avon and Valentin were aware that corruption led to more corruption and money couldn't guarantee anything. They realized that people who didn't reside in the same country and became genuinely *in* Love had to go through the agony of waiting away from each other and many couples even gave up discouraged without pursuing Love at all.

Avon also learned that immigration officials' decision was based on the evidence the couple provided demonstrating true Love, and randomly, any request could be denied at once or delayed when insignificant mistakes were made. Therefore, the verification process could have taken years, while Valentin and Avon couldn't stay away from each other one more day.

Separation wasn't an option, absolutely not, because when learning and understanding the process; Valentin told Avon in a final tone, "We won't allow a forced separation due to an immigration status princess. Come to Provence and let's get married. Once we are together, I won't allow us to separate ever again. Not even for one day." And so, Avon was ready to put into practice every expertise and aptitude she possessed combined with her limited knowledge aiming for success on their first request and at expedite pace.

Their wedding wasn't going to be the typical wedding most celebrate; for as far as Avon and Valentin were concerned; they had already consummated their commitment the night in the caravan. So, they focused on complying with immigration official's requirements, laws, permits, forms, requests, demands, and their marriage statutes.

They also realized that for an interracial genuine couple to demonstrate their hearts' truthful meaning of Love before an immigration officer could be torturous at times; as no one would be exempt to follow the strictness of the process developed through the years due to others' fraudulent behavior when abusing the system. Notwithstanding Avon and Valentin had nothing to doubt in regards of being *in* Love; they were willing to follow every rule and regulation from any of the countries involved in order to obtain permission to unite in matrimony under the respective immigration law.

Tossing a reflection to the air...

"Thanks to the cruelty of consistency, discipline, laws, principles, and order; the Universe works in perfect harmony. Thus there is nothing cruel about human beings complying equally to form a civilized world."

So when Avon joined Valentin again; Valentin had rented a townhouse for a few weeks close to the farm where the caravan was. In the meantime, they were supposed to figure out where to create their temporary nest as a couple and sort-out their future. Nonetheless the more time they spent together sharing activities and responsibilities, the more they learned about each other and small details as well as big details began to emerge.

Naturally, during the first couple of weeks they were excited to be together and Valentin took Avon for short trips traveling around the south of France. He romanced her like she had never been romanced before. He brought her flowers, wined her and dined her. He took her to Niece for breakfast, Monte Carlo for

"When the philosopher points to the stars, the fool's eyes are fixed on the finger."

lunch, and San Remo for dinner visiting three countries in one day trip. However, Avon noticed that Valentin didn't allow her to pay for anything at all. He was spending to indulge her. He took her to Saint-Tropez, Cannes, and one day; they even went out into the Mediterranean Sea in a sail boat that he hired. What's more, he had taken her on a motorbike ride along Côte d'Azur and he seemed quite comfortable when letting her know that the BMW K 1600 GT bike belonged to him, and now, also to her.

By the end of their adventurous reencounter the townhouse rental term was about to expire and Avon had plenty of things to be concerned about. She seemed rather preoccupied. She was still pondering how she had managed to get fired from her job and a pile of paperwork was yet to be produced and organized. In addition, as much as she enjoyed the tiny caravan, when thinking that besides the motorbike the caravan was Valentin's only material possession; she considered that living in such a small area would be uncomfortable for both of them. So, one morning after breakfast while they were sitting at the table she suggested, "We should stay in this townhouse renting temporarily until we settle our affairs luv."

After Avon's suggestion Valentin expressed, "Do not concern about a place to live princess. You could pick one of the houses in the farm, and if you would like, I could even build a new house especially for you."

The farm was immense and Valentin was ready to please his loving future wife. Then again, Avon was serious and not joking around and with everything she had in her mind; she failed to pay attention to her loving Valentin. Thinking that Valentin was kidding she replied kindly but a bit bitter, "I would prefer not to complicate matters. It is temporary and I don't find appropriate to request from the owners of the farm to vacate the premises because *we* need a place to live. I will be pleased renting this small cottage

which is close to the farm for you to work and close to the caravan."
So then, Valentin realized that Avon actually had no clue that the
farm practically belonged to her. However, he had to be prudent
when explaining because Avon was frustrated.

Valentin stood up from his chair and he approached her
tenderly. Then, he tried to openly explain to his bride-to-be saying,
"My precious Avon, I know we are making serious decisions and
that you are not toying around."

"Correct" she stated.

"Well, allow me to explain something to you precious, I didn't
mean to sound witty with my suggestion and would you listen to
me attentively?"

"I am listening" she replied in a tense tone.

Then, looking intensely into her eyes he said firmly, "Both
houses in the farm where my caravan is—" and he paused for a
moment making certain that Avon was paying attention and he
repeated, "Both houses in the farm where my caravan is belong to
us precious because I am the owner of the farm."

At that moment Avon couldn't feel, sense, perceive and she
could hardly breathe. Avon was frozen momentarily while her mind
traveled in the highest speed and she remembered a reflection:
Nothing is the way it seems to be or not to be.

Logically, Avon couldn't avoid ignoring the unknown; or else,
she wouldn't have much to learn and explore in life, and most
certainly, she couldn't know it all. And even though the surprise
was pleasant; she was just learning that she wasn't exempt to be
fooled whenever she got distracted; so, she felt dumbfounded and
she didn't know how to react.

Valentin knelt down and held her tight where she was frozen
sitting at the table. He caressed her and Avon start apologizing for
not knowing; then, Valentin said kindly, "Some say, 'What you don't

"When the philosopher points to the stars, the fool's eyes are fixed on the finger."

know doesn't hurt you' but you seem to be hurting yourself for not knowing something that you weren't supposed to know in the first place."

"What do you mean I wasn't supposed to know Valentin?" She asked defensively, irritated and suspicious.

So, Valentin stood up and he walked to the kitchenette which was steps away from the dining area leaving Avon sitting by the table. Then, he spoke from where he was, "We are discovering each other and we have the rest of a lifetime to learn about the treasures that we hold in our hearts for one another. However, in the process we will also discover what we have materially and each others' flaws." She looked at him embarrassed and he added, "I told you that your innocence hits me like an arrow aimed from above entering directly into my heart and I mean—"

"I am sorry, luv, I didn't mean to underestimate you," she said interrupting him.

He waited for her to finish and then he said serenely but resolutely, "Do not interrupt me when I am speaking Avon. If you are not interested in what I have to say tell me so and I would be glad not speaking at all. I grant respect to everyone for *free*. Therefore, I will not make the slightest move to *earn* anyone's respect. Everyone is entitled to give out respect or to disrespect whoever they like. However, I will not tolerate anyone to disrespect me while I am present. I might not know much about myself; but I do know that one of my flaws is impatience; another one is that I dislike to be interrupted when I speak; let alone repeat or explain myself to someone who isn't paying attention. I must have other flaws and I'll discover them as I live life. So, I beg of you not to interrupt me when I speak. You are experiencing relocation and many changes. You lost a job, I know. I'll be tolerant and considerate toward you in that regard. Nonetheless, distrusting the unknown *about me* will only bring *you* conflicts. I have traveled a long path to encounter you; being *in* Love with you is the greatest happiness I have experienced in life so far. So, I am willing to compromise my flaws and I'll tolerate yours. I know it's a lot for you to assimilate thus let us allow things to unfold as they come." She was frozen again and terribly embarrassed. So, he continued, "As I was saying when you interrupted me, I mean what I express and there are many things that we will discover from each other and we should embrace those discoveries instead of challenging them, do you agree?"

At that point, tears were rolling down Avon's face out of guilt and embarrassment for overreacting and all she could say while sobbing was, "I Love you Valentin."

While Valentin was talking from the kitchenette he was preparing tea and he brought a cup to her. He sat at the opposite end of the table and he gained strength to be patient and explained himself to his loving princes. "When I was married, I lived in the main house of the farm." He paused and sipped tea.

"Yes, we delivered a Christmas card with Jaidee there," said Avon sniffling.

"After the divorce, I didn't need that much space for myself; so, I rented the main house. The cottage further away is rented as well." Then, Avon recalled that they also delivered a Christmas card there. Valentin continued explaining, "When the children visit, we usually travel and we stay in hotels."

"Who works the land?" Avon asked.

"I lease individual land parcels to farmers who don't have land and by working with *our* equipment, in *our* farm; they are able to generate an income to support their families. It's been a long time since I worked those parcels of land. Being by my own, the only thing that I enjoy doing around the farm is repairing the equipment when necessary, and at times, when I'm occupied with

"When the philosopher points to the stars, the fool's eyes are fixed on the finger."

other affairs, I just hire someone to deal with the repairs, but I keep busy enough," he replied.

All of a sudden, it seemed that the farmer and Avon had some things in common after all. However, Avon was feeling almost sick for not realizing that she wasn't to decide by herself anymore, as she had to make decisions with Valentin and even if she was *in* Love with him; she was just beginning to learn to be his companion in life. At the same time, she felt like a bubble adrift wondering if she deserved so much Love. She didn't doubt or reject any of the blessings she was finding along the way and she was receiving them as gifts with grace; but she also recognized that by then; she was settling in the soilless area where she had entered when she made her pact. She felt like she was in a different dimension where she would be exposed to unforeseen and endless possibilities which she would have to adapt at her own pace and as they came from the unknown to her.

Avon appeared to be completely distracted and floating in the clouds; so, Valentin suggested, "Princess, would you like to go and visit our farm?" Then, Avon got up, she approached him and she sat on his lap cuddling him and holding him tight.

Valentin caressed her for a long while, and finally, she suddenly let him go and she stood up exclaiming, "Yes, let us go and visit the farm!"

Valentin was experiencing the floating sensation in a different way, as he absorbed the purity and innocence Avon projected. He actually perceived his own reflection when being around her giving him a great sense of confidence trust and satisfaction. While Avon felt embarrassed for underestimating him, Valentin felt fortunate and he was the happiest man in the world; for he was enjoying the fact that she wasn't demanding anything from him but her intention was purely to be by his side and nothing else. She truly had come to him ready to give him everything she possessed intangibly, physically, and materially if necessary. Therefore after that incident, Valentin allowed things to unfold naturally and although his greatest challenge in life was patience; he had to be patient with his princess and he just enjoyed while observing her through the process amorously.

They went for a ride in the car around the farm; it was midday and the sunshine was at its fullest *joie de vivre*. They passed by the main house in the farm, but Avon didn't ask to stop thus he continued driving her around. Then, they drove by the cottage and Avon didn't seem interested either. So, he continued driving her around and suddenly, Avon seemed fascinated appreciating the structure of some glass-greenhouses perfectly aligned. There were about ten greenhouses on each side of the path where they were passing by, and as they drove a bit further, in between the greenhouses lined up in parallel, at the end of the path, she distinguished a barn. "What is in there?" she asked interested.

Valentin replied, "It's an old barn."

"Is someone living there?" she asked oblivious.

Containing his amusement he replied, "No, barns are used to store harvest or equipment; although some barns are used for animals, there are no animals living in this barn."

"May we see inside it?" she asked.

And while parking the car he replied, "But of course my darling."

When they entered and she sensed the space inside the barn, she asked, "Could people live here luv?"

"Well, this barn has not been used for a long time. As you can see I've been using it to store the things that were left behind in the main house after the divorce. Is here where you would like to live my princess?" He asked pleasantly.

"When the philosopher points to the stars, the fool's eyes are fixed on the finger."

"Yes," she replied pausing for a moment and she turned around admiring the greenhouses from inside the barn. Then she added, "I really like the view of the perfectly aligned greenhouses from here." Approaching her from behind, he grabbed her waist and he turned her around tenderly to face him. He observed her with his indigo eyes driving her romantically insane again. He held both of her hands bringing them to his lips and he kissed them. Then, he embraced her and swiftly whirled her around and around rejoicing in their new home-to-be, right in the center of the barn.

As he put her down, "Here is the bike and you told me that the barn was vacant," said Avon in a teasing tone; as she noticed that the motorbike was sheltered in the barn. Then she asked, "What is up there?" Pointing at the hayloft and stepping up on a wooden ladder. Valentin helped her up and he encouraged her to satisfy her curiosity by herself. The first thing she noticed was the view. The magnificent horizon of fields against the background of the Alps in the afield distance combined with the greenhouses and trees, looked absolutely splendid from the elevation through a triangular window exposing the full front peak of the barn facing a spectacular view of the farm. Then, she looked around and once again; she was impressed by her connection with Valentin. He had followed her up there and he was standing close by with his hands inside the jeans pockets and observing her.

"Do you spend time here luv?" she asked.

"Yes, I do" he replied.

"You have a library in here!"

"Yes, I do."

"Luv, is this your favorite place in the farm?"

"Yes princess, it is."

There was a couch, a coffee table and a couple of end tables in the hayloft. But when Valentin spent time up there; he mainly read. The area looked dusty and uncared for; in desperate need of a woman's touch. Avon presumed that there was no electricity in the barn because it seemed as though Valentin enjoyed candle light. There were books and candles everywhere. He had a couple of bookcases, but there were books on the bear wooden floor corners and there were books in between the bare studs on the walls. In general the area had great potential to do wonders with it, Avon thought. However, she wouldn't intrude Valentin's private corner and she appointed the hayloft in the opposite side of the barn for her to do their paperwork. "I would like an interior bridge to join one hayloft with the other luv," she said pointing out and asked, "Would it be all right if I do paperwork over there? He didn't reply verbally. He approached her, he passionately kissed her, and they ended up on the couch.

From then on, a new facet began.

Tossing a reflection to the air...

"A man could live out of a lunchbox, if it weren't for women demands castles wouldn't exist perhaps."

"When the philosopher points to the stars, the fool's eyes are fixed on the finger."

18

৪৩

Avon offered to help with everything she could manage to do to renovate their new home and she input her ideas for the barn to be transformed. So, Avon and Valentin remodeled, refurbished and painted away creating their nest and bubble of Love by their own selves. Valentin had knowledge of carpentry, electricity, plumbing and much more; making reality every thought she expressed and manifesting her imagination when passing through his hands. She had never considered refurbishing a house; yet, remodeling the barn turned out to be one of her most cherished experiences in life.

When they started to clean out the barn and preparing for the renovations; they found boxes of old toys, clothes, kitchen stuff, furniture, and many things from Valentin's previous household. His memories revived here and there and he expressed some but others he kept for himself.

Cleaning around, Avon discovered a grand piano under a cover and as she looked closer; she noticed other musical instruments guarded by the piano as well and she asked, "Do you play music luv?"

"When the philosopher points to the stars, the fool's eyes are fixed on the finger."

"Yes, I do." Valentin replied while taking out some trash. So, she could hardly wait for him to play music for her, but first, she had to select a special corner for his musical instruments in their new home.

An uneventful morning, Valentin was sorting out boxes with old toys and among the things he was unraveling; he found a small old dusty Earth globe. Playing around, he tossed the Earth globe to Avon for her to toss it back at him as if they were playing ball. She caught the old dusty Earth globe in the air. She held it for a moment. She gazed at the sphere between her hands and it wasn't until then when Avon realized that her childish dreams were attained, one by one. She observed the small old dusty Earth globe following the continents' lines with her index finger and remembering her entire journey fully aware of having bounced from continent to continent, country to country and she recalled the places that she had lived at and visited. Tears rolled down her face because from that point forward; her endeavors didn't involve childish dreams anymore. Valentin approached her expressing his vibrant affection and Avon felt entirely satisfied by his side.

She accepted and grasped at that moment that she couldn't have accomplished any of her childhood dreams by herself and she credited her realization to her true source. Because no one else knew in detail about her childish dreams; especially her ultimate dream which she had secretly confided to Arolf. Just then, deep in her heart, Avon recognized that Energy had been the only presence guiding her through Earth each and every step of the way, placing her where she was supposed to be so that her childish dreams could be attained; because from the time when Avon was only a child her ultimate dream had always been to live in France and there she was.

Up till then, Avon had experienced everything she had asked for as a child and she even learned the languages she was supposed to, perfectly synchronized with her dreams cause for a perfect effect. However, she couldn't even begin to imagine how the wishes she requested from Energy as an adult would manifest.

Tossing a reflection to the air...

"When life becomes a dance floor; the ideal partner to Tango with is Love. Love's Tango steps tangle-one-in, tangle-one-out, untangle one with kicks of bliss, toss one's wits to the air instead of a red rose and finish one off with an ardent wink of inspiration to Tango on."

Working with Valentin Avon discovered what eagerness in progress to advance at once was all about. She always tried acting upon any situation without procrastination or vacillation. Nevertheless, Valentin's concept of beginning any project was to finish it. Avon found herself rapt by the speed Valentin possessed in his hands. Her ideas where captured in his mind like photographs reproducing in detail exactly what she had imagined and combined with his magical touch; everything he created worked in perfect functionality. Valentin's mind allied in harmony with his hands bringing out result faster than most. Thus in the shortest reasonable period of time their home-barn was ready, being a restroom bigger than the caravan the first thing they built for Avon to be comfortable and fine.

After they were established in their new home, one morning while they enjoyed a *latté* in a back porch that they had built next

"When the philosopher points to the stars, the fool's eyes are fixed on the finger."

to the kitchen, Avon said, "This farm is enormous and gorgeous; it must be expensive luv."

Valentin replied, "Not really princess, the farm wasn't expensive, although it's worth a lot of money."

"Tell me the difference."

"Well, expensive is when people pay more than they should for something and usually the extra money is hidden in fees and the interest, or people also pay extra money for prestigious brand names. Most of the land in this farm was a good investment and it's worth the money spent because with the return, slowly but surely it has paid back itself."

She looked at the distance and deeply inhaled saying, "It would be great if we could stay here."

"We can always return here; we ought to go back to America to settle our financial affairs with Angelina and Gabe."

"I was wishfully thinking, I guess." She said. He gave her a peck on the cheek and he left to check on a plowing machine in need of repairs.

Valentin was prudent regarding anything to do with finances; for as time passed by, Avon would realize that Valentin was in a much better financial position than she was and from personal experience Valentin understood that finances could dissolve relationships. He also understood that, if not managed properly, money could destroy the purity of someone's heart. In addition, he knew that more often than not, due to ego, money could get in between two people *in* Love.

In the meantime Valentin continued working in the farm and occupied with whatever it was that he did when he went out, while Avon's focus was on preparing their marriage paperwork; because she took charge of the task. Their objective was to return to America as soon as possible together. Therefore, Avon had to concentrate on the length of the process and she was able to find the timelines outlined on the embassies' website guidelines. Nevertheless, every country had different procedures. For instance after getting married; the timelines were different if she submitted the permanent residence petition to sponsor Valentin as her husband at the American Embassy in Paris, than if she submitted the petition at the American Embassy in a lessen public demand city as Belgrade, Budapest, or Sofia. From professional experience, Avon was able to determine the demand of requests at an American Embassy in the countries involved depending on the scale of the population, and once she gathered the information, she narrowed the alternatives down focusing on their objective and from that point; she began to explore their options in reverse. Avon utilized the tactic to obtain best results when working on projects attaining goals from a fail-safe approach and totally free of mistakes. It was crucial to file the paperwork correctly the first time to avoid delays, or worst yet, being rejected due to an error.

Valentin was originally from Bulgaria which made their options simpler. Because Avon found out that the Bulgarian immigration scheme neither force a separation between a foreigner and a citizen when applying to get married, nor forced the two in Love to separate after getting married while waiting for sponsorship approval. So, if they got married in Bulgaria, the process to sponsor Valentin for U.S. permanent residency at the American Embassy in Sofia would take from thirty days minimum to three months maximum; which was by all comparisons the most generous length of time Avon was able to find in the guidelines among the countries involved. Yet, due to the Language barrier; she had to think twice about researching in the Bulgarian website, because not every detail was translated into English and Valentin wasn't always around to assist her.

"When the philosopher points to the stars, the fool's eyes are fixed on the finger."

On the other hand, the paperwork required from two people that had been previously divorced in two different countries and applying to get married, yet in a different country, was intensive. Avon's paperwork from her divorce was in English and issued in Quebec; Valentin's paperwork was in French and if they got married in Bulgaria, everything had to be translated into Bulgarian. Still when considering their timelines, Avon couldn't disregard the option.

If they got married in France, and then, they went to the American Embassy in Sofia trying to submit the paperwork thinking that they could take advantage of the quickest process, the results would have been nothing but complications; because if the marriage certificate was issued in French, their petition would've been assigned to different category for translation, delaying their request. The quickest process applied only if their marriage certificate was issued in Bulgaria. Moreover if they got married in France and submitted the petition for Avon to sponsor Valentin at the American Embassy in Paris, the process would've taken minimum one year. Besides, when studying their backgrounds, if they got married in France like in any other country involved, they would've been forced to a separation and sadly, as glamorous as getting married in France could've seemed to Avon; she had to prepare to abandon the idea.

Tossing a reflection to the air...

"When willing to understand, the apparent hard way disentangles into simplicity leading to best results; whereas the apparent easy way leads to nothing but complications."

When Avon was ready to convey to her husband-to-be that they had to go to Bulgaria to get married; she revised the guidelines one more time discovering that at the Bulgarian Embassy in Paris the Consul was allowed to perform marriages on site. Therefore, Avon and Valentin could get legally married in Bulgarian territory and modestly celebrate their wedding in one of the most romantic cities in the world—Paris.

Avon was enthusiastically surprised when finding out that the Bulgarian immigration marriage statutes were rather merciful in contrast to other countries, because by not forcing an interracial couple to separate in order to get married, the Consul was allowed to perform marriages on site. So from that point forward, Avon focused on complying with every request required by the Bulgarian Embassy in Paris for the Bulgarian Consul to perform their marriage ceremony and to issue their marriage certificate. And even though, Avon had brought most of her divorce documentation with her, paperwork was being sent from the farm to San Fran and San Fran to the farm while documents were sent to Sofia to translate. By using translators from Bulgaria avoided future mistakes when they submitted the request at the U.S. embassy in Sofia for the officials' verification of seals, along with legalization of the documentation; because after the wedding, the newlyweds still had to go to Bulgaria for Avon to sponsor Valentin as her husband at the U.S. embassy in Sofia to get his permanent resident visa.

By the time Avon had compiled official copies of the original documents and all the required paperwork to obtain a marriage certificate, months had passed. She found herself occupied spending most of her time studying the aspects of international marriage when two people were not official residents of a common land and the couple *in* Love happened to be in a neutral country, because neither one of them were Bulgarian residents nor originally from

"When the philosopher points to the stars, the fool's eyes are fixed on the finger."

France. Therefore, during that period of time, Avon began to reflect on physical belonging. Because even though when she received her Canadian residency she had already realized that she had lost her origin roots. She had never reflected on the fact that once her umbilical cord had been cut; she had no roots at all and by being out in the world, she really didn't belong anywhere.

In the interim, Avon and Valentin had been dealing with their neighbor Xavier and he was manipulative and controlling. Eventually Avon was so busy; she didn't get involved and Valentin dealt with him. Still, Avon suspected that Xavier was shielding something and she felt as though Valentin knew his secret, but she respected their privacy and she didn't pry; although she wondered if Xavier was aware that Valentin owned the farm. In any event, Xavier didn't allow the girls and Jaidee to spend much time with Avon and considering the impression that Jaidee projected to Avon about Valentin during Christmas, the few times they got together, the ownership of the farm was never mentioned.

Tossing a reflection to the air…

"Just like everything that exists, magic is part of a Universe working in perfect harmony and it might not reveal through an instant effect like an illusion trick would; however true magic manifests in perfect timing."

For their wedding day in Paris, Avon had only one request for Valentin and he gladly pleased her when she asked him to let his hair down for their special occasion.

The ceremony was performed in Bulgarian. Avon didn't understand a single word the Consul said and the two *in* Love didn't make vows or promises to each other. After the Consul spoke briefly, Valentin surprised Avon with a set of precious wedding bands. Then, the Consul allowed Valentin to indicate to Avon when to say "Yes," because up till then, *"Da"* was the only Bulgarian word she had to learn so as to conquer her Valentin's heart and take him back to America with her.

Following the ceremony, they gathered in a private dining room at a fine hotel where they celebrated intimately with a few guests. Avon was pleased appreciating Valentin's glow. He looked handsome and stylish; especially with his loose golden locks. She enjoyed observing him dressed up and without a ponytail for a change. On the other hand, Valentin could not keep his eyes off his new wife. They toasted with fine champagne, ate well, danced, and they had a natural good time. At the end of the festivity; the guests went to their suites and the newlyweds went up to theirs.

When the bride and groom got to their honeymoon suite, there was a butler holding the door opened for them. Valentin picked Avon up swiftly carrying her through the threshold and he put her down for her to appreciate. He had made arrangements for their own private wedding celebration to spend the rest of the night at the heart of what *Dark Matter* meant to him and what Arolf meant to her. The suite was prepared for their souls to meet not as much their bodies; soft music was playing, aromatic candles were lit and brewing herbal tea fragranced the air. Some details were in place for them to enjoy their first night as husband and wife.

Avon felt relief in her heart; as she didn't feel like they were celebrating their wedding but rejoicing a victory. They had managed to leap the first mountain in order to cross the ocean for their next objective which was to be legally together wherever they went.

"When the philosopher points to the stars, the fool's eyes are fixed on the finger."

Avon was the happiest woman in the world looking at the marriage certificate holding the piece of paper like a treasure tightly between her hands despite the fact that it was issued in Bulgarian and she didn't understand.

As Avon stood looking at the marriage certificate enthralled; she sensed Valentin's eyes penetrating each pore in her body. He was observing her from where he was standing with his right hand slid in the pocket of his trousers and his left shoulder leaning on a column holding a cigar in his left hand. All of a sudden, Avon realized that they weren't in the same suite where they had first checked-in. She looked around and for what she could gather; it seemed like they were in an upgraded suite of the hotel. She noticed the butler, she paid more attention to the live music coming from the balcony and just then, she was able to tell that they were in the presidential suite of the hotel because she had been left standing in middle of the elegant foyer.

The entire living area was illuminated with candle flickering flames and the flare burning in the fireplace. The sensation Avon felt standing in the middle of Jaidee's kitchen returned intensified a thousand times, except that she was able to identify it. The sensation she felt was the pure Love connection between her and her Valentin.

Avon stood still allowing Valentin to admire her and he did. Keeping his eyes fixed on her, Valentin paced slowly from the column where he was leaning at to the opposite side of the room. He leaned his back against another column crossing his right foot over the left one and he lit the cigar. Then, she didn't know if he was admiring her or she was admiring him. She smiled firmly holding the marriage certificate in her hands and he kept looking at her while smoking his cigar. They admired each other a short time listening to the music background and conveying silent vibes of Love.

For him, Avon looked like a princess wearing a plain bodice and spaghetti straps silver Charmeuse A-line floor length gown delicately embroidered with beads and pearls by the fluffy base combined with a sheer shawl covering her shoulders under her naturally curled long hair. For her, Valentin's handsome silhouette looked like the form of a perfect male covered by a dark blue tuxedo along with a snow-white shirt, tie and vest; intensifying his bronze skin tone with the white and the dark blue enhanced his azure eyes. Just like Christmas night; he observed her while she observed him and the Energy magnetism between them was immense.

Valentin waited for Avon to make the first move and when she did, she walked slowly through the glossy marble floors and when she reached him; he put his arm around her back-waist directing her to the balcony. A trio of classical musicians was playing violins out in the terrace and the butler brought two glasses of bubbly leaving the bottle of *Dom Pérignon* inside a standing cooler next to them.

Soon after, Valentin asked Avon to look at the stars crowning the moon and she couldn't find the moon, let alone the stars; however, there was a bright red glowing sign floating in the midst of the dark sky flashing his words: *I Love you more for saying "Da."*

Valentin stood behind her holding the cigar and the glass in one hand while he held her front-waist tight against his body with his other hand, allowing her to feel each inch of his masculinity while she contemplated his words written on *Dark Matter,* afar, but close enough.

After a good while appreciating the melodies and enjoying Valentin's words written in the middle of the dark sky, unexpectedly just like fireworks, colorful arrows, stars, and hearts puffed up in the air dissolving the sign and poof! The magic trick was gone. The helicopter that was holding the sign approached on top of the

"When the philosopher points to the stars, the fool's eyes are fixed on the finger."

terrace spreading fresh white rose petals and sparkling hearts of red, silver and gold confetti mix all over them. She turned around kissing him passionately as her eyes suffused with tears of joy.

After their shower of romance; they walked back into the living area. She sat on the sofa appreciating the music and Valentin knelt on one knee taking her shoes off making her feel like a real princess once more. Then, he stood up and took the marriage certificate from the center table where she had left it and asked, "Wife, would you like me to translate it for you or should we put it away in a safe place?"

She looked at him getting comfortable and with a grand smile replied, "Safe place husband."

Valentin handed the marriage certificate to the butler indicating to put it away and he sat on an armchair across his wife observing her while sipping *Dom* and smoking the cigar. "You are so handsome my loving Valentin." She said.

He modestly mentioned, "Do not brush me princess, I am a simple man. I definitely needed a lot of assistance for what I have prepared for you tonight."

"What do you mean by saying not to brush you luv?" She asked.

"I dislike socializing and showing off among others. I like being unpolished. That's all, princess." He replied.

Valentin waited for Avon to react patiently. He could sense that Avon was in seventh heaven absorbing every minute of their moment. She didn't seem overexcited regarding the luxury though and he was amused by her vagueness about it. He felt mysteriously fascinated with her, as she reacted like a natural princess. She fit so well in the extravagant atmosphere that he had created for her and she didn't seem the least curious. When the butler refilled their glasses; she knew instinctively how to handle the etiquette, since with a gracious glance from Avon, the butler got her hint to serve some strawberries deepened in chocolate to her new husband. Valentin continued observing her; he remembered the night in the caravan and the way Avon genuinely had accepted to be with him for who he was demonstrating the same indifference toward material stuff. He also recalled with appreciation the way she had physically worked by his side in the barn expressing the same elegance, finesse, and gracefulness she naturally possessed and he continued observing her.

Avon delicately pulled up her legs on the sofa and finally reacted saying, "Last time I checked this suite rate was over twenty thousand dollars a night luv."

Valentin said, "I got a special package princess."

"It is precisely what I am wondering, how much did you save negotiating the package, eh?" He looked at her intensely, and she added, "You are not like the clients I worked with in the past who splurge money to brag. My heart giggles wondering how much you saved." He sat next to her as she continued, "I admire your sense of consciousness my Valentin. You are the greatest man in the world. I do not care if you are polished or not, I just Love your rare manner and the way you approach everything with certain vim."

"I am glad, because now we are married for life." He said tossing her a flirty wink.

Avon felt that Valentin wasn't ready for intimacy just yet. He was being his natural flirting, affectionate and romantic intriguing self; as some Europeans seem to behave. But he was not being sensual as she knew that when he wanted sex; he expressed more physically than vocally. Then again, she had no idea that she was on the verge to receive the answer of her own requests and a taste of the blessings that Arolf had in reserve for her.

"When the philosopher points to the stars, the fool's eyes are fixed on the finger."

So, she caressed Valentin's hair looking at his eyes asking, "Would you like to take your jacket off?" He agreed and while he was standing up; she admired his attractive backside and sighed.

"What?" He asked bashfully and she smiled moving over indicating for him to sit and to get comfortable because she sensed that he was eager to talk to her.

During the last months Avon had been so absorbed preparing and researching paperwork for their marriage; Valentin was thirsty for her words as she was for his and being in the perfect surroundings; they were finally able to relax enjoying each other to the fullest.

"I have a wedding gift for you, but first, I would like to tell you a story." He said.

Avon's reaction was surprising to him, because she seemed more excited about the story than the gift. "Tell me, luv, tell me," was her response.

Expressing some discomfort he said, "I don't know where to begin though."

She said chuckling, "Well, if you start at the end, I suspect that the end of the story is your gift to me and I can assure you from my heart that whatever your gift is, I will accept it and treasure it. So, start at the beginning and my gift to you will be listening."

"I accept; but really, don't interrupt me princes, be kind to me," and Valentin commenced telling his tale, "When I was a young boy, about eight or nine years old, somebody in the next village was getting married and our family attended the wedding. Right after the ceremony finished, when the newlyweds were walking through the aisle, was when I first noticed the bride. She looked like an angel and she was the most beautiful woman I've ever seen." He recollected thoughts pausing briefly and expressing unease; he carried on, "Then, I just remember that a very strong desire inside possessed me and I chased the twosome alongside the aisle. I wanted her to see me but she didn't look at me and as a young boy surrounded by so many people, I couldn't make myself noticeable." He seemed tense. He cleared his throat and continued, "At the reception I saw my opportunity when the bride and groom were getting ready to dance, because everyone was out of the way and the bride would notice me then.

"So, I squeeze amid people to the edge of the dance floor platform and as I looked at the distance I noticed that not only the bride but everyone else will see me. Yet, my desire for her to look at me was more intense than the fear I felt and I walked through the dance floor until I reached the center where the newlyweds were set to have their first dance as husband and wife." Valentin seemed timid but he carried on, "I stood next to the bride and found myself in front of her looking up realizing that she finally noticed me. She looked at me with her angelical smile and as she bent down to pay attention to me, instinctively, I embraced her neck and I kissed her in the mouth."

Avon was listening attentively and she sensed that Valentin memories were not pleasant. He seemed nervous and she said gently, "You must have been a naughty boy; but, you managed to kiss the bride luv!"

Valentin went on, "Well, I guess I was the happiest boy in the wedding hanging from the bride's neck for a second, because nothing but embarrassment followed next. I didn't let her go and I messed up her dress, her hair style and her veil. She lost balance and we fell down on the floor. It happened so quickly, I basically ruined the wedding. I don't even know what happened next because my father took me back home right away and he punished me."

"How did he punish you?"

"Well, the usual, he sent me to the dining room corner with my arms up and I wasn't allowed to put my arms down until he said so."

"When the philosopher points to the stars, the fool's eyes are fixed on the finger."

Avon smiled asking, "So, what happened then?"

"When mum returned home from the wedding reception with my brother; she found out that I was still punished by the corner and she got angry. Dad and mum started arguing and I couldn't hear the entire discussion although I remember my mum saying to dad, 'You didn't need to punish the boy for this long, we have to pay for the bride's dress damage anyway and if you want your sex, you better pay for what you've done to my son.' Then, mum came to the dining room; she released me from the punishment telling me to go out and play with my brother but I stayed around because my arms hurt and the last thing I wanted was to go out and play."

"What did your father say?"

"My father was angry and he was pacing around; so, trying to justify himself he yelled back at mum, 'The boy embarrassed the entire village before a French bride, her French family and her French friends.'"

"The bride was French!" Avon exclaimed. Valentin nodded assent.

"Did you fall in Love with her?"

"Well, platonic Love you know." He continued, "Then, my mum's anger rose from angry to mad, because she yelled back, 'If you are torturing my son to honor the French, let's see if they give you what you want. You might even find out if in fact, French women are as good in bed as they say.' At that point my father didn't reply and I think that dad was feeling guiltier than anything else, because he probably forgot about me watching TV waiting for mum to come home and deal with me herself.

"So, while dad paced around, he passed by me distressed. Then he stopped and said, 'When you pick a woman to be your bride beware Valentin; a bride is like a bribe. If you don't have money to give them whatever *they* want, they won't give you what *you* want.' I was annoyed wondering what exactly I have done wrong, because as a mature man I understand now, but back then no one was clarifying the cause of the punishment to me. And even though I only had a vague idea of what sex was all about at that age, I guess after all the information I gathered from the argument that mum and dad were having, I felt confident and I said to dad, 'I'll marry a French woman and she'll give me sex all the time.' So, my father approached me looking deep into my eyes and he said, 'If what you want is to have sex all the time Valentin, you need lots of money; but if what you really want is to have sex all the time and with a French woman no less, you better start playing the lottery son.'" Valentin paused for a moment and they laughed. The butler approached to refill the champagne glasses and Avon requested, "Tea and sweets, please."

"Certainly Madame," the butler replied. Avon was pleased enjoying her husband's childhood story and she continued attentively listening.

Valentin felt comfortable and asked, "Are you actually enjoying my story princess?"

"But of course I am. Anything you say is important to me. You must have been the cutest naughty boy in the village." She replied.

"I am embarrassing myself, but I am enjoying too, you have a sparkle that makes me feel vivid and I mean every time I call you princes." He added. Avon looked at him smiling and glowing from his flattering words encouraging him to continue and he went on, "Little did I know, I trusted my father's advice and from a very young age, I began playing the lottery. I remember that when I was a boy, it was hard for me to collect coins for the ticket but I managed and I played devotedly without ever missing a week. I picked my numbers and mum or dad bought the ticket for me."

"How old were you?"

"When the philosopher points to the stars, the fool's eyes are fixed on the finger."

"Nine or ten years old perhaps," he continued, "Obviously weeks, months, and years went by and I played the lottery every week. In the mean time, I grew older and I don't remember ever missing a week; especially, when I was old enough to buy my own ticket. As time passed by, the world was advancing and even the regime changed in Bulgaria. However the older I got, the more intense was my confidence to win the lottery one day and I was certain that I will have enough money to marry a beautiful French woman and have lots of sex."

Tossing a reflection to the air…

"Whishing aimlessly manifests one's dreams at random; however ideas inspired out of life-force manifest as creativity on purpose."

19

☙❧

*T*he butler brought an exquisite tea brewing display. He delicately poured steaming water in a gorgeous glass-teapot resting on a high-silver-stand warmed by a candle flame. Then using silver tongs; he skillfully dropped a blooming tea ball inside the teapot. After that, the blooming tea ball infused slowly floating and unfurling gradually before their eyes releasing the most delightful aroma and forming a set of interlaced hearts.

Avon glanced at the presentation politely and she continued listening to her husband's story attentively. Then, Valentin picked up where he had left off, "When I finished college in the field of machinery mechanics and engineering; I got a job at the nearest town airport servicing planes and I really enjoyed working there. At that stage buying the lottery ticket every week became merely a routine; nevertheless one day, my lottery number was drawn and I won the lottery."

Valentin paused hoping for that part to be the end of his story and waited for Avon's reaction, but instead, Avon exclaimed, "Really! You won the lottery luv?!"

"Yes, I did." He replied.

"When the philosopher points to the stars, the fool's eyes are fixed on the finger."

"With your determination and your drive, you focused and you actually won the lottery! Then what? Tell me more!"

So, since she didn't even give a second thought to his point because she never asked him how much money he had won; he didn't have much of an option and he continued telling her more, "Well it was exciting, I had all this money; but when it finally happened I seemed to have forgotten what I wanted the money for." Avon listened and he kissed her. Then he said, "My gorgeous wife, it pleases me that you spoil me to have my sweets with tea." By then, seeing that Avon wasn't interested in the amount of money no matter how many times he brought up the subject, he relaxed. He took off his shoes, he pulled his feet up on an ottoman and he sipped tea enjoying sweets while telling his tale, "And so, after I had all this money it was the worst part because the whole village was after me."

"What do you mean?

"Well, my brother and mum were excited and basically they took care of spreading the word; besides, it's such a small village, everyone knows everybody. Of course, I was going to share the money with my family; but when something as exciting as winning the lottery happens people can become mad. What am I saying? Now that I am a mature man, I know that money is the primary reason why people murder each other; but as a young man I didn't know that; however my father did." He paused briefly. He seemed uneasy again and he continued, "Suddenly, everyone in the village wanted to be my relative. I had to quit my job, because most of my peers were asking me to pay for surgeries."

"Surgeries…" She wondered puzzled.

"Yes, after people learned that I won the lottery, one day I was in my lunch break at work and one of my peers approached me with a sad story about his mother suffering from a terminal illness.

He said that she needed a surgical procedure in Germany. So, thinking of paying my luck back, I was trying to do a good deed and I gave him money to help out. After that, everyone had ill relatives needing surgeries and depending on my lottery money to survive. During the last few weeks I worked there, everyone was asking me to give them money for surgeries. Even my superiors were asking me for money to invest and they were aggressive. They pressured me to the point that I became frightened to go to work. Then, I found out that the peer I gave money for his mother's surgery in Germany had lied to me. So, totally disappointed, I quit."

Avon noticed that Valentin was getting sadden and she was able to perceive that the harassment had affected him profoundly. But she didn't interrupt him and she allowed him to continue, "After I quit my job, I couldn't go anywhere because at the same time as my ex-coworkers were stalking me around the house, every girl in the village wanted me. The girls were on the door step at my house waiting for me to come out. I felt everyone's eyes watching me and what they really wanted was the money. This is embarrassing and uncomfortable for me to talk about. I've never said this to anyone before but when I was a young man, I didn't feel like my friends did around girls. I remember being apprehensive around girlfriends. I didn't want to kiss them right away and I was interested to learn more about them first, not just kiss them or have sex and the other boys would tease me. So, as a young man, it was difficult for me to be close to girls, much less have sex; especially when living in a small village.

"Back then, I didn't have a steady girlfriend because not one girl took me serious, but as soon as I won the lottery, most girls in the village were ready to nearly sell themselves to me without scruples. In that regard my father was right when saying that some brides allow to be bribed I guess." He paused and the memories

"When the philosopher points to the stars, the fool's eyes are fixed on the finger."

brought tears to his eyes. So, Avon allowed him to release what he was experiencing and she robbed his legs. She looked at him with kindness and with a graceful smile she conveyed that she loved him even more. The butler handed her some tissues and she lovingly dried a couple of tears rolling down his cheeks.

Eventually, Valentin carried on, "I was completely lost in despair, because I wasn't going to pay every girl that came to me for sex, and most certainly, I wasn't going to marry any of them. So, I locked myself in my room and I didn't talk to anyone. I was devastated and mum brought me food, but I didn't come out or speak at all. I was terrified to come out of my room."

He paused reflecting for a moment and Avon said, "The entire village was harassing you, your reaction was natural."

He looked at Avon kindly and he continued, "While I was locked up in my room, I didn't do anything for weeks and a couple of months must've passed by I suppose. I just wanted to sleep and never wake up. I was drowning in a sea of agony absorbed by fear, wondering what others will do to me or to my family just to take the money and I couldn't tell the anguish my mum was experiencing to see me in that state of mind every time she brought me food.

"Until one day, there was a knock on my bedroom door and I knew it wasn't mum. So, I didn't open and I wanted to hide. I was horrified thinking that someone had broken into the house and they had killed my family and I was next. I hid under the bed and when I didn't respond; the next thing I knew is that the strong man who was knocking on the door kicked it and he broke the door in half. He entered aggressively. He pulled me from under the bed where I was shaking of terror. He grabbed me by the neck and with a rigid tone he said 'Don't you think it's time for you to go to France; find your French bride; and have sex all the time?' I looked at him crying feeling mortified and the only thing I could say was

'Father, I forgot my dream and what I wanted the money for' and he said 'Go on son, you have half of life figured out at this point, only remember this: Love isn't a lottery and doesn't come to you by luck. Live! You have plenty of money. Go and enjoy it, leave!' My father had tears in his eyes, I know he didn't want me to go, but I had to, and I left."

At that stage of Valentin's tale, Avon's heart was wounded and ready to erupt of sadness; however, she didn't cry. She breathed serenely and she was calm. That moment was her husband's cry desperately needing support from his wife. Avon let Valentin shed as many tears as he wanted surrounded by her arms. She caressed his hair and she held him tight for a long while. After that, she untied his bow tie, unbuttoned his shirt collar for him to breathe better and she poured him a glass of water. Then, she slid a chair in front of the sofa and she sat facing him. She bent her knees pulling her feet up on the sofa next to him. She rested her arms on her knees, her chin touched her left wrist and her eyes were fixed looking at him for a few minutes. In the meantime, the butler had stopped the music and he was serving some refreshments to the musicians allowing Avon and Valentin total privacy. Then she asked, "Do you feel relief luv?" He nodded.

As he regained some senses while holding the glass of water between his hands; he stared aimlessly and said, "I always dreamed of marring a French woman in Bulgaria, but I never considered the fact that I had to leave my culture, my family, my traditions, and everything I was familiar with to attain my dream. It didn't make a difference where I went, however it's precisely what I had to do and I left my family totally against my will." He cleared his throat and in discomfort he said, "Leaving my parents and brother is the worst experience I had to face in life. We were a united family and all of a sudden, one day, I found myself so far away; I couldn't see

"When the philosopher points to the stars, the fool's eyes are fixed on the finger."

them daily and when I realized that I was so lonely thanks to my money, I was sad, very sad indeed." He looked at Avon's tender smile as she attentively listened trying to hold her tears back and he said, "Well, I didn't think that the story was going to take this long, but this is the way is coming out. Are you still enjoying or did I make you sad princess?" She shook her head smiling drying tears off her face and she allowed him to go on. He inhaled deeply and carried on, "Before I left, I remember my father giving me the best advice he had for me to be able to manage the money and not to lose everything out of despair. I arrived here in Paris and I followed my father's advice and instead to abominate money, which was my instinct at the moment, I decided to establish a healthy relationship with finances. I rented a small apartment where I was comfortable and I registered in advance French classes to learn to communicate. I started to learn how to manage money from books that I brought with me on the subject. I already knew some English back then, because besides learning Russian as a mandatory second language from an early age, I had to learn English at school to understand manuals and mechanical stuff due to my *métier*. So after I learned some French, I felt confident to go out and I found a nice *café* not far from my place where I went to read. I got familiar with the owners of the *café*, as well as with the servers and while I read, I used to observe one of the girls who worked there. She was a student in Paris, but she was originally from Provence. She was French and she was beautiful. She had the attributes that I was looking for, but most importantly, she seemed to like me for who I was."

He paused for a moment and he sipped water. Then Avon asked, "Did she become your ex-wife?"

"Yes! As a matter of fact, that's exactly who she became, my ex-wife." He replied smiling and he went on, "Well back then, we became close. We went out on dates. One thing led to the next and we ended up living in my small apartment together. By then, I had already been here Paris for a couple of years and despite of the beauty of the city, living here isn't as glamorous as it seems, plus, we both enjoyed the country life style. So, when we found out that she was pregnant we moved to the south and it was then, when I met Xavier's parents—"

Then, Avon interrupted him asking, "What do you mean Xavier's parents, are you getting ahead of the story?"

"No, I am not, princess; since the story took this course, I may as well tell you everything now. I don't want you to be a wife like Jaidee. Xavier keeps Jaidee in the dark about things and he might only be trying to protect her, or perhaps he's protecting himself. This concerns you and I'll tell you openly." He said.

Avon smiled saying, "I am listening I didn't mean to interrupt."

"It's alright, you had a point. Besides, it's different when you interrupt me out of innocence than when you interrupt me questioning my intentions, or worst yet, when you unduly apologize. I don't have a logical explanation but your innocence allows me to cope with patience. I will not tolerate interruptions from anyone else though." He said winking at her and ongoing with his tale, "So, when I went to Provence with my ex-wife, she brought me to her parent's house and *then* is when I met Xavier parents." He waited for Avon to react.

"Are you telling me that your ex-wife is Xavier's sister?" Avon asked.

"Yes, she is." He replied.

Avon expressed the greatest smile and suddenly; she was energized. She stood up and she hinted the butler letting him know that they were ready for a splash of *Cognac*. While the butler performed the *Courvoisier* serving ceremony; she allowed her husband to enjoy it and she walked out to the terrace.

"When the philosopher points to the stars, the fool's eyes are fixed on the finger."

She acknowledged the musicians with a kind nod and she said in a courtly tone, "Gentlemen, this might be an average night in the city of Paris; however memorable to me." She inhaled deeply and exhaled smiling in grand. Next she asked, "Would you allow me a request?"

By then, the three musicians were standing and one of them replied performing a respectful nod saying, "Most certainly Madame."

So, speaking softly she said in an intriguing tone, "Shall we invite *Mr. Vivaldi* to join us in celebration? Any season of the year will do. If the *Four Seasons* reverberate will do just as well; and if the *Storm* passes by will do better yet." Still smiling in grand, she performed a poised curtsy and instantly; the trio started to perform *Storm*, by *Vivaldi* followed by the rest of the *Four Seasons* excerpts, one by one.

Having reinstated the music background; she walked back to join her husband and as her ear-sense enjoyed the melody, appreciating the fragrance with her smell-sense; she selected a cigar. The butler immediately did the honors lighting the cigar for her and Valentin simply observed.

She raised her *Cognac* glass performing a graceful curtsy delicately lifting her dress with the hand holding the cigar and said, "I Love you husband."

Being amazed, "I Love you more and more, princess." Valentin said. Then, he also picked a cigar. They sat facing one another enjoying one melody after the other accompanied by *Mr. Courvoisier* and *Mr. Vivaldi* while enjoying the pleasant subtle aromatic herbal flavors of the aged *Montecristo Cuban* cigars smoking patiently between their fingers.

They delighted themselves listening to the melodies and Valentin was completely pleased observing his wife's sense of fulfillment. She was radiant and smiling like he had never seen her smile before.

Then again, when Avon had interrupted Valentin, a thought had passed at the highest speed through her mind and when Valentin revealed that his ex-wife was Xavier's sister; her thought connected with her remembrance path. Avon recalled that she had written an affirmation being grateful for what she didn't have at the time; however, she was willing to receive it with grace as a gift from the Universe which was what she called requesting in gratitude:

In accordance to the will of the Universe, expressing intention of peace and harmony to the entire world, under the grace of a perfect path, I am grateful for the person created to be my intimate companion in life. Thank you for listening to my request and for giving the order for my intention to manifest.

Just then, Avon recognized undoubtedly, that she had just married the person who had been created for her; as their encounter wasn't a twist of fate. At that moment she was the happiest woman in the world thinking how much she was going to enjoy the pleasure of sharing everything with her new husband. Although, she didn't realize then that, except for the pure and genuine Love that Arolf was reflecting all over them, most of what she had to share with Valentin was debt.

On the other hand, Valentin felt relieved and fortified enjoying the great musical performance. He was absorbing the melodies, his wife's smile, and the fact that he finally had been able to open up to Avon was giving him a great sense of satisfaction. Avon expressed what she was feeling vocally, "Everything seems to indicate that we were meant to meet and to be *in* Love together."

"I agree because I am the happiest man in the world, but I don't know exactly what is it that you mean princess." Valentin said.

So, she clarified, "Well, I was just thinking that if Jaidee and I did not keep in touch with each other, I would have never

"When the philosopher points to the stars, the fool's eyes are fixed on the finger."

been invited for Christmas dinner. Although she is one of my few friends, I have no explanation to justify keeping in touch with her except that she was supposed to be the link for you and me to meet." Valentin absorbed her thought and Avon added, "Then imagine, if Xavier did not marry Jaidee or if he didn't have a sister; we would have never met. I am simply reasoning the cause; because I am utterly thrilled with the effect. I Love you!" She exclaimed. She stood up approaching him. She bent and she kissed him while he sat marveling her. Then, she sat by his side again.

After that, she was trying to encourage him to continue his tale and she asked, "So, when did you get married luv?"

"Today," Valentin replied and they both laughed. He continued his tale, "Not long after my ex-wife and I arrived at her parents' farm, we had to get married because she was starting to show the pregnancy. Xavier was abroad and her father treated me like a son. So, they gave us one of the houses in the farm and I started to work the land." He paused for a moment.

"So, when did you meet Xavier?" Avon asked.

"I met him out and about when he came to visit from Bangkok. Then soon after he returned for good from abroad, I got divorced and all I knew about him was that he lived in Marseille with his wife. I didn't meet Jaidee until they sold their house in Marseille and they moved into the farmhouse a few years ago."

Then Avon said in wonder, "If Xavier never told Jaidee that you were his brother in-law, I wonder if your ex-wife met Jaidee."

"They probably saw each other in social events, but I was the one who was never around."

"What do you mean?"

"Well, it's hard for me to explain, but more than anything else it comes down to embarrassment."

"If you are embarrassed you do not have to talk about it, never mind I asked."

Valentin clarified smiling, "I am not embarrassed with you. I have already told you the most awkward things about me. When I say embarrassment I refer to them. I will not generalize saying that all French people are the same, except, my ex-wife and her mother were always covering up the truth with appearances. I was never invited to social events because *I* used to embarrass them. Well, I guess I still do; as you can see, after all these years and Xavier doesn't accept me for who I am; I do not hide my naked truth. As men, we do not discuss these matters and he knows that I am not going to fake who I am. Their father and I were never in social gatherings, because *I* embarrassed them by not going along with their dishonesty and their father didn't socialize at all. So, we always stayed home working. Their father was a hard working man."

"Is that why Xavier did not want you around for Christmas dinner?" Avon asked.

"Not only Xavier, I keep away from socializing as well." He replied.

"Why did you accept the invitation for Christmas dinner then?"

"You," he said chuckling.

"Me!?" said Avon puzzled.

"Remember in Xavier's kitchen after we brought the Christmas tree into the house?" Valentin asked.

"How could I forget, but of course I remember."

So, he expressed his experience, "Well, when you asked me directly what my plans were, I didn't know what to say. I had no idea who you were, or what you looked like; while I was facing the sink, I didn't even notice that you were in the kitchen. I hadn't seen you at all and although I am welcome to do dishes and things

"When the philosopher points to the stars, the fool's eyes are fixed on the finger."

around their home, I hardly speak to Jaidee for not to embarrass Xavier and the last thing I wanted was to say something and end up embarrassing him in front of their guest. However when you spoke, it was as if your voice rhythm and vibes froze me for a moment. I felt like someone had just pushed me into a pool of frozen water. It was the most intense Energy I have ever felt before. I felt cold and somehow hot at the same time. I hardly remember what I replied, because I couldn't move and I just recall looking out the window and thinking *Dark Matter I need guidance now more than ever before*."

Avon start laughing and she encouraged him to continue, "Tell me more about that evening luv."

So, Valentin joined her in laughter and expressing amusement he went on, "I was in desperate need of *Dark Matter*'s guidance at Xavier's kitchen looking through the window while doing dishes. Then, I noticed a small star in the distance and I thought *if I could reach that star, I'll through it to this lady that has me under inquisition*."

"No wonder. You had to accept the dinner invite then! You came prepared to have a war of stars with me and you were well equipped with imaginary arrows for full attack, eh?" Avon said. Then she expressed her experience in Jaidee's kitchen and they laughed for a while.

Tossing a reflection to the air…

"A war of romance is just like any other war; except for the weapons employed for the attack, for as soon as one of the leaders concedes victory to the adversary, the results are as simple as a resolution of agreement."

20

After laughing for awhile Avon said, "You are a great romancer Valentin and the scary part is that you seem to know it luv."

He modestly shook his head chuckling and continued with his tale, "So, where was I?" He asked.

Avon reminded him, "Embarrassment."

"Well, that's about it for embarrassment; the purpose of that marriage was bringing two healthy and beautiful children into the world and I was divorced longer than I was ever married when you and I met."

"So, how did you manage to purchase the farm?"

"Good point, because in part, I didn't." He replied. Avon looked at him baffled and he added, "I was wrong. I do have to mention embarrassment again." Avon just listened, "It seems like while embarrassment is people's worst enemy, their shame transforms into my benefit and I approach their guilt as a friend. I cannot logically explain it, but money has never been difficult for me to obtain; except when I was a boy and I had to collect coins for my lottery ticket. I must have a magnet to attract money and I don't even trust luck. Yet in spite of all the money, I couldn't

"When the philosopher points to the stars, the fool's eyes are fixed on the finger."

purchase Love; let alone have sex all the time like I thought when I was a boy.

"I find that due to ego people deprive from pleasure because most reject who they are in their hearts. Instead of accepting themselves and embrace their higher self with joy and happiness; most allow ego to take over through embarrassment, guilt and disgrace; and they rather focus on being accepted by society ending up refusing their true essence and source." He paused and looking profoundly into her eyes said, "After Christmas dinner while we were playing Chess, my father's wisdom manifested and materialized; because when looking into your eyes his words echoed in my mind *'Love isn't a lottery and doesn't come to you by luck.'* Right then, I realized that only Love would bring happiness, allowing a couple to have sex any time they want. Money is simply a tool to survive in life and is not what makes a person who they are.

"My ex-wife and I were not *in* Love like I and you are, princess. We thought we were until one day; she actually fell *in* Love with someone else. For many years, the picture of her eyes looking at him, the way she never looked at me, stock in my mind. And I saw her looking at him just the once. She loves him. I was hurt, but at the same time, I wanted her to be happy and I didn't oppose to detach from her. I divorced her as soon as she asked allowing them to enjoy the happiness that she and I never had. So, the ex-wife was embarrassed for being unfaithful to me and she gave me her half of the farm."

Valentin was serene and calm. Avon was listening to him drying tears off her face. He carried on, "Of course, she knew that eventually, Xavier would get his half of the farm. She also knew that at the end of the day, I'll be the only one working to keep the farm in the family, and in the future, our two children would benefit from it. She went to London with her executive new husband who looked neat and clean. Well you see; her mother and she never accepted that her father and I were hard working men. Therefore, we didn't look like executive men. I always worked on heavy machinery and she said that I looked like a vagabond just like her father did. By the way, you and I never talked about it; do I look like a vagabond to you?" Avon looked into his eyes thinking the many times she had dressed down as a vagabond to hang about Union Square with the doctor and she didn't reply. So, he tried to elaborate, "You know, I work with machinery and I am usually dusty and with black grease all over me, does it bother you?"

Then, Avon smiled and replied, "I enjoy seeing you dressed up; yet, I also enjoy seeing you at home working and taking pleasure in your daily activities. I Love you and as long as I can look into your eyes, I do not mind if you are dressed up or not my Valentin."

He looked at her eyes penetrating her most profound senses and she pulled his hands with hers toward her face. She caressed and observed the two rough palms which indeed, looked like they had dirty oil stained in every line. Then, she lowered her head approaching her lips kissing his hands several times and saying, "These hands are the finest working hands I have ever had the privileged to kiss." At that moment, he felt like the greatest man in the world and full of enthusiasm he continued his tale.

"So, I didn't purchase the whole farm, princess. Considering that the ex-wife and her new husband were going to the city; the only thing they could've done with the farm land was to sell it to strangers and since I was already working and used to the equipment, I accepted the farm to ease her embarrassment and guilt; although I could have perfectly bought it. I don't know how she's doing now, but back then, it was hard for her. She couldn't ask me *for* what I didn't have to *give* her. I agreed to everything she requested to ease her emotional state because she was distraught.

"When the philosopher points to the stars, the fool's eyes are fixed on the finger."

I let her be and I released her from any attachment to me without objection at all, out of pure Love. However, everything she was giving me was out of embarrassment and shame from the guilt she felt for cheating. And still, she wasn't in peace within. So once, she asked me if I could *for-give* her and I wasn't going to lie to make her feel better telling her what she wanted to hear. I told her the naked truth. I said that the day that she accepted who she was in her heart; she would find forgiveness within.

"Plus I told her that falling *in* Love wasn't a sin to ask for mercy. I encouraged her to embrace being *in* Love and to feel fortunate to be happy. I told her straight forward that forgiveness was in her heart and I clarified that I do not possess competency to forgive anyone; except myself, because I wasn't any greater than she was for her to ask me to forgive her as if I had more human attributes than she did.

"I assured her that after she learned to forgive herself; she wouldn't need to request forgiveness from external entities ever again. I didn't allow her to humiliate herself in front of me to justify her actions; for agreeing to forgive someone is precisely to humiliate another human being, making them feel as if they are in the wrong path just because they made a decision unrelated to one's, when everyone is entitled to follow their own heart.

"Once accepting an inner source and understanding liberation of guilt, there is no need to justify one's actions requesting forgiveness from an external source; I am a simple man, however I clearly understand the difference between being humble and humiliation.

"Forgiving someone is like enabling them to continue their guilt trip and guilt trips don't have a proper destination."

He paused for a moment and drying tears off her face Avon said, "No wonder she gave you the farm."

He glanced at Avon kindly and added, "Of course, by now, I have multiplied the lottery money and the value of the farm through investments and my real estate business; but I never had the chance to share my money with her; something inside me didn't fully trust her. When her father passed away, her mother was ill and it was then when she transferred her half of the farm into my name. She married well. My children have half-siblings. Her husband loves her and he's a wealthy man. So, it pleases me to see them and the children happy."

Then Avon asked, "Did Xavier agree for you to own the farm?"

"No, *au contraire*, there are business matters that you already learned and other matters you will find out as we get to know each other princess; but I'll tell you this much: except for the area of land where Xavier's house is, Xavier sold his half of the farm, and of course, I am the one who bought it discreetly, ending up in my hands." He winked smiling and continued, "Xavier is not interested in farming or anything to do with hard work. I don't think that Jaidee was ever aware that he owned half of the farm. He has no idea that I possess ownership of the farm either. Xavier is under the impression that his sister sold her half of the land long time ago. That's why he doesn't enter the private areas of the farm and he doesn't want Jaidee to come to our barn. As you know, I don't explain myself to anyone, so from what appears to be; he thinks that I worked something out with the owners of the farm and that we rent the barn."

He gathered thoughts and staring aimlessly he said, "Naturally when I first got divorced, the experience affected me tremendously. I remember giving up and I didn't follow my own advice because I distanced myself from romance. I abandoned myself completely and then—"

He inhaled deeply and exhaling loud he said, "Well it was then, right after the divorce, when I decided to move into the

"When the philosopher points to the stars, the fool's eyes are fixed on the finger."

caravan. I didn't need anything or anyone. Life became all about *Dark Matter* and my money. As years went by, the money multiplied and multiplied. I focused on multiplying the money even more. So, I felt fulfilled because at least I was doing something that I was competent about and productive."

He sighed deeply again and he added in a paradoxical tone, "At the end of the day, I didn't even have the chance to show my French wife to my parents. That wedding was so improvised; my parents didn't come and they met my children after I got divorced. When the kids were old enough, I took them a couple of times a year to visit dad and mum. Now, my boy is over adolescence and my girl is in the teen phase. They don't even call me dad. They have their own plans and I wouldn't be the least surprised if my own children are embarrassed of me as well."

Avon sensed that that part was the end of the story and she was so impressed by Valentin's tale; she ignored what was coming her way. She didn't realize what her new husband was desperately trying to convey to her.

Valentin was ashamed, except his shame wasn't caused by guilt; his shame was caused by his rare bashful and humble ways; because through the years; he had multiplied his small fortune into millions and he had never been comfortable to share his wealth with anyone until he met Avon. Valentin was ready to unveil his riches to his new wife and he didn't know how. He certainly didn't want to wait until he passed away for Avon to find out about their reserves via an attorney reading a testament to her.

Valentin was tired of repressing his financial aspect in life. Because in his case, he wasn't only a pure, rare, soiled, naturally kind, impatient, impulsive, and embarrassing individual thanks to his truthful manners; but he also happened to be a multimillionaire who lived in a small caravan due to rejection thinking that he had lost the chance to ever be *in* Love with someone else. The time for Avon to receive her wedding gift was coming soon and she had no idea what it was about, at the same time, Valentin was on the verge of exposing his princess to an overwhelming revelation and ready to support her during the difficult moment; because he understood the emotional turmoil and the sensation that a person experiences when acquiring an amount of money that they could have dreamed on spending; however, they might have never dreamed on managing such an amount of money through a lifetime. Especially, after the experience he had when telling Avon about owning the farm. Valentin was prepared for any reaction Avon could develop as a result of his overwhelming news to her. He was ready to see her in any state of mind in case she reacted hysterically crying and laughing all at once; or if her reaction was silence for awhile; he was ready to be patient and wait for her to assimilate the news. He was familiar with Avon's emotions and although the odds were low; he was hoping that she didn't suffer some sort of physical trauma which he was prepared to manage as well. However, he was sincerely hoping that she didn't turn mad, or even worse, as she could turn against him seeing that he was risking for her to embarrassedly refuse him, due to ego, which could've been more often than not the case at their relationship stage.

He took into consideration her reaction when he first told her about owning the farm; because if then, when Avon felt embarrassed she was inclined to distrust him acting defensive and suspicious toward him; when revealing his riches to her; she could turn against him if he wasn't cautious. Valentin found himself in a situation not many would like to be in and he didn't have idea how he had gotten there. He loved his princess and he wasn't going to renounce being *in* Love with her. He understood the irony of living as well as the inevitable truth regarding money, as lack or

"When the philosopher points to the stars, the fool's eyes are fixed on the finger."

abundance of funds could not remain unnoticed for long and for him there was no other way than being embarrassedly truthful. Therefore, he figured out that the best way was to tell Avon about his wealth on their wedding day presenting it as a gift to her.

☙❧

Tossing a reflection to the air...

"Living life *for-getting* what one is for Love; is not the same than living life *for-giving* what one is for Love."

☙❧

Valentin beckoned the butler and the butler brought a silver tray holding an envelope to him. "Dominique we certainly made you wait to present the gift, didn't we?" He said to the butler expressing gratitude. Dominique smiled, nodded politely and he walked out to the balcony to join the violinists.

Valentin placed the tray on the center table close to Avon and he said, "I Love you more for saying '*Da*' princess. My wedding gift to you, remember?"

"Ooh my gift, thank you luv." She said still in seventh heaven thinking of the story he just shared.

He added, "It will please me greatly if you accept."

He remained seated by her side observing her and waiting for her reaction. Avon noticed that there was a pen on the tray. Then, she picked the envelope, she opened it, she took a folded leaf out and before reading anything she said, "I will sign whatever it is that you want me to sign. Although at this point, is rather too late to sign a pre-nuptial agreement luv." They both laughed.

She then unfolded the leaf finding her gift to be a proposal for her to join Valentin's wealth giving her full access to his assets worth half of billion Euros and there was a dotted line with her new name as his wife for her to sign if she accepted.

Avon stood up shaking like a feather blowing away in the air and she said, "Luv, according to this proposal you are a multimillionaire and I have said that I will accept your gift with grace," she looked at him inhaling deeply and exhaling slowly adding, "I need to assimilate this." She was silent for a slight moment and then she said, "Would you hold me? Please hold me tight." He immediately stood up and held her.

While Valentin held her firmly, Avon's mind traveled at the highest speed as she remembered when she wrote in her *affirmations journal*:

In accordance to the will of the Universe, expressing intention of peace and harmony to the entire world, under the grace of a perfect path, I am grateful for being financially independent. Thank you for listening to my request and for giving the order for my intention to manifest.

Then, Avon held Valentin like she had never embraced him before. Her arms felt too short for the immensity of her hug; as she was aware that when she wrote her affirmation she didn't even know what financial independency meant. Afterward she realized that she had nothing to share with Valentin; except for their connection through Arolf and *Dark Matter* and she felt entirely where she belonged surrounded by his arms sensing peace in her heart admitting that being *in* Love individually was what had attracted them like magnetic Energy to fall *in* Love together.

Valentin held her, but he didn't want her to pass out in his arms. He released her a bit and her entire body was trembling like she was on Christmas night. So, he carried her and he sat holding her tight on his lap. Then, he released her again to be able to see her

"When the philosopher points to the stars, the fool's eyes are fixed on the finger."

face. He needed to make certain that she was well; but she asked him once more, "Would you hold me? Please hold me tight luv." So, as long as she was talking, he thought that she was fine. But he didn't want to suffocate her between his arms and he remembered when he disclosed to her the ownership of the farm and the way she reacted. Back then, after he suggested visiting the farm for the first time; she approached him and she held him for a long while until she was ready to go to the farm.

So when having his new wife trembling in his arms; he tenderly looked at her and he allowed her to hold him instead. She couldn't tell exactly what she wanted, but it wasn't his embrace that she was looking for; she was rather looking for support between her trembling arms. Not knowing what to do for her physically, Valentin spoke softly to her while caressing her, "*Da, da*, princess, I am holding you. I am holding you, *da, da*," he said hardly touching her; but she felt safe holding him tight.

In the meantime Dominique had a laptop on a console table by the foyer and he was wearing head phones communicating with the paramedics who were in a suite close by and with an ambulance ready; waiting for Avon's reaction in case she needed to be taken to the emergency room.

Two violinists were in the living area standing on alert. The other violinist had taken his jacket off, his shirt sleeves were rolled up, and he had the medical essentials prepared as well as a doctor's fist aid carry bag next to Avon. Everyone was silent and observing her.

After a long while, Avon moved slowly from Valentin's lap and she sat next to him. Every man in the room was watching her. Suddenly she spoke and asked, "Is your performance over gentlemen?" They smiled and no one replied.

So, Valentin asked her, "Princess; are you alright?"

"Yes, luv, I am fine." She confirmed.

"Well, I hope you don't mind if our friends stay until being certain that you are totally fine." He said.

Then, she looked around. She noticed their unanticipated preparations and the gentlemen attention toward her and she said, "I don't mind at all; as a matter of fact, let us celebrate and toast with some *Dom*."

Then, Valentin said, "But of course princess" and he called out, "*Dom*-inique" teasing the butler.

While Dominique did the honors serving bubbly she asked, "Would you joining us Dominique?"

"My pleasure Madame," Dominique accepted.

When she was ready, she stood up. Valentin stood next to her holding her back-waist with one hand and with the other hand he held the glass. She courtly said, "Gentlemen, allow me to express my gratitude in humble words. I would like to make a toast in honor of the *forgotten, knowledge,* and especially the *unknown*." Valentin squeezed her ribs expressing satisfaction for her mention of the unknown. She continued, "I also would like to quote my loving husband's words when not long ago he shared an adage with me which goes, 'What you don't know doesn't hurt you.'" She smiled looking at Valentin and carried on, "Just now, after receiving my wedding gift, while I was surrounded by my husband's arms, I reflected learning from those words and I realized that, if the *unknown* does not hurt me nor should *knowledge*; for in the midst of tomorrow I will *forget* about many things and when *forgotten*, *knowledge*, will rest in the midst of the *unknown* anyway." Everyone expressed wonder and she kept talking, "The emotions I am experiencing at this moment due to my recent *knowledge* will fade away and without me knowing, these emotions will be *forgotten* and return to the *Unknown*. However, it is precisely the management of

"When the philosopher points to the stars, the fool's eyes are fixed on the finger."

emotions what makes people react in different ways. The source of the gift that I received today derives from Love; hence harmless gentlemen. I am privileged and I *do* accept my husband's wedding gift. I am grateful to all of you for your kindness. Cheers!"

After they toasted joyfully, one of the violinists who was standing on alert approached her and said, "Madame, I happen to enjoy playing the violin but I also happen to be Valentin's attorney. Would you mind signing the proposal?"

"Not at all," she replied and signed accepting. However she was surprised when she realized that the talented violinist was Valentin's attorney and she didn't even notice. Then, the other Violinist who was standing on alert and the one who had his sleeves rolled up signed as witnesses and Valentin signed next to her signature. As the attorney congratulated her; he slipped the document in his jacket inner pocket walking away to play his violin next to a silent grand piano that seemed to be decorating the living area.

The violinist who was standing on alert and served as a witness approached to congratulate Avon as well saying, "I also enjoy playing the violin and *I am* a violinist. It's a pleasure being your witness today Madame." He walked away to join the attorney by the piano playing his violin.

After that, the violinist who was also a witness and had his shirt sleeves rolled up, approached Avon to congratulate her too and while rearranging his cuffs, he said, "I am pleased that you are fine and I do enjoy playing the violin as well. However, at times, I play the role of a doctor." They laughed and she was totally amazed with their musical talent, but almost in shock for not noticing that the gentlemen were in there fulfilling more than one role. Then he added, "Don't hesitate to let me know if you need my medical expertise. I'll be on site purposely at your service Madame." And he went to join the others playing his violin by the piano.

Afterward, Valentin and Avon sat looking at each other for awhile listening to the music. Then, Valentin stood up and he said, "Princess, it's time for me to express my gratitude for being *in* Love with you the only way I know how." He beckoned her to come along with him. They walked toward the musicians; he lifted Avon up and sat her on top of the grand piano. He sat positioning himself to play and as the others introduced the melody with their violins, Valentin blended in playing *Air* by *Bach*, just for her.

Although Avon had listened to Valentin play piano at home before; she had never sensed the fulfillment he expressed playing on their wedding night.

She didn't know that Valentin also played the violin and he surprised her playing violin as a wedding gift as well. Valentin and his friends had been practicing for several months especially for that night which Avon didn't notice because she was busily in charge of the paperwork and research. And most certainly until then, Avon wasn't aware that Valentin practiced living a double life looking like a vagabond in the open and being a passionate musician as an unknown multimillionaire; just the opposite of what she did with the doctor wandering around Union Square.

At that point, Avon had obtained from Arolf exactly what she had requested combined with what she had *attracted* by her own decisions and actions in life, and at freewill, she could whether bless what she was receiving with an open heart, or due to ego, decline. Since as a result of her request to become a great performer in life, from the moment she made her pact, many blessings were sent her way and she had to go through much more to fully understand, assimilate and appropriate the truth from her source.

"When the philosopher points to the stars, the fool's eyes are fixed on the finger."

Tossing a reflection to the air...

"Passion is the sensation burning like a flame of desire in one's heart. Some ignore it and very few follow it. However when one's passion is developed and shared with others; one's flame remains lit beyond death, and that, is the closest to immortality."

The talented musicians delighted her with the finest classical melodies getting completely over-involved performing as an expression of their pure Love to the musical art. She absorbed to the fullest the perfection of their harmony listening to them as they conveyed the reflection of their passion ecstasy to her.

Then, when they played *Adagio* by *Albinoni*, Avon perceived that her new husband was ready to be intimate with her.

Except for Dominique, everyone retired to their respective sleeping quarters and Valentin carried Avon to the master bedroom of the presidential suite. Dominique was holding the door open for them and as soon as they entered; the most enchanting romantic milieu was sensed. Dominique closed the door behind them and the instant they came in; the fragrance of herbal tea intensified.

Valentin put Avon down allowing her to appreciate the setting. Enormous aromatic candles were lit. White roses and petals were spread all around, and in the right front corner, a giant green-tea bag was brewing inside an in-ground glittering hot tub ready for them to immerse.

While Avon was observing the setting, Valentin pulled up his hair and the next thing she noticed; Valentin was like his truth, totally naked. He approached her from behind and as he kissed her shoulders and neck; he helped her getting undressed. She tied her hair up as well and they slipped into the tub facing each other. "After such an eventful day this hot bath is the best remedy to relax you princess." Valentin said.

"I hope you relax as well. Your day was as eventful as mine; especially with everything you prepared for me" she said and then teased, "I am also hoping that you did not spend the whole fortune tonight; although I am having a great time. I am a very happy bride!"

"I can respond to your initial question now; as you asked me how much I saved getting a special package for the suite. Let me tell you in brief, Dominique is my right-hand man and he has been by my side from the time when I first came to France. He was my French and English tutor and we became business partners ever since. When I want something, I just ask Dominique and he takes care of everything for me. So actually, we got the suite for free. We are shareholders at this hotel along with several others around Europe making us part owners princess." She smiled in grand feeling completely satisfied and she relaxed looking at his heavenly eyes.

After awhile, Valentin had his eyes closed and he felt Avon coming out of the tub. He then heard the fizz of *Dom* being poured into glasses.

He came out of the tub and all he felt was a fluffy towel drying him with Avon's soft and sensual touch.

She handed him a glass of bubbly and as she sipped from her glass; she kissed him.

Valentin sensed wet kisses on his back neck and then lower. He felt her wet kisses moving slowly down to his backside gradually into his front waist and she kept going slowly up to his front shoulders and neck. He felt her wet mouth kissing his chest and she began to go down again. He felt shivers as she kissed him slower and lower. He tingled all over and all the way down to his toes.

"When the philosopher points to the stars, the fool's eyes are fixed on the finger."

He sensed her moist kisses lower and slower; yet a bit lower. The next thing Valentin felt was Avon enjoying him to the fullest as her lips surrounded his erected virility until he was ready to explode.

He walked away beckoning her and he laid on the bed. She crawled on top of him and they immersed within each other as husband and wife afresh.

Tossing a reflection to the air...

"The mechanics of the Universe work in perfect harmony being lovingly amused by the rest of its components; meanwhile terrestrials take the Universe faultless performance too serious overlooking its everlasting witty functionality."

21

⚭

From France to Bulgaria

Avon's mind couldn't register a single word. Strange faces smiled. Unfamiliar eyes were looking at her. She heard odd voices. She was surrounded by a mystifying ambiance and she couldn't talk or understand at all.

In the meantime during the day, the sun rose in the mornings and bright matter glowed all over the blue skies, and at night, the sparkling stars crowned the moon while *Dark Matter* hid behind. Giving Avon a sense of relief for she might have found herself feeling like an alien in a concealed area; yet, appreciating the well-known sun, moon and stars brought her to realize that she was in familiar territory for she wasn't much further than Earth.

At that point, everything seemed to indicate that Avon had drifted away; far and beyond anything she had been familiar with up till then; because the following was an entirely isolated phase provided that her only link to the world out there was her husband Valentin.

"When the philosopher points to the stars, the fool's eyes are fixed on the finger."

Following the wedding, Avon and Valentin enjoyed some time in Paris. Then, they went back to the barn at the farm in Provence to make arrangements to go to Bulgaria. After acquiring their marriage certificate most of the complicated paperwork had already been handled and as soon as they submitted the request for Avon to sponsor Valentin as her husband at the U.S. Embassy in Sofia; they only needed plenty of patience while waiting for approval.

However, unlike fairytales ending in a glamorous wedding and living happily ever after, Valentin and Avon were well aware that, "Happily ever after," was simply it, a fairytale. For till then, being married didn't mean much to them; except that they had a legal marriage certificate justifying their loving union. Their challenges were just about to begin. They still had to provide evidence substantiating their merger; because the U.S. Embassy Officials were about to evaluate and scrutinize their loving intentions to one another in any thinkable defying scenario and not even if Avon and Valentin gathered all the money in the world, they could do a thing about it. Simply, their loving union was at the mercy of the U.S. Homeland and Security Department.

Or so it seemed in the midst of the ordeal, because they did have a couple of other options; they could've overlooked Avon's communication issue and stay in Bulgaria, or they could've reversed the communication issue toward Valentin and go to tropical Thailand. Also, since Avon was a Canadian citizen; they could've explored those territories as well. Although, being that Valentin was a French citizen; they could always go back to France. Once being married, as long as they were together; they just had to sponsor one another and select a country to reside at, and that country was the U.S.A.

Something Avon learned about immigrations when she first entered Canada, then in College and throughout her career was to respect Immigration Statutes in any country; for toying around with Immigrations wouldn't grant her the privilege of traveling or residing legally all over the world. Therefore, once they submitted the petition forms and the application at the U.S. embassy in Sofia; it didn't really matter if they paid a third party to represent them; as the embassy would summon the newlyweds at random for interviews. So, Avon and Valentin were prepared and ready to respond to their call at any time of the day while in Bulgaria. And just like Avon had found out through her research, the Sofia U.S. Embassy Officials confirmed that their petition process would take from one month to three months to get resolved.

Therefore, spending some time in Bulgaria introduced Avon to experience a new facet in life. They spoke Slavic written in Cyrillic. For the first time, Avon was in a place where she couldn't communicate with anyone at all; except for one person, Valentin. As a result, Avon and Valentin became inseparable. Avon couldn't do much without him, and during that phase, he demonstrated the most profound sense of kindness in all aspects toward his wife not giving importance to certain characteristics the woman he had married revealed in the process.

On the other hand, during the period that followed, a frequency of silence turned out to be a fascinating dimension for Avon's learning life lesson; although back then she ignored it, and so, she struggled. Unable to communicate through voice; not by option, but by force; she had to trust Valentin with serious matters which she had never allowed anyone else to handle for her before. She entered Bulgaria as an American tourist and she was allowed the minimum stay at the port of entry. A few weeks later, when her permit was about to expire; she had no option but to trust Valentin to handle her visa renewal. From Avon's perspective, English didn't seem to be too popular in Bulgaria, because even if people spoke

"When the philosopher points to the stars, the fool's eyes are fixed on the finger."

it, they wouldn't express it, period. Also dealing with the local immigration office was a challenge from Avon's viewpoint, while a simple process from Valentin's. Once again she was skeptical regarding the unknown about her husband because she had never heard of renewing a tourist permit without having to leave the country and reenter; yet, such, was not the case in Bulgaria. Her only option was to trust their system without torturing herself by double checking, or pressuring Valentin. Because except for him, no one would speak English to her, much less any of the other languages she spoke. In the past, her communication skills could have been an asset; however, being multilingual and capable to interact professionally as an educated communicator didn't seem to be useful in Bulgaria.

And so, while in the core of a silence frequency; Avon realized that every time she had disagreed with Valentin so far was due to her constant need of being in charge, which became evident to her in Bulgaria where she was totally unable to understand having to depend on him entirely. Valentin had never brought up the issue regarding her constant need of being in charge because it didn't affect him. He did as he considered best for both of them anyway and he didn't mind when she tossed a couple of fits for no reason now and then. However, when Avon realized the naked truth; she struggled about it within exposing more of her inner senses still.

Then by reading and researching; she figured out the difference between interior silence and exterior silence; forced silence and voluntary silence; and overall, when comprehending the complexity of silence she became even more aware of her inner-self. Basically, an egress silent wave vibration was the only tool Avon possessed when communicating with others while in Bulgaria. The short period of time turned into an intense lesson for her to learn because she felt like she was incompetent; not only regarding the most important documentation she had ever handled, but also feeling that when Valentin needed her the most; she was unable to assist him and *then* was when Avon immersed into learning about *silent waves*.

In her effort to understand what was happening to her and studying her senses; she discovered an instinct within. She found herself trying to identify if her instinct derived either from manipulation or control and when looking for strength to let it go; she became aware that the process was as difficult as when releasing *willpower* to Arolf because confiding and trusting another human being, Valentin, felt at the moment like the ultimate challenge for her to surmount.

Perhaps due to the fact that Avon didn't play much with dolls becoming a mother was never one of her goals. However, given that she had been exposed to fecundation long enough and she had never been in the position to perform a pregnancy test; she accepted the fact that if fertilization didn't happen naturally she wasn't going to become a mother by forcing the situation. And of course eventually, she had to trust Valentin as he trusted her, but not before identifying that the instinct awakening slowly within her, shielding her husband as if he was her child, revealed as her maternal instinctive sense.

At first when Valentin was appointed to do things, Avon instructed him step by step and in detail telling him how to proceed. Meanwhile, Valentin didn't appreciate to be treated like a kid. He tried to be patient, but he didn't follow his wife's directions to the tee like she rigorously indicated. Avon didn't seem to understand that not every person in Earth was going to follow structure as she had been trained. Obviously she ignored then what later she discovered, since as a male, Valentin was much more direct and practical than she was when achieving a task, because Valentin

"When the philosopher points to the stars, the fool's eyes are fixed on the finger."

didn't get emotionally involved like Avon did as a female. Besides, as long as he accomplished the objective properly, it really didn't matter the steps he followed.

And so, although Avon was the one who filled out the forms and applications by thoroughly complying with the U.S. Embassy guidelines; the Embassy Officers wouldn't speak English to her during the interviews. At the U.S. Embassy in Sofia only the Consul spoke English, and naturally, the Consul didn't talk to the public unless it was absolutely necessary. And provided that the petitioner wasn't Avon but Valentin; the Consul didn't find necessary speaking to her. From the Embassy Officers' viewpoint, Avon and Valentin's request was just a simple and ordinary case and not such a big deal as it represented to her. Hence, Avon felt like she was in loud silence unable to understand what the Embassy Officials were saying to Valentin and vice versa.

At first, Avon wanted Valentin to translate every single word they were saying as if her understanding would influence the interviewer's perception of their true Love intention which just caused a couple of uncomfortable moments for both of them during their initial interview. However, it didn't take long for Avon to understand; not to understand Bulgarian and what everyone was saying but she finally grasped that, she had to let it be allowing Arolf to set whatever they needed into place. Above all, Avon had to trust Valentin blindly as her intimate ally, because she realized that deep inside; her struggle was about trusting the man that had been created for her—her husband.

Then again, eventually she understood that by not employing translators indicated the effectiveness of a practical and economical Bulgarian society. Also, thanks to the low demand of English speaking population in the area; the U.S. Embassy was able to process formalities efficiently and quicker than in other countries.

All things considered, every time they went to Sofia for an interview at the U.S. Embassy, sooner than later, Avon found out the results of the paperwork they submitted when her beloved Valentin translated for her while driving back to the village from the city. Just like the ceremony of their wedding, when the only part which concerned her was to know when to say "Yes." Then, as a result of the paperwork she had prepared; the marriage certificate was issued and every word said in between had gone with the wind.

Clearly, the fact that she was in Bulgaria with Valentin in person provided evidence to the American Embassy to take their petition serious and not as a fraudulent request; but at the same time as Avon's physical presence was important she secluded herself instinctively and she isolated to be within; unlike the past when she had isolated from within for not to be. And since she didn't have much to do but wait; she was able to think in silence without interruptions and her thoughts began to reflect on paper. So she continued encountering much more expansion of wits. Through the same silence she was experiencing in the exterior; she silently allowed thoughts to exit her mind as they entered exposing every idea in writing through pure inspiration. Although back then, she ignored what was happening to her, and at times, she even wrote through the night.

During the waiting silent frequency phase, Avon discovered another meaning of the gold and fire metaphor while practicing the art of Alchemy focusing on her emotions. She began with her truest faculty: *Her Will*. She was able to study the implementation of Alchemy when transmuting *will*power by releasing it into the *will* of the Universe. She learned to transmute ill-*will* into good*will*, and she was left with a quest regarding transmutation of her last-*will* as her free*will* allowed. In the process, her sharpness expanded one more time experiencing a diminishing sensation detecting a

"When the philosopher points to the stars, the fool's eyes are fixed on the finger."

gradual void in her interior. The void wasn't of emptiness but a void of space increasing and expanding slowly; in and out, back and forth, up and down, stretching her inner-self like when a bubble is tenderly blown within its elements allowing the breath of being to pass expanding throughout; to the point where she sensed her heartbeat merging with her breathing pace next to a symbolic flame which remained with Arolf's presence as a permanent resident in her heart bonding through Love, the will of the Universe and silence.

Tossing a reflection to the air…

"Not every word spoken is heard, and not every word heard is necessarily spoken."

In the interim, as boring as Avon's silence phase sounded up till then, being in silence didn't impede for Avon to capture some pleasure out of the experience as well. The fact that Avon was unable neither to speak nor to understand meant practically nothing to Valentin's mama, because his mama didn't give up communicating with her. Initially, Avon remained quiet listening and making an effort to sense what his mama was trying to say. Meanwhile, his mama talked, talked, and talked. Then, as Avon's sensing attempts failed; the only remedy was to request from Valentin to translate what his mama was trying to convey. Otherwise, the longer Avon waited to ask Valentin to interpret; the louder his mama spoke to her. Seemed as if the association between understanding and volume might have been universal; although Avon thought that volume had nothing to do with understanding whatsoever; for it didn't matter how loudly his mama spoke; still, she couldn't understand a single word.

So, while waiting for the American Embassy's summons, in the midst of a silence frequency, inspirational writings, and more silence; Avon and his mama learned to communicate through gestures, looks and senses. They managed to understand each other fairly; however, their communication ended up developing into pure silence.

One day, Avon noticed that his mama was struggling with a safety pin trying to patch up a dress seam. Avon observed her wearing the dress while dealing with the repair and as soon as his mama pinned the seam; she carried on with her daily routine. A few days later the same dress hung off the drying line after being washed giving Avon an opportunity to mend it. His mama wasn't home. So, Avon asked Valentin to set up an old sewing machine that rested by a corner in the living area of his parents' house. The sewing machine might've been old, but it worked. Once Avon repaired the seams needing reinforcement on his mama's dress; she left the dress on a specific spot for his mama to understand that the dressed had been fixed.

When his mama found the dress and she understood that Avon had mended it; she spoke, she talked, saying something and adding more. Of course, not understanding a single word; Avon approached smiling, nodding, signing and showing his mama where she had repaired the dress.

Excited, his mama brought out several items putting them by the sewing machine and indicating that they were in need of repairs. Avon smiled and nodded assent slowly trying to convey agreement

"When the philosopher points to the stars, the fool's eyes are fixed on the finger."

to mend the items. However, when his mama noticed that Avon nodded in response to her request, *she* called Valentin to translate. Apparently, Avon ignored the gestures in Bulgaria as much as their language, because it turned out that in Bulgaria, nodding meant "No" while shaking the head meant "Yes."

The misunderstanding took some effort from Valentin's part to clearly convince his mama of his wife's genuine intentions, and at the same time, Avon wished being able to communicate openly with the lady who had birthed her beloved Valentin.

After the anecdote, Avon was a bit surprised with the fact that his mama was wearing outworn clothes and one evening after dinner; they were sitting at the terrace playing Chess and enjoying a nightcap and she asked, "Luv, do you think your mama would like us to take her shopping for a new dress?"

He replied, "No, if she wants new dresses she can go herself. She doesn't need us to take her; would you like dresses for yourself? Let me know and I'll go with you to translate."

So, Avon said smiling, "No, I do not enjoy shopping in person. I was thinking that your mama might need a new dress. That's all."

"Why, because of the repairs?" he asked.

"Yes" she replied.

Valentin said, "My darling, do not concern about my parents' wellbeing. They enjoy *weal* and are *healthy*; therefore they are *weal*thy. They lived the majority of their lifetime under a different regime. They are happy to have what they need. They are not like other people who compete to have the most, even when they have no use for it. Mum and dad live a life of abundance not a life of waste. Their frame of mind is different. They don't lack of anything but everything they have they produce themselves through natural resources and they respect their reserves. Well, I am not far from living the same lifestyle, for I am a simple man as well."

Avon was attentively listening and she asked, "Would you tell me more about your parents?"

So he added, "Well, after I shared some of the lottery winnings with them, plus the money they have reproduced through the years; they could've relocated to a popular city like Sofia, or they could be living by the Black Sea. But they didn't relocate. They still live here in the same small village and in the same house that they built together with their four hands when they first got married. They own properties in other cities and by the Sea, but those are investments to keep money circulating in order to produce cash flow; they are happy and wealthy though. Mum enjoys spending most of her days in the garden and preparing preserves. She probably doesn't find the need to get a new dress to perform her daily tasks. However, when they came to Paris for our wedding; my parents were happy to indulge visiting the most exclusive clubs, theaters, opera houses, and restaurants entertaining themselves. They enjoyed privately, and afterward, they returned home to carry on with their simple daily activities."

Then Avon said, "I understand, because when I got into real estate; I learned to live under my means in order to invest with Angelina and Gabe."

"As far as I understand your friends introduce you to real estate with rentals and flipping houses which is a good way to begin, but that isn't what real estate really means. I am sure Gabe must know that real estate has a more profound meaning. For instance, in Bulgarian the meaning of real estate is immobile, solid, fixed assets; and those are the kind of assets I look for in order to invest and produce cash flow."

Then, she added, "Let me see— in Thai translates into grounded assets and in French means the same, immobile and permanent assets, yes?"

"When the philosopher points to the stars, the fool's eyes are fixed on the finger."

"Yes, and in Spanish?" he asked.

"In Spanish translates into something like rooted assets luv," she replied.

"Ooh well, that should tell us enough, but just for the fun of it, have you realized what real estate means in English?"

"Real estate—" she said in wonder. Then she added, "Real estate meaning that the rest of an estate is not as *real?*" Valentin winked. They smiled and the evening went on.

Few weeks later during an uneventful morning, Valentin brought his passport with the U.S. Permanent Resident visa stamped on it to Avon. The U.S. Embassy had sent his passport through currier and the visa granted him thirty days to enter the U.S.A.

The evening prior to their trip to America, Avon and Valentin were preparing dinner and they noticed his mama walking in the hall toward the kitchen. She hid her hands behind her back as if she was holding something and they also noticed that she was mumbling. The closer his mama approached the clearer the words she mumbled became. Then, they perceived the words that she was murmuring and sounded familiar. When his mama came closer; they were able to clearly hear his mama speaking English saying, *"From my heart to yours! From my heart to yours! From my heart to yours!"*

As his mama advanced close enough; she stopped facing Avon. Then, his mama pulled out a gorgeous bouquet of rare Orchids from her back. She handed the flowers to Avon as she repeated like the echo of a *mantra chant*, "From my heart to yours!" His mama gave signs of an accomplished mission, turned around affectionless and walked away.

As a response, Avon reacted with a radiant smile not being able to give his mama a hug nor to contain tears of joy. Meanwhile for his mama physical affection didn't mean much. Afterward, Avon asked Valentin if he had told his mama the phrase, "From my heart to yours!" And he said that his mama didn't learn it from him. So, during dinner Valentin asked his mama where she had learned the phrase and he translated for Avon explaining that his mama went to the shop to buy the Orchids for her. After that, his mama walked a couple of blocks to her friend's who had lived in England and spoke English. So then, his mama asked her friend in person because telephoning her would have been impolite to translate what she wanted to say from Bulgarian into English and once her friend told her the phrase, for not to forget it; his mama kept repeating, "*From my heart to yours!*"while walking all the way from her friend's house until the moment when she handed the Orchids to Avon.

In the midst of communication, there was a connection between Avon and his mama feeling like a frequency of rhythmic vibrations at the heart of the Love that they shared for the same man in silence–Valentin.

Tossing a reflection to the air...

"Even in the quietest frequency of silence, Love emits the highest volume of rhythmic vibes among an intertwined world of people living on the Earth globe which like a hot air balloon, miraculously revolves in the thick of the Universe."

"When the philosopher points to the stars, the fool's eyes are fixed on the finger."

22

٭

*A*von had fallen *in* Love without a companion. She had met Valentin who was also *in* Love and willing to be her intimate ally in life. They had accomplished to get married and just like they had planned; they were living in San Fran. Nevertheless, she was unaware of her own growth and inner wealth.

The truthful moment began unraveling for her a few days after they arrived in San Fran from Bulgaria when Valentin approached her at the library where she was absorbed reading and he asked, "Princess, shall we talk about our finances regarding the mortgage on this building with Angelina and Gabe and the bank?" Avon's response was silence. She stared aimlessly for awhile and Valentin patiently waited for her to react.

Suddenly she said, "I am intimidated to use the money luv."

He then said, "Well, your reaction is natural although you must realize that every day passing by we are wasting funds with the interest paid. We are not paying hundreds of dollars in interest for thousands of dollars. We're actually paying thousands of dollars in interest for millions and once we pay it off, being our asset, we will profit from the rentals cash flow or we can decide what to do

"When the philosopher points to the stars, the fool's eyes are fixed on the finger."

with the building. As you know, real estate is not our asset until the mortgage is paid off; meanwhile, this building and *we* are assets to the creditors and the bank."

"I understand, but it's precisely the amount what I feel intimidated about. I have never spent so much money before; you do it luv," was her response.

While trying to contain his amusement, he added, "So we seem to have an issue, because what motivated me in the past was to provide for my children. Now that you are my wife my motivation is to provide for you as well and thus far I have demonstrated competence to provide. However, I am not a spender and I was hoping you helped me to distribute the money properly."

"So, am I supposed to spend your money now?"

And he replied smiling, "No, it's not *my* money. It's *our* money. I am still producing more money. The fact that we have been traveling and not established didn't stop me from managing businesses. You know that Dominique and I keep in touch regularly and all we talk about is work. I provide for you by bringing money, I see your smile and we share happiness; but if I sense tension and pressure from you, I feel like I'm not providing enough or unfulfilling my role which blocks happiness from flowing. It's *our* money."

"Am I to administrate all the money then?"

"No" he replied holding back a laugh. Then, looking intensely into her eyes he added, "Jimmy administrates the rentals here with the money we allow by making our own decisions. Dominique administrates the farm in Provence and a great deal of business for us, with the money we allow by making our own decisions. However, with creditors is the reverse. When we don't make decisions in our favor and we hold money instead of allowing cash to flow; the creditors decide how much interest percentage and fees we pay administrating our money and cash flows in *their* favor.

You see princess by now, you have more money than any amount you ever needed to borrow in the past and it's our responsibility to make decisions and channel the funds appropriately."

"Luv, what else can I ask for? I appreciate your patience to explain these matters to me. Should we make decisions together until I learn then? I have a slight idea about managing such an amount of money; however, no clue about spending it," she said.

Then he teased, "Finances are like sex; nobody likes to talk about it, and yet, everyone wants to enjoy it. But of course we will do it together and not only until you learn. We should always maintain financial matters clear between us, just like sex princess, just like sex." She looked at him smiling and he added, "This is only the beginning; eventually you will discover the pros and cons to be a multimillionaire; however for the most part, the greatest sense of satisfaction reveals when trusting someone to share everything with." He winked and she tossed her arms around his neck kissing him.

Tossing a reflection to the air...

"When it comes to finances and sex, many provide their opinion. Sadly due to lack of one or the other, just a few of those 'many' understand their own judgment."

As soon as Avon and Valentin arrived in San Fran; they had decided to refurbish the entire floor where the library was to create their new home with enough space for his piano and their

"When the philosopher points to the stars, the fool's eyes are fixed on the finger."

general comfort. Except the project was going to be different than remodeling the barn, because they depended on workers helping, city permits and inspections which prolonged the end result a bit longer than the time Valentin would have taken. Still, after they worked renewing their new home, Avon went to the library and she was in silence most of the time. She kept distant from the doctor and Jimmy. She wasn't able to find a new routine and she didn't gather in the garden with them as they used to do in the past.

In the interim an uneventful evening, due to their forthcoming financial settlements, Avon received an e-mail from Angelina conveying that they were coming to San Fran to meet Valentin and to reconcile their financial affairs. Avon was excited to see her *sunshine* again and when they arrived; they landed in a private jet. To Valentin's surprise; Gabe was the pilot. As usual, Angelina and Gabe had leased a private jet taking pleasure when crossing the country by avoiding the commercial flights hassle. Angelina, Gabe, and Valentin met and aside from settling their business affairs; the couple enjoyed a week in the West Coast with them. They went dinning and wining through Napa Valley; they hired a sailboat to go around the bay; and they explored some restaurants in Sausalito as well.

Angelina was impressed when she learned about Avon's latest adventures and especially surprised with Valentin turning out to be a multimillionaire. Avon shared some of her recent writings with her and she encouraged Avon to pursue writing her memoirs. Avon received Angelina's words with an open heart and she explained that although she had plenty of material; she had no idea of how to gather and organize her memoirs but that she would try. In the meantime, Gabe and Valentin acquainted with their related interests and after playing musical instruments while sipping *Brandy* and smoking *Montecristo* cigars; it didn't take them long to agree on building their own aircraft. Both of them had the means and share certain enthusiasm about flying; Gabe had knowledge and experience as a pilot and Valentin in engineering and mechanics.

They enjoyed a week together and after Angelina and Gabe left; Avon and Valentin settled their financial affairs with the bank liberating them completely from debt. Then while Valentin had found a new endeavor around mechanics building an airplane, Avon began revolving around life as a multimillionaire. She adapted to the administrative factors of managing greater amounts of money in contrast to what she had managed in the past and with Jimmy's accounting assistance, Valentin introduced her to charity concepts in order to keep finances flowing.

So, since Avon had learned from her own failure after the complimentary hot air balloon ride adventure; when becoming a multimillionaire it was time for her to decide her true intention to assist the homeless and she asked advice from Jimmy regarding strategies to give them support. Naturally, the best policy was to unite to organizations that were already functioning under the guidelines that the homeless trusted for resources when they felt a spark in their hearts. Therefore, just like when Avon united to the Universe in order to live a perfect and harmonious life because it was the only thing that she knew already functioning in perfect harmony; she allied with a couple of charities that were already organized to aid the homeless volunteering a couple of times a week. Her contribution was to motivate the homeless to write their stories through dynamics she created for the cause. However, as Avon began breaking the silence within and she began to communicate with others besides Valentin; just when Avon thought that life couldn't get better; she emotionally collapsed.

In the previous months, Avon had experienced intense expansion and life didn't even resemble to the normal life she knew

"When the philosopher points to the stars, the fool's eyes are fixed on the finger."

at all. She realized that she had accomplished her childhood dreams one by one. She no longer chased a career. She had relocated a couple of times in less than a year. She had encountered an intimate ally and she was married to a multimillionaire. Avon's inner-self was stretched to the greatest of her capacity and she had to learn how to adapt and cope with the effect of each cause. In the midst of her mind set; she decided to go back to the book that illuminated her through the darkest moments in life and when she tried to read "*The Greatest Salesman in the World*" one more time; she felt hopeless and nothingness inside.

The book's words were ingrained in her mind and not one of the *scrolls* that the book exposed gave her the satisfaction she felt when reading them in the past. Then, Avon encountered the cruelest phase in life realizing that she was far and beyond her own knowledge. She had reached a dead end and in order to find new methods to manage her emotions and thoughts; she had to start all over again. The awards that she had accepted from being a great performer in life were far too much for her to absorb and to assimilate all at once. In the past, when she thought that she was unequipped to accept one blessing; she didn't recognize the effect that would be produced when accepting more than one blessing at a time. She didn't even consider the ramification that would be generated by the immensity of pleasure when attracting more than one blessing mighty at once. Previously, when she accepted one blessing; she felt physically sick. However just then, she wasn't feeling at all, she felt numb. She felt hopeless, hollow, and bare inside.

Avon was still to discover that blessings weren't completed until accepted responsibly by the receiver; for acceptance of a blessing meant to implement the blessings received in a constructive way; however she assumed that being submissively grateful sufficed to accept the blessings she had requested and due to her excessive meekness; her ego ended up in a dormant state and apart from the Love that she shared with her beloved Valentin; she was torpidly gliding in the air with no objective or goal, let alone an aim.

In the middle of her desperation, she began to read her own writings finding some anecdotes from her past and the phase in Phoenix popped out. Reading alerted her memories recalling the instance when she sent money to her mama for the electricity reconnection in the house, and still, her mama had died in the dark. Then, she reflected on the expectations list that her friends advised her to make at the time, which consisted of listing the desired qualities and the tolerable flaws focusing on a potential partner. In the midst of angst, not having much to go by; she created an expectations list. And of course, considering that at that point she had a solid and hermetic unity with a genuine intimate ally; she didn't focus on a potential partner, quite the reverse, she focused on herself. She had no idea where her exploration was driving her at but she needed to occupy her mind discovering yet, more inside.

"Which qualities and flaws would I accept and tolerate from myself?" Avon self quested. Her intention was to find ways to fulfill her own, for she felt emptiness within and she understood as clear as the sunshine that Valentin was incompetent to provide fulfillment to her; the same way that Valentin was incompetent to provide Love, happiness, or forgiveness to her. While being *in* Love as a couple was extraordinary, as individuals they were unable to take emotions away from each other, for they could only share their emotions from heart to heart with one another; just the same as Lek was incompetent to take the source of Avon's dreams away. So she found herself by her own in the midst of solitude again.

Obviously, when making the expectations list, her natural instinct led her to note down her flaws first and when evaluating the

"When the philosopher points to the stars, the fool's eyes are fixed on the finger."

faults revealed; she concluded that most of those flaws developed from *one emotion* buried deep in her heart. After having been practically distilled by all the experiences she had endured so far; she was diminished into the capacity of meekness allowing her to discover that she had much more *resentment* in her heart than she ever cared to take in hand.

Avon resented her parents for sending her away on a deceiving student exchange. She resented her siblings' rejection and rivalry toward her. She resented not being able to see her dad. She resented that she couldn't share any of her accomplishments with the residents in her heart. She resented, she resented, and she resented. However sadly, the fact that she sensed resentment indicated solely one truth to her and the truth being was that she resented herself, mainly, because her mama had died in the dark and she wasn't there for her.

Valentin found Avon crying inconsolably in the library that evening and she couldn't tell him what was wrong with her. So he reached his violin and, standing next to one of those gorgeous tables where Avon was sitting with her face down buried on the tabletop surrounded by her arms drowning in her own tears and used tissues all over the floor, he began to play *Vivaldi*'s *Winter Excerpt* just for her.

After she listened to him passionately playing for a while; she realized that she hadn't only married the man created to be her intimate ally in life, but by listening to *Vivaldi*'s melodies over and over again with such an intense enthusiasm in her heart; she had attracted a man that played the *Four Seasons* especially to her. Then, she calmed down a bit. She lifted her head and absorbing his extraordinary talent she said, "I wish to be a man."

"Do you really princes?" He asked without stopping his performance.

"Yes" she said while he devotedly played his violin.

"Any man in particular?"

"Yes, I want to be able to manage my emotions like you do" she replied.

"Aha!" he exclaimed smiling and after executing *Staccato* notes in fast movements ongoing with the piece, he added, "For a minute you scared me princess, as I thought you wanted to be any man but seems as if you would like to be closer to me."

"No, not exactly closer but I would like to be able to feel accomplished like you do," she said pausing and listening to his amazing talent. Then she added, "I feel empty Valentin. A couple of weeks ago I said to you that there was nothing else I could ask for and look now, my feelings, my emotions seem to be failing me luv."

"Well, what gives you the impression that I feel accomplished?" He asked passionately playing his violin.

"Look at you right now. You project fulfillment playing your violin." She replied.

"Aha!" He said again stopping his performance for a moment and looking profoundly into her eyes.

"What?" she asked. He closed his eyes without replying and he resumed the piece dedicated to her.

When he finished playing he said, "Come here and sit with me for a moment." So, she approached him and he sat her on his lap asking, "Do you know what passion is my darling Avon?"

"Yes"

"Well, what is your passion?"

"I do not really know what it is luv."

"Aha!" he exclaimed yet again. Then, he stood up letting her sit on the chair and while tossing her a wink; he took his Zippo lighter out of the pocket of his jeans. Next, he picked a decorative candle that had never been lit from a shelf; he set the candle on

"When the philosopher points to the stars, the fool's eyes are fixed on the finger."

the table in front of her; he clicked the remote control with his index finger turning the lights off and closing the drapes followed by sudden pure darkness.

After that, he lit the candle and the tiny flame illuminated the entire library. Then he asked her, "Would you like to play a game? Avon was stock-still and she remained silent. Thus Valentin extended his invitation with an explanation, "When I was a boy, I learned to focus playing games in the dark with my brother."

"What do you mean in the dark?" She asked.

So he explained, "Well during the previous regime in Bulgaria; the electricity was turned-off in the village at random and usually my father lit a candle on the center of the dining table. He would tell my brother and me to gaze at the flame until we couldn't keep our eyes open and our eyelids naturally closed. Then, dad said that it was magic, because the flame remained in our mind motivating us to be still and silent. After a while, I realized that when I focused on the candle flame I was more focused myself. So, I used to look forward to playing the flame game and the village blackout. And then, I started playing the flame game by my own every so often and when I began playing music; clearly, being focused allowed me to play better. Although I could tell that every time I played a musical note; the fire I felt in my heart was the reflection of the flame. I guess my father's intention was to save money and not light more than one candle at a time keeping my brother and me in one room and by the light instead of letting us wander in the dark. So, if you try playing the flame game, perhaps you can feel the fire in your heart leading you to your passion. Would you like to play?"

Avon agreed and while she gazed at the flame, Valentin glanced at some papers that were on the table and he read a couple of lines standing up next to where she was sitting. Then, he got interested and he moved the papers a bit to be able to read straight and closer to the flame's light and by then, Avon's eyes were closed and a smile radiated all over her face. So, Valentin felt at ease reading and after a few minutes she opened her eyes standing up and saying, "The flame vanished, it's gone!"

"Princess, you never played that game before?"

"No."

"Well now, you can play the flame game any time you want. Just focus on the flame as long as you can and once it's gone, you can focus on the fire that is burning in your heart. Let me ask you, I know you are not as talkative as I am and you rather keep silent at times; even so, would you like to tell me your story like I told you my story on our wedding night?"

"Ooh luv, telling my story would take me a lifetime even if I were as talkative as you are," she said and they laughed.

"Well, I didn't mean for you to tell me your story talking, would you like to write it for me instead?"

Avon's face illuminated with the most cherished smile Valentin had memorized from her as of yet and she teased, "Only if you tell me that you liked what you just read." He didn't reply verbally; he held her kissing her.

She said softly, "I didn't realize you liked what you read this much. I should let you read more to get extra kisses and hugs."

He added, "Princess, there is a force behind your prose that I have sensed from you as your essence but you seldom express it anymore."

"The past months have been challenging for me to express vocally. I have been surrounded by paperwork, listening to stories and in places where I could not really talk much. However, as I reacquaint with our friends and I find a new routine; I will express more often; especially when we gather in the garden to play Chess."

"I can hardly wait," he said and by then, she was calm and serene again. So, the evening went on.

"When the philosopher points to the stars, the fool's eyes are fixed on the finger."

After doing some research, it didn't take long for Avon to get acquainted with the candle flame and she began practicing and exercising with candles. From then on, she became emotionally involved with the flame and without even noticing; she was burning the resentment inside her and at the same time, she was purifying by breathing the flame's glow; just like impure gold purified from lower into higher karats in the *golden pact* metaphor; bringing her back to living, given that Avon returned to breathing and thinking again.

Most importantly, Avon discovered the colorful dark side of Energy illuminated by a tiny flame allowing her to *for-give* herself for being where she was supposed to be at any given moment; because she then understood that her mama didn't die in the dark; as her mama seemed to have died surrounded by the flickering magical glow of candle flames illuminating the dark side of Energy, just like the stars crowned the moon at night in the dark skies.

Tossing a reflection to the air...

"Life has no beginning and no end. Life doesn't belong to a person for whether one enters or exits life lives perpetually."

23

An ordinary morning after playing the flame game, Avon sat in the library gathering her memoirs for the story that she was affectionately compiling for Valentin. She had been struggling for awhile, as she didn't know how to seal the ending of the tale. Nevertheless, that morning while on the laptop checking e-mails, *Voila!* An e-mail from Angelina popped up captivating Avon's attention at once when reading the subject:

"This is the e-mail that I told you about Avon, '*Learning when teaching*'"

Avon opened the e-mail and the contents read:

One learns:
Ten percent from reading;
Twenty percent from hearing;
Thirty percent from seeing;
Fifty percent from seeing and hearing;
Sixty percent from reading, seeing and hearing;

"When the philosopher points to the stars, the fool's eyes are fixed on the finger."

Seventy percent from discussions;
Eighty percent from personal experiences;
Ninety percent from teaching... Hence teach **Love***!*

—William Glasser

Immediately, Avon felt shivers from her crown to the tip of her toes. Her mind traveled at the highest speed self questing, "*Who learns?*"

Instantly a *silent wave* replied, "*A Student,*" making Avon realize that she had been a student in life's path all along. Although if her parents truly wanted her to become an ordinary student they could've perfectly sent her to England eliminating most of the challenges she confronted by going to America, being that her father was English and Avon had citizenship rights in The U.K.

However, Avon was totally satisfied with the facts just like they were. Mostly, she was grateful for having had the opportunity of surmounting every challenge she had encountered up till then and becoming an extraordinary student in life instead. So, she deciphered that by teaching Love to herself; she could become a ninety percent student and by learning at least ten percent from reading other people's writings; she could accomplish to become one hundred percent student. Just as the Shoe Shiner had said, "*Regardless of what a person's purpose is; everyone should focus on developing their passion one hundred per cent to reach their highest potential in life with no excuses.*" Even though her rationale made sense only to her; Avon had finally established a symbolic meaning of the alleged student exchange arrangement between her parents and Lek leaving her with a quest to discover what she could possibly give in exchange.

Also, when reading Angelina's e-mail, Avon realized that the *learning when teaching* citation exposed as a metaphor would make a perfect ending for the story that she was writing. So, having the end of the tale figured out; she began to compile a sort of manuscript which later became her book of memoirs. She was pleased with the information she had gathered to expose how she had attained her childhood dreams and it was then when she decided to title the story:

"My Childhood Dreams"

Of course at the time, Avon had no clue that she would end up publishing a book, but deep in her heart she felt like dedicating her writings to her siblings and to her niece Mae. She also trusted that the Universe would inspire her with an idea to get the story to her siblings one day thinking that they might want to learn about her, but ignoring that when she finally did; her siblings would put the book out-of-the-way inside a garbage can ending up in Mae's hands instead.

Some time passed and one evening, Avon and Valentin watched a documentary exposing interesting material about a secret and although most of the information was impressive; Avon was fascinated with a quote that was told by a spokesperson one too many times saying, "*Attention goes where Energy flows*" or something to that effect.

Thereafter, Avon's passion began to surface. First of all, she understood what Energy meant to her and second; she also understood what attention meant to her when focusing on her connection to the source of Love allowing Arolf to be present inside her at all times. Not necessarily paying attention but being aware of her intentions. So, she began practicing awareness and finally she was able to listen to her heart following the rhythm. At last, she found herself practicing what she had learned from her

"When the philosopher points to the stars, the fool's eyes are fixed on the finger."

own experiences and from the book she had read so many times allowing her heart to perform at its greatest potential. Her heart was expanding through her senses emitting words of reflection into her mind in any language to think not to remember and transmitting those words to the Universe in sequence in order for the Universe to manifest her ideas back to Earth in material form. She was manifesting her thoughts by creating the story that she was writing. Energy was flowing where her attention was exactly going and she was captivated receiving inspiration from the source and unfolding in her heart. Her thoughts activated by Energy awakened the *silent wave* setting her senses into motion reviving within her the emotion of *hope* again through lucid inspiration from the greatest muse of all—Love.

In retrospect and contemplating on her emotional collapse; Avon admitted that when accomplishing too much too quick the emotion of *hope* could get lost in the midst of the oblivion and as a result she felt hopeless, unfilled, bare, and numb. However she wasn't empty at all, quite the opposite; she had fulfilled everything she had ever dreamed of and much more; she was rather filled to the top and in the process, she didn't find the need to hope anymore because she seemed to have it all.

Hence after regaining hope again; it was time for her to practice every lesson she had learned during her journey and since she didn't have any more childish dreams to pursue, regardless of Arolf and her intimate connection with Valentin; her only option was to follow objectives in life to create. Breathing and thinking without a goal resulted in hopeless extremes of emptiness or fullness and neither sentiment was pleasant to her. Thus practicing the lessons she had learned became her new endeavor.

Thanks to a candle flame; Avon discovered that being a 100% student was her passion. Her thirst to learn indicated that her internal fire kindled by being a student of whichever thoughts Energy transmitted to her. Thus, she focused on Metaphysical Sciences being the subject that absorbed her at the time, and she began learning about beings' most profound intangibilities like mind, emotions, and feelings. So, just as Valentin expressed through music or the Shoe Shiner shone shoes; she expressed through writing. Her fascination became the study of the connection among breathing living souls with their respective physical body and the principles of the Universe and its law. Therefore intangible topic and she couldn't express her passion in any other way than in written words; hence her affirmations, her written reminders, her attraction to Metaphysics and learning through reading others people's writings. She was finally able to practice the link among emotions, the *silent wave*, the *sealed wave*, words and manifestation of thoughts. And not by writing out of aspiration or even desperation like some professional writers would; but writing out of pure inspiration from the source of Love.

Tossing a reflection to the air...

"After all, the only lessons in life are the ones that one admits to have learned; therefore the only student one could ever teach is oneself and being one's only teacher is just another lesson to learn along the way."

"When the philosopher points to the stars, the fool's eyes are fixed on the finger."

24

⁊t was Christmas season and incidentally, Avon and Valentin's first anniversary from the day they had first met, so they spent the holidays away from the city at one of the most gorgeous and relaxing havens in the world located in Half-Moon Bay. Besides their first year anniversary; they were looking forward to celebrating their first New Year's Eve together. Thus, they enjoyed the Health Spa treatments, the restaurants, the lounges, the bars, and they even played some golf during the time they were on the grounds of the *Half-Moon Bay Ritz-Carlton Resort;* including the traditional daily *High Tea* delight accentuated with sweets, per Valentin's request.

Avon and Valentin approached Christmas different than the norm; Jimmy had assisted them to organize a group of volunteers distributing food and gifts to the homeless in the Bay-Area, and not only through the holidays, but also year-round in gratitude of discovering their hearts during the Christmas season. Then, since Avon and Valentin had already received, claimed and conserved the most treasured gift they could ever obtain for Christmas by blessing each other *in* Love; they established exchanging gifts between one another on New Year's Eve.

"When the philosopher points to the stars, the fool's eyes are fixed on the finger."

Therefore after enjoying a week of room-service and first class treatment when they checked-out of the resort on New Year's Eve; Valentin drove Avon to the Half-Moon Bay Marina unveiling a Yacht as his anniversary gift to her and he was enthused. He said that she could pick a name for the Yacht and that they could go cruising around the bay for her to enjoy anytime she felt like getting away from the city. Valentin had made arrangements hiring a crew with a Captain, a Steward and a Chef. His intention was to enjoy the midnight fireworks from a good angle and afar from the crowds in the comfort of their own privacy. Avon wasn't as impatient and impulsive as he was and she waited a bit longer to disclose her gift to him.

Later on, on the eve to welcome the New Year; they celebrated in their Yacht. They dressed up for each other and the sunset was glorious. They sat by the aft deck dining casually and appreciating the most colorful exposition of the sun gradually going down from the middle of the bay. Avon didn't eat much and Valentin wondered if she felt unwell. However, Avon was just anxious, as she was a bit embarrassed to present her humble gift to him. Then she realized that even if she had spent their entire fortune buying the most expensive gift; she wouldn't have been able to come up with what she had created especially for him. So, the same force that she was so familiar with drove her to proceed presenting the gift to her husband as she had initially intended.

They were seating by the table enjoying the breeze before dessert was served, which was Valentin's favorite part of any meal, and suddenly, Avon excused herself leaving for a few minutes. Awhile later, she returned with a rectangular box between her hands wrapped as a gift which contained her rare writings imprinted on paper disclosing her memoirs. After going through so many years of effort gathering thoughts, having a copy finally organized and printed gave her some sort of relief. However she also felt a bit sad since thereafter, except for tossing reflections to the air, she probably wouldn't have much to write. So, she approached him with teary eyes saying, "From my heart to yours, dear husband."

Valentin was enjoying the Yacht so much; he had forgotten that the Yacht was his gift to her and not his. For during the few minutes Avon had left; he got fascinated checking the mechanics of a Jacuzzi that rested on the fly bridge and when she handed him the present; he was surprised and he reacted a bit oblivious about it. On the other hand, Avon had no idea of what to do with her new Yacht; although her intuition indicated that most likely *he* would assist her on that regard.

When Valentin look at the rectangular box with a ribbon wrapped around it forming a gorgeous bow on the top; he was certain that his gift was a shirt or some sort of chemise. He received the gift placing a quick peck on her cheek and as she observed; he took off his shirt. Avon just smiled. Valentin was shirtless and ready to wear whatever the box contained. He unfurled the ribbon. He opened up the box and when he saw the first page showing the title: *My Childhood Dreams*, out of excitement and being half naked; he impulsively dove off the Yacht for a quick test of the bay waters deep right under the Golden Gate Bridge.

As Avon laughed out loud and tried to talk to the Captain via the intercom, Valentin had already saved himself and he was back on the Yacht. Obviously he was dripping wet but he didn't care and he embraced Avon swiftly spinning her around and around many times. "You finished your story princess!" He exclaimed.

"Yes." She replied.

"Let's change clothes quickly; I want to read it"

"Now, before dessert?"

"Ooh yes, now!"

"When the philosopher points to the stars, the fool's eyes are fixed on the finger."

So when they were changing clothes in the master stateroom; she tried to seduce him, but he wasn't interested on playing around with her; he actually meant it, and in no time, he was in the main deck living area reading about his princess childhood dreams. Then Avon changed into informal wear and without disturbing him; she went to the upper deck checking out her new gift and she talked with the Captain at the cockpit. After that, as she passed by the living area, Valentin was reading. So, she went downstairs to the lower deck and she noticed that besides the master stateroom, there were another five guest staterooms. In addition, there were cabins for the crew and the Yacht was not only gorgeous but huge. Then she went to the galley and she ended up eating dessert talking with the Steward and the Chef while Valentin had dessert by himself reading away.

For a moment Avon wondered if every time she was absorbed reading or writing, Valentin missed her as much as she was missing him then; but at the same time, she realized that he was reading her memoirs. So, letting him be, she established a conversation with the Chef and the Steward talking about life and such things. They prepared special snacks for her, time went by and hours passed. The next thing they knew it was midnight and Valentin had fallen asleep on the sofa during his reading. Avon tried to wake him and he didn't wake up. Thus Avon had bubbly with the crew enjoying the New Year's firecrackers and overall, it was a great New Year welcome for both. They were practically together and Valentin didn't miss much; except for drinking some bubbly and looking at fireworks; however, Avon spent New Year's surrounded by strangers and without a New Year's midnight romantic kiss once more.

Afterward, Avon sat next to Valentin in the living area observing him sleep. She admired his vigor and his amazing glow; even when his eyes were closed his golden eyelashes looked heavenly to her and as sad as she felt for not being kissed on New Year's Eve, a *silent wave* emerged in her mind saying *Avon, you have lived half of a lifetime without being kissed by Valentin on this date because you didn't even know him. So now, you can perfectly live the rest of a lifetime kissing Valentin at any time of the day and at any given date.* Happily smiling; she reached a blanket tenderly covering her husband. Then she crawled up on the other end of the sofa and she fell asleep next to him.

The following morning Avon woke up comfy in the master stateroom and there was no sign of Valentin. Clearly looking after her wellbeing he had carried her into the bed while she profoundly slept. Then as she came out to the aft bridge; the Steward greeted her asking if she'd like some breakfast and Avon replied with a smile requesting a simple *latté*. Valentin was sitting on the sundeck reading, sipping a *latté*, and smoking a cigarette. When Avon gave signs of being around; he stopped reading. He greeted her with the most amorous embrace, a kiss, and wishing her a great New Year. "Are you enjoying my rare writings luv?" She asked.

"Well, it needs some work yet, but your tale is superb. Your story is intense and last night I wasn't in the mood to celebrate. I was rather sad for what you had been through princess. Your sense of genuineness is transparent in your prose and I am captivated by the way you expose your learning lessons in life," he replied.

"What do you mean it needs some work yet?"

"Don't take me wrong. I understand clearly; however the more I read, the more I think that this story should go to print. I am sure there will be modifications by the editors."

"Have you any idea of the uncomfortable sense of exposure I feel just by knowing that you are reading what I have written lacking of literature guidance luv? Not considering the fact that I have put out in the open my most treasured memoirs. Why should I publish my very personal writing?"

"When the philosopher points to the stars, the fool's eyes are fixed on the finger."

"No, I didn't consider any of those thoughts you've just mentioned. Although it's precisely the reason why I say that it needs some work; you have to make it work to expose it to the world. I can tell that you wrote the story for me, however if you modify it and write for *Dark Matter* instead; I can only imagine where your creativity would lead you. It's just like music. When I read musical notes I don't enjoy playing as much, most of the time I play by ear and for *Dark Matter*, and then, I could care less who is listening when I play. Every time I play the same melody I improve my talent because the creativity I extract from *Dark Matter* is what makes me look accomplished to you when I play, do you understand what I am saying princess?"

"Yes" she replied smiling, and by then, a delicious *latté* was brought to her.

Tossing a reflection to the air...

"The power of imagination is such; creates childish dreams testing peoples' drive to achieve goals so as to expand the mind to be able to extract inspiration directly from Love and create on purpose from the heart."

Not long passed before Avon grasped the concept of extracting inspiration from life-force creating as she wrote and her modest rare manuscript became only her first draft. From then on, she taught literature related matters to herself and she wrote her story from a first person point of view. Several drafts came after the first one. She felt as if she was buffing each word enhancing the paragraphs to spark; just like the Shoe Shiner buffed shoes to shine. Or maybe she was polishing each word to make the paragraphs glow, just like burnishing gold to glitter, because the phase of polishing the manuscript felt endless to her. At any rate, when she finished polishing her manuscript to wink; she had countless possibilities to publish her book and she did.

Once in that phase, if Avon felt a sense of emptiness and numbness when her childish dreams were attained; she had no concept of what fulfillment was when attaining passion extracting inspiration from life-force; given that at that juncture, fulfillment or emptiness weren't important anymore. She finally grasped what the completion of a blessing meant accepting and expanding the blessings received by sharing those blessings with the rest of the world.

Up till then, Avon had not confronted her purpose as a human being *tête-à-tête* just yet and she was simply allowing the Universe to drive her through Earth just like any other element in space out there.

While the book was being published, in between the manuscript corrections and modifications, Avon named her Yacht: *The Flame Remains!* Nobody could guess why she selected that name, except for Valentin who had a notion of her intent. However, she named the Yacht in relation to a project keeping her occupied prior to manifesting her intentions which she had structured all by herself, because despite the time that had passed by; she never forgot about her homeless friends and the idea had been lingering in her heart ever since the doctor invited her to the very first *high tea* party at Union Square; only she was unable to execute her plan due to lack of many things; especially, clarity in her mind.

She was planning to get involved in a program with the U.S. Army veterans who were returning from wherever they had been

"When the philosopher points to the stars, the fool's eyes are fixed on the finger."

at into the Bay-Area. She had submitted a proposal and at that time; she was waiting for approval so that they could convert the 30 rental units in the building into private quarters with the aim of welcoming soldiers with a warm home and assist them before they ended up homeless, since she was aware that many of her genuine homeless friends from Union Square were war veterans. So, she needed official legislative authorization for such an endeavor and in order to organize and implement her proposal; the process took years to develop.

Valentin supported her and assisted her with ideas to find a constructive use for the Yacht besides enjoying it for personal pleasure, but mostly, he encouraged her; because in the meantime she was also studying to obtain a degree in Holistic and Metaphysical Sciences which would grant her therapeutic counseling credentials to aid the war veterans.

As soon as the book was published, Avon sent a copy to her *sunshine*, Angelina, and she hand-wrote a dedication saying something along the following lines:

I am grateful for your encouragement; your brilliant ideas; your sense of trust; your healthy mind; and your approval. But most of all, I am grateful for allowing me to manifest one of your thoughts; for in spite of everything, the idea to write my memoirs came from you my sunshine.
Enjoy!

Tossing a reflection to the air…

"Laziness develops best in idle minds, regardless of the means available to practice a variety of personal physical activities and pleasures."

About a year had passed after Avon got her Yacht and by then, they had finished refurbishing their home. She was satisfied with a new routine and she had also reacquainted with the doctor and Jimmy gathering in the garden regularly. During the previous months, Avon had been busy with the veterans' project, studying for her degree, going in tours promoting the book with Valentin and she also began to write another book, since due to the deal made with the publisher; she was expected to present new material in the future.

One evening while Valentin and the doctor played Chess in the garden, Avon and Jimmy observed knowing that most likely the doctor would be defeated again, because Eastern Europeans seemed to have mastered the art of playing Chess. So, after Valentin placed the doctor in Checkmate; the doctor said, "It is great to have you both back. Although during the time you were touring what I missed the most was Valentin playing the violin. You will not be traveling as much, I suppose."

"No, at this point the book is selling itself by word of mouth and I am not much of a lecturer, so we are home for now doctor," Avon said.

Then, the doctor teased, "I know you are passive and not activist like I am my dear; for I rather protest out loud; but if not lecturing or voicing how you would approach a cause, in silence?"

She replied giggling, "Yes, collective contemplation would accomplish any cause and even if I do not express myself out loud or lecture that much, I respect any expression of voice. Yet in my experience, Energy does not seem to flow properly when interacting with more than one person at a time."

The doctor and Valentin found her comment humorous and so did Jimmy; however Jimmy was thinking *while the doctor protests out loud, Avon talks to one person at a time; but as to getting the attention, when playing the violin, Valentin leaves them behind.*

"When the philosopher points to the stars, the fool's eyes are fixed on the finger."

Then, the doctor said, "Talking about voicing, I would like your insight regarding a project my dear."

"Certainly" said Avon.

And the doctor explained, "I am preparing for a speech about gay marriage and as advocate in the gay community I know about being gay; however apart from traditional material and as a celibate, I don't seem to come up with much to motivate my group regarding marriage and I was wondering if you would not mind sharing your personal perspective as a married couple."

"Gay marriage..." Avon said wondering.

"What defines a gay?" Valentin asked. Avon and Jimmy were just listening and their eyebrows rose.

"What do you mean?" Asked the doctor.

"I mean what I asked; what defines you as a gay doctor?" Valentin repeated.

"I am attracted to my gender," the doctor said.

Then Avon thought out loud still in wonder, "Love and marriage—"

"Are you anti or pro gay marriage my dear?" The doctor asked interrupting.

Avon replied, "Neither. Regarding human beings, I am pro Love and Peace. Regarding marriage, I find that it is a contract of convenience between two people, just like I consider divorce. Marriage is about trust, not about sexual preference. Anyone can have sex without trust, but only Love allows the trust that two people require to marry each other; since marriage grants certain civil rights over one another."

Then Valentin said, "I can tell you that in our case; we confronted challenges to be together and even though marriage was the remedy, societies around the world complicate matters regarding interracial marriage and we're not the same gender, gay is just a label."

"Yes gay is just a label, but gays face different challenges to justify being *in* Love, luv. I will take the liberty to mention that I would define gays as a manifestation of the highest power in the midst of humankind due to their neutrality." Avon added.

"What are you referring to my dear?" The doctor asked.

"You know that after mama passed away you were the only person I spoke with during several months;" she said.

"Yes, those were the circumstances at the time my dear," the doctor agreed.

"Well, during that time, I pondered for months about your kindness and the way society perceives your personal sexual preference. Hence you played a major role influencing my ability to find validation for mama's death," she acknowledged to the doctor.

"I still do not understand what you are talking about my dear," the doctor insisted.

"I am referring to life-force; *Energy beyond gender* doctor, here in the West goes by the label of *God*. As you know I was brought up sort of agnostic under Eastern philosophy worshiping an enlightened male figure and although I strongly felt, sensed, and perceived an almighty presence within me and not in the exterior, after mama passed away nothing validated my perception of the almighty presence under Eastern or Western philosophies. So, I had to come up with my own conclusions about being, existing, and life-force. And during the process while interacting with you, I personally identified gays as *beings beyond gender* and it is the reason why society rejects them. Society is totally unfamiliar with your nature doctor." Avon said.

Jimmy was just listening; however thinking, *God is rejected just the same.*

"*When the philosopher points to the stars, the fool's eyes are fixed on the finger.*"

"I am flattered!" the doctor exclaimed.

Valentin added, "Societies around the world seem to focus too much on sex regarding marriage. Unfortunately due to sexual abuse and crime, everybody seems to judge others based on sexual preference."

The doctor said, "I understand your first query now Valentin; as I just defined my own self by gender and sexual preference without even thinking."

Valentin said, "Precisely, lacking of a person's physical *neuter genital* doesn't help; however you might find new material for your speech focusing on trust between two beings as *neuter gender*, instead of focusing on the already existing marriage contract between a male and a woman. For instance, the *asexual* working bees and ants in *Zoology* are as productive as the other ones. In *Botany, Flora* reproduces perfectly having neither stamens nor pistils. Those are simple examples of *neuters* in nature and being *asexual* doesn't make *neuters* less productive or incapable to develop within their natural environment; because *neuters* exist beyond male or female, in other words, *beyond physical genitals*."

Avon said, "Sadly, marriage does not validate being *in* Love for gay or heterosexual couples. I find—"

Jimmy said smiling, "I don't mean to interrupt Avon; but I have to say that Love is as blind as your heart and your perception is romantic."

Avon said, "Ooh, you know that there are times when I do not sound romantic Jimmy. Allow me to brainstorm, for I may have a point; however, if I get carried away feel free to stop me at any time, would you?" They smiled and she said, "My understanding is that societies around the world have been trying to manipulate people for generations inducing everyone to read material about the Universe law and while the Universe principles and law are intangible and may only be expressed vocally or through written words; everyone without exception is able to feel the Universe life-force in their hearts. Hence the conflict for allowing other people's thoughts to control and manipulate one's mind through a misinterpreted written Universe law, would lead anyone to feel guilty for not complying with it. Then again, the civil right of marriage should not have anything to do with organized dogmas. The Universe exists beyond genitals or sex, and still, most of the writings about the Universe law that humans create seem to be based precisely on humankind reproduction and lineage having nothing to do with trust between two people *in* Love. There seem to be more threats, demands and rules listed on the writings than elucidation about the art of sharing Love for a married couple, let alone among all. So, establishing marriage based on those writings does not make much sense at all." Jimmy, the doctor and Valentin just listened.

"As a writer, I understand that every book has been written by a human being and as a thinker, I understand that inspiration comes from the same source to one and all; thus it is my responsible decision to manipulate inspiration or not when I write and I write universal truths for readers to find their own truth when reading my writings, not my truth; because each soul holds their own truth in the heart. However when people read the writings of a misconstrued Universe law, then follow and practice it without finding their own truth is like manifesting other people's manipulative thoughts and twisted inspiration; not manifesting the Love that is perceived in one's heart from the Universe life-force. I do agree with Valentine when he says that societies focus too much in sex regarding marriage. I find that when two people enter the contract of marriage does not necessarily mean that they will be sexually active, because marriage is irrelevant to sexual preference.

"When the philosopher points to the stars, the fool's eyes are fixed on the finger."

"Sexual preference is broad and so is marriage because there are many people married to the opposite gender using a husband or a wife as a cover just to be accepted by society as heterosexuals. Then, when they feel like exploring Energy through sex; they enjoy sexuality with a person of their same gender and behind their spouses' back. Others are not even heterosexuals, bisexuals, or unrevealed gays; as they just want to explore sexuality with someone anonymously, nameless, or wearing a mask. Yet, they have the right to hold a conveniently arranged heterosexual marriage contract with a person of the opposite gender, even if it's not their sexual preference. I won't mention any other sexual preferences for I presume you got my point.

"However, when studying the Universe principle of *Generation*, I learned that allows nature to expand as feminine, masculine, and neuter in conjunction with the rest of the Universe. *Generation* is not linked to the physical genitals attached to a human being like gender is thus the focal point is creation and not humankind procreation. Sadly humankind seems to be arrogant, as they tend to separate from the source and relate everything to themselves and not the other way around. For instance, exploring Energy through stimulation of genitals whether solo or with another person equal sex and sexual preference emerges. *Generation* though, is beyond gender and much further than human beings' general understanding. Especially if one is in an arrogant and obstinate state of mind; for not until setting the reproduction of terrestrials aside and then focusing on *Generation* as the properties that distinguish organisms on the basis of their productive roles and considering every life form and element in the complexity of the entire Universe as *One* creative force, my wits began to expand in areas that I never intended to explore and so did my heart."

Jimmy looked at Avon amazed as she didn't sound romantic at all and Valentin exclaimed, "I must say how pleased I'm to listen to my wife speaking again!"

"Indeed!" the doctor added.

Then Avon said, "You wish I never did gentlemen for I am just getting started." They laughed.

Avon then shared her own views regarding marriage, "I am grateful to my marriage and divorce rights. By divorcing young, I understood that I got married the first time ignoring what merging in Love was all about and I got divorced without finding out. After the divorce, I didn't even consider marriage. Even so, the experience taught me well and I moved on. I dealt with it and I extracted the lesson from my miscue by myself. Now, when I encountered Valentin, I experienced the exploration of Energy by being in Love with a person that is in Love as well and we share Love from heart to heart fully; because we don't provide or extract Love from one another. Our merge was genuine and sharing Love became a romantically insane priority. So, we decided to be together at all times. We merged in Love attracting each other like magnets exploring Energy through sex and most likely exploring Energy in Love will maintain us sexually active.

"For Energy in motion arousing the emotion of Love during sex, is the most sublime expression of being. Hence some might still label the action of sex "Making Love," as no other activity *generates* such a loving Energy exchange which as a result even creates human beings every now and then."

She smiled looking at them and continued, "In essence, thanks to marriage, Valentin and I are as one today. However, since the length of a marriage cannot be measured by a set of vows which would have been recited in a ceremony and by the end of the first honeymoon night forgotten, because no vow lasts for a lifetime,

"When the philosopher points to the stars, the fool's eyes are fixed on the finger."

we base our marriage on loving actions and loving words to one another daily and we do not input 50/50 in our marriage. We contribute 100/100 because it is our individual responsibility to be one hundred percent fulfilled so that we can share full happiness." As they listened, she continued passionately expressing.

"In our case, after marriage surfaced as the only option to be together without physically separating we focused on complying with society's rules. I learned long time ago that I will be an immigrant wherever I go. So, in order to avoid any type of discrimination, the only way to survive in peace and harmony within society is by obeying their rules and also paying dues; and not only financially but socially as well. Paying dues is a duty no one escapes, as sooner or later it will catch up with one anyway. Law, dues, and rules are acceptable to structure a civilized world; however when it comes to control and manipulation of thoughts, no one is competent to enter one's mind unless one allows it. We got married to be together and when we decided to get married, we didn't even consider the social benefits of the merger. Our focus was Love. When Love is the priority, anyone should follow their hearts even if they have to move to another State or Country where they are openly accepted. And then, they would be able to Love each other in peace of mind. At the end of the day, many well formed societies in the world welcome everyone to pay their dues." Jimmy, the doctor and Valentin could sense her passion.

She kept talking, "So the rest of the world does not expand and advance just because I say so. Of course ideas manifest best collectively and thinking prior to manifesting will bring even better results; but I personally rather think so, than say so. Therefore, would you allow me to contemplate about the subject of gay marriage doctor? I certainly do not have a personal opinion. However, I am willing to think and create a couple of ideas, and as usual, when working in our projects, we will aim for a faultless outcome. Focusing on your expertise in human law and the insights from the Universe law and principles, I am confident that we will figure out some fresh design for your speech." Jimmy and Valentin simply observed.

The doctor nodded adding, "Well, I am impressed with your *beyond gender* concept and as we discussed in the past you know that here in the West some claim that *God* created heterosexuals to his image and likeness; so comparing *God* to gays is a bit extreme my dear. Although I should admit, I am still flattered."

"So was I, doctor, so was I." Avon concurred and serenely said, "With all due respect because I recognize your faith; when I learned about the Western *God* and *its* similarity to me, I was quite flattered as well. Until of course, I realized that the story sounded more and more as though a group of human beings gathered to create a *God* for *their* advantage, *their* image, and *their* likeness than the other way around. After that, they seem to have written long and confusing stories about it. And as it seems, those who wrote the stories must have been a group of gentlemen for they refer to their *God* as a male; just like some do in the East, North, and South, I guess. Like I mentioned before I repeat confidently; humankind is arrogant because if we don't pay attention, we could fall into ego's trap at any time; however regardless of the varied versions that the story carries in books all over the world about one *God* or another, not much applies to my nature anyway and what makes me different from the male *God* defined in those books is not relative to my sexual preference either because I am not gay." She paused and they waited.

She added, "You see gentlemen, I turned out to be as defective as a woman could be in relation to the image and likeness of the *God* those writings expose for I seem to be a *barren woman* and although

"When the philosopher points to the stars, the fool's eyes are fixed on the finger."

there is a probability that nature is in debt with my maternal instinct and still owes me a child; if I never engender, I certainly would not meet the criteria of the image and likeness of the *God* described in those writings. I take the liberty to say that comparing *God* to heterosexuals is just as extreme as comparing *God* to gays; or are gays not human beings then? You see doctor, not only Western people, but also Eastern people comprising North and South I suppose, have created *Gods* for generations in a heterosexual image and likeness in which regardless of gays old age existence, gays are banned from the image and likeness of the *Gods* they come up with. Yet, last time I checked the meaning of the words *hetero* and *homo* had not changed. Of course, it will be a matter of contemplating both words in relation to the whole as *One* or *Generation*, not gender or sex.

"I would confidently say that unless otherwise proven, such likeness between humans and *Energy Life-Force* do not resemble truth at all. Humankind is merely driven by an inescapable *Will-Life-Force* to exist; just as the rest of the Universe is. There is no need to be arrogant and confuse matters dividing *Energy Life-Force* and humanity and then, make comparisons between the two. Through lessons I learned about competition playing Chess I understood that arrogance's core is division and separates one from the source; hence disconnection and not unity. Without omission *Energy Life-Force* is within each individual gay or not and integrates one and all. We are not *similar* to Energy Life-Force or *like* Energy Life-Force. We *are* it!

"However, for some arrogant reason humankind tends to segregate from the source. As a matter of fact, Energy Life-Force is so very inescapable that even I, as a *barren woman*, sense it in the heart.

"Then again, from any other life form in Earth, humans seem to be the only kind unable to distinguish the Energy driving them within and unifying them to the Universe as specie. Need not to divide and then make comparisons just to feel flattered. Everyone without exception is rightly capable to attain unity in peace of mind by accepting Energy Life-Force as Love in their hearts and thinking of the same objective individually expands into collective contemplation, need not to say a word out loud. I was not comparing you to the highest power of powers; I meant that you are a manifestation of Life-force doctor. You may accept it as compliment or with the Peace that is in each individual's soul; a Peace that will most likely surface once humanity collectively acknowledges Energy Life-Force when falling with one voice *in* Love." She concluded followed by silence.

Suddenly, Jimmy exclaimed, "Avon you're like a *Tango* dance!"

"What do you mean Jimmy?" Valentin asked.

Jimmy replied, "Back in my day, I used to take dancing classes with a friend and Tango was one of the most challenging dances to learn; but once you learn to Tango, Valentin, feels like you're levitating. Same when listening to Avon speak because she introduces with sensuality and romance; then she tangles-in and tangles-out. After that, she kicks aggressively and at the end; she tenderly tosses you a delicate flower in one word: Love."

They expressed amusement and then, the doctor stood up reaching for an embrace from Avon. It was the very first time the doctor ever expressed physical affection to her in all the years they had shared. And of course Avon was so passionate about her doctor friend aspects, tears rolled down her face. As they hugged affectionately everyone expressed enjoyment. Then, the doctor asked Jimmy and Valentin to stand up and tossing his arms around their necks he said, "I feel so loved around you people; you understand me better than my own family does. I had no idea that I influenced Avon with my humble presence in such a way and you

"When the philosopher points to the stars, the fool's eyes are fixed on the finger."

are kind and genuine. I would like the three of you to address me by my name. Do not call me doctor anymore as if there is a barrier between us, would you?"

"I have no objection; I will certainly address you by your name," said Valentin.

"So, will I," Jimmy said.

"We do Love you Leopold!" Avon exclaimed.

Tossing a reflection to the air...

"It is not the same to seek one's equality of rights than equally seek for everyone to rightly be who they are."

25

⚭

Avon and Valentin spent Christmas traveling through Europe with the Children that year. Then, they went to Provence for New Year's and stayed a couple of months in the farm. When they returned to San Fran, Valentin kept occupied building his plane and managing the finances with Jimmy and Dominique's assistance. Avon helped administrating as well spending some money here and there; but she was mostly focused on saving. She continued working on her projects and they socialized with the doctor and Jimmy enjoying the Yacht cruising on the bay. They gathered in the garden every so often and besides playing Chess and conversing; Valentin would entertain them playing the violin and also with candle flame games exposing the almighty power sealed within a flickering flare.

In the interim, the doctor had been the *liaison* between Avon and Mae, because Avon didn't allow her siblings to have direct access to her. So an uneventful afternoon; the doctor transferred a call from Mae to Avon saying that her dad wanted to speak to her. When Avon picked up the phone, her sister Kalaya was on the other end. Kalaya said that she needed to speak to Avon before

"When the philosopher points to the stars, the fool's eyes are fixed on the finger."

her father did. Avon wasn't the least surprised, as her sister had
been using Mae for some time to contact Avon employing the same
trick to get money from her; and although Kalaya ignored Avon's
marital or financial status, that time she didn't asked for hundreds
but for thousands of dollars explaining, "My dear sister, we started
remodeling my house and I don't have enough money to finish; I
promise you that as soon as I receive my share of dad's fortune, I'll
pay you back." Avon spoke with Kalaya briefly and afterward; she
spoke to her dad. When the phone call ended thinking about her
doll, Avon wasn't interested in discovering the pleasure of *lending*
as she was enjoying the pleasure of *giving*. So, she sent some money
to Kalaya as a gift, just as she always did; specifying that she didn't
have to pay it back. However, Avon didn't send the full amount
Kalaya requested, because Avon was rather irritated by her sister's
uncontrollable expenditure habits and during the following few
days; Avon got almost obsessed focusing on the fact that none of
her siblings seemed to learn how to live by their means, let alone
under their means.

Tossing a reflection to the air...

"Whoever has been face to face with evil most likely created
the scene by manifesting their thoughts."

A couple of days had passed since Avon had spoken to
Kalaya; however Avon couldn't stop thinking about her siblings'
capriciousness, unfairness, and constant lack of responsibility. That

morning after being in the dark, Avon lit a candle and she observed the small flame growing firmer and larger absorbing the flickering flame brightening the library powerfully. She sat still gazing at the flame until her eyelids naturally closed and a bright reflection of the flame remained floating in her mind's eye. Then, just as she was beginning to focus on the flame remains to relax in contemplation; she sensed a *silent wave* say, "*Avon, you became a great person. You are remarkable. You are successful. Have you realized how much power you possess? You are not Avon Felix anymore, now you are Avon Dinev. Your book is a success and your readers give you the attention you deserve. If your siblings only learned who you are; they would be ashamed and humiliated by the way they have been disrespecting you through the years. Would you like to retaliate against your siblings?*"

Avon was unfamiliar with the *silent wave* and she wasn't relaxing with the emotion she felt, so she asked, "Who are you? I truly do not recognize you."

The *silent wave* replied, "*You do not recognize me? I am Energy in motion. Usually you call me Arolf.*"

"You could not possibly be Arolf" Avon said trembling a bit, and added, "Arolf never communicated with me in such ways."

"*Which ways are those Avon?*" asked the *silent wave*.

"I sense arrogance. Why should I humiliate my siblings? I do not trust *you* being Arolf." Avon replied.

"*If I am not Arolf, the only Energy there is revolving throughout the Universe; who could I be then? What else could have the power to transmit to you the way I do?*" asked the *silent wave*.

Avon replied perplexed, "I do not know but I sense negativity from whoever you are."

"*Have you not sense negativity before?*"

"Yes, I have felt negativity before thus I recognize it; but never from Arolf. Arolf is the source of positivity." Avon replied upset.

"When the philosopher points to the stars, the fool's eyes are fixed on the finger."

Then, the *silent wave* expressed tenderly and kindly, *"Avon, your sense of innocence is so pure; you actually deny to yourself the truth. Some venerate their God as the Alpha and the Omega, the First and the Last, the Beginning and the End and you still think that negative and positive come from two different sources? I am the only Energy there is and the only source of all things.*

"Avon, if you only pay attention and comprehend the correspondence among the Universe principles; you would not be distrusting me at all. You are naturally inclined to trust my positive pole and it is the reason why you still fear the unknown. Clearly, you are only willing to trust my positive aspect of polarity; rejecting, ignoring and disregarding my negative pole. You do not will to admit or recognize that negative is as much part of me as positive is; hence you stimulate me, the only one Energy there is, to set your fear emotion into motion inducing you to distrust the unknown. Trust me Avon, I am Arolf."

Then, Avon felt Energy's presence in motion realizing that the *silent wave* she sensed was in fact, Arolf. And by then she was crying. So, sobbing like a child Avon asked, "How can you be negative and positive at the same time Arolf? It does not make sense."

The *silent wave* replied questioning Avon's last sentence and clarifying, *"It does not make sense? Perhaps it does not make sense to you. However, if you only think setting off your thoughts through the proper channels everything would make sense. You do not seem to be fully aware Avon, nevertheless if you were, by now you would have already realized that I, Energy, am neutral. I cannot be created and I cannot be destroyed. Energy is fundamentally everything there is and everything that would ever exist comprising both polarity forces negative and positive. Otherwise balance would not be and disorder would take over the entire Universe along with the tiny Earth. Would you like to retaliate against your siblings?"*

Avon was overwhelmed and she took a moment to assimilate trying to understand what she was sensing from Arolf that day. Then, Avon asked, "How come I never sensed this emotion before?"

"Which emotion is that?" the silent wave asked.

Avon replied, "I feel arrogance. I feel a sense of superiority toward my siblings."

"Have you not felt arrogance in the past?"

Then, Avon remembered when she had felt self-important trying to prove to her mama that she was able to help and financially support her entire family by herself. She also recalled when she felt overconfident thinking that she could change the homeless world with a hot air balloon ride. So she replied, "Yes, I have; but I felt different."

"You must have felt different since you allow your sense of self to take over keeping you distracted from awareness. However the source is the same; I am the only source of each and every emotion you sense. Would you like to retaliate against your siblings?" The silent wave tempted Avon again.

Avon was distress and she expressed frustrated, "This is cruelty; how could you be kind and cruel at the same time Arolf?"

The silent wave said, "I ought to be cruel only to be kind Avon; as you know the Universe woks in perfect harmony. Perfect; thanks to the constant cruelty of its mechanics moving forward and stopping for no one. Harmony; thanks to its kind core of Love. In brief, it is just like a human being is formed. Would you like to retaliate against your siblings?"

Troubled, Avon said, "The emotion I feel is taunting me why are you tempting me to retaliate against my siblings?"

The silent wave replied in a derisive tone, "Taunting you, yes; you were created to amuse me, remember? Tempting you, yes; it is my intent to tempt you in order to keep balance for you to differentiate bliss from misery and you are free to decide which emotion to permit me to set into motion Avon. Temptation does not come from society as you keenly try to convince yourself. Temptation comes from me; Energy. Would you like to retaliate against your siblings?"

Desperate for mercy Avon said, "You provided the money I have and I will give everything back if I have to in order to be in peace with you Arolf."

"When the philosopher points to the stars, the fool's eyes are fixed on the finger."

Then the *silent wave* retorted, *"What could I possibly need from you Avon, a tithe of your fortune? Or are you trying to purchase something that is not for sale with currency from your world? You truly amuse me. You are ready to give everything back and you do not even understand because—What in the Universe am I supposed to do with your offer? Are you trying to bargain with me instead of taking responsibility and making a decision? I have no use for money, let alone access to money. Do not flatter yourself thinking that I have handed you the money you have. Currency was created by humans. I have no money; therefore I give no money to any, and most certainly, I need not a thing from your world. What can you possibly offer me, to negotiate, that I need from the human race? With no exception, everything that humanity could ever utilize or need derives from Earth's natural resources which I have no use for at all and despite the fact that everything in your world is at no cost; you humans negotiate, bargain, exchange and trade just about everything for money which is entreating to me because apparently possessing currency seems to make some of you worth more than others and I cannot help to amuse myself observing.*

"However Avon, if the arrogance you are feeling is inducing you to reject the blessings you have attracted through the reflection of your own selected thoughts, which for all I can tell is what you deserve in life, go ahead; give all your possessions back to whoever you got them from if you want. Yet, you might like to consider the fact that you could always give from the heart; as in sharing Avon. But if you think that by giving back something that someone is sharing with you through the art of Love you will be somehow paying back and balancing out the guilt of arrogance, you will only be bringing misery to your own experience in life. Would you like to retaliate against your siblings?"

Then, Avon replied defensively, "I am not free to decide which emotion to permit you to set into motion, if you have all the power and I seem to be nothing but your pawn."

The *silent wave* replied, *"As a pawn in the Chessboard, you have the freedom to decide the very first, next and last move Avon. As a matter of fact,* **freewill** *is the only freedom you, as a human being, possess.*

"You are freely where you will to be, do not blame me. Think, even if you were free from all the laws and rules in your world; you would still depend on Earth's gravitational atmosphere to survive and to be. Every human being depends on the Universe principles and law without escape. You will never be free, except for your greatest power, **freedom of will**.

"Humankind is certainly amusing for they utilize creativity against them. Instead of allowing elemental unity as it was created to be; they divide Energy from themselves. Then, they divide Energy into positive and negative, while Energy is purely neutral. In addition, they even segregate Energy into two different gods; one seems to be evil and the other one appears as divine. All in all, only to unsuccessfully justify laziness trying to get away from responsibility and not making decisions; blaming alleged energies and gods for the result of their foolish actions, just to avoid honoring their only freedom and most powerful aspect: **freewill**. *Would you like to retaliate against your siblings?"* the *silent wave* tempted her again.

Avon asked sobbing and trembling, "Why do you insist on tempting me?"

Then, the *silent wave* replied serenely, *"This is simply my response to your husband's communion Avon."*

"I do not understand." Avon said confused.

The *silent wave* said, *"Well, it's precisely what happens when others pray on your behalf. The result of their prayers will expose you to situations that you were not anticipating to confront. Beware of what you wish for; especially in the presence of others Avon.*

"Remember some time ago when you wished to be a man in order to be able to manage your emotions?"

"Yes" Avon confirmed.

"When the philosopher points to the stars, the fool's eyes are fixed on the finger."

The *silent wave* added, *"That evening your husband invoked my presence in one of the most sublime expressions of Love and while passionately playing the violin; he devotedly requested for you to be able to manage your emotions; hence today I am responding to his plea. Would you like to retaliate against your siblings?"*

By then, Avon was dumbfounded and she said, "I do want to be able to manage my emotions and I do not seem to find a lever to maneuver. I cannot employ freewill if I ignore where the luring desire of retaliation and arrogance comes from."

Lovingly the *silent wave* said, *"It comes from me, Arolf."*

"Yes, I know, it comes from your negative pole though, let me think." Avon said distressed and the *silent wave* remained silent patiently waiting.

After reflecting for a moment Avon said, "You are the will and Life-Force in me and I have no doubt that I am connected to your positive pole. What could possibly be the negative pole, would you tell me? I cannot identify the emotion. Yet, I can sense that is stronger than arrogance, I feel it in my core."

"Do not act surprised for not being able to identify the emotion you have been neglecting for a lifetime Avon. It is obvious that you ignore the emotion and it is precisely why I keep bringing it up to you. Would you like to retaliate against your siblings?" the *silent wave* tempted her again.

Then, Avon was frozen, shivering for some time and tears rolled down her cheeks uncontrollably. She couldn't move; although, she was still breathing.

Avon reflected for a long while searching within to identify where the shivers eating her up deep inside were coming from; triggering such a feeling of superiority and conceit. She struggled to focus on her most intimate senses and she managed to concentrate leading her to her core and basically identifying sense of self.

Suddenly, with a trembling tone Avon whispered, *"E-G-O."*

The *silent wave* affirmed enthused, *"Energy-Goes-On, Energy-Goes-Off, yes!"* And added, *"However, understand this: nothing belongs only to one pole Avon. Everything there is and exists possesses equal measure of both, positive and negative nevertheless. Ego is the switch to each and every emotion within you.Without ego you would be a vegetable. Ego allows humankind to think and discern; ego is merely logic. A soul without ego would be like a hot air balloon ride without the flame floating in the air aimlessly and torpidly gliding in the clouds. Ego is the lever you were looking for to be able to employ your freewill willingly; as ego is the precise force to execute decisions properly.Without ego, you couldn't distinguish the difference between ill-will and freewill, let alone will. However, bear in mind that ego is powerful, just like the flame of the hot air balloon which at the same time as it is fundamental for its function could set the whole thing on fire and destroy it.The same way ego could take over the will spreading into your being as willpower disconnecting and isolating you from the source and making you pretend that you are the driver of such force."*

So, Avon asked, "How to manage ego then? I always ignored it trusting that ego is the root of evil."The *silent wave* replied, *"The core of the Universe is Love Avon. Ego is the bond between Love and human beings separating themselves from the rest of the other organisms in Earth as rational.While lack of Love could turn into odium, excessive ego could turn into evil; the difference is a matter of degrees. Hence equal measure of the two Energy poles negative and positive; as both poles are distributed evenly into everything and all that exists; dividing Energy and suppressing one pole or the other produces nothing, except for unbalance bringing disaster into your world.*

"Spreading Love among all would not turn into excess; as Love is the only faculty that once you accept it, could be shared without being diminished nor increased into glut. However, spread ego all over yourself not only in your head; diminish ego by dissolving and distilling it within your inner-self to the capacity of meekness and differentiate each emotion

"When the philosopher points to the stars, the fool's eyes are fixed on the finger."

*you sense just as you discover your resentment, and perfect management of emotions will emerge.Would you like to retaliate against your siblings?"*The *silent wave* asked tempting Avon again.

Tossing a reflection to the air…

"The name given to evil is just another god created by manipulative people from previous generations aiming to scare humankind."

By then, Avon had pushed herself into a corner between the bookcases, like a *King* on the Chessboard facing some sort of Checkmate, just like she usually found herself when playing chess. Avon was on the floor curled up into a ball. After crying for a very long time; she moved slowly. She stood up. She sat in front of the candle gazing at the flame. She had run out of tissues and she rubbed her nose with the sleeve of the sweater that she was wearing and she wondered why she was wearing the old sweater because the cuffs were worn to shreds and she recalled the origin of the value attaching her to the shabby sweater as well as the reason she still wore it.

The sweater was in one of the black garbage bags her designer friend had given to her when she was just a young girl full of hope and inevitably the tag tied to the bags reading: *GOODWILL* popped up in her mind. So, finally she felt serene and calm. Then, she thought of what Arolf had just said to her, *"You may always give from the heart, as in sharing."* All of a sudden the same force that she was so familiar with drove her to regain her senses and blindly trusting life-force; she selected the emotion she wanted to set into motion determinately.

Eagerly, the *silent wave* tempted her again, *"Would you like to retaliate against your siblings Avon?"*

Once making her decision, Avon felt a bit reluctant as she was about to defeat her inner-self by symbolically placing Arolf in Checkmate; yet she had to and she did.

Closing her eyes, Avon replied like she was igniting a flame in the deepest areas of her soul and in the midst of Energy darkness she said, "No Arolf, I determined not to retaliate against my siblings. I am *in* Love and I will let ego rest in a warm corner of my heart treating it with kindness and most importantly with respect. I will not react with cruelty as it is not my place. So, just like I shared the pair of sapphire earrings with mama and when I gave the doll to Mae. I decided to be kind by sharing with my siblings instead of retaliating. I have just determined that my *freewilling* decision is not to feed my sense of self with malice, but to dissolve and diminish ego with a flame of Love and with the same flame of Love I will transmute *ill-Will* into practicing *Goodwill* once and for all."

Apparently the *silent wave* didn't care about Avon's selection when making a decision, because once Avon firmly made her decision to share with her siblings; the *silent wave* remained silent and didn't tempt Avon about that subject anymore.

Tossing a reflection to the air...

"Granting that thoughts manifest, if evil's best trick is to convince others to *think* that it doesn't exist, what would be the

"When the philosopher points to the stars, the fool's eyes are fixed on the finger."

cause and effect of such trick? Perhaps the entire trick is a cruel and controlling idea passed from mind to mind just like every thought is. However, ignoring that thoughts manifest, the cause and effect of such a trick would be: Boo!"

After that, time passed and a couple of productive years had gone by since Avon's first book was initially published, but still she was unable to complete the new manuscript. She had written thousands of words and she felt like her story was missing something. Although, the editor was patient and satisfied with the material, Avon was uncertain about her story's point of view, voice, and her foreign perception. What's more, she had tossed reflections all over the manuscript and she didn't know how to get rid of them. At the same time; her first book was being translated into other languages; meaning, that the first book was successful. And of course, at that point, Valentin and Avon had noticed that the royalties of the book were bringing a small fortune into their already existing reserves.

An uneventful morning after Valentin left to the garage where he was working on the plane, the doctor found a message from Mae recorded in his voice mail. Mae had probably called in the middle of the night and it sounded urgent. The doctor listened to the message and he considered for a moment because he didn't know how to approach Avon.

In the interim in the library:

Love, peace, and harmony were in the air as Avon was meditating that morning. She sat in the dark with her eyes closed bonding to the surface by inhaling deeply, exhaling gradually and sensing truth from each of her heartbeats. Stillness and silence combined filled the space as she connected to her soul and experienced an instant of bliss. In the midst of the darkness; her smile reflected delight like she had just joined infinity. Suddenly, the sound of a spark broke the silence as she opened her eyes to light a candle and the tiny flame illuminated the entire library.

In the meantime, the doctor decided to go and talk to Avon, as he couldn't wait much longer for Valentin to return. The doctor could have called Valentin, but he was affected by the news and he couldn't think properly. However he knew that it was imperative for Avon to learn about Mae's massage and he headed to the library.

On the other end, Avon observed the small candle flame growing firmer and larger appreciating the fact that not long before; the space was as dark as matter in the sky at night beyond the stars and she absorbed the flickering flame glow brightening the space powerfully. She gazed at the flame.

Meanwhile, the doctor hesitated for slight moment pacing in the hall by the door outside the library. He wasn't sure how to convey the message to Avon; but then, he thought that there was only one way and he decided to be brief and straightforward.

At the same time inside the library, Avon sat still gazing at the flame until her eyelids naturally closed and a bright reflection of the flame remained floating in her mind's eye and she began to focus on the flame remains.

Right outside the library; the doctor decided to knock on the door and he heard Avon asking who it was from the other side of the walls. "I do not mean to disturb you my dear," he replied and as soon as she opened the door he cleared his throat adding, "Mae left a message, your father passed away."

Not having much of an option, Avon received the news with grace. She stared down aimlessly for a moment. Then she raised her eyes looking at him and she said in a soft tone, "I am deeply grateful for your assistance in this matter Leopold."

"When the philosopher points to the stars, the fool's eyes are fixed on the finger."

"It is my pleasure. Let me know if you need me for the trip arrangements my dear."

She smiled in response to his kindness saying, "I might indeed need help. I have not been in Bangkok since mama passed away and considering the situation, I foresee a confrontation with my siblings approaching my way." Hesitant she asked, "I guess I could not elude being present at father's will distribution, could I?" He looked into her eyes concurring with her guess by shaking his head and he walked away. Avon closed the door behind him and turned around gazing at the candle flame from the distance while sensing Arolf, whose presence have been motionless all along. She sighed deeply and quietly said, "Father is gone."

Just then, Avon's thoughts traveled at the highest speed trying to recollect the last time her father spoke to her and she remembered that she had last spoken to her dad a couple of years earlier, when her sister Kalaya was asking for money to remodel her house. On that occasion, after talking to Kalaya on the phone, Avon tried to talk to her dad but it was an incoherent conversation.

Earnestly disclosing, from the time when her mama passed away; her father had been lost in the midst of death and he never regained his wits again. Her father had been suffering from dementia ever since her mama died and every time Avon spoke to him; he brought up the topic of a fortune that he was about to receive and he would retell once and again that he would leave a fortune to his children after he died. Her father reiterated the same story over and over like a *mantra chant*, which was the same *mantra chant* that Avon had been hearing since she was only a child.

Avon was brought to tears at times reflecting on her siblings, because besides the fact that they seemed to be lost in the midst of death along with their mama and their dad; her siblings were possibly suffering from dementia as well; for they trusted their father's word and they were convinced that, after death, their dad would leave a fortune to them. The situation was sort of a paradox for Avon to assimilate due to her siblings' resentment and rejection toward her, as she couldn't share openly among them; besides her siblings would have felt offended if she shared her success with them *in lieu* of accepting her accomplishments with grace. Also, Avon had to consider that, although she didn't mind sharing some of the money she had generated from royalties with them, Valentin's words resounded in her mind *"This is only the beginning. Eventually you will discover the pros and cons to be a multimillionaire. But for the most part, the greatest sense of satisfaction reveals when trusting someone to share everything with."*

Avon didn't trust her siblings, because if she shared her riches with them openly, most likely they would have not rested until extracting up to the last penny of a fortune accrued by a hard working man, Valentin, who didn't deserve to be impoverished in such way. On the other hand, Avon couldn't tolerate the idea to see her siblings disappointed by their dad.

So back then, after listening to her father's voice for the last time, repeating over and over *"I am about to receive the fortune I have worked during a lifetime for my children..."* It didn't take long for Avon to make a decision and put in practice her goodwill faculty by allowing Energy to set the elements required into motion and manifest her intent of sharing with her siblings.

Therefore, a few days after the last conversation with her dad, when Avon had the meditation session and determined to share with her siblings instead of retaliating against them; she also prepared for her father's death. She realized that her father sounded sick; his death seemed to be approaching and she wanted to be ready for the moment. So back then, a couple of years prior to her dad's actual demise and when her father's voice was still fresh in her ears; Avon assigned a portion of her *last-will* favoring her siblings.

"When the philosopher points to the stars, the fool's eyes are fixed on the finger."

The day when she had confronted her ego meditating; she approached Valentin in the evening after dinner and asked, "Luv, do you remember when we got married and the violinists were playing in the balcony?"

"Yes, how could I forget princess?"

"Well, I was just curious about how did you manage to set everything up without me noticing who the violinists really were until the end?"

Valentin exclaimed, "Aha!" asking, "Do you want to plot a set of events?"

"Well, I was thinking that my siblings are getting old and I would like to share some money with them in this lifetime, not after I am dead. Besides, I am the youngest and probably they will die before I do anyway. I have an idea regarding a testament or a sort of will; however, if things turn out harsh during the actual will distribution event, I would like my siblings to think that the fortune came from my dad," she replied.

Then, with a mischievous intriguing smile and while rubbing his palms together Valentin added, "Dominique is my right-hand man in these matters and we would probably have to prepare everything in advance and wait until your dad dies. Let's talk about it and when the intention is Love, everything is possible. We'll plot and stage a will distribution princess."

As soon as Avon returned from her stroll down memory lane remembering when she last spoke to her dad; she called Valentin letting him know that her father had passed away.

After that, they prepared the last minute details and made the necessary arrangements for the trip in order to attend the will distribution in Bangkok which they were ready to execute, because they had been planning the event during the last couple of years with the assistance of their friends. So, two weeks after her father's demise, Avon was emotionally equipped to confront her siblings at the plotted and staged set of events.

Tossing a reflection to the air...

"A book could be worth more than fixed assets, as it can be taken anywhere feeding the soul for a lifetime not just satiating a dwelling desire for some time."

"When the philosopher points to the stars, the fool's eyes are fixed on the finger."

EPILOGUE

Bangkok, right after the Will distribution took place.

*G*iven that Avon had traveled from abroad for the distribution of the funds; she was by the hotel lobby waiting for the valet to bring a car she had rented and thinking *this might be the last time I am stepping on the soil where I was born.* All of a sudden, she noticed Chet's son standing outside by the hotel entrance door talking on a mobile phone. During the meeting; she had also noticed two suspicious men roaming around the hall. She was aware of the corruption, danger, hijacks, kidnaps, and risks she took when traveling around the world; so, Bangkok wasn't going to be the exception. Therefore, she was prepared for the worst but hoping for the best while there and the two men were not that suspicious for they were Valentin and Gabe watching over her.

When she drove away, the steamy evening was slowly dissolving the scorching beams from the sunset reflecting everywhere and as she spotted the car following her; she remained calm because she knew that the helicopter that surfaced monitoring her course was a sign that Gabe and Valentin were in the copter to protect her and aware of her location. Avon was planning to go to Mae's house and

"When the philosopher points to the stars, the fool's eyes are fixed on the finger."

deliver other books that she had in the trunk for each of her siblings; but when she recognized her nephew through the rear-view mirror, because despite of his ski mask disguise he was wearing the same clothes, Avon understood that sharing the book with her siblings was in vain and when her nephew's companion tried to attack her she thought *Arolf at times you are just a presence, aren't you?*

And she sensed a *silent wave* saying, "Always, not just at times. We got into this mess; we will get out of it, no doubt."

After that when the helicopter came down startling everyone, Gabe and Valentin jumped off rushing toward her and they were the ones that grabbed her loading her into the copter which flew up in the air right away. Thus Avon wasn't the least bit kidnapped as her siblings thought she was.

Tossing a reflection to the air...

"Pursuing the will gets anyone wealth and success but it doesn't stop there. One has to always have a high aim to be hopeful in life."

Whoosh-whoosh, Angelina heard the helicopter's blades whirling as they descended to land not far from where she was standing by the door of a private jet at one of the Bangkok private airports. In the midst of the darkish evening; she distinguished Gabe's bright blue eyes inside the chopper looking at her through the window and indicating an accomplished mission. As soon as they landed, Gabe opened the door, his robust shape jumped off the copter in the shadows and he rushed toward the jet to greet his wife.

Inside the helicopter in the dark, Valentin' indigo eyes glowed. He got off the chopper in the midst of dusk right after Gabe. Then Avon was distinguished. Valentin helped her out and when he put her down; she looked at his azure eyes saying, "Your eyes are my heaven Valentin." Just then, Arolf's presence lit up their hearts in the midst of *Dark Matter* disguising behind the moon and the stars.

Angelina, Gabe, Valentin, and Leopold, were wearing latex masks and heavy makeup to disguise. Avon and Valentin along with Dominique's assistance and the rest of the group had been plotting the set of events during the last couple of years to stage the distribution of the will. They had been preparing to protect Avon at all times through her last foreseen visit to Bangkok for when her father died. They all accompanied Avon to give to her siblings the money expected from an imaginary fortune their father had promised to leave them in a will after he died, and at the same time, Avon honored her dad's dreams and his last will.

Avon's main intention to execute her plan was the last sane words she heard from her dad when she saw him for the last time after her mama died and her father share his dreams with her saying *"My only drive to live without your mother is the dream to fulfill her will of leaving an equal amount of money to each of our children from the fortune I am about to receive and hopefully my children will unify"* or something to that effect.

However, as much as Avon did to unify with her siblings; she perceived that they might attempt to take more from her due to their greediness. So, she had prepared the backup package and if her siblings only expressed an effort to at least read the book she left in the package exchange; she also had a backup plan to share the truth with them. Yet, her siblings' sense of greed allowed money to triumph over their father's humble wish and in truth, Avon wanted to share with her siblings much more than she could actually give.

"When the philosopher points to the stars, the fool's eyes are fixed on the finger."

However at times, no matter how genuine a person's intention might be when giving, as only the receiver's freewill would allow them to accept blessings with grace. So, even if Avon accomplished sharing some money with them, she couldn't disclose the truth and unite with her own siblings as their father wished; for in their case, only they were competent to allow truth and Love into their hearts. It appeared that her siblings would rather live in a sea of deceit than learning how immense their potential could reach. And as a result, Avon allowed her siblings to perceive what the whole scenario seemed to be in the surface for she understood that it was more feasible to share Love with strangers than with her own blood.

When Avon exposed her plan to Valentin for Dominique to assist them to plot the set of events; her intention was to share with her siblings out of Goodwill. Little did she know; for unaware, she ended up precisely manifesting her father's words and thoughts; her father's dreams; and as if it wasn't enough, Avon even manifested her dad's last will which was to fulfill her deceased mother's will.

Then Avon realized the inescapable truth when confronting purpose *tête-à-tête*. For at that moment, Avon understood as clear as the sunshine that her purpose as a human being in Earth was passing thoughts from head to head. Bringing her to appreciate that it didn't matter what she achieve in life or not. Because, truly, her purpose revealed as being neither more nor less than an *emissary* of thoughts, and literally, passing those thoughts from head to head in order for those thoughts to manifest. Then she figured that if her purpose as a human being was to manifest thoughts; she was better off manifesting her own ideas by creating constructively out of inspiration and sharing truth and Love with the world, not manifesting by listening to other people's thoughts which might have developed out of aspiration or even worse, desperation.

Tossing a reflection to the air...

"It is not the same to pursue a created purpose than to create out of inspiration on purpose."

During the will distribution; Leopold, the doctor, with his legal expertise played the role of the attorney. Angelina was the brilliant assistant. The butlers were Dominique's contacts. Gabe and Valentin had a helicopter that they had hired with a pilot on the roof of the hotel. Dominique and Jimmy stayed in the private jet at the airport coordinating and monitoring the event and Avon played her own role. With Dominique's assistance; they concealed the doctor's identity from Mae for her to assist with the meeting suite reservation at the hotel keeping the whole affair appearing legitimate.

As Avon and Valentin boarded the jet, Angelina, the doctor, and Gabe, were cheerfully retelling Dominique and Jimmy the occurred events while taking off their makeup. Then, Avon observed her siblings through a monitor that Dominique had set up connected to the suite at the hotel and she realized that she had never seen her siblings as happy as they were celebrating their fortune. Watching through the monitor Avon noticed that the book had ended up inside a garbage can; therefore, Dominique made the necessary arrangements for the book to end up in Mae's hands, and of course, once reading the book and knowing the circumstances; Mae understood clearly the fortune's source. Mae didn't know about Avon's intentions when she gave the doll to her as a little girl until she read the book and it turned out that the doll had a name engraved under one foot, reading: *Flora*. So Avon's deciphering

"When the philosopher points to the stars, the fool's eyes are fixed on the finger."

mind and such triggered her to reverse her name, Avon, into *nova* creating her *nom de plume* as *Floranova*; and when Mae received the book, it was simple for her to figure out that the book came from Avon. They had leased an intercontinental private jet with an attending crew which Gabe flew with his new copilot Valentin and as soon as all of them were back in the plane; they left Bangkok.

Tossing a reflection to the air...

"While some are busy manifesting other peoples' thoughts in desperate search for a created purpose, others rather think so as to manifest their own ideas by creating on purpose."

After they returned to San Fran from their Goodwill distribution escapade; an uneventful morning, Avon received the official authorization to proceed with her proposal to work with the U.S. Army veterans. She always perceived that warriors and soldiers attended their duty hoping to protect a country from war not to provoke war for a cause. So her intention was to share methods that she had developed to auto-deprogram thoughts with them, supervised by professionals until she could practice as a Metaphisicist by herself.

Avon was willing to convey the power of a tiny candle flame implementing an effect to think not to remember distilling the memories of their actions one by one after they had returned from a war which whether for a cause or only to keep appearances they have had the courage to fight exposing themselves to die.

And after working with several U.S. Army veteran groups, Avon realized that her so-called adversities in life didn't mean as much in relation to what the souls returning from war had intensely experienced when representing and defending the entire population of a country by facing combat and witnessing one of the cruelest ways to end life.

On the other hand, the war veterans enjoyed cruising on the bay during their holistic healing sessions; as every meeting was held on Avon's Yacht, "*The Flame remains!*"

Tossing a reflection to the air...

"Being a soldier is not far from being a monk. Not everyone has the luxury to live in a monastery in silence defending a code of belief; and not everyone has the courage to expose themselves to the luxury of dying by following a code of honor to protect a country from war."

In the interim, soon after they had returned from the Bangkok adventure, Avon visited the editor at the publishing house because she still had a new unfinished book pending to submit. Valentin was with her along with Jimmy and the doctor for they represented Avon as an accountant and attorney in her publishing events. While she made arrangements for an extension to submit her new manuscript; she also had arranged to meet with the publisher's attorney. So, after getting an extension to submit her new book; everyone sat at a meeting table and Jimmy handed a briefcase that

"When the philosopher points to the stars, the fool's eyes are fixed on the finger."

he was holding between his hands to Avon. She put the briefcase on top of the table, she opened it and she took out a package. The package looked like one of those bubble padded mailers. She opened the package taking out her published book containing her memoirs and she reached inside the envelope taking out what was left to be disclosed to her siblings in case any of them selected the package during the will distribution. She was in effect, opening the original package which contained the book: *My Childhood Dreams* and a document granting her siblings a percentage of her royalties from every future book sold under her *nom de plume* from the date when the will distribution took place forward. Naturally, the document was to take effect only if Avon's siblings reached an agreement to share from their hearts with hers and she reserved certain rights as a preventive measure. She had organized the meeting with the publisher's attorney to nullify her request of granting future royalties to her siblings through a trust that they had established and to void them as the beneficiaries. Then, she also requested to redirect the payments to her and Valentin as they originally were.

Avon's intention was to share with her siblings much more than she could afford, exceeding the amount that the certified checks reflected all together; which was five million dollars and a speck compared to Avon and Valentin's reserves. However, if her siblings united and agreed to share the five million dollars with her; she was willing to share her royalties for life with them. In addition, she was willing to assist them with financial management information; because she understood the effect of obtaining an amount of money that one might have dreamed on spending but not manage to last a lifetime.

Unfortunately her siblings' eyes seemed to be blinded by greed, not allowing Energy to flow in their favor, and as a result, they only got crumbs of what could've been a true fortune. Because eventually, when Avon's second book was published and several books more as years passed by; Avon and Valentin not only recovered the small fortune that she shared with her siblings but her books turned out to be much more valuable than her siblings could ever imagine when refusing a package in exchange for cash.

&

Tossing a reflection to the air…

"Money is ego materialized. The difference is that in order to balance evenly in society and in life, one ought to be diminished and the other ought to be multiplied."

&

Avon was liberated at that point, feeling totally detached from any attachments and she wrote her emotions and thoughts ceaselessly devoting her attention to her second manuscript. She didn't have a quest trying to find out what to give in exchange for having become an extraordinary student in life anymore. She had a different message besides writing her own reflections and more of a story to tell. She was a complete, experienced, wise, and accomplished person.

She knew in her heart that her essence was beyond gender and in order to manage her emotions she no longer longed to be a man because gender and ego promenaded through life hand in hand. At that point, she understood that her great ignorance would always triumph over her limited knowledge and she was freely willing to let it be, blindly trusting the unknown.

Sadly disclosing, although Avon thought that by giving such an amount of money to her siblings would fulfill her heart to the extent of bliss experiencing the same sensation that she felt when

"When the philosopher points to the stars, the fool's eyes are fixed on the finger."

giving the doll to her niece, she didn't. On the contrary, the feeling of liberation she felt at that point had nothing to do with bliss as her heart and soul reflected true Peace.

When Avon's second manuscript was completed, there was one last detail missing because she had not titled her new book just yet. So an uneventful evening while they were in the library's balcony appreciating the sailboats' glitter cruising in the bay from the distance; Avon was listening to Valentin playing *Vivaldi's Spring Excerpt* in the violin surrounded by the glow of candle flames and she sensed Arolf's motionless presence. She then smiled thinking of her idea to name Arolf after her doll *Flora*, except that she had reversed the name, of course; but she also remembered Valentin's words:

"In Botany, Flora reproduces perfectly having neither stamens nor pistils."

"Just like Love" said a *silent wave* in her heart.

So, since the main character in her second book was *Will* and her mama seemed to have been the main cause of every effect Avon had experienced in life up till then; she reached her laptop looking forward to the many blessings and the new causes with successful effects coming her way and with a bright smile filled of hope in her face; she titled her new born manuscript typing:

"Her Will"

Tossing a reflection to the air…

"The *'Flame'* remains!"

~The End~

AUTO-BIO

$\mathcal{I}$ am from Canada; although at this point, it doesn't matter anymore because just like any other person I have been exposed to different adversities through my path in life and I sincerely feel that I belong where my heart is which is a place not represented in the physical realm.

Years ago, after adjusting to remain distant from a greedy and emotional contaminated family by moving to the U.S., I went through a deceiving marriage ending up in divorce. Then I faced financial bankruptcy, yet I kept going picking myself up. I had my share of romantic break ups, I confronted challenges to accomplish objectives and I shared misfortunes with others as well as happiness, but unlike most, I wasn't the least afraid to change. I was able to navigate through hard times transferring from country to country, city to city, and I easily relocated anywhere; as working in the tourism field allowed me to travel giving me the opportunity to reside in other countries and learn about different cultures in the world. I always advanced without hesitation making certain that my career was not going to be affected by my personal matters and

"When the philosopher points to the stars, the fool's eyes are fixed on the finger."

nothing stopped my willpower from accomplishing every goal I set for myself; until one day, mother passed away.

When mother died, I was living in Arizona and my existence was turned upside down. To my surprise, I found no instructions to surmount the affliction left deep in my soul and heart after the fact. So, I had to make a conscious decision to either move forward, or drown within my own sadden solitude; and after I gained some strength, I decided to transfer to San Fran. My experience in San Francisco was vast in every area, except I noticed that change wasn't "change" anymore, because at that point, I began to expand in mind and soul–a practice I never thought of exploring before.

Thus far, I had been studying Metaphysics and Holistic Sciences for some time, although different than the norm, I don't perceive metaphysics from the general approach. Instead of focusing on the afterlife, tarot cards, crystals, astrology, or divination, I focus on the metaphysical aspects of "living and breathing human beings;" emotions, mind, thoughts, and feelings. My studies concentrate in the merger of body and mind; unity of Science and Spirituality; fusion of the intangible and the tangible.

So, back then, I also learned a lesson by observing the homeless people at Union Square and as I continued my studies and research; I began to learn to select my "mental vocabulary" carefully when I thought, awaking in me an enthrallment with words in the languages I know which generally reveals through my prose, and I began a new quest to discover the magic that writing holds. After learning some and experiencing more, a few years later, I transferred again and I relocated in Florida.

I was never homeless. I only learned from them and I often pondered about the homeless for they impacted a connection within my inner power greatly. So, while settling in Florida I realized that perhaps the homeless people were where they were for lack of a drive, something I used to have plenty of: willpower; and at the same time, I wondered if they were where they were as a result of "The Will" of the Universe. Little did I know, as later on, I discovered the drive to live through a sort of disguised sense of hope that only a homeless person's heart could give off.

In the interim, an average evening, I received a long distance call from a family member and after hanging up the phone, I was left with a taste of distrust when realizing that none of my family members cared about me, but instead, they were willing to extract every financial resource I had if I allowed them. So I wondered once more about the word "Will," only on that occasion I was thinking of how would my family members react if someone left a will in a sort of testament and they found themselves in the position of sharing money with me and give, in place of always taking away.

"Her Will" comes to light:

After wondering about a will distribution, naturally my fascination with words arose bringing me to reflect profoundly on the word "Will" and its deriving terms. I thought of "The will" a person leaves behind after they die; I thought about goodwill, freewill, willpower and the fact that, we, as human beings are supposed to allow "The Will" of the Universe to provide. Then I realized that a will distribution, just like I set it up in the novel, would make a good ending for a book.

The idea of the ending of "Her Will" came to me in 2003. Back then, I didn't know where to begin; all I had was the end of a story which was burning like a flame in the deepest areas of my heart. After that, some time passed and I lived through more experiences. I even transferred to Europe residing there for awhile and, when I returned to the U.S. married to a great Bulgarian man, my vocation led me to earn a degree at the University of Metaphysics of Arizona becoming an Non-denominational Ordained Minister.

"When the philosopher points to the stars, the fool's eyes are fixed on the finger."

An uneventful morning in October of 2009, Avon, literally began to meditate inside my mind; I started to write about Avon developing the character and as time passed, other characters joined the tale as well. I wrote continuously through days and nights nonstop until nearly two years later when the last word in the manuscript was written–WILL–bringing to light a novel which for many reasons I titled: Her Will.

*In memory of the great minds that had left a
remaining flame behind so that later generations could
find comfort in their hearts... Just to mention a few:*

⚮

Albert Einstein

Antonio Vivaldi

Aristotle

Claude Monet

Confucius

Frank Sinatra

Galileo Galilei

Rumi

Hermes Trismegistus

Isaac Newton

John Lennon

Ludwig Van Beethoven

Og Magdino

Plato

Pierre-Auguste Renoir

René Descartes

Socrates

Quotes and proverbs from the unknown

Vincent Van Gogh

Voltaire

William Shakespeare

Wolfgang Amadeus Mozart

⚮

"When the philosopher points to the stars, the fool's eyes are fixed on the finger."

Made in the USA
Lexington, KY
15 February 2015